Christmas Carl

A Garland Grove
Holiday Romance

Robin Paul

Lakewood Ranch, Florida

FRIDAY, NOVEMBER 25

NASHVILLE

*B*rooke Summers counted eleven media types scattered about the restaurant as she slipped through the busy dining room. Two of them, a Nashville blogger and a freelancer for one of the big country music websites, would not make it into the press conference scheduled in two hours. The blogger had been warned repeatedly about her fictionalized headlines. The freelancer recently sold comped tickets to a Blake Shelton concert and pocketed the money. It was Nashville, not New York City. And in Nashville word gets around fast.

The remaining nine would be joined by another twenty who would arrive at the last minute. For whatever reason, they passed on Wainwright's Chop House's Friday lunch special. Ribeye, baked potato, and salad for $19.50. Their loss.

"Hey, Brooke." She nearly made it through the dining room before Clive Naylor caught up to her. Clive was always looking for a little extra edge, some nugget to share with his listeners on the overnight show he hosted on one of those satellite radio stations. Brooke slowed but kept moving. Stopping would bring a swarm of reporters. One press conference a day was enough.

"What's up, Clive?"

"Can I ask you about—"

"C'mon now. You know that if I answer your question, I'll get twenty more."

"But really, it's something that—"

"Save it for later, Clive. If you don't get what you need during the presser, see me after."

She didn't wait for his reply as she pushed open a door and stepped into a private banquet area. The walls had dark paneling. The chandeliers were old wagon wheels. The place screamed manliness. A small stage was set up. Twenty chairs were arranged in front of it. And in the rear, seated alone at a table meant for ten, was the person Brooke Summers loved and admired most in the whole wide world. Her father, Bobby.

"Hey darlin'," he said, glancing up from a porterhouse the size of a catcher's mitt. He was in full Bobby Summers regalia. Pressed blue jeans, black leather vest over a white shirt, black boots, and a leather belt engraved with his initials. And of course, the signature Stetson Diamante Premier, his fifth as best as Brooke could remember, all gifts from clients. When Brooke came close, he tilted his head so she could kiss his cheek, just like always.

"What time is she getting here?" Brooke asked as she pulled out a chair to his left.

"She's in the limo, so it depends on how good Milo does getting through traffic. Want something to eat?" Bobby picked up the receiver of a thirty-year-old desk phone in the middle of the table, just another of the curiosities that made Wainwright's his favorite dining establishment.

"Just a glass of iced tea. I already had a salad."

Bobby repeated her request into the phone. He had barely replaced the receiver when the owner's college-age grandson hustled in with her tea.

"How's the steak, Bobby?"

"Perfect as always, Ernesto. Let your granddaddy know, please."

"I will, sir. Are you going to the game tonight?"

Brooke sipped her tea and looked on as Bobby and young Ernesto debated Vanderbilt University's chances for basketball success in the Southeastern Conference. There was only one perfect man in the world as far as she was concerned, and he was tearing through a steak large enough for three men while chatting about Vandy's anticipated rise from the conference basement. It was only when she looked closely that she could see evidence of his sixty-seven years. The crow's feet and laugh lines were deeper. The skin more weathered. From ten feet away, though, he still appeared just as he had when he taught her to reel in large-mouth bass from the big lake on their place out at Percy's Crossroads.

"Are you ready to take the lead?" Bobby asked after Ernesto left.

"The question should be, is she ready for me to take the lead?"

"I've been working on her, sweetheart." He leaned over and retrieved his leather briefcase. "I found some old songs she recorded back before she got to town. We'll start by going over those, then I'll tell her you're going to be running the Christmas tour."

"Wait until after the press conference, Dad. She's always in a great mood when those are over."

Bobby's cellphone buzzed on the table next to his plate. "Hey Milo...that works...yep, just like always...and Milo, another thing...Brooke will be your contact through Christmas. You've got her number, don't you?"

He tossed the phone on the table, took another bite of steak, and wiped his face with a linen napkin.

"Milo said they're ten minutes out. He'll make sure the alley is clear before he brings her in."

"Twenty chairs won't be enough, Dad. Want me to have Ernesto bring in more?"

Bobby gave his trademark sideways grin. "Did you forget your daddy's first rule of press conferences?"

She hadn't. She just enjoyed hearing him repeat it.

"If you expect thirty, set up for twenty."

Yep, there it was. Bobby Summers was never caught by surprise. Empty seats at a press conference would make people think the star's appeal was waning. Bobby's stars never waned. At least not while he represented them.

Again, his phone buzzed. He sighed as he reached for it.

"What's up Raquel?"

Raquel Doney had managed Bobby's office longer than Brooke had been alive. It was a big job because Bobby rarely went to the office, and he paid her well to keep promoters, talent agents, and overzealous fans at bay.

"Yeah, give it to him, but let him know I only have a couple minutes." Bobby sighed again. He said to Brooke, "Smokey Yarber's gonna call."

"Is his contract with Steele and James expiring?"

Bobby nodded. "I knew he would do this. He wanted to drop the stage name and go back to his real name back when we repped him. I kept telling him, 'People have known you as Smokey since you hit it big back in ninety-four. Nobody is going to buy country records from a guy named Sven Yarber,' but he had his heart set on it and Steele and James said they could make it work."

"Hey, Smokey," Bobby said as soon as the phone buzzed. "I've got Brooke here with me, so I'm putting you on speaker."

"Sure enough, Bobby. Hi, Brooke, it's been a while."

"Sure has, Smokey." The last time she saw him was at a post-concert party at some hotel in Bismarck, North Dakota. She was twenty-two. Smokey was forty. He stuck his hands where they didn't belong and she slapped him so hard it left a mark. That was eight years ago. Brooke remembered. Smokey probably didn't.

"Hey, Bobby... I was thinking that maybe you and me could team back up. My contract expires at the beginning of the year, and it's time for a change."

"Why, Smokey? Courtney Steele is good at what she does. I'm not sure we could do anything for you that she's not already doing."

Brooke knew better. Bobby was spouting a bunch of hooey. Smokey's days as a headliner were long gone, but they could easily send him on a fifteen-city tour opening for any of a dozen country legends. The best Steele and James were doing for him was weeknight gigs at county fairs.

"You have contacts she doesn't have, Bobby. You know people out west who—"

"Hold on a minute, Smokey." Bobby cut in when Ernesto stepped into the room.

"Four more reporters showed up for the lunch special, Bobby. One of them is that guy from Huntsville who stiffed us on the check last time."

"Don't serve him, Ernesto. And if he puts up a fuss, tell him to see me after the press conference, because he sure as heck ain't going to be at it."

Ernesto nodded and left the room.

"I'm back, Smokey."

"Where are you guys?"

"Wainwright's. We've got an event here in a little bit."

"That place?" Smokey said. "I heard it ain't worth a damn since them Mexicans bought it."

Bobby was quiet for a moment. Brooke steeled herself for a glimpse of his edgy side.

"You heard wrong, Smokey. It's better than ever, and that kind of talk won't help you get back on top. Maybe you need to ride it out with Steele and James. Sign on for another four years and get yourself some of that diversity training."

"I'm sorry, Bobby. I just meant that since the Mexicans—"

"Look, Smokey, I have to run, but I wish you the best. Maybe they can find you some more county fair gigs. Tell them to try western Montana. I hear good things about the county fairs out there."

Bobby punched the disconnect button and placed the phone in his vest pocket. Brooke noticed how he was slower getting up than he used to be. Part of it was his knees. Summers men were born with bad knees. His back was acting up, too, as a result of forty years of tossing hay bales and breaking strong-willed horses—two of Bobby Summers's favorite things to do when he wasn't managing the careers of some of Nashville's biggest stars.

"Are you ready?" he asked.

Brooke stood up and smoothed her skirt. "As ready as I'll ever be. Are you sure that me taking her on tour instead of you is for the best?"

Bobby didn't hesitate. "You're going to run this outfit eventually, aren't you?"

She said she was.

"Then, yeah, it's for the best." The words were barely

out of his mouth when the door banged open. Milo said a quick hello before stepping aside as if he was clearing a path for royalty.

Because he was.

Royalty by the name of Raven McCloud.

RAVEN MCCLOUD WAS the darling of country music. Everyone loved her. Her reputation was beyond reproach. She visited sick kids in the hospital. Her terrier mix was a rescue. She even did TV commercials for macaroni and cheese.

Over the years, Brooke had met country music's biggest stars. None of them intimidated her.

Raven McCloud intimidated her.

But why?

Was it her perfectly styled jet-black hair?

Or the sky-blue eyes that peered into your soul?

She was so... Brooke couldn't think of any other way to say it...*put together*.

Her eyebrows—perfect. Skin—perfect.

Toned arms, long legs, and a butt hard enough to crack walnuts.

She had chosen a short black skirt and a tasteful Christmas sweater for the press conference. And black boots. All flipping perfect.

And perfectly intimidating.

Get over it, Brooke said to herself as she watched Bobby's easy interactions with his star client. There was no intimidation there. The way Bobby spoke to Raven McCloud was little different from the way he spoke with Milo the limo driver or Ernesto the restaurant owner's grandson. He walked her through a stack of documents with the same tone he would use to describe a favorite fishing trip. Raven listened intently for the most part, but when she appeared to drift off, Bobby gently brought her attention back to the paperwork. He was a marvel, her father.

Could she ever be as good at the job as he was?

"Brooke, you checked these bond ratings," Bobby asked, in the same calm manner that had gotten Raven back on track a few moments before. "Should we increase the investment or stay where we are?"

How could he tell she had been off in la-la-land?

Brooke pulled her laptop closer and opened the file he was referring to. "I would stay where we are for now. Maybe reevaluate the performance in March."

"You okay with that, Raven?" Bobby asked.

Raven flashed Brooke a friendly smile. "If the two of you say wait, let's wait."

Brooke remembered when Raven used to balk at meetings. She would tell Bobby that she trusted him and didn't want to be burdened with money stuff. Bobby responded the same way he responded to any client who shied away from the numbers. "The further you get from the financials, the closer you get to becoming Vance Whitney." Vance Whitney was a legend in Nashville entertainment circles. An up-and-coming country star with crossover potential, Whitney entrusted his manager with all the financials only to find himself after five years with a manager who vanished and debt in excess of four million bucks.

"We still have some time before we let the press in," Bobby said, moving things along. He reached down and brought up a cardboard box of old tapes and CDs. "Raven, I was cleaning up my attic last week and I found this. It's got your name on it, but the date is twenty years ago, well before you came to Nashville. Any recollection of what's in here?"

Raven pulled the box closer and peered inside. She picked up a CD and squinted to read the label. "These are from college."

"I didn't know you went to college," Brooke said. "That's not in your bio."

Raven rolled her eyes. "I didn't really go *to college* as much as I was *at college*."

She rolled her eyes when she saw they didn't understand. "Missouri State University. I was a Sugar Bear."

Bobby cocked his head. "What's a Sugar Bear? Don't tell me if I'm going to be embarrassed by your answer."

Raven slapped his arm playfully. "Sugar Bears are the college dance team, silly Bobby. We performed at football games. I was only at Missouri State for a semester, though, so the evidence is pretty scant."

Bobby stroked his chin. "How did I not know this?"

"I'm more complex than you think, Bobby Summers. A girl likes to keep a guy guessing." Then, turning to Brooke, she said, "I came to Nashville over Thanksgiving break and knew I had found home." She laughed as she said, "And after six long years of waiting tables and getting my butt grabbed while singing in dive bars, I became an overnight sensation."

"Hmm," Bobby said, more to himself than Brooke and Raven. "Maybe we need to work the college thing into your bio."

"No way," Raven said quickly, her piercing eyes growing dark. "The press will call me a college dropout."

"Not a chance," Brooke said. "The press loves you."

"Not that blogger who writes those mean headlines," Raven replied.

Bobby shook his head. "He won't be attending. Now, Raven, about these tapes? I thought we might go through them real quick and see if anything's worth keeping."

"No thank you," Raven answered. "I recorded that stuff at one of those pay-by-the-hour studios. The songs are stuff other people already recorded. Let's not waste our time."

"Fair enough." Bobby pulled back the box. "I'll take care of these. You get yourself ready for the press."

"How do I look?"

"Perfect. Just like you always do."

Raven ran her hand through her hair and smiled into the mirror mounted over the restroom sink. "You're sweet, Brooke. Just like Bobby." She rolled the waist of her skirt to make it a tad shorter, appraised the results, and said absently, "I wish I could've won the Daddy Derby like you did, sugar."

"You've done okay for yourself, Raven."

The spit-shined version of Raven's childhood was that she grew up the happy and well-adjusted daughter of a schoolteacher mom and CPA father in the tiny mountain town of Salmon, Idaho. The occupations were true enough, as was the hometown. Her father was cold and distant, though, and rumors persisted he had carried on a love affair with his much older secretary right up to the moment it was discovered that she had been pocketing client fees. Bobby sometimes wondered aloud how Raven's old man hadn't caught her in the act, being an accountant and all. Raven's mother was the surly fourth grade teacher that smart parents steered their kids away from. Fortunately for Raven and her parents, folks from Salmon weren't the kind to disparage their hometown hero, so the press never really picked up on the tawdry stuff.

Brooke wondered sometimes if Raven's childhood was the reason she had developed such a close relationship with Bobby. She had heard the rumors. Some Nashville insiders had speculated early on that Bobby and Raven carried on a love affair of their own while he guided her to the top of the country charts. If there was any truth to the rumor, it happened between the hours of midnight and five-thirty in the morning, because most of Bobby's time other than when he slept was consumed with deal making, fence mending, hay baling, and doting on his daughter out at Percy's Crossroads.

Still, sometimes Brooke wondered.

Like she had wondered about Sophie Maxwell back when Brooke was in junior high. Sophie's career never lifted off like Raven's, but then again, she never worked as hard. When she had asked out of her contract a decade before, Bobby was quick to let her go.

Bobby rapped on the restroom door and pushed it open just enough to say, "Brooke, c'mon out here and help me get the media situated." Brooke touched Raven's arm, said a few words of encouragement that weren't necessary, and left.

"She okay?" Bobby asked.

"Yeah. But she's not going to like it when you tell her I'm going on tour with her."

"She'll be fine. She's a big girl."

She's only nine years older than me, Brooke thought. *And I'm not feeling so big right now.*

THE PRESS CONFERENCE was orchestrated to perfection. Bobby decided who got to ask questions and who didn't. Raven cheerfully answered creampuff queries about her upcoming Christmas tour and the album she had in the works. The male media fell all over themselves to seem glib and worldly. A couple practically swooned when Raven called them by name. The women tried to be sophisticated and unaffected by their proximity to stardom, but Brooke saw the way they checked out Raven's clothes and makeup. Sexist? Maybe, but it was the way things were in Nashville.

After thirty minutes, Bobby said there was time for one more question. He called on a girl who was there representing her high school newspaper up the road in Clarksville. Most kids her age wouldn't usually get within a mile of the gathering, but Bobby thought it was good for business.

While Raven described how she chose the songs for her albums, Brooke looked over the assembled media. Clive Naylor, seated near the rear, caught her eye. Brooke leaned over and whispered to Bobby, "Call on Clive."

"We're done."

"I kind of promised him."

Bobby nodded, then when Raven was finished with the high school kid, he said, "I guess there is time for one more." He searched the gathering as if trying to decide which raised hand to call on. No one knew the decision was already made.

"Clive. Make it quick, though. Raven's due back at the studio in a half-hour."

No, she wasn't, but Clive nor anyone else knew.

Clive glanced at his notepad, then used his index finger to push his heavy black glasses up on his nose. Brooke thought he resembled what Buddy Holly might have looked like had he lived to fifty and eaten too much pizza.

"Yeah, Raven, thanks for taking my question. It's regarding your relationship with Travis Horton."

Wait a minute.

What relationship with Travis Horton?

Clive was obviously confused. Travis Horton dated Olivia Price, the nineteen-year-old Mississippi dime piece who wore her skirts too short and her neckline too low for old-timers but appealed just fine to the college crowd. Word was, Travis already had her hooked on whatever crap he had been ingesting since his last album pulled in the kind of money that allowed him to afford the stuff.

Brooke was stepping forward to correct Clive when she noticed that Raven looked like a cornered cat. The others in the press corps noticed it, too. Cameras buzzed and whirred. Cellphones flashed.

"You taking this or want me to?" Bobby whispered.

"Take it."

"There's nothing going on between Raven and Travis Horton," he announced in his casual, slow drawl. "Somebody fed you a line, Clive. That's all it is."

"Maybe, Bobby," Clive said. "But that somebody saw the two of them coming out the back entrance of the building where Travis rents his penthouse."

Raven had recovered enough to shake her head. "I don't have a clue where Travis Horton's penthouse even is," she said, laying on a little extra southern charm. Her response seemed to appease the rest of the press who were already packing up. Brooke could tell that Clive Naylor wanted to push the issue, but he wouldn't get the chance. Bobby escorted Raven back to the restroom and told her to wait there for a couple minutes while Brooke cleared the room.

When their paths crossed as they herded the media toward the door, Bobby whispered, "Raven is all fired up about us taking Clive's question."

Brooke would have to answer for herself.

RAVEN KEPT them waiting for twenty minutes.

"She must be on her phone," Bobby said as he checked his watch for the third time. "What else is there to do in there?" He had known and dealt with Raven long enough to recognize it was best to let her have her moment, then set about straightening things out. Brooke had to work to keep her knees from shaking as she and Bobby sat on the edge of the stage with their legs hanging over the side.

"Maybe not the best time to tell her I'll be going on tour with her," Brooke observed.

"Nonsense. We manage Raven, darlin'. Raven doesn't manage us."

"Promise me something, Dad? If you don't hear from me after a few days on the road, call the cops, okay?"

Bobby chuckled and made things a little better.

Raven was smiling when she stepped out of the restroom. That made things even better.

"Okay, guys," she said cheerfully. "We have six days until we start the Christmas tour. What town do we go to first, Bobby?"

"We kick it off here in Nashville. Bridgestone Arena. It'll be the biggest Christmas show anybody does this year."

"Oh darn, not the Opry?"

"It only holds 4,300, darlin'. What do we tell the other fifteen thousand nice folks who want to hear you sing? Besides, you're at the Opry tomorrow night."

"That will be fun."

"You're the final performer for the opening night of their Opry Christmas show. Lorrie and the Gatlins and all the others are opening for you. It'll be you that everyone sticks around to see."

Raven beamed.

Bobby continued. "Memphis is a week from Sunday, then Cincinnati. Both are sellouts. You have two days off after that."

"Good, good," Raven said. "That'll give me a chance to rest my voice. I truly love the Christmas songs."

Brooke knew it was time for Bobby to say something, but he seemed in no hurry. That was his way. Don't rush things. Everything in its own time. Instead, he told Raven about some of the backing groups that would accompany her, from the Tennessee State University Gospel Choir in Nashville to a Kansas City community chorus later in the tour. All were thrilled to be on stage with the great Raven McCloud.

"I can't wait," Raven said, clapping her hands.

"You'll be wonderful," Bobby said, reaching out and squeezing her hand. "I'm sending Brooke out with you. She'll do all the things I usually do."

The color drained from her face.

"Bobby? No. I need you there."

There was an uncertainty to Bobby's soft laugh. Did Raven notice?

"Now, sweetheart, you and I hardly cross paths on tour. Brooke is better suited to help you than an old broken-down cowboy."

"I signed on with that broken-down cowboy because I wanted him to manage my career."

"Yeah..." Bobby's voice trailed off. They had reached a

standoff. Brooke searched her father's face and saw something she didn't recognize. A sadness, perhaps? Or was it just an act to get Raven to acquiesce?

"Raven, this is your sixth Christmas tour," Brooke said. "I've been with you and Bobby for the last two. I know what the job takes, and I'll work my butt off to make this your best tour ever."

"You couldn't even control the press conference, Brooke."

There it was.

Brooke's stomach took a deep dive, but she refused to look away. "I'll own that. Clive Naylor tried to speak to me one-on-one and I blew him off. I apologize and promise to learn from my mistake." She paused and focused her attention on Raven. "But Raven, Dad isn't getting any younger. He needs a break now and then, and it's time for me to pick up some of his workload. You and I can make this work."

The room was quiet as Raven's gaze shifted from Brooke to the ceiling and finally to Bobby. She approached where he was seated and wedged herself between his knees. Their eyes met, and Raven placed her hands on his shoulders.

"I don't want you to get older, Bobby."

He smiled but didn't reply. His eyes said plenty. Raven continued, "If you need some time off, I'll allow Brooke to go with me, but if I hear you're out at Percy's Crossroads busting broncs or whatever it is you do that makes your back hurt so much, I'm dragging you back on the road with me, understand?"

Bobby nodded. He opened his arms and accepted Raven's embrace. Brooke watched and knew with certainty that the rumors of Raven and her father were just that. The look that passed between them, the way they embraced, reminded Brooke of her and Bobby. Father and daughter. Nothing more.

Raven hugged them both and went to the back door where Milo was waiting. She wiggled her fingers in farewell, then disappeared.

"That went well," Bobby said after a few moments.

"Do you think there's any truth to what Clive said?" Brooke asked. "Raven and Travis Horton?"

Bobby sighed. "I suspect so."

"That can't be good. Dad, I know you don't like bad language, but Travis Horton is an ass."

"Yep. Why do so many of you girls go for bad boys?"

"Don't toss me into that," she said, slapping his arm. "Tristan isn't anything like Travis Horton."

Bobby grimaced but said nothing. It wasn't that he disliked her boyfriend of three years as much as he just didn't see much about Tristan that was worth hanging on to. He never said it, but a girl just knew those things.

"Travis will find his way onto the tour somewhere along the way. I just know it." Bobby removed his Stetson and ran a hand through his white hair. "Maybe I should go along. Just in case."

Brooke eased herself off the stage and placed herself between his knees, exactly as Raven had. "No. If I'm going to make it in this business, I have to learn to handle those situations. If Travis Horton starts hanging around, I'll take care of it."

Bobby tipped her chin so their eyes met. "No shooting, though, right?"

"Dad, if I shot Travis Horton, it would be from long range. Nobody would have any idea who did it."

That made him laugh. "You're certainly a good enough shot."

"FFA skeet shooting champion two years in a row." She hugged him. "I learned from the best, and I learn more from you every day."

Brooke pushed open her apartment door a few minutes before eleven. The living room was dark, other than the glow from the TV. Tristan was stretched out on the couch with a half-eaten bag of microwave popcorn. The room had a stale smell. Burnt popcorn, stinky feet, and maybe tuna. She bent over and kissed him.

"Hey," he said. "Long day, huh?"

She sunk down onto the couch next to him and grabbed the popcorn.

"I botched up the press conference, but other than that everything was great."

She thought he might ask what she messed up, but he was focused on Jimmy Fallon so she munched popcorn and waited for a commercial break. The next thing she knew, Tristan was rubbing her shoulder.

"You dozed off."

"That kind of day," she said through a yawn. "How about yours?"

"Same old, same old. I'm pitching reverse mortgages this week, so that's different."

"Aren't those sort of predatory? Don't some of those companies take people's homes and kick them out?"

"A few of the less reputable ones," Tristan said as his hands drifted from her shoulder to her back. "Unfortunately, I think I'm shilling for one of them. It pays okay though, so there's that."

There was, Brooke had learned, some mysterious inner

sanctum of telemarketing. Probably in a dark corner of the web reserved for devil worshippers and unscrupulous used car salespeople. Wherever it was, they were aware of Tristan Fleming's aptitude for separating people from their money. Especially elderly people. He was turning out to be a much better telemarketer than guitarist. After three years of gigs in small venues all over town, they had hoped things might be the other way around. Tough town, Nashville.

"There is some good news though," he said as his hands continued to explore. "I'm playing next Saturday with Rance Troup's house band at Knucklehead's. His regular guy's grandmother croaked."

"Congratulations, I guess."

"Thanks. Can you come?"

Brooke stretched and allowed Tristan's fingers to move lower on her back. It felt good. Therapeutic and in other ways, too.

"I'll be on tour with Raven."

His fingers stopped.

"She's performing here in Nashville on Saturday night, though, right? Isn't that what I saw on the announcement?"

"Yes, but I'm taking the lead."

"Can't Bobby cover that night? I would love your opinion on how I sound with Rance's band."

"Sorry, Tristan, but I'm committed. I'll be home Tuesday and Wednesday, though. How about then?"

Tristan shook his head. "They don't play on Tuesday and Wednesday."

Brooke wrapped her arms around his neck and kissed his ear. "I'm sorry. There will be a next time, though." She kissed his ear again. "You're going to do great things. I know it."

SUNDAY, NOVEMBER 27

NASHVILLE AND GARLAND GROVE

Bobby was at his kitchen table when Brooke arrived at ten-fifteen. The day was gray and cold, and she didn't expect he would stray far from the farm, other than perhaps a quick run to Percy's Crossroads General Store for one of those disgusting scrapple sandwiches he loved so much. You couldn't tell anything of his plans by looking at him. The outfit was a near match to the day before, except the shirt was light blue and the vest and belt were dark brown. The $5,000 Stetson was on the shelf, replaced by an older and cheaper version, but could be called into duty should someone show up unexpectedly.

"I brought doughnuts," Brooke said, setting a bag on the table.

"The good ones, or that foo-foo kind with nuts and stuff?"

"The good ones." Bobby reached for the bag and grinned when he found a coconut cream.

Brooke asked, "You want milk?" as she moved to the refrigerator.

"I'm not sure I have any, sweetie."

She checked. He had milk, but the expiration date was eleven days past. She poured it into the sink and threw away the container. Bobby wasn't much of a cook. Never had been. When Brooke was growing up Miss Ruth came by daily to clean up, buy groceries, and leave something in the refrigerator for dinner. Miss Ruth had reluctantly quit four years earlier after her son Troy signed a baseball contract with the Minnesota Twins and said he didn't want his mama cleaning houses anymore. Bobby had planned to hire someone to replace her but never got around to it. The fridge and cupboards were mostly bare, and Bobby took most of his meals at local diners where people either didn't know or didn't care about his show business connections.

"Hey, Brooke, have you got time to listen to something?" Bobby went into his office and returned with a CD player. "I've been going through those old songs of Raven's."

"And you found her next hit?"

"I wish," he snorted. "Most of it is Raven trying to sound like Reba or Shania Twain, but I found one that kind of piqued my interest."

He hit the button and sat back. After a moment of silence, a guitar started playing—not bad guitar, but not especially good, either. Just okay. The melody was slow like a ballad and reminded Brooke of some of George Strait's older stuff. Then someone started singing. A guy.

"That's not Raven."

Bobby shook his head.

It was a Christmas song, Christmas Eve, really. About a couple wrapping Christmas presents for their kids and doing all the stuff moms and dads do the night before Christmas.

Until the mom started putting the moves on the dad.

Brooke didn't see that coming.

The hook, she had to admit, was quite good.

"Making Santa smile."

She listened closely as it played out, then asked Bobby to play it again. He did.

"What do you think?" he asked as it ended the second time.

"You realize that the Mama and Daddy are getting it on, don't you?"

Bobby snickered. "I'm old, darlin', but not dead."

"Right there in the middle of all the Christmas presents, they're...and she..." Brooke felt her face start to burn. "...to him right there in the living room."

Bobby nodded.

"Dad, it's kind of...*risqué*, don't you think?"

"Yeah, but in a sneaky way. Listen to the lyrics again." He fired up the CD one more time. The quality wasn't the best, but Brooke could still make out the words.

"See what I mean about sneaky? Little kids won't pick up on what's going on, so it's an okay tune to play on the car radio. Mom and Dad will hear it and kind of look across the room at each other like maybe this Christmas, we'll...you know."

"How about the Baptist church?" Brooke asked.

"A few of them will preach fire and damnation for anybody who listens to it, but we get that anyway."

"Good point. Are you thinking Raven should record this?"

Bobby raised his hands. "Heck no. Remember how much backlash we got for that song she did about the reformed prostitute?"

Brooke remembered.

"This isn't for Raven. Or any female singer for that matter. But maybe if I can get it in the hands of some up-

and-comer we can score a quick Christmas hit and jump-start a career at the same time."

That was Bobby in a nutshell. Salvaging something from a bunch of old demo tapes that most everyone would have tossed to the curb. Who knew if it would work? But Brooke knew how much her father enjoyed the pursuit of new talent.

"There's one problem, though," Bobby said as he removed the CD and examined the label. "Someone wrote this song. And someone performed it. Maybe they're one and the same, but if we decide to do anything with it, we have to at least make a good faith attempt to find them." He slid the CD across the table to Brooke, then finished off his doughnut. "Will you ask Raven if she remembers who this fella is?"

"Sure, Dad. I'm going by her place to make sure she's ready for the Ryman tonight."

"That's a good idea. She putters around that big old house and forgets her commitments sometimes. After you leave her place will you stop by Country 98's studio? Tommy Watkins does his show today from noon 'til six. Ask him to put this on and see what kind of response it gets.

"No problem. Anything else?"

"Yeah." Bobby stood up and came around the table. He planted a kiss on her forehead. "Next time you come out bring me more than one doggone doughnut."

Raven's maid had Sunday off, so she answered the door herself. Brooke noticed how she glanced toward the drive-way, probably checking to see if Bobby had come along.

"I'm making sticky buns," Raven said after a quick hug. "Want one?"

The doughnut from ninety minutes ago was still weighing her down, but Brooke never refused sticky buns. "Just one, though."

Raven's choice of a home had always puzzled Brooke. Five bedrooms and more bathrooms than she could keep track of. Six secluded acres a half-hour southwest of downtown Nashville. Plenty of stars lived in the area, but none were single. Brooke wondered sometimes if Raven spent a lot of time getting lost in her own house while wishing she had invested in a high-rise condo close to midtown's restaurants and nightlife. Maybe she would ask her sometime.

Raven was wearing sleeping pants and an Idaho State University sweatshirt. No shoes. No makeup. Bedhead. And she still looked great. Brooke caught a glimpse of herself in the door leading to an outdoor patio and wished she had opted for jeans and a sweater rather than business attire. She was working, though. Anytime she was with a client she was working. Bobby was a stickler that way, and it had worked out okay for him. She sat at an oversized kitchen island while Raven prepared the buns. The kitchen was so white that it nearly hurt her eyes. Nothing was out of place, despite being the maid's day off.

"What's new?" Raven asked as she spread icing across a half-dozen buns that filled a large baking pan.

Brooke removed the CD from her purse. "Dad wants you to listen to a song and tell us what you know about it. I left my CD player in the car, though."

"Second drawer, next to the stove." Raven pointed with an icing-covered index finger. "It doesn't get much use anymore, but I still keep it around just in case."

The player was small. Probably from the late nineties.

Brooke suspected there was no way the batteries were still good, but she hit the power button and saw a light come on, so she jammed the CD in and clicked play. Raven didn't say anything until the song was over.

"What about it?"

"Any idea who it is?"

"Should I have any idea?"

Brooke removed the CD and held it up. "It was in those old tapes and stuff that Dad showed you yesterday. From back when you were in college."

The mention of college caused a light to go on for Raven. "Yeah. I remember. I dated him."

"This is great. We need to find him and see if he's okay with us recording it with another singer. Any idea where he is these days?" Brooke grinned as she added, "Or don't you keep up with your old boyfriends?"

"There weren't that many, believe it or not. I liked lots of guys, but never really let any get too close." She pointed to the CD. "That guy was an exception. We dated from midterm until Thanksgiving."

"You broke up at Thanksgiving?"

"I didn't go back after break. I liked him, but not as much as I liked Nashville."

"And that was the end of it?"

"Remember, Brooke, we didn't have cellphones and stuff back then. I had a school email account, but when I didn't return they shut it off. Maybe he tried to call Mom and Dad's place, but I wasn't there, so I guess we just..." her voice trailed off.

"You ghosted him." Brooke said with a smile.

Raven put the sticky buns in the oven, then leaned against the island. "Yeah, I guess I did. That was inconsiderate of me, wasn't it?"

"Maybe I'll ask him when I track him down. What was his name?"

Raven shrugged.

"Wait a minute." Brooke stood up. "You don't even remember his name?"

"His first name was Carl. I think."

"You think?"

"Or maybe it was..." Raven pushed her hair away from her forehead. "Yeah, I'm pretty sure it was Carl. But as far as his last name? No idea."

"You're not making this easy for me, Raven."

Raven laughed. "It's for stuff like this that I have you and your sweet Daddy."

The timer went off and they dove into the sticky buns. Unlike at Bobby's house, milk was abundant in Raven's fridge. Large frothy glasses of chocolate. The whole stuff, not that watery skim. Brooke drank hers a little faster than she should have and belched. Raven laughed, then belched too. For a few minutes, it seemed less like a recording star and her agent and more like two old friends. Was it too much to hope that it stayed that way?

"I have to run into town for a couple appointments," Brooke said after a half-hour of chit-chat. "I'll be back at six to ride to the Opry with you. Did the messenger come by for the music this morning?"

"They have it. I'm doing one of the new Christmas songs we'll use on the tour. They begged me for an encore, but I put my foot down."

Brooke knew better. The contract specified one song. But if it made Raven feel good to say they begged her for more, who was Brooke to correct her? They hugged again as Brooke was leaving.

"This was fun," Raven said as she showed her out. "Maybe having you on tour will be pretty good after all."

"You better believe it. Now if you hear from your old boyfriend Carl between now and this evening, promise me you'll give him my number, okay?"

Raven made the pinky promise. "Who knows, Brooke? The two of you might make a great couple."

If there was any doubt that the Christmas season had started it was put to rest as Brooke drove to the Country 98 studio on Fourth Avenue. City workers along Union Street were busy hanging decorations in Public Square Park. The Metro Christmas tree lighting would be later that night, at about the same time that she and Raven would be arriving at the Opry.

Country 98 was housed on the first floor of a century-old seven-story hotel, in space that legend said had housed everything over the years from a haberdashery to a chili parlor. As it was the weekend, the door was locked. A sign instructed visitors to call the studio number for access. The voice on the other end sounded like a kid but was probably one of the many underpaid college interns who kept things humming around town. When Brooke said who she was and why she was there the kid buzzed her in. There was no sign of the intern when she stepped into the studio, but Tommy Watkins himself was waiting for her.

"Well son-of-a-gun if it ain't the legend's daughter!" Tommy extended his liver-spotted hand. "Your daddy ain't out fishing in this weather, sweetheart, so I'm guessing he's on the road."

"He's home, Tommy. Since I was coming by, he wanted

me to stop in and ask a favor." Brooke fished the CD from her purse. "We found this song in some stuff at the house. Dad thinks it might have potential and was hoping you would put it on and see what people think."

"If Bobby Summers thinks it has potential, then it must have potential. Let's hustle on in there and play it." Brooke followed Tommy through the reception area and into the studio. Anyone who expected palatial digs with high-tech equipment would be disappointed. The space was cramped, with barely enough room for Tommy to turn around. The walls were covered with sound-absorbing foam and yellowed concert posters. The carpet was threadbare. Tommy was sort of threadbare, too, come to think of it. Two generations of Music City listeners had made him a celebrity around town. His morning drivetime show topped the ratings year in and year out. Radio was a tough business, though, and Tommy's best years were far behind him. Age, changing music tastes, and falling ratings forced his demotion from the morning airwaves, first to a midday spot then, as he entered his mid-seventies, to his current show on Sundays. Brooke gave him credit, though. Tommy handled his reduced role with humility and good humor.

"What's on here exactly?" Tommy asked as a Waylon Jennings tune played in the background. "We don't play many CD's anymore."

"A Christmas tune. The title is—"

"Brooke, honey, I don't start playing Christmas music until next Sunday." Tommy handed the CD back. "If you want to come around then I'll give it a spin for you."

"Oh, darn. Thanks anyway, Tommy. The guys over at Nashville 105 are playing a few Christmas songs. I'll run by there." Brooke stood up and stuck the CD in her purse, hopeful that Tommy wouldn't call her bluff and let her walk out the door.

He didn't let her walk.

"Wait a minute, darling. Those guys are so far behind us in the latest ratings books, there's probably not anybody even listening." He glanced over his shoulder at the sound board. Waylon was a minute from winding down. "What's the song called?"

"Making Santa Smile."

"And who sings it?"

"Well...we don't exactly know."

Tommy's face had a pinched expression that made Brooke think he was about to back out again. He glanced at the CD, then said, "No name?"

"His first name is Carl. We think."

Tommy nodded and slipped the CD into an auxiliary player. He turned on his microphone and said, "There's a little Waylon to spice up your Sunday, folks. Now I've got a treat for you. A little holiday ditty from a performer..." He paused, pursed his lips, then said, "A guy who goes by Carl... *Christmas* Carl. Yesiree, folks, here's Christmas Carl with his latest, 'Making Santa Smile.'"

"That's Christmas Carl right there folks. 'Making Santa Smile.' Yes indeed. What did you think of that one? Why don't you call us and let us know? You're listening to the Tommy Watkins Weekend Show here on Country 98 and here's an oldie but a goodie from Miss Loretta Lynn. Tommy lowered the studio volume and turned to Brooke.

"That song is kinda dirty, ain't it?"

"No, Tommy. I mean, it's a little suggestive, but so are plenty of songs today."

He placed his hammy forearms on the control board and stroked his chin. "Yeah, but the mama in that song, she...did she... I guess that would make me smile, come to think of it. Or maybe it would have twenty years ago."

Brooke laughed. "Will the phone calls come to you, Tommy?"

"Trang takes the calls on weekends. He's the kid who let you in."

"I'll stop and see him on the way out. Thank you, Tommy."

"You betcha, darlin'. Tell Bobby I'll be at Wainwright's this Wednesday. He can buy my steak."

"I'll let him know. Take care."

With ninety minutes to burn Brooke decided to make a quick stop at her apartment. From the parking lot, she could hear TVs blaring from every direction. That wasn't uncommon on a fall Sunday in Nashville. Everybody loved their Tennessee Titans. When they were playing in town, fans clogged the interstates and filled the bars. More people in Nashville could tell you who the Titans were playing than could name the Governor of Tennessee. While not a hardcore fan, Brooke kept up enough to know how the team was doing and who the stars were. She had other things on her mind, though, as she left her car and walked up the stairs to her place. She needed to check back with the kid at the radio station, call the stage manager at the Opry to make sure there were no last-minute changes, and confirm with Milo the time he would pick them up. She would also change clothes. It was getting colder as the day wore on, and by golly, if Bobby could wear blue jeans, so could she.

All that was momentarily forgotten when she stepped into the apartment and found Tristan and three guys watching the game. Two of them she had never seen before. She wished she had never seen the third.

Julian Freeport.

"Hey, hon!" Tristan stumbled as he scrambled out of the recliner. "I thought you weren't getting home until late." He glanced at the food spread that covered every inch of their round coffee table, except the corner where Julian Freeport had parked his bare feet. "Titans and Broncos are tied in the second quarter. You want some nachos?"

"No thanks. I only have a few minutes before I head back out." She looked from Tristan to the strangers, then back at Tristan.

"These guys work with me. That's Zane." A big guy with a cheese-stained Titans jersey waved from where he was stretched out on the floor. He had a beer in front of him and three empties nearby.

"Wandy's over there." Wandy was a stringy-haired guy with peach fuzz on his cheeks and chin. He probably didn't weigh a hundred pounds. At least he got to his feet and stuck out his hand. "Hi, Brooke."

"And you already know—"

"Damn right she knows me," Julian said from the far end of the couch. "How's the music biz, Brookster?"

Brookster?

"Great, Julian. How's the dope business?"

That sucked the air out of the room. Except for Julian. Nothing fazed him.

"I wouldn't presume to have any idea what you're talking about, Brookster."

Julian knew damned well what she was talking about, but what good would it do to argue with Tristan's dopehead buddy? "I have to change and head back out," she said instead. Tristan followed her into their bedroom and stood silently while she launched her clothes toward the overflowing hamper.

"Why are you changing? You know how much I like—"

"Why is Julian here?" she snapped.

"He didn't have any place to watch the game. His dad's TV is broken."

"He can go to a bar or that wing place you guys like so much."

"You know he can't go to a bar, Brooke." Tristan's voice was rising. "He still has the ankle monitor. If his probation officer—"

"He wears an ankle monitor, *Tristan*, because he was convicted of dealing pot outside a high school. And what the hell difference is there between a bar and this place? There are beer cans all over the living room, including two empty ones on the end table next to Julian. And I'm sure that smell in the air isn't that cheap cologne you guys love so much."

"Hold on a minute!" Tristan's eyes narrowed. He straightened his usually stooped posture to stand at his full height, which wasn't much taller than Brooke. If he was going for intimidation, he wasn't succeeding. "Yeah, the guys probably smoked weed on their way over, but I told them not to bring it in. And they didn't. And what's the big deal anyway, Brooke? The shit is legal practically everywhere in the country except here. And sooner or later, it will be legal here too."

"It's not just the weed, Tristan." Brooke lowered her voice, which had been escalating to match his. "It's that..."

She took a deep breath. It was the same song, different verse. Tristan not only supported legalization of weed, but he was also an occasional user. How occasional Brooke couldn't be sure. There were so many things about him that had attracted her. The dope continued to trip her up, though. That and her suspicion that he had started experimenting with other stuff. Stuff that would never be legalized. Part of it was the time he spent at home. He used to do his work from a small desk in the corner of the apartment's second bedroom, but in recent months had relocated to the kitchen table. It was hard being stuck in the cramped apartment all day, she got that. But until his music started paying the bills, his options were limited. Waiting tables never paid very well. He had tried and failed miserably at being a substitute teacher. That left telemarketing.

"Look," she said, coming to him still in her underwear and wrapping her arms around his waist. "You go enjoy the rest of the game. I'm going to make a couple calls and head to Raven's place. She goes on stage at nine-thirty, so if things go according to plan, I'll be home before midnight."

He kissed her. His breath smelled of beer and cheese and maybe grass. At that point, she didn't care. When his fingers traced down her spine she shivered but stepped back.

"Later," she said. "I really have to go. And you have to get back to your friends."

"They're fine," he said breathily.

"What if they're stealing the silverware."

This made Tristan laugh. Friends or not he knew a good zinger when he heard it. He kissed her again and stepped out. Brooke locked the bedroom door and threw herself onto the bed for a few blissful minutes of rest.

❄

GPS showed Interstate 65 was backed up, so Brooke jumped on Hillsboro Pike. Traffic cleared a couple miles out of downtown. She punched Bobby's number and he answered on the first ring. Brooke heard the Titans' game playing in the background.

"Darn it, Dad, I forgot the game was still on. I'll let you finish watching."

"This one's in the bag, darlin'. Titans are ahead by three touchdowns at the two-minute warning. What's up?"

"Tommy Watkins played the song."

"I heard. He called and left a message after you left. Something about me owing him lunch at Wainwright's."

"Yeah, you do. I just got off the phone with the kid who takes calls for him."

"Trang?"

"You know him? Dad, how? He can't be more than seventeen."

"He's older than that. He's a sophomore at Austin Peay. Communications major. He thought he had landed in high cotton when he caught on with Country 98, but they stuck him with Tommy and he's bored to death."

"But, Dad, how do you come to know the weekend intern at a local radio station?"

"The same way you come to know people, honey. By reaching out. By being nice. It ain't hard. You're already real good at it."

Brooke felt a pang of guilt for having barely given Trang the time of day. She had to get better at that. But anyway...

"The kid...Trang said they didn't get any calls about the song."

"Nothing?"

"Nothing."

The line was silent for a few beats before Bobby said, "Maybe I misjudged it."

"No way, Dad. You have an ear for these kinds of things."

"Not always. Did I ever tell you the story about how I passed on Dwight Yoakum?"

He had shared that story many times. And she knew he was about to share it again.

"I was still just a kid myself, but I thought the business was headed toward the urban cowboy music. Old Dwight didn't fit that mold, so I passed. How big would this farm be if I'd signed him when I had the chance?"

"Everybody makes a mistake now and then. Do you want me to reach out to another radio station, Dad?"

"Nah. You've got enough going on. I guess old Carl what's-his-name just missed his chance at a million dollars. Have a good evening with Raven and call if you need anything."

"I love you, Daddy."

"I love...so they didn't get any calls about the song?"

"Nope."

"None at all?"

"None at all."

"Hmm... I love you too, sugar. Give my best to the folks at the Opry."

Brooke surfed the internet while she waited in Raven's living room. She had arrived a half-hour early. Milo had just texted that he was topping off the gas tank and would be there shortly.

The semi-circular sofa was arranged in front of a huge fireplace where Raven kept a roaring fire going from Thanksgiving through New Year's. The warmth it put off felt good as Brooke relaxed against the plush white leather upholstery. The sky had begun to spit snow on her drive out. It probably wouldn't amount to anything, but any threat of winter weather in Nashville brought out the craziness. People flocked to the supermarkets for bread and milk, and, like Milo, topped off their gas tanks. It was usually all for nothing, as temperatures would probably be back in the fifties by midweek.

Brooke was surprised to hear Raven coming downstairs a few minutes early. She tucked away her phone and turned to catch a glimpse. Jeans that cost more than twenty pairs of the ones Brooke wore, a beautiful cashmere sweater, and boots. Raven could go on stage in the outfit and leave the fans speechless, but she would change into something even nicer when they reached the Opry.

"Can we leave a few minutes early and see some Christmas lights?" Raven asked as she stopped to check herself in a mirror at the bottom of the stairs.

"That will be fun. We have some time to kill. Are you ready?"

"Let me grab a coat."

Brooke nearly gasped at the white puffer coat Raven retrieved from the closet. "Did you get that at Saks?"

"Is it too much?" Raven asked, suddenly self-conscious. "Brittany recommended it."

Raven had met Brittany, the young woman who served Raven and other Nashville elite as a personal shopper.

"Brittany was right," Brooke said. "I'm ready to fight you for it right here and now."

Raven grinned and pointed her finger at Brooke. "I

would win." She demonstrated a shuffle step and several jabs and uppercuts. "Cardio-boxing three times a week, remember?"

"Okay then, you can keep the coat. Milo is outside waiting. Let's go see the lights."

Milo recommended they backtrack to the Nashville suburb of Franklin, a community that had maintained its small-town vibe. Brooke rode in back with Raven, and upon Milo's suggestion, they stopped for peanut brittle and cider at a little place Milo knew about. He pulled into the parking lot, scoped out the situation, and said, "It doesn't look like there's many people inside. Do you want to go in, Brooke? I'll wait here with Miss McCloud."

"Why don't we all go in?" Raven said suddenly.

"Raven, I don't know." Brooke looked about, certain that little good could come from parading one of the biggest names in show business into a country candy store, but also remembering Bobby saying that their clients sometimes craved a bit of normalcy. It was rather dreary out, with the precipitation alternating between snow and rain. She counted just four cars in the lot. Maybe they could pull it off.

"Milo, pull around the side where no one will see who gets out."

Once they were parked, Brooke stepped out of the car. Milo followed. "Lead the way, Milo. If you see anything weird, get her out of there."

Milo opened Raven's door and she emerged, one beautiful blue-jean-covered leg in front of the other. She pulled her puffy coat around her, and she and Brooke followed Milo to the entrance.

"Make it quick, folks," a matronly woman behind the

counter called out. "We're closing in ten—*holy smokes, you're Raven McCloud!*"

There were seven other people in the store. Three were elderly women. They gawked but posed no threat. A man was alone, immersed in the store's selection of fresh pies. He took a quick look, then went back to his browsing. Probably not a country music fan. The other three customers were a family. A couple not much older than Brooke and a little girl probably in preschool. The husband made a beeline for Raven, pulling his wife behind him, who pulled their daughter behind her. Brooke moved into the space between Raven and the father, ready for whatever might happen. Milo did the same. Behind them, Raven exclaimed, "Hey everybody. It's so good to see y'all. We stopped in for some of that yummy peanut brittle y'all sell here."

The man slowed. He was smiling from ear to ear. So was his wife. Their daughter appeared to be on the verge of tears from having her arm nearly torn from its socket.

"Come here, sweetheart," Raven said, bending down and extending her arms to the child. "There's no reason to cry. It'll be Christmas in a few weeks. Do you like Christmas?"

It was as if she had cast a spell. The little girl nodded and said that she did indeed like Christmas. She let go of her mother's hand and went to Raven who hugged her and said, "You want some peanut brittle... What's your name, sweetheart?"

"Hattie."

"Would you like some peanut brittle, Hattie?"

Hattie nodded. Raven stood up and turned to face the others. "How about y'all? Does everyone like peanut brittle?" Everyone did, except the man who was checking out the pies.

"I have a peanut allergy."

"Oh, well in that case, just pick yourself a pie and take it to the nice lady at the counter." She stepped to the case where the peanut brittle was displayed. "Why don't you just divide all of that into..." she stopped and counted the people around her, including Milo and Brooke. "Why don't you divide it into nine and box it up for us all to take home? It's my gift to y'all."

Unsure how to respond, the customers applauded, except the pie lover. The shopkeeper was speechless as she filled the order.

"I'll take apple," the pie lover said to Raven. "What was your name again?"

"I'm Dolly Parton," Raven said with a giggle. The others laughed along with her.

"I've heard of you," the man said. "Thanks for the pie."

"We're going to have to hustle to make it to the Opry," Milo said when they returned to the car.

"That's fine," Raven said. "We can see the lights another time." She turned to Brooke. "That was so much fun! Thank you for going along with it. Bobby would have made me wait in the car."

Uh-oh.

"Sometimes you just have to take things as they come," Brooke answered gamely, quoting another Bobby-ism. "But if it's all the same to you, Raven, let's not tell him."

They gossiped and munched peanut brittle while Milo cleared the windshield. After a couple minutes, he put the limo into gear.

Nothing happened.

He revved the motor and tried again.

Nothing happened, except the engine died.

"Milo?" Brooke said mid-chew.

"Must be flooded," he said. He turned the key, and the engine came back to life.

And died again.

"It's getting cold in here," Raven said, looking up from her cellphone. "Is everything okay?"

"Cold might be the least of our worries," Brooke answered, trying to keep the panic out of her voice. "Milo?"

"I'm trying, Brooke."

And he was. But nothing was happening.

"Brooke..." Milo said, alarm creeping into his tone. "It isn't going to start."

"It has to start," Raven said. "I go onstage in less than an hour."

Milo kept trying. And trying. It was a lost cause.

What would Bobby do in a situation like this?

Bobby wouldn't *get* in a situation like this.

But Brooke was, and she had to do something quick.

"Milo, how long will it take to get another limo?"

When he turned to face Brooke he was sweating. "Longer than we have. They're all giving Christmas light tours."

Brooke pulled out her phone and her eyes were drawn to the Uber app she used while traveling. A ride from their location to the Opry would be pricy, but preferable to Raven missing her appearance. She plugged in the destination and was dismayed to see that it would be seventeen minutes before a car would arrive to pick them up. That was cutting it close, but what else could they do?

A rap at the window next to her head nearly caused Brooke to pee her jeans. It was the pie lover from the shop.

"Are you having trouble?"

Could they?

Should they?

What if he turned out to be a serial killer? Brooke could only imagine the headlines.

RAVEN McCLOUD LATEST VICTIM OF PIE EATING SERIAL KILLER!

"Brooke?"

MANAGER BROOKE SUMMERS TO BLAME!

"Brooke, honey?"

"What? Did we? Oh, Raven, I'm so sorry that—"

"Honey, put the window down."

"I don't know if we should—"

"Put down the window, sugar. He's not going to do anything bad."

Brooke lowered the window, her eyes locked on the pie lover's hands, checking for a gun or knife. They were empty, except for the pie.

"Our car won't start and I need to get to the Opry," Raven said. "Any chance you can give my manager and me a ride?"

"The Opry?" he asked.

"Yeah, sweetie. It's in Nashville."

He stared at her for a few moments before recognition seemed to come.

"Is that the place by that big shopping center?"

"Yes! Yes, it is!" Raven exclaimed. "Do you like to shop?"

"No, but my wife does. I usually take the kids to the Rainforest Cafe while we wait for her."

"You're a good man, Mr... I don't believe we caught your name."

"It's actually Doctor. I'm a philosophy professor at Lipscomb. Just call me Ahmad. You'll never be able to pronounce my last name. Sure, I'll give you a ride. My friends will be impressed that I spent Sunday night with Dolly Parton."

They arrived at the Opry with twenty minutes to spare. Ahmad was a sweetheart who, while disappointed that Raven wasn't really Dolly Parton, gratefully accepted four complimentary tickets to her show the following week. What he wouldn't accept was the hundred-dollar bill Brooke offered him.

"This is Nashville," he said, waving off the cash. "I've only been here since June, but I understand that people go out of their way to help each other here."

Brooke was ready to dash for the building, but Raven McCloud never ran, even if late. They took their time passing through security, then strolled through the stage entrance as if Raven owned the place. Which, based on her current popularity, she kind of did.

"Now Brooke, I'm glad to be here, but I don't want to stay long after the show is over. If some of the folks want to bend my ear, please step in and rescue me, okay?"

"I'll say the limo is waiting and you have friends in town."

"Good! Now you go on and enjoy yourself. I'll get changed and wait for my cue. I'll see you back here later. And thanks for a fun evening!"

Brooke strolled around the building while other stars performed their holiday tunes. She reminisced about her first visit to the Opry, with Bobby of course. She was four years old, yet she remembered many details of the magical night including meeting the legendary Ronnie Milsap and being surprised to learn he was blind. "These are good people," Bobby said that night as they watched the performances from seats in the second row. "And you'll get to know a lot of them as you grow up."

He was right. On both counts. Sure, some weren't the most morally upright people in the world. They had affairs, drank too much, and blew their money, but they and the business had been pretty good to Bobby, and after six years of working alongside him and learning from him, Brooke felt blessed that it was treating her pretty good, too.

The snow was coming down hard when Craig Callaway stepped out of Hanson's Fine Italian. If the forecast was correct, the fifteen inches on the ground would be covered by another foot by Tuesday morning.

That was winter in Garland Grove.

"Wait here under the awning," Craig said to his girlfriend, Jenna Waite. "I'll run up the street and get the car."

"Blow the horn when you pull up." Jenna smiled as she stepped back to the door. "I'll be waiting inside next to the fireplace." Craig jogged north to where he had parked his pickup, nearly tripping over a bump in the sidewalk in front of Haley's Bicycle Shop.

A man passing by with his wife called out, "Careful there, Craig. It's slicker than sin out here."

Craig acknowledged the man, a long-time customer of his drugstore, and paused for a moment to get his footing. Though Haley's was closed on Sunday, an amazingly flexible mannequin named Manny still pedaled an old-fashioned cruiser bike, just as he had for decades.

"Hey, Manny," Craig called out because it was supposed to be good luck. Snub Manny at your own peril, Craig's friend, Amy, had admonished him last winter.

Thanks to remote start, the pickup was warm when he jumped in. The tires were new, as were the wiper blades. He hadn't grown up in Garland Grove, but nine years in town had taught him not to underestimate the weather.

The community's Decoration Committee, a team of sturdy men with sturdier ladders, had worked with the city maintenance crew to get the downtown Christmas decorations installed the previous afternoon. Some locals argued that the weekend after Thanksgiving was too early and that Christmas needed to wait its turn. They were in the minority, though, and the Santas, angels, and candy canes suspended from streetlamps would remain lighted through the second week of January. All night, every night.

It took a couple horn blows before Jenna emerged from Hanson's. She had her phone to her ear, probably chatting with her mother. Though Nancy and Homer Waite lived in Freeport, just 30 miles away, Jenna rarely missed a day of catching up with them. She finished the conversation and tucked the phone into her coat pocket.

"Even a minute out there is too long tonight," she said as she got in and reached for the heat control.

"Your house or mine?" Craig asked.

"Umm, how about mine. I'm recording that Grand Ole Opry Christmas special that's on tonight."

Craig was disappointed but tried not to let it show. Going to Jenna's house meant he would be returning home later in the evening. Whenever he and Jenna spent the night together it was at his house. He never quite understood why, other than her place was just off the main road while his was tucked away in the back of one of Garland

45

Grove's older residential districts. It was the twenty-first century, and the two of them were in their thirties. Unmarried and unattached, except to one another, but Jenna didn't want people to see his truck parked at her place overnight and get the wrong idea.

Craig drove carefully through the four-block downtown area, cognizant of slippery roads and the possibility of Officer Greg Claggett lying in wait just beyond the feed store to enforce the strict twenty-five mile an hour downtown speed limit.

"How's Nancy?" he asked.

"What?"

"Your mom? Are you zoning out over there?"

"No, I'm just enjoying the snow. I guess she's okay. Why?"

"Weren't you talking to her when I picked you up?"

"What? Oh, yeah. She's fine. Are you okay with watching that Christmas special?"

"Sure. I know you like it."

She smiled. "We went to the Opry at Christmas time when I was in junior high school, but I know you're not a big country music fan."

"I like it well enough. It'll be fun. Do you have popcorn?"

"Sure, but how can you be hungry after that big plate of spaghetti and meatballs?"

Craig grabbed her hand. "Christmas music and popcorn go well together. And maybe romance. Romance and Christmas music? And popcorn?"

Jenna laughed. "I guess we'll just have to see."

Brooke felt the crowd rippling with excitement when Larry Gatlin took the stage following the next-to-last performer of the evening. While he spent a couple minutes plugging upcoming shows and performers, several people called out from their seats.

"Bring out Raven!"

"We want Raven!"

Gatlin handled the interruptions with his usual good-natured charm, then, after a moment's hesitation to build up the excitement, said, "And here she is, the one...the only... Raven McCloud."

The crowd erupted. Raven kept them in anticipation for a few moments while the band played and repeated the opening riff of her top-five holiday smash from the previous year. And then, in a flash of lights and fake snow, she emerged to a wall of sound. Guitars, keyboards, drums, and an adoring audience not afraid to show their love. Raven McCloud was in her element. And off she went.

Brooke had moved to the back of the auditorium where she could take in everything. Raven held center stage like a queen held her scepter. Her appearance commanded total attention, from the short black skirt trimmed in white Santa fur to the sweater with *I've Been Good!* emblazoned across the front. It practically screamed, *look at me*. And boy did they look. Brooke's eyes swept over the 4,300 people, most on their feet, swaying and singing along. Some were dancing. Raven had them right where she wanted them. And when the song was over after four minutes that seemed like four seconds, they showered her with love and applause and stomping of feet and calls for more.

"Encore!"

"Play us another one, Raven!"

But that was all they would get. Raven bowed, blew

kisses, and waved. She pointed at strangers in the crowd as if they were old friends, calling out, "I love you!" and "Merry Christmas!" at least a dozen times. And then she was gone. The houselights went up the minute Raven left the stage. Larry Gatlin came out to thank people for coming, but they barely heard him.

Holy smokes, it was spectacular.

Brooke remained near the exit, watching and listening as waves of people passed by. None had any clue who she was or that an hour earlier she had been stranded with Raven McCloud at a Franklin candy shop. She was just another face in the crowd. And she always would be. Bobby never allowed himself to become the story. *Unless your name is Colonel Tom Parker, stay away from the spotlight*, he said, referring to Elvis Presley's longtime manager and master showman. Very few country music fans knew the name Bobby Summers, but the people they worshipped, the performers they came to see? They knew Bobby. They respected him. Many wanted him to manage their careers. If there were a hall of fame for country music managers, Bobby would be Babe Ruth and Willie Mays all in one.

And Brooke was his kid. His only kid. And his heir apparent.

Oh, my goodness.

"Oh. My. Goodness. Isn't she amazing?"

Jenna had been lying with her head in Craig's lap until the show's final performer took the stage. Craig knew of Raven McCloud. He could even name a couple of her songs, but mostly he listened to the oldies station out of Freeport. He could bang out from memory most any hit by

Hall and Oates or Billy Joel on the piano at Garden Grove's Vogue Opera House or the keyboard he kept in the back of his closet. He could play the opening chords of Lynyrd Skynyrd's Free Bird or the Eagles' Desperado on his old Yamaha guitar.

But country music? Nah, it never moved him like Dire Straits or Toto.

He had to admit, though, that Jenna was right. Raven McCloud was pretty amazing. And damned beautiful. He had googled her while Jenna fast-forwarded through the commercials. They were about the same age, he and Raven McCloud. That was all they had in common, though. At thirty-nine, she still looked great in short skirts and tight sweaters. The thirty-four inch waist on Craig's khakis was starting to feel snug. Raven's face was perfect, angelic even. No beginnings of a double chin there. No glasses, either. Lush, full hair. She looked twenty. The thought of someone his age being in such great shape made Craig consider renewing his membership at Garland Grove Fitness.

"Don't you think?"

He definitely would renew that membership. After Christmas, of course.

"Craig? Don't you think?"

"I sure do."

Jenna plopped down next to him. "You weren't hearing a thing I said."

He reluctantly admitted that he hadn't.

"I said she's sexy, isn't she?"

"Who?"

Jenna slapped his shoulder playfully. "Don't lie. It's okay. Raven McCloud is incredible. I mean, I'm at least five years younger than her, and if I had the thighs to be able to rock that skirt, I would buy it tomorrow."

"It would be hard to birth a calf in a skirt that short, wouldn't it?"

Jenna laughed for what Craig realized was the first time all evening. Was he losing his comic touch?

"You're right," she said, "but the farmers would enjoy it."

She sat back down next to him and kissed his cheek. "My appointments start early tomorrow."

That, he knew, was her way of saying hit the road, Jack. No romance tonight. He stood up, stretched, and went in search of his shoes. She followed, grabbing his coat from the closet doorknob where he always left it.

"I nearly forgot to ask," he said as he pulled on his shoes. "How does tomorrow evening work for going out to Blankenship's Tree Farm? I was thinking we could go to Smack's for dinner, then pick out our trees."

"Oh, darn, Craig. I can't commit. I'm meeting Mom after work and maybe doing some shopping."

He paused with one shoe on and the other in his hand. "We've gone to Blankenships' the Monday after Thanksgiving the last three years. Did you forget?"

"I guess so." She came close and placed her hand on his shoulder. "I never really thought of it as a tradition or anything."

"Well, then, I guess we can wait until later in the week."

"How about this? You go and pick out two perfect trees, then I'll meet you for a late supper when I get back. Is that okay?"

Craig thought on it a little, just to let her know he was miffed that she didn't consider three years of tree shopping a tradition. He could wait until later in the week, but the best trees might be gone by then.

"Sure. We can do that." He smiled. There was no need

to go home grumpy. Jenna's work was hard. There were only three veterinarians in the county, and she was the only one who tended to large and small animals. If she needed some mall therapy with her mom, he could live with that. "I'll find you the best tree ever. And send Nancy my love. Tell her that I'll stop in to see her and Homer when I'm in Freeport to pick up that new computer monitor next week."

"She'll like that." Jenna stretched on tiptoes to kiss him. He met her halfway. "Thanks for watching the Christmas special with me."

"You're welcome. And let me know when you decide to wear a short skirt to work."

She laughed. "Mark your calendar. It will be in exactly...fifteen pounds."

"You look perfect." He kissed her again to let her know he meant it.

"I'm glad you think so. And as far as Raven McCloud, from what I hear she is as sweet as she is gorgeous. Something to live up to, I guess."

Craig hugged her close, buying an extra couple moments while the remote start got the truck warmed up again. "I love you, Jenna."

She buried her head in his shoulder. "Mm-hmm. See you tomorrow night."

Brooke stood across the room checking messages while Raven held court with a half-dozen Opry regulars. Milo had texted to say he was en route with a backup limo. She would wait five more minutes before rescuing Raven as she had requested.

Home by 11:30, she texted Tristan.

See you then! Love you! He texted back. Exclamation points were a sure sign that he was trying to make up for their earlier rift. That was okay. She was past it. He had a lot of potential, if only he could figure out how to tap into it. And he needed to spend more time practicing his guitar. He was close to being able to make the leap from bars to stage shows, but the gap between where he was and where he needed to be was the same as a lot of Nashville hopefuls who were waiting tables or, like Tristan, doing telemarketing from their kitchen tables. Only a little more practice. And fewer distractions, like doper friends with ankle monitors.

I love you! See you soon. She texted and included a heart emoji for emphasis.

It was time to get on the road. Brooke approached the group surrounding Raven. A couple people had joined the scrum. One, a long-time stagehand smiled and said hello.

"Hi, Tony," Brooke said softly.

"She was great, wasn't she?" he asked, nodding at Raven.

"She sure was."

Though most were stars in their own rights, they were like moths drawn to Raven's bright light. They laughed with a bit more enthusiasm than her witticisms deserved, but that was typical. Sadly, as Brooke had seen over the years, the descent from being a headliner to not having your calls returned often came without warning.

Enjoy it, Raven. You've earned it.

Brooke cleared her throat, raised herself as high as her flats would allow, and said sweetly, "Raven?"

Raven was midstory and didn't respond. That was okay. It was Brooke's mistake to interrupt. She waited until she saw another opening, then a bit louder, "Raven, we really need to go. Your guests are waiting at—"

The world suddenly turned weird.

"Brooke!" Raven snapped. "Can't you see that I'm visiting with my friends?"

"I understand, Raven, but we need to—"

"Brooke, I said *I'm visiting with my friends*. Now, why don't you go wait by the door. I'll be ready when I'm ready."

Brooke turned away so they wouldn't see the color drain from her face. She swallowed, took a deep breath, and walked away. She wondered if the others, some she had known for years, were watching.

You're a big girl, Brooke. You're strong. Dad said there would be days like this. She's a star. Maybe you caught her at a bad time.

The hell you did. She was laughing and swapping stories. She shouldn't have treated you that way, especially after asking you to help her out.

Chin up, Brooke. And for gosh sakes, don't cry. Never let them see you cry.

What would Bobby do?

Raven wouldn't have done that to Bobby. If she had, she would be looking for a new manager.

Well, Brooke, you don't have that option. Not yet. Maybe someday, but for now, you take it.

And she could have, had she not overheard what Raven said next. She lowered her voice, but Brooke's hearing was off the charts.

"She's trying so hard to become her Daddy, but there's only one Bobby Summers...and she's never going to be him...or anything close."

❄

It was fifteen past midnight when Brooke arrived at the apartment. She had cried in her car for most of the ride from Raven's but could find solace that she hadn't cried in the limousine.

Raven knew she had acted like a prima donna ass. She bounced into the limo as if the ugly scene had never happened.

"Wasn't that great?"

"Weren't the other performers wonderful?"

"And the audience! They were sublime. Don't you think so, Brooke?"

"They certainly were," Brooke had responded with fake cheer. That would be all she could muster until Raven apologized. She might be a huge star, but she was also a person, and people didn't treat other people that way.

But Raven didn't apologize, and Brooke wondered if success had pushed remorse from her personality. It would be sad if it had.

Despite all that, she was determined to put on a happy face for Tristan. At least he had been sweet enough to reach out and tell her he loved her.

But Tristan wasn't up when she walked in. All the lights were off, and she could hear him snoring in the bedroom. Okay, she was late. He had probably tried to stay up, but how long should someone have to wait? And she could have called and let him know, but she was busy bawling her eyes out.

She flipped on the living room light and nearly started bawling again. The room was much as it had been when she left hours before. Congealed cheese covered the coffee table like a kid's finger-painting project. Plates of chicken bones were stacked on the end tables, and bits of tortilla chips crunched under her feet. It needed to be cleaned up if she didn't want mice or whatever scary crawly things that came out looking for nacho cheese and chicken wings in the middle of the night.

But she didn't have it in her. Not after the evening she'd had.

So instead, she headed down the hallway in the direction of the master bedroom, stopping along the way to use the bathroom. She did what she needed to do, brushed her teeth, removed her makeup, and stepped back into the hall. Tristan was still snoring. She looked toward their bedroom, then at the door to the spare room. The bed in there was tiny, but it was empty. And if she closed the door she could barely hear the snoring.

Some choices seemed so easy.

Morning walk-in business was slow. Elderly customers stayed home when there were two feet of fresh snow on the ground, availing themselves of the free delivery Craig had added soon after opening. It was a good way to keep the big pharmacies from poaching his customers. Walgreens might have four rows of greeting cards and nine different kinds of foot cream, but they didn't have Stacy Pike showing up at customers' front doors, week in and week out, with their pill refills, the latest gossip, and the biggest smile in Garland Grove.

"Stacy!" Craig called out so she would hear him in the back. "Can you run a scrip over to Mrs. Donaldson?"

"Alveera or Lettie?"

"Lettie."

Stacy came up front. Her insulated coveralls, parka, and leather snow boots swallowed her petite frame. "Ring up some gumdrops, too, Craig. Miss Lettie loves her gumdrops."

Craig and Stacy were about the same age, but Stacy still looked twenty-five. She kept her blonde hair pixie short, and while Craig had never seen her wear makeup, she was still one of the prettiest women in town. Pretty in that pure-as-the driven-snow, girl-next-door kind of way. Since she and her husband Melvin had four kids, that pure-as-the-driven-snow part might be a reach, but there was no denying that she possessed that quality. And she was Callaway Drugstore's most valued asset.

"Are the roads getting better?" Craig asked as he handed off the pills and gumdrops.

"The county boys are on it. Things will be back to normal by lunchtime."

The bell over the front door tinkled as Dr. Sam Griffin bounded in with his usual enthusiasm.

"Hey, Sam!" Stacy called out as she buttoned her coat. "Oh, my goodness, is that who I think it is under that blanket?"

It was, and Stacy swept in with arms open wide to get her hands on little Christopher Claus Griffin, the most passed-around baby in town. Sam pulled back the blanket and held his youngest out as if he was passing a bowl of mashed potatoes. Little Christopher did his part, cooing and giggling at the sight of the little woman in the oversized winter gear.

"Does anything scare him?" Craig asked as he came around the counter to greet his friend and take his turn holding little Christopher.

"He gets a little cranky when we leave him on the porch overnight," Sam quipped. "Other than that, he's pretty chill."

They spent a few minutes catching up and cooing at Christopher before Stacy headed out for deliveries.

"You know I'm going to hire her away from you sooner or later," Sam said after she was gone.

"Do it and I'll be out of business in a month."

Sam laughed. "Nah. You know better than that. How long have you been in town now, anyway?"

"Nine years. I'm practically a local."

"That's where you're wrong. Local status can't be earned in Garland Grove. Either you were born here, or you weren't. If you didn't have Stacy running deliveries and saying good things about you, people wouldn't even know your name yet. You'd just be that pharmacist from Minnesota."

It was a running joke between Sam, the local boy, and Craig, the newcomer. Truth was, Craig felt very accepted, and if it was because of Stacy running interference, that was fine.

Craig returned to his raised perch in the back of the store. "Is strep throat running amok at your place, Sam?"

"I guess you heard from Dr. Patel's office. The older four have been coughing and whining about sore throats. And this morning Beth's sick too." He raised Christopher in the air. "Me and this guy are tough, though. Real Griffin men."

Craig held up a bag. "Four bottles of the pink stuff and pills for Beth."

"Ahh, Amoxicillin. The miracle drug. Thank you, brother."

"I'm required to ask if you have any questions before I hand this over," Craig said.

"Yeah, as a matter of fact, I do." Sam pulled a flyer from his pocket. "Can I hang this in your front window? It's the prize list for the hospital's first Christmas baby contest. Can you believe that Laslow's Furniture donated a recliner?"

"That's great. Nothing that good last year, was there?"

Sam laughed. "We made out okay, let me tell you.

Thanks to this chip off the old block, we didn't have to buy diapers until July. And the ten free portraits we won are already wrapped and under the tree. The grandparents, aunts, and uncles are going to love them."

The story of Sam's quest to win Garland Grove Memorial Hospital's Christmas baby contest had already reached legendary proportions in less than a year. His wife, Beth, had delivered Christopher with just minutes to spare.

"We have three potential winners this year," Sam continued. "I'm lobbying the hospital to rename it the Sam Griffin Christmas Baby Contest, but I'm not getting far."

They chatted for a bit longer while gazing out the front window. Sam was the most likable and down-to-earth physician Craig had ever known. He considered him one of his closest friends but knew that many others in town did, too. That was Sam's way.

"What was Jenna doing out so early this morning?" Sam asked as he gathered his scrips and started bundling Christopher. "I passed her on the county road outside of Templeton."

"Probably giving the new guy over there a hand. He only tends to small animals. The large animal vet they use had knee replacement, so Jenna's been filling in."

"Must've been an emergency. It was six-fifteen when I saw her." Sam sighed. "I was on my way to my Aunt Phyllis's house. Her pipes froze again."

"I thought she was moving to an apartment in town."

Sam threw his hands in the air. "Don't get me started. She was supposed to but can't bring herself to give up the family house. Four bedrooms on the second floor and she can't even climb steps anymore. Oh, yeah, Beth wanted me to let you know that she's bowing out of the Christmas concert this year. She sends regrets."

"No, Sam. Tell her that is unacceptable."

"You have her number. You tell her. She enjoys it, but between ringing the Salvation Army bell downtown and taking care of this guy..." He held up a blanket-covered Christopher "...she's on holiday overload."

Craig leaned on the counter. "I guess that means you're taking her place?"

Sam grinned. "Sure. Allow me to audition right now."

His rendition of White Christmas was perfect. Perfectly off-key. Perfectly awful. So bad that Christopher wailed. After two verses, Craig raised his hands in a time-out gesture.

"Tell Beth she gets a pass for this year, but she has to take a solo next time."

"What about me? When do I need to be at the theater?"

"You focus on getting your family healthy again, Doctor. And maybe consider singing lessons."

Sam shook his fist, winked, and pulled his coat tightly around him as he balanced Christopher against his chest. "See you later, alligator!"

Craig walked past and opened the door for him. Something Sam had said about Jenna had stuck with him. She had mentioned early appointments but said nothing about going out of town.

"Sam, when you passed Jenna this morning was she on her way to Templeton?"

"Coming back," Sam said as he stepped out into the snow.

Raquel Doney looked up when Brooke strolled into the office. Her natural brown hair was frosted to a tone she called champagne beige. Her lipstick was fire-hydrant red. One false eyelash was crooked. She was pushing seventy and trying not to look it, which only made her look older.

"I have to put up with two Summerses today?" she asked good-naturedly.

"Dad's here?"

"Got here at nine, went to lunch at eleven, just got back."

Brooke hadn't planned on running into Bobby. She was still sorting out how much to tell him about the evening before. Particularly the part where Raven humiliated her in front of the other performers. She grabbed the stack of messages Raquel had left in her box and took the back stairs to where their offices were located. Bobby had moved into the present location, a two-story brick structure built in the twenties, two decades earlier after the previous owner, a three-person law firm, went under. Given its proximity to the nerve center of Nashville's music industry, it wasn't uncommon for them to receive purchase offers many times over what Bobby had paid. He wasn't going anywhere.

"Brooke?" Bobby called out. "Is that you out there?"

"Yes, Dad."

"Come here, sweetie. You need to hear this."

Had Bobby heard from someone who witnessed Raven's actions at the Opry? Given how many friends he had around town, it wouldn't be a surprise. She considered making up an excuse to go straight to her office, but as she collected herself, she heard Bobby say, "Hold on a minute, Gary Gene. I want Brooke to hear what you told me. She won't believe it, either." She knew it had to be Gary Gene Pickler, a local deejay. How many Gary Genes could there be? It was Nashville, though, and names like Gary Gene were nearly as common as Bill or Mary. She still felt safe enough to step inside.

"Sit down, honey. Gary Gene, Brooke's here. Tell her what you told me."

"Hiya Brooke, how ya doing?"

"Good, Gary Gene. How are things with you?"

"Fine as frog's hair. I was just telling your daddy that I was listening yesterday when Tommy played that little Christmas song you dropped off."

"Yes, Gary Gene."

"You left it behind when you took off. I found it in the control room, so I gave it a spin this morning during my first hour."

"That was nice of you, Gary Gene."

"Well, Brooke, I'm not surprised that Tommy didn't get any response. About the only people listening to his show these days are the nursing home set, if you know what I mean."

Brooke smiled. Gary Gene was suggesting that Tommy's audience was about the same age as Tommy.

"So, anyway, I'm on from ten to two, as you know, so I put it on at about twenty past ten this morning, and the phones lit up."

Brooke looked across the desk at Bobby. He was smiling and shaking his head.

"We got twenty-four calls between ten-thirty and eleven-fifteen. It's a crappy demo and the sound quality isn't very good, but folks are going nuts over it. They want to know who Christmas Carl is and where they can get the song. One old boy said it was funnier than Grandma getting run over by a reindeer." Gary Gene chuckled. "The way he said it made me wonder if he was talking about the song or if his grandma really got run over by a reindeer."

"That's amazing," Brooke said. "Are you going to play it anymore, Gary Gene?"

"I already did. Twice. Once just after eleven and then at twelve-thirty. The calls picked up each time. I'm putting it on again just before I go off the air at two. We'll see if the requests keep coming on Tammy's show from two 'til six."

"I can't believe this. Dad, your intuition was right."

"It just happens sometimes, sweetheart. Gary Gene, tell her about the other calls."

"Oh, yeah, we got calls from stations in Murfreesboro, Chattanooga, and up in Paducah asking for a copy. Do you want us to send them?"

"Can you do that, Gary Gene?" Brooke asked.

"Sure. They would do it for us. We can just copy and send it in an email."

"Gary Gene, that's awfully kind of you," Bobby said. "How much do we owe you for sending out the copies?"

"Not a cent. Just promise me that if this thing blows up, you'll give us the first interview with whoever Christmas Carl turns out to be."

Bobby disconnected, then sat back in his chair and stretched his legs out on the desk. His boots made a clopping sound as the heels met the mahogany.

"We have to find that guy, Brooke."

"There's not much to go on." She stood up and walked to a window that overlooked Nashville's famed Music Row. The dismal weather of the previous day was long gone. Skies were sunny and temperatures were in the upper forties. From Bobby's second-floor window, she could see the recording studios and marketing firms that earned Nashville the title of Music City USA.

"Now, as I see it," Bobby continued. "We could hire J.R.

Potter and put him on this. He did a good job hunting down that gal who owed—"

"I can find him, Dad. We don't need a private investigator, especially one as over the hill as J.R. Potter."

"But how, Brooke? All we know is that his name is Carl and he went to... What school did Raven go to?"

"Missouri State University. I'll start there. Maybe we'll get lucky. But first I'm going to see if Raven remembers anything else that might help. I'll call her. She should be back from rehearsals."

"No, let's drive out and see her. I want to find out how rehearsals are going. Besides, there's something I need to see for myself."

"What's that, Dad?"

Bobby pulled his feet from the desk and stood up. He tried to hide his discomfort, but Brooke caught the wince.

"Maybe nothing. I hope nothing. Will you drive?"

"Sure. And if I need to, I'll head to Missouri first thing in the morning."

"That's a good idea. We need to find that guy fast. With the song getting airplay, there will be other bloodhounds hunting for Christmas Carl."

Stacy restocked eye drops and then did a quick look up and down the drugstore's three aisles before saying, "If you don't need anything else today, Craig, I'm going home. The kids have been by themselves all day, what with school being cancelled."

Craig walked to the front of the store and looked out. Main Street was cleared of snow, and people were venturing out. "School should be back in session tomorrow," he observed. "You go on home, Stacy. Thanks for everything."

It was four-thirty when Stacy took off. Craig usually stayed open another hour but was planning to close early to drive out to Blankenship's tree farm north of town. On a lark, he called Jenna's number to see if the plans she had with her mother had changed. There was no answer, which likely meant she was already on her way to Freeport. Phone service was abysmal for about ten miles once you left Garland Grove.

"Just checking in to see how your day was," he said to voicemail. "I'll see you at Smack's later tonight. Tell your folks I said hey. Love you."

Craig laid the phone aside when Sadie Trout and Willa McKenzie walked through the front door babbling excitedly.

"Oh, thank goodness you're here Craig," Willa exclaimed. "We have thrilling news about the Christmas concert!"

Willa and Sadie were on the concert committee. Willa was chairperson and Sadie was secretary. There were three other members, but they knew their places. Willa, a local attorney's wife, was a fervent Presbyterian who could chop people into tiny pieces with her sharp tongue. Sadie was a lapsed Baptist schoolteacher who understood that whatever power she wielded in Garland Grove came from being Willa's best friend. Many, including the other committee members, found them impossible to deal with and left them alone. Craig escaped their wrath, probably because he was the only person other than Willa's husband who was privy to her ongoing battles with bromodosis, or stinky feet. *Bad* stinky. Like, really really bad. Or, as Willa's husband

Leland had once confided, smellier than a hog's ass in summer.

Sadie took the lead. "We got word today that—"

"Sadie, let me." Willa took back the lead. "Craig, we found out today that Hal Richie is available to perform on the day of the Christmas concert! Isn't that fantastic?"

Sadie, silenced but no less enthused, was practically jumping up and down in her denim jumper embroidered with little chalkboards. It was evident that Hal Richie was a big deal, but the only problem was...

"Ladies, who is Hal Richie?"

Silence.

Both stood with their mouths open in astonishment. Sadie recovered first. "Craig? How can you not know Hal Richie?"

Craig shrugged. "The name doesn't ring a bell."

"The Hal Richie Quartet?"

Craig shook his head.

Willa threw her hands in the air as if she was dealing with a child. "Only the best gospel quartet in the upper Midwest, Craig. Where have you been the last twenty years?"

"And they want to perform at our little Christmas concert?"

Willa said, "People from all over know about Garland Grove's concert, Craig. Don't sell us short."

"We had people from as far away as Minneapolis come last year," Sadie interjected. Craig didn't have the heart to remind her that the Minneapolis attendees were Jeannette Mincher's parents, who were in town for the birth of their first grandchild.

"The Hal Richie Quartet were regulars on that televangelist's TV show," Willa said, building her case. The televangelist's name she tossed out wasn't one Craig was familiar with, either, but it certainly was exciting to Willa and Sadie.

"And they want to perform here?" Craig asked.

"Not all of them," Willa said. "Just Hal Richie. He and the other three parted ways last spring. He's out on his own now and thought Garland Grove would be ideal for a performance."

"How much?"

"Does it matter?" Willa said quickly. "It's Hal Richie. People will come from miles around."

"I respect that, Willa, but our budget is limited, and we have recurring expenses we need to take care of."

Willa threw up her hands again, which led Sadie to do the same. "He only needs seven-fifty, but I think we could—"

"Seven hundred and fifty *dollars?*"

"I think I can get him to take less," Willa said, with less certainty. "I'll tell him seven hundred is the best we can do."

"Willa..." Craig leaned against the counter. "You're in charge of finances. Where can we get that kind of money?"

"We just raise ticket prices. People will gladly pay extra to see Hal Richie."

Craig knew he had reached a point of no return. Though he was the concert director, his authority was limited to music selection and deciding who performed solos. Tickets and budget were the board's domain, and they were welcome to it.

"You decide what you want to do and let me know," he said. "We start rehearsals tomorrow night, so the sooner the better."

Willa and Sadie went on their merry way, and Craig knew that their first words to the rest of the board would be that Craig wanted Hal Richie. He would speak privately to the others at the next evening's rehearsal but knew it was futile. If Willa McKenzie wanted Hal Richie to perform at the Christmas concert, Hal Richie would perform.

Brooke was chatting with Raquel in the office's smallish reception area when Tristan called. She hadn't heard from him all day and suspected he was brooding because she spent the night in the spare bedroom. If that was the case, she preferred that Raquel not hear the conversation, so she stepped out the front door.

"Hey, babe, what are you doing?" he asked cheerfully.

"At the moment, I'm on the front step at the office waiting for Dad to finish setting up a fishing trip with a couple of his singing buddies, then I'm driving him out to Raven's house."

"How about later today?"

"It depends on what happens at Raven's house. Why?"

"Want to go to the Sundrop tonight? Maybe eight-thirty?"

"Like on a date? That would be fun, but could we go earlier? Maybe seven?"

"We could go earlier, but Tyler Paxton's band plays at eight-thirty. You might enjoy hearing them."

"The Dusty Shades?"

"Yep."

Brooke had seen Paxton's band a few times. They were a pretty good rock band that was starting to find its niche in a town that craved country. Tyler's creds were solid. He had played keyboards and sang backup for a couple of performers who moved on to bigger and better things, and in his early thirties hoped that the Dusty Shades might be his ticket to the next level. Reviews were mixed so far, but he was working hard.

If the set started at eight-thirty, though, it would go until eleven or later. And if Brooke had to go to Missouri in the morning, it was a lot.

"I don't know, Tristan. I like the band well enough, but I was hoping to—"

"You're going to *really* like them tonight, babe. Guess who's sitting in on guitar?"

Brooke shrieked, grabbing the attention of a couple of pedestrians. One asked if she needed help. She shook her head and pointed to the phone. "That's wonderful, Tristan! You bet I'll be there. How did that come together?"

"Tyler's drummer is Melinda Keller. Her boyfriend is Layne Fanning."

Brooke had no idea who those people were and what it meant, other than Tristan had a gig. And that was reason to celebrate.

"I need to get there by seven-thirty to set up, but I'll have a spot reserved for you." He sounded like a kid at Christmas. It was far from his usual mellow tone, and that made Brooke as happy as him scoring the gig.

"Brooke? You ready?" Bobby had stepped outside.

"Dad, Tristan's playing with Tyler Paxton's band tonight."

Bobby whistled. "That's a pretty good outfit. Congratulations to Tristan."

"I have to run, Tristan, but I'll see you tonight at eight-thirty. Break a leg and all that stuff."

"I'm glad you're coming, Brooke. I play better when I see you in the audience."

❄

"Are you going to tell me why you're coming with me to Raven's?"

Bobby gazed out the passenger window. "I hope it's nothing, so let's leave it at that. How did last night go at the Opry?"

They stopped at a light at the corner of Twenty-First and Grand while a delivery truck squeezed into a tight spot in front of a pizza place. Brooke pretended to be focused on traffic when she was actually trying to figure out how to answer Bobby's question. How much did he know? Anything? And if he had heard, what would his response be? He was her father, her Daddy, and from the time she was a little girl he had been the person she could tell anything, the person who made things right.

But that was kid stuff. Mean girls in grade school, things boys said in junior high, who she hoped asked her to prom. This was work. And she had decided the previous evening, while trying to find sleep on the lumpy guest room mattress, that she needed to be her own woman at work. By giving her responsibility for Raven's tour, Bobby was saying as much.

Put on your big girl bloomers, Brooke.

"The limo broke down, but we got her to the Opry in time. Besides that..."

The moment of truth.

What should she say?

Remember! Big girl bloomers!

"Besides that, things went okay. Raven was great on stage. She stuck around a bit longer after the show than I expected, but things were good."

"Any sign of Travis Horton?"

Brooke shook her head. "Nope. And I would have seen him if he were there. Is that why you're coming along today?"

"Yeah, it's just a hunch, but Milo called me after he dropped you guys off last night. There was a white Lamborghini parked in the turnaround the trash trucks use just past her front gate."

"Why did Milo call you instead of me?" There was more anger in her tone than Brooke wanted to show. Bobby heard it.

"Don't get ticked off at Milo. I had asked him to. Travis Horton drives a white Lambo, and if there's any truth to what Clive Naylor said at the press conference, we need to know."

"That means I drove right past him and didn't see him."

"I suspect that after Milo spotted him, Travis pulled back further into the trees," Bobby said. "There's no trusting that boy, and if he's got his sights set on Raven, we're in for trouble."

"Do you think he's there now?"

"I hope not, darlin', but that's why we're showing up unexpected."

Lloyd Blankenship's four-wheel-drive truck rolled through the snow like it wasn't there. In every direction Craig looked, there were Christmas trees. They stretched out over acres and acres. The snow gave them an angelic flocked appearance that made them even more beautiful.

"As I remember you had a blue spruce last year," Mr. Blankenship said as they bumped over the narrow road between fields. "And Jenna had a Scotch pine."

"I'll take your word for it, Lloyd. The only trees I know by name are real and artificial."

The old man chuckled as he hung a left onto a side trail. "Let's change it up for you guys. We have fir trees over here, and some real nice cedar further back. We only got a half-hour of daylight, so let's pick and tag 'em, then head back to the house for hot cider."

It didn't take long to complete the job. Mr. Blankenship loved Christmas trees as much as Craig loved Beverly Blankenship's hot cider, and a few minutes after choosing a nice six-foot fir for Jenna and a seven-foot cedar for Craig, they were pulling up behind the old frame house that served as the office and gift shop for Blankenship's tree farm.

"I reckon that's Amy Edwards's car over there," Mr. Blankenship said as he pointed to a maroon SUV parked off to one side.

"You need to remember to call her by her married name," Craig said. "But then, I do, too. I filled a prescription for her the other day and put Edwards on it without even thinking. She scolded me good."

"I do indeed. You go on in and warm up, Craig. I'll put the truck in the barn and be in directly."

Craig climbed down from the truck and walked along the cleared blacktop toward the back door. As soon as he stepped inside, the Christmas season overtook his senses. Scented candles were stacked on shelves along one wall. Greenery, garland, and mistletoe covered nearly every square inch of wall and counter space. Four of the Blanken-ships' most majestic Christmas trees, fully decorated, created a path from front to back while Johnny Mathis crooned *White Christmas* over speakers concealed in the ceiling and paneled walls. Craig stopped for a couple of moments to warm up and enjoy the holiday vibes. From the front room, he heard Beverly Blankenship chatting with Amy Edwards Bennett. They were talking about him.

"I don't know, Beverly. If he were going to ask her, don't you think he would have told someone?"

"Like who?"

"Well," Amy paused. "Like me or Andrew. Or Sam. He and Sam are close."

"Or Stacy Pike?" Beverly offered. "She's there with him every day. She would know if anyone would."

"I asked her," Amy said. "She doesn't know anything. I even asked Buckshot Kelly. If he was buying Jenna a ring he would get it from Buckshot's place."

Craig did his best to keep from laughing. Gossip was as much a part of Garland Grove as burgers at Smack's and Manny the mannequin pedaling away at the bicycle shop. And though she had only been back for a year, Amy Bennett was proving quite proficient at doing her share to keep it going.

Mrs. Blankenship said, "Of course, he would buy it from Buckshot. Craig's not the kind to shop for something so important at some out-of-town store. What did Buckshot say?"

"He told me to mind my own damn business."

That did it. Craig couldn't contain the laughter any longer. They looked up just as he came around the corner.

"How long have you been back there, Craig Callaway?" Mrs. Blankenship asked. Amy stood behind her, trying to avoid eye contact.

"Not long," Craig said as he rubbed his hands together. The women appeared to relax. "But long enough to hear that I'm supposed to do all my engagement ring shopping at Buckshot Kelly's jewelry store."

Amy crossed her arms and tried to feign irritation, but her smile gave her away.

"I thought Andrew had warned you about gossiping," Craig teased.

"Andrew Bennett is my husband, not my father." Then, a little softer, "So, are you?"

"Am I what?"

"You know what," Mrs. Blankenship said.

Craig looked around, checking to see if the coast was clear, before saying, "I bought Jenna something very special."

The ladies leaned in, eager to hear more.

"But I didn't get it from Buckshot. Please keep that to yourself."

"We won't tell a soul," Mrs. Blankenship said, crossing her heart. "Where did you get it? That big jewelry store in Freeport?"

"I got it...right here. It's a beautiful fir. A six-footer."

Amy stuck her tongue out at him. Mrs. Blankenship gave him the stink eye as she moved to her spot behind the counter. "You're impossible, Craig Callaway. Do you want some cider or not?"

He wanted cider. Mrs. Blankenship poured a glass and handed it over. She took a seat at a stool she kept close by. Craig knew she was experiencing some issues with arthritis, and that the long days behind the counter of the tree farm contributed to her discomfort.

"Speaking of Jenna, why isn't she with you?" Amy asked as she sat down in one of the folding chairs arranged around the center of the shop. Craig followed suit. The place reminded him of an old-time general store, except with Christmas on the shelves instead of groceries. He also knew that the location had special meaning to Amy, as she had grown up in the house. Her parents had sold it to the Blankenships years before, prior to moving out of state. The space where they were seated used to be Amy's family living room, and there was a dream quality to her eyes as they sat and chatted.

"Jenna went shopping with her mom. I'm meeting her later for supper."

"How's the Christmas concert shaping up this year?" Mrs. Blankenship asked as she sipped cider.

"We start rehearsals tomorrow night. It will be fine if I can keep Willa McKenzie out of the way."

Mrs. Blankenship nodded. Amy smirked. Willa's reputation was known far and wide.

"That reminds me, do you ladies know who Hal Richie is?"

They didn't. Mrs. Blankenship thought that might be the name of the man who bought the tire store out on the old highway.

"No, his name is Racine. Neither of you has heard of Hal Richie? He used to front the Hal Richie Quartet."

Nothing.

Mrs. Blankenship looked at him quizzically. "Why do you ask?"

"Just curious."

Raven's evening security detail appeared alongside Brooke's car as she entered the code and pulled through the main gate onto the drive leading to Raven's house.

"Good evening, Khalid," she called out.

"Hey, Brooke." He bent over and peered past her. "Good evening, Mr. Summers."

"Howdy, Khalid. Everything okay?"

"Yes, sir. Just double-checking to make sure it was you. A security light blew out over the entrance, and it makes it hard to see who's coming and going after dark. The company is coming out in the morning to replace it."

"Do you have lots of people coming and going, Khalid?" Bobby asked.

Khalid appeared hesitant to reply. Raven employed the security firm he worked for, and it was natural that his allegiance would be to her. He was also aware of how close Brooke and Bobby were to his client. And that they ultimately paid the bills.

"Not really a lot, Mr. Summers. But some." He glanced in the direction of the house, which was three hundred yards in the distance and surrounded by trees and multiple security zones. There was something in the way he said it that made Brooke suspicious.

"Khalid, is somebody—"

"You keep up the good job, Khalid," Bobby interrupted. "Raven is darn lucky to have you on her detail." Then, to Brooke, "Drive on up to the house, honey."

Brooke raised her window and proceeded up the drive. "Why didn't you want me to ask Khalid who's here?"

"We don't want him to break Raven's confidence. She needs to know she can trust him. Khalid is a smart man, though. He knows that we have her best interest in mind, too." Brooke sighed with relief when they rounded the last corner, and the house came into view. There was no white Lamborghini in sight.

"It's in the garage," Bobby said, reading her mind.

"How do you know?"

"I just know."

Bobby was out of the car first and led the way up the

front steps. He wore an expression of anger, disappointment, and sadness. Brooke had experienced all those sides of her father, but never at the same time.

"Dad, if Travis Horton is here, let me handle it."

Bobby stopped on the top step and turned to her. Brooke could see past him into the living room. The fireplace where she had warmed herself the evening before was fully stoked, but the room appeared to be empty.

"What will you do?"

Brooke jammed her hands into her coat pockets. The sight of the warm fire burning just a few yards away gave her a chill. "I'll talk to Raven. Woman to woman. I'll tell her she's making a mistake, and that Travis can be toxic to her career."

"Don't you think she knows all that?"

Bobby had a point. It was that whole bad boy thing he'd mentioned before. For whatever reason, some women were drawn to men who needed fixing. She had seen it. Heck, some might think she was living it. They would never say it to her, but Brooke could see where they could think it. Successful young Nashville talent agent in a relationship with a musician telemarketer whose career prospects were limited to fill-in gigs on the local bar circuit. What if one of her friends confronted her with those facts? How would she respond?

She would become angry. She might tell them to mind their own business, and that her personal life was hers, not theirs. She would defend Tristan, describe his potential, and how close he was to breaking through. If they pushed the issue she would shut them down, even if they said they were telling her for her own good.

Yeah, she probably was the last person to walk in and tell Raven McCloud that she was making a mistake.

But then, so was Bobby.

Or anyone else.

"Dad, let's leave."

"What?"

She took his arm to lead him back down the steps, but he didn't budge. "Raven has the right to make her own life choices, Dad. We're her agents, not her parents. And even if we were her parents, she's almost forty years old."

He gazed at her for a few beats while he considered what Brooke was saying.

"Maybe she's just lonely," Brooke continued, wondering if she was speaking about herself or Raven. "Maybe she wants a man in her life and Travis Horton is the only guy able to break through the protective bubble she lives in."

Bobby nodded, slowly at first, then with a bit more certainty. Brooke wondered if he was also thinking about her and Tristan. "What about Christmas Carl? We wanted to see what else she might know."

"I don't know how much more she can tell us. I'll head to Missouri and find out what I can."

When she reached out a second time, Bobby wrapped his arm in hers and they retreated to her car. No one spoke until they had cleared the gates and were on Hillsboro Pike headed in the direction of the office. It was dark and rush hour was in full swing. It was Bobby who broke the silence.

"You made a wise decision back there, Brooke."

Brooke reached out and squeezed his hand.

"I don't think I would have handled things as well," he continued. "Travis Horton is getting his shifty self in between my client and me, and that makes me mad."

"Raven's not the first unmarried client you've had, Dad."

"Yeah, darlin', but she's the first who didn't have family

or close friends around her. The others had people close to them who could talk sense into them when needed. Raven, though." He removed his Stetson and set it on the dashboard, then rubbed his eyes. "Raven is vulnerable."

"She didn't seem too vulnerable when she ripped into me at the Opry last night."

"Yeah, I heard."

Brooke tightened her grip on the wheel. *How in the world? And why hadn't he said anything?*

"You didn't deserve that," Bobby continued. "But I also heard that you handled it with grace and dignity."

And then she knew why he hadn't said anything sooner.

She had handled it.

With grace and dignity.

Maybe she could someday come close to being as good at the job as Bobby after all.

Probably not, but at least she was carving out her own niche, and that would be plenty good enough.

Craig was seated at the bar, working his way through a bowl of Smack's homemade chicken noodle soup when Jenna entered. Amy and Andrew Bennett were right behind her. Amy's cheeks flushed when she spotted Craig, but she recovered quickly. Andrew patted him on the back. Jenna kissed him on the lips, a departure from the way she usually greeted him in public.

"You started without me," she said.

"I walked from home. By the time I got here, I couldn't feel my face."

"I'll give you a ride home," she said with a wink that said even more. "Let's get a table."

"Andrew, you guys want to join us?" Craig asked, hoping they didn't. They were great friends, but Jenna was giving off vibes that the evening might go places he hadn't anticipated.

"Nah, we're picking up a pizza," Andrew said. "I had an emergency at the hospital this morning and spent the rest of the day catching up on appointments. I just got done and I'm toast."

"Where was Sam during all that?" Craig asked. "He came by the drugstore this morning but didn't say anything about how busy things were."

"Yeah, some partner, huh?" Andrew joked. "Nah, Sam came down with a sore throat after lunch."

"Strep," Craig said. "The whole family has it."

"Not baby Christopher," Amy interjected. "He's as healthy as a horse and is staying with his Grandma Griffin until the rest of them get better."

The server, a young guy with the unlikely name of Pilgrim, called out, "Dr. Bennett, your pizza is ready." The Bennetts grabbed their order, said goodbye, and took off for home.

"How about we do the same?" Jenna suggested, rubbing her hand on Craig's back. She didn't have to suggest it twice.

Brooke arrived at the Sundrop with two minutes to spare. The guy at the door recognized her.

"Scouting talent tonight?" he asked casually.

"Actually..." she searched her brain for his name, trying hard to be as good at names as Bobby was. It wasn't there, though, so she asked. It was Lindall.

"Actually, Lindall, I'm with the band."

They both got a laugh out of that. Then he led her to a table to the left of the small stage. It was a different vantage point, as Brooke usually stayed close to the back when she was checking out musical acts. She flagged down a server and put in an order for a bowl of chili and a beer just as the houselights went down and the manager introduced the Dusty Shades. The crowd, medium-sized and made up mostly of tourists, offered enthused applause. It was Nashville after all, and the chance to hear live music–any live music–in Music City USA brought out the best in people. Tyler Paxton, a seasoned performer, knew exactly how to play to an audience. He kicked things off with an old Charlie Daniels number that had the crowd yelling for more. He followed it up with two more familiar country crossover hits, each progressing from traditional country to the rock genre that Tyler was becoming known for. To Tyler's right, no more than fifteen feet from Brooke's table, Tristan played his guitar with a look of pure joy. The band was into its second song before his eyes adjusted to the lights and he spotted her. He winked, mouthed *I love you*, then retreated into his blissful guitar-playing cocoon. He looked great, having shaved and put on one of the outfits he saved for performances. That was the man Brooke had fallen for two years earlier. A man full of potential and willing to put in the work to live up to it.

They ate pizza and made love. Craig's house, of course, but still. Wow!

The temperatures hadn't made it above freezing, but in Craig's bedroom, there was panting and perspiration. If he hadn't known that the thermostat stayed on sixty-eight, he would have thought it was a hundred and twenty. Jenna laid beside him with an arm across his chest. It was some of the best love they had ever made.

So, what gave?

Jenna was staying over. On a Monday night.

Relax, Craig. Enjoy the moment.

"How was shopping?" he murmured.

He thought for a moment Jenna might be asleep, but she moved her arm, then sat up and walked into his bathroom for a drink of water. "Fine. It's always good to see Mom and Dad."

"So, what stores did you hit?"

She returned, pulled back the covers, and slid into bed. "Is there any more pizza?"

The room was dark, and Craig wanted to keep it that way, so he felt around for the pizza box. There was one slice left. He handed it across and she took a bite.

"Umm, that's delicious."

He listened to her chewing for a few moments before saying, "Did you guys go to that coat store at the outlet that your mom likes so much?"

Jenna stopped chewing. "What?"

"The outlet store? The one that sells coats?"

"Why are you asking so many questions?"

"I'm not asking many questions, just making conversation."

"You never care about what stores I go to."

What the heck? "Like I said, just making conversation."

"Fine, but about shopping?"

"Geesh, Jenna, I'm sorry."

She sat up and laid the rest of her slice on the bedside table. Craig wished she would put it on a plate, but figured it wasn't the time to go there. "I just screwed your brains out and all you want to talk about is where I went shopping?"

Craig sat up. "Man, Jenna, what's up with you? You screwed my brains out? Since when do you say stuff like that?"

"It's what you wanted, wasn't it Craig? Last night when we were watching the Christmas special? All you came over for was sex."

Craig turned on the light on his side of the bed. The romance was over. "I came over because you invited me," he said testily. "And sure, I asked about staying, but is that so bad? I'm a guy for crying out loud, and you're a beautiful woman, so sue me. I like sex!"

Jenna became quiet and her face softened. Then she veered in another direction.

"I saw Sam Griffin this morning. Did he tell you?"

What to do? Throw Sam under the bus? Lie?

Enjoy the view from under the bus, Sam.

"He said he saw you coming back from Templeton real early. I told him you've been helping the vet over there."

If Jenna was expecting more, maybe a follow-up question or ten, she wasn't getting it. Craig was done arguing. He didn't know why they were having a spat in the first place. She pursed her lips, then spoke softly. "The shopping was good, but getting to see Mom was the main reason for going. I worry about her and Dad getting older and me not being close."

"They're in their early sixties. That's not old."

"Yeah, but Mom has high blood pressure. Diabetes runs in her family. And Dad still works too many hours." She shrugged. "I just want them to be okay, you know?"

She leaned in close and kissed his forehead. It was Jenna's way of apologizing, that and caressing his chest and belly. Craig turned the light back off and happily accepted her apology and then some.

It was five after eleven when the set ended. By then, most of the tourist crowd had drifted back to their hotels, leaving only a couple dozen diehard locals for the Dusty Shades' final number. Brooke waited while the band convened backstage. Tyler Paxton was the first to reappear.

"Thanks for coming, Brooke," he said, offering his hand. "Are you ready to sign us up for a world tour?"

Brooke laughed. Tyler was one of the nicest of the nice guy regulars on the local music scene. If there was a chance of his succeeding, she would be happy to represent him.

"Keep working on your own songs," she said. "Have you considered gigs up north, maybe Cincinnati or St. Louis? Places where country music isn't as ingrained in the fabric?"

"As a matter of fact..." He pulled out a chair and sat down. "I've got a little tour set up this spring that includes St. Louis."

"Congratulations, Tyler!"

"Well," he grinned his self-deprecating grin. "I had to schedule us in West Frankfort and Mount Vernon, Illinois, too. And in Effingham and at a biker bar in some little town on the Mississippi River that I can't even remember the name of. Gotta pay the bills, you know?"

They chatted about music and the music business for a few moments before Tyler stood up. "I need to get home to the wife and kids, but good talking to you, Brooke. Tell Bobby I said hey and that I'll be waiting next to the mailbox for a fat contract." He leaned closer and said, "Tristan did a nice job for us tonight. He was rusty at first, but he got with it after a bit."

"Thanks for inviting him, Tyler. And if I don't see you before then, good luck on your tour."

Tristan came out just as Tyler was leaving. They swapped high-fives, then Tyler was gone.

"You were great!" she said as Tristan kissed her.

"Thanks, babe. Are you headed home?"

"Yes, aren't you?"

Brooke followed Tristan's eyes to the back of the club where two men were waiting. Each had a woman on his arm. Brooke recognized one of the men as the band's bass player, Antonio. The other she didn't know.

"I was hoping you might want to go out with the guys and me. Just for a little while. We're going over to Attaboy's for a nightcap, then maybe over to Freddie's house to jam a little." He nodded at the taller of the two men. "That one is Freddie."

"Who is Freddie?"

"He's trying to get started in the business. Antonio and me are going to work him out and maybe offer some tips."

"I don't think so, Tristan. It's been a long day and I leave for Missouri in the morning."

"Will you be back tomorrow night? I think Tyler is going to ask me to come back."

"I don't know yet. It depends on how much luck I have chasing down the guy who recorded a song we like."

Tristan's eyes narrowed. It was a look Brooke had seen before.

"It would really be nice of you to come back and support me, Brooke. I mean, I'm always there for you."

"I'll do what I can, Tristan. That's all I can promise."

"Fine then," he said in a tone too loud for the nearly

empty room. He waved her off like a smartass and headed to where the others were waiting. No goodbye. No wishing her safe travels. Brooke watched him stalk out of the club and wondered again how she would react if someone said the things to her she had considered saying to Raven about Travis Horton.

Maybe she was ready to listen after all.

Their apartment was a fifteen-minute drive from the Sundrop. She arrived a few minutes before midnight, too wound up to sleep. After consulting a map and seeing that Springfield was four-hundred and fifty miles due west, she packed an overnight bag and hit the road. She could drive the speed limit and still be standing on the steps of the Missouri State University registrar's office when they opened at eight the next morning.

"Christmas Carl, I'm coming for you," she muttered to herself as she exited the apartment complex. "Just don't make yourself too hard to find, okay?"

TUESDAY, NOVEMBER 29

SPRINGFIELD, MISSOURI AND NASHVILLE

The man across the counter was the prototype of what someone in a university registrar's office should look like. Short, balding, and portly. Owlish eyes behind wire-rimmed glasses. Everything except the bowtie.

"I'm sorry, ma'am, but I cannot help you. That kind of information might take weeks to locate."

"Look, Mr..." Brooke paused and checked the nameplate on the counter. "Mr. Millstadt, it's imperative that we find out who this man is. He recorded a song years ago, and—"

"You know he recorded a song, but you don't know his name?"

"It's complicated, but yes. He recorded a song and no, we do not know his name. That's why I'm here."

"I'm sure you can appreciate how understaffed we are. Now, if you would like to fill out an information request, I'll have my boss run it up the chain of command. If they say it's okay, we'll have one of our archivists research your request. There will be a charge of course, but within six weeks they should come up with something."

Millstadt's phone rang. He excused himself to take it. Brooke took a step back and gasped when she caught a glimpse of herself in a frosted glass door to her left. Driving straight through from Nashville was hard, and even after a twenty-minute nap in a university parking lot, she looked rough. Why hadn't she touched up her makeup? It was a dumb decision, but she had wanted to be first in line when the office opened. A lot of good it was doing her now.

Then she wondered if maybe she was overreacting at what she saw. Millstadt was still on the phone, so she dared another look.

Yep. Terrible.

The door she was gaping at herself in opened suddenly, and an attractive, well-dressed woman of about fifty stepped out. She looked at Brooke, then did a double-take. Their eyes met for a few seconds before the woman came over. She leaned in close and said, "I think you're bleeding."

Brooke recoiled in horror as she checked as much of herself as she could see. No blood on her shirt or jeans. The woman whispered, "Just below your left ear. Come with me."

Brooke obediently followed her through the frosted glass door. They proceeded down a hall to a washroom. The woman held the door open for Brooke. "It may only be a small cut, but you should check it. My office is across the hall. Come by when you finish and let me know you're okay."

"Thank you so much," Brooke said as she closed the door and turned to the mirror. She had checked her reflection in the car's rearview mirror, but her hair had probably covered the wound. She pulled it back and felt a moment of panic before she realized she wasn't bleeding at all. It was a dab of dried ketchup from the fries she'd grabbed at a 24-hour burger place in Poplar Bluff, Missouri. She washed it off, then gave her entire face a good scrubbing before reapplying makeup and running a comb through her hair. She didn't look nearly as scary.

She stepped out of the washroom and considered sneaking away before the nice woman saw her again. Then she noticed a placard on the wall next to her door.

Dr. Julia Hargraves, University Registrar

Talk about screwing up in reverse.

She tapped on the open door. The office was spacious, with windows on two sides and a conference table with room for twelve. Registrar Hargraves was at her desk. She looked up and smiled when she saw Brooke.

"Everything okay?"

Brooke ventured in a step. "Ketchup."

Dr. Hargraves laughed. She was kind, Brooke could tell.

"Unfortunately, you'll be at the rear of the line when you go back out," she said. "What year are you?"

"Oh no, ma'am. I'm not a student. In fact..." Brooke approached the desk, ready to make her pitch. "I left Nashville at midnight and drove through the night to see you."

"To see me?" Now she had the registrar's full attention.

"May I sit down?" Dr. Hargraves pointed to a chair. Brooke pulled out a business card and placed it on the desk as she took a seat.

"We're looking for someone who went to school here about twenty years ago."

When Dr. Hargraves didn't cut her off, Brooke dived in and told her about the song and about her search for Christmas Carl.

"How can you be so sure he went to school here?"

"Well, you won't believe this, but he dated Raven McCloud. She remembered that his—"

Dr. Hargraves nearly came out of her chair. "Stop! Raven McCloud did not attend Missouri State. Trust me, Miss Summers, if she had, I would know it because I adore Raven McCloud."

"I'll bet you lunch she did."

The registrar pulled her laptop closer. "You're on. Mizzou maybe, but she certainly didn't go here."

Brooke sat quietly, aware that Dr. Hargraves would come up empty, but content to let the suspense build while she punched away on her keyboard. Sure enough, after a couple minutes, she turned the screen so Brooke could see.

"Three McClouds. Two are male. The only female attended from 1948 through 1951. Sorry, Miss Summers, but you owe me lunch."

"Please call me Brooke. Now search for Megan Stackhouse from Salmon, Idaho."

Dr. Hargraves' eyes became wide. "You mean..."

Brooke nodded. "She changed her name." She didn't mention that it had been Bobby's suggestion that Raven McCloud might sell more records than Megan Stackhouse.

"Oh...my...goodness." Dr. Hargraves stared at the screen for several moments. "Raven McCloud attended Missouri State." She looked up. "I cannot believe this."

Brooke giggled. "She didn't stay long, but she was here."

The registrar turned her attention back to Raven's school record. "She took five courses...three C's, a B, and a D in—wait a minute... What the...*she was in my Psych 101 class.*" Dr. Hargraves shrieked. "I taught Raven McCloud... and I have no recollection of her."

"There you go," Brooke teased. "You were that close to greatness and didn't even know it."

"And I gave her a D." Dr. Hargraves looked up. "Oh, my goodness, Brooke. I might be the reason that Raven McCloud is singing instead of working as a psychologist."

Brooke laughed. "I know Raven very well, Doctor. She would have been a terrible psychologist."

It took a few moments for reality to set in, but when Brooke thought Dr. Hargraves was there, she circled back to Christmas Carl. Dr. Hargraves jotted some notes, then said, "It's too early for lunch, but how about a late breakfast? And while we're gone, I'll have my people pull together a list of Carls who would have been here at the same time as Miss McCloud."

"Are you sure you want to be seen with me? I smell like I walked from Nashville, and I look a mess."

"You look fine, but how about this instead..."

Brooke had no doubt that had Julia Hargraves lived in Nashville they could have become the best of friends.

Rather than breakfast out, Julia—that's what Brooke was calling her by the time they returned to campus—had invited her home for a shower and a delicious quiche prepared by Julia's much older, happily retired husband, Irving. And when they walked back into the office, there was a printout on Julia's desk.

"Seven males named Carl attended the same semester as Raven," Julia said as she scanned the list. "Sadly, one has passed away. We have addresses and contact information for four of the remaining six."

"That leaves two unaccounted for," Brooke said.

Julia handed the printout across the desk. "Here is what we have. It should be easy enough to find out if any of the four are your Carl. As for the other two, you're on your own."

They hugged and traded phone numbers. Julia promised to come visit. Brooke promised to take her shopping and show her all the popular tourist destinations.

"One more thing," Julia said as she walked Brooke to the door. "Back then there was only one recording studio I know of that allowed people to walk in. It's not there anymore, but the guy who ran it is still around."

"Really? Should I try to see him?"

"Maybe, but be ready, because he's kind of a jerk."

The story was typical in growing cities. The recording studio was among a row of businesses in the path of a major highway expansion. And while he received a generous purchase price, he had become anti-government and anti-university.

"But he remembers everything," Julia said as they parted. And as Brooke followed GPS to the location Julia had given her, she placed a quick call to Raquel back in the office, asking for help in running down the Carls whose whereabouts they knew.

Buster's Burgers was in an alley between a vape shop and a laundromat. The smell of fried food tempted Brooke as she stepped inside. The lunch rush would start shortly, so she knew if she was going to have any luck getting anything out of Buster Vogel, she would have to be quick. He was easy enough to find, a grizzled little man with a spatula in his hand and a scowl on his face. Brooke considered how to approach him before deciding to try her feminine charm.

"Hello," she said, batting her eyelids. "Are you Mr. Vogel?"

"It depends? Who the hell are you? You're from the city, ain't ya? If so, you can get the hell out of my place."

So much for feminine charm.

"Buster, I'm Brooke. I'm a talent manager from Nashville."

Was that a glimmer of curiosity? If so, it was gone as fast as it appeared.

"You're in the wrong place, sugar britches. I got—"

Sugar britches?

"I'm in the right place, *Buster*, and if you call me sugar britches again, you're going to see my mean side. And trust me, Buster, my mean side can kick your mean side's ass."

Buster's face turned red, and he appeared to be loading up to give Brooke what-for. But then the storm disappeared as quick as it came. He actually smiled.

"Well, I don't want my mean side to get its ass kicked. What can I do for you, missy?"

"I'm looking for someone who recorded—"

"Come in back. I gotta cook. Don't touch nothing. Your hands ain't clean."

Brooke followed him into a stinky, greasy kitchen where five deep fryers were waiting to be filled with onion rings, fries, and whatever else got deep fried at Buster's Burgers. Her shoes slipped as she walked, and the air was heavy with food smells. It was gross, but it made Brooke's stomach growl from hunger. Gross or not, if Buster accidentally dropped an onion ring, Brooke might lunge for it before it hit the floor.

"What were you saying?" he asked as he tossed six burgers on the grill.

"We're looking for a guy who recorded a song in your studio about twenty years ago. All we know is—"

"Twenty years ago? Are you serious? We were turning out thirty recordings a week back then. You expect me to remember one of them?"

"Maybe. It was a Christmas song called 'Making Santa Smile.' The guy's name was Carl."

"Nope. Don't remember it."

"He would have come in with a student at the university. Her name was Megan Stackhouse, and she—"

"Look, sugar...lady, everybody was coming in to cut demo tapes back then. They thought they were the next Lionel Richie or another Raven McCloud. The only thing was, none of them was."

"You sure of that, Buster?"

"Yeah, I always had an ear for talent, but there never was any. I got the guys who couldn't hit the high notes or the girls with voices that sounded like fingers on a chalkboard. If the checks cleared, I made the tapes and sent them on their way."

"Well, Buster, what would you say if I told you that Raven McCloud actually did cut some demo tapes in your studio?"

"Bullshit."

Brooke shrugged. "Believe me or not, I don't care. I have a box of songs she recorded at your place, but that's not why I'm here. It's the guy I'm looking for today. And you don't have any memory of him?"

"Raven McCloud was in Springfield?"

"Yep."

"At my place?"

"Uh-hm."

"Well, son of a gun. And the guy you're looking for? Is he a star?"

"Not yet, but if we find him, who knows?"

Buster leaned against the counter while the burgers sizzled. He rubbed his hand across the stubble on his chin, then, to Brooke's amazement, actually sang a couple lines of "Making Santa Smile." His voice was quite good.

"That's it! Buster, you do remember."

Buster grinned. "I got a good memory, even after breathing fry grease for the last eight years. I don't remember the kid's name, but I remember the song. And the girl who he came in with. Pretty thing, good voice. She... *holy smokes*, that was her, wasn't it?"

"Can you remember anything else, Buster?"

He thought some more. "He was a good kid. Not cocky like a lot of 'em who come in. And he was from someplace up north."

"North Missouri?"

"No. Out of state. I saw him around town a few times after that, and he would always speak."

"But no last name? We know his first name was Carl, but nothing else."

"Nah, missy, I can't help you there. He never came back to record anything else, and I never saw... I still can't believe it was Raven McCloud...dammit, if I'd known I would have helped her get started in the business."

"She turned out okay, Buster, but thanks." Brooke laid one of her cards on the counter. "Call me if you remember anything else. And turn those burgers. They're burning."

Brooke cut a sliver from the T-bone, put it in her mouth, and moaned with ecstasy. "The best steak ever!"

Bobby laid his tongs on the edge of the patio grill and stepped into the kitchen. The temperatures had reached seventy in Nashville during the day, and even at eight-thirty in the evening, it was still in the low sixties. "You say that every time,"

"Because your steaks are perfect every time."

It was late for supper, but Bobby had waited until she was back from Missouri. They sat at the kitchen island with Bobby's go-to meal in front of them. T-bones, baked potatoes from Publix, and canned peas and carrots. He was the first to admit that he wasn't much of a chef, but his grilling was sublime.

"Is Tristan back at the Sundrop with Tyler's band tonight?" he asked as he sat down beside her and pulled his plate close.

"He didn't get back to me today. I think work has been kicking his butt lately."

Okay, not completely true. Tristan hadn't returned her calls or texts, so she didn't know if he was playing with the Dusty Shades or sitting at home with a six-pack. After doing her best to forget the way he'd abruptly left the Sundrop with his friends the night before, the last message she left as she was driving through Nashville on her way to Percy's Crossroads was more pointed.

"Tristan, I'm tired of the game playing and your constantly changing moods. We need to figure things out. Soon."

Still no response.

Bobby pulled a slip of paper from his vest pocket and smoothed it on the bar. "Here's what Raquel was able to find. You gave her information for four Carls who were at Missouri State at the same time as Raven. She spoke to three of them and the wife of the fourth. One, Carl Stoker, said he was in the college choir, but didn't remember ever making a recording. Then there was Carl Kappstein. He's a lawyer who still lives in Springfield. He threatened to sue Raquel if she called again."

"Seriously?"

"Old Raquel doesn't get flustered by some silly lawsuit. She dug some more and found the guy's Facebook page, then she called a friend of his who also went to Missouri State. Raquel claimed to be from the college and said they were giving Kappstein an award and needed some background. The friend was happy to help. Long story short, it's not him either." Bobby chuckled. "Raquel gave him the okay to tell Carl Kappstein that he was getting an award. Won't he be disappointed?"

They shared a laugh over poor Carl Kappstein.

"And the other two..." Bobby said as he reviewed the notes. "One said he can't carry a tune in a bucket. And the other is...get ready for this, darlin'...he was Carla in college. He only became Carl about fifteen years ago."

Brooke paused mid-bite. "You mean...?"

"Yep. Really good guy, too. Just not our Carl."

Brooke replayed her earlier conversation with Julia. "That leaves us with two Carls unaccounted for."

"Raquel has a note about that. You said the recording studio guy—"

"Buster."

"Yeah," Bobby said. "Buster told you Carl was from up north. Raquel called your registrar friend and learned that only one of the two other Carls was from the north. He grew up in a small town in North Dakota. The other was a Louisiana boy, so we can cross him off the list."

"So, Dad, we're down to one Carl. We don't know anything except he was from North Dakota. We don't know where he is or even if he's still alive."

"Sounds about right," Bobby said, as he wiped his face with a napkin.

Brooke's phone buzzed. She checked who it was, then held it up for Bobby to see.

"Hey Raven," she said.

"Brooke, I am so angry at you right now. You have ruined my career!"

The words that came from Raven's sweet mouth for the next couple minutes would never make it into any of her songs. Missouri State University's social media pages were full of the news that Raven McCloud briefly attended their fine institution. The resulting comments, according to Raven, were vicious personal attacks. While they listened to her rail, Brooke pulled up the pages. She skimmed them, then handed them over for Bobby to see.

Any civility that was in Raven's tone when the call began was long gone. "You let my personal information get out against my wishes. Now everybody thinks I'm a dumb hillbilly who can't do anything but sing."

Bobby's genial smile disappeared. He leaned in as if to speak, but Brooke shook her head.

"Raven, we'll release a statement before the night is over. It will acknowledge that you attended college for one semester, that you passed your classes, but decided after visiting Nashville that your future was in music."

"Not good enough!"

"Raven, it's the truth. What's wrong with the truth?"

"Bobby would never have done what you did. He would never have gone to the college looking for records of some guy who cut a demo tape a thousand years ago. He would never have let things get like this. I will not watch my career get blown up just so Bobby can let you be..." she paused, then sputtered as she said, "...so you can figure out how to make it as an agent, because, Brooke, honey, you're not."

Brooke's breath caught. She felt the sting of the words but knew she needed to respond. Bobby slapped the table with his fist but didn't speak. "I'm not what, Raven? I'm not going to be a success as an agent?"

"No! You don't have what it takes. And it's Bobby's fault for not seeing that."

Brooke didn't know what she could say in reply. She felt the tears welling up but fought against them.

Big girl bloomers!

Right now! Put them on!

"Raven, you need to—"

Bobby cut in. "Raven, it's Bobby."

Silence.

Brooke started to speak but didn't when Bobby held up his hand.

Still silence.

Then, "Bobby? Why are you at Brooke's place?"

"She's at my place."

"Oh... Bobby, she never should have told that college—"

"Raven, listen to me." Bobby kept his voice steady. "Don't speak. Just listen."

"Okay, but Bobby I—"

"Listen. It's pretty obvious that you're unhappy with us, so I want you to—"

"I'm not unhappy with you, Bobby. It's that Brooke—"

"Brooke and I are a team. If you're unhappy with her, then you're unhappy with me, so sit down tonight and send me an email requesting to be released from our agreement. Send it to me by eight tomorrow morning, and we'll send the release back to you before noon."

Silence.

Bobby yawned. And waited. When Raven didn't speak, he did. "Unless there's anything else, I guess this conversation is finished. I wish you the best, honey. You're at the top of your game right now. Plenty of agents will line up to represent you."

Raven's voice was barely audible when she said, "But... what about—"

"I'll always put my family first, Raven. And that includes you because I think of you as family. But that's changing, so it's just best if we part ways. Like I said, send me the request by eight tomorrow. Good night, now."

He took the phone from Brooke's trembling hand. Bobby hit the button to disconnect, then stood up and started clearing plates.

"Dad? Why?"

Bobby set the plates in the sink and started running water. "We're going to see what Raven is made of."

"Did I just witness one of the greatest examples of bluffing this side of the world poker tour?"

"No, sweetheart, you saw a daddy who doesn't like people messing with his daughter. You saw a businessman who doesn't like people messing with his investment and you saw a man standing up for what he thinks is right."

"But...what if you wake up in the morning and find an email from Raven?"

Bobby offered the slightest of smiles. "Then I guess we go client shopping." He took a deep breath. "You better get busy finding Christmas Carl, because as of tomorrow he might be the only client we have."

❄

Brooke lifted her head from the pillow when her phone buzzed at 3:00 a.m. It took a minute to remember that she was in her childhood bedroom. She had intended to drive back to the apartment, but Bobby put his foot down when he learned she hadn't slept in over thirty hours.

It was Raven. And she was an emotional wreck. The words spilled out. "I treated you terribly, Brooke. I was rude to you in front of all those people at the Opry, and I went off on you earlier tonight for something that doesn't even matter. If you guys want to fire me as a client, I understand, but if you give me a second chance, I'll do better by you. I promise."

Brooke gave her a minute to get her breathing under control.

"What made you change your mind?" she asked.

"I talked to a couple of people in the business."

"Was one of them Travis Horton?"

There was a pause before Raven said, "Well, I talked to him, too. He thought I should drop you guys and go with his team. But the two other people I spoke to reminded me that Bobby is the best there is and that you're smart and hard-working. And that I was a bitch to you at the Opry and I need to realize that nobody else out there will look out for me like you guys do. Lots of people will look out for my money, but they won't treat me like family." Raven gulped back a sob. "You and Bobby treat me like family. And I appreciate it."

Brooke had to fight her own emotions. "Thank you for saying those things, Raven. Dad and I think a lot of you, too."

It was hard not to giggle when she heard Raven honking her nose. "Does that mean you'll keep representing me?"

"It does indeed. And we'll do it proudly."

As soon as the call ended, Brooke jumped out of bed and scampered down the hallway to Bobby's bedroom, much as she had as a little girl during thunderstorms. She didn't want him to lose any sleep worrying about their biggest client, so she pushed open the door and peered in.

Bobby was fast asleep. The small amount of light from his bedside clock was enough for Brooke to see his face. Peaceful. Without worry.

The man was amazing.

WEDNESDAY, NOVEMBER 30

NASHVILLE

Coffee was brewing, but there was no sign of Bobby when Brooke entered the kitchen at seven-twenty. She had slept like a rock, and even after Raven's call, she had fallen back to sleep almost immediately.

She checked his den, then took a pass through his bedroom in case he had slept in. The bed was made; the den was empty. She went back downstairs, poured a cup of coffee, and glanced out the kitchen window at one of the most heavenly views in Tennessee. Bobby had purchased the place when it was a run-down tobacco farm a few months before Brooke's birth. The outbuildings had been falling down, and the land was over farmed and worn out from a lack of crop rotation. He had nursed the place back to health by leaving the land fallow for several years while he built lakes and replaced old barns with modern sheds. There was no farming at Percy's Crossroads. Just tallgrass and trees full of birds, woods where deer and squirrels roamed, and Bobby's beloved ponds teeming with all manner of fish and wildlife. Percy's Crossroads kept Bobby grounded and gave him peace. Brooke could envision him as a younger man, seated on the back porch, staring into the distance while dealing with a divorce he didn't want. She was only thirteen months old when her mother left, telling Bobby she didn't love him and never wanted a child. Brooke had no recollection of that period. Bobby had willingly answered the questions she'd asked as a little girl, but since she didn't remember her mother and suffered no issues with separation, the questions had ceased by kindergarten. She was a happy little girl whose daddy adored her. And when Bobby picked her up from school one day in eighth grade and told her that her mother had died in an auto accident, Brooke had felt no grief.

She was immersed in the scenery when Bobby came into view. He was wearing a spring-weight jacket and carrying his fishing rod. No fish, but that wasn't important. He threw back more than he kept. Mostly, it was his time to think and meditate and sometimes pray. Bobby had never stopped praying. He gave up church after Brooke's mother left, more because of the way he was received by the other parishioners than by feelings of guilt or shame. His church was, Brooke knew, just over the hill where the fish were plentiful and thinking was easy.

He smiled and waved when he saw her gazing out the window, then stepped onto the porch and beat his boots against a post to knock off the mud before removing them and leaving them next to the door. When he stepped inside, his cheeks were rosy and his eyes were alive. Brooke went to him, raised up on tiptoes, and kissed his cheek.

"Raven called and wants to stay with us," Brooke said.

Bobby nodded, then went to the sink and washed his hands.

"You weren't worried, were you?" Brooke said.

"Not really."

She moved up behind him and wrapped her arms around him as he dried his hands on a dish towel. "I love you, Daddy. Thanks for having my back."

"Always, daughter. Always."

He took a seat at the kitchen table while Brooke got started on breakfast. "You really need to get some groceries," she scolded gently. He said he knew. Brooke eventually settled on French toast made with the heels of a loaf of bread she found in the pantry. While it cooked, she checked the usual entertainment sites and other news until something caught her eye.

"Dad, look at this!" She hurried to the table and held out her phone where Bobby could see the screen. "Somebody uploaded our song onto the internet."

"Is that even legal?"

"Not really, but right now it's fair game since nobody knows who recorded it. That's not even the biggest news. Dad, it's been downloaded eighty-one thousand times."

"I'm guessing that's good?"

"For a poor-quality song by an unknown singer? That's only been played in the south? It's crazy good. We need to find this guy before somebody else does."

"I was thinking about that this morning," Bobby said. He sniffed the air and said, "The French toast is done. Anyway, since we're running into a dead end, why not try a little old-fashioned public relations trick?"

Brooke brought their plates to the table and sat down. "Tell me."

The idea was certainly old fashioned. Real old school. And real good. It bypassed social media and, for the most part, the entire internet. If he's on social media, Bobby concluded, he would have already heard the song, since it was trending on Twitter and was linked on Facebook and Instagram. Bobby's idea? Network television. And Bobby being Bobby, he knew just the people who could make it work.

Perhaps it was hurt feelings, or maybe it was stubbornness. Whatever it was kept Brooke from swinging by the apartment for a showdown with Tristan. She kept a change of clothes in her office closet, so after breakfast and a shower, she left Percy's Crossroads excited about how the day might play out. Who knew? Maybe by the next day, if Bobby's plan worked, they would have located Christmas Carl.

Raquel greeted Brooke with a quick hello followed by, "Raven is coming in at one-thirty."

"She's coming here?"

"That's what she said."

"But...how is she getting here?"

"She's driving. She said to leave the garage door up."

Raven had largely given up driving. She still had the red Mercedes convertible, her pride and joy when she'd purchased it five years earlier, but Brooke couldn't remember the last time she'd driven it. The guys who serviced it took it for a spin every few weeks, but Raven? Was her license even valid? Brooke hurried to her office and dug through her records until she found what she was looking for. Yep, Raven's Tennessee driver's license was good for three more years. Brooke considered calling her and telling her she would happily send Milo in the limo but decided against it. Raven was entitled to make her own decisions. Brooke just hoped she didn't try to make a quick run through some fast-food drive-through.

The intercom on Brooke's desk, a relic from the nineties that Bobby and Raquel still used entirely too much, squawked to life. "Brooke, Harley Willard's on the phone."

Just hearing the name made Brooke smile. She grabbed the desk phone and blurted, "If it isn't my favorite bluegrass singer from Adelaide, Kentucky!"

"And if it isn't the prettiest and smartest member of the Summers family!" Harley exclaimed with a laugh. "Dang it, Brooke, how old are you now, sweetheart? Fourteen?"

It didn't matter how often they spoke, it was always the same.

"How's the tour, Harley? Are you bringing the house down?"

"I'm home for Christmas. Mary Alice demands it. She says she's too old to buy and wrap the grandkids' presents by herself."

They chatted for a few minutes about life and music. Harley's career as a bluegrass picker had peaked in the sixties, but every eight or ten years brought a resurgence of the genre. Harley would reemerge from his hog farm in Adelaide like a bear coming out of hibernation, driving his own 1980s RV to places like Frostburg, Maryland and DuQuoin, Illinois. Not big venues, but places with plenty of fervent bluegrass fans willing to pay fifty bucks a ticket to hear an eighty-year-old perform songs their grandparents listened to on their Philco radios.

"Brooke, my reason for calling is that my second guitarist is moving on, and I need a replacement."

Brooke fired up her laptop and opened a file of names she was willing to recommend. "What do you need, Harley?"

"I prefer someone young. There's plenty of old boys like me who can pick a little, but they don't have the energy I need. The boy who left is twenty-four and he's got a lot of career in front of him. I'm hoping to find someone like him. Someone hungry to move ahead. If they stay with me six months, that's fine, as long as they've got the drive."

"How about I do some calling around and get back to you, Harley?"

"Well, that's good, but actually I have someone in mind already. Your boyfriend, Tristan Fleming."

"You know Tristan?"

"Not at all, but I know some boys who do. I heard he's between gigs and since you and him are together, I figure he's good people."

"Well, yes, Tristan is good people. Want me to have him get in touch with you?"

"That would be good. Of course, Brooke, you know..." Harley became difficult to hear. "I'm trying to keep it down. One of my grandsons is in the next room. You know about the troubles I had with the booze and the pills."

It was long before Brooke was born, but yeah, she knew. Everyone knew about the hell that Harley Willard used to raise.

"I still got my rules, Brooke. And I hold my band to them, too. No booze. No drugs. No pot. Now I know it's old-fashioned, and people are going to say, 'Harley, there ain't nothing wrong with a shot of whiskey or a toke now and then,' but I have to protect myself."

"I understand, Harley."

"I've been clean and sober for thirty-four years and still go to meetings every week. If I didn't go I reckon Mary Alice would feed me to the hogs, but those are my rules and I'll stick to them. So as long as your boy is clean and sober and doesn't do any of that stuff, I'm interested in bringing him on."

Brooke didn't know what to say. Tristan had done all those things at one time or another. She had no idea how much or if he could even quit when he wanted. But he would be great with Harley. She was certain of it. Tristan, for all his shortcomings, could be one of the kindest and most selfless people there was. And he loved bluegrass. A lot more than she did. He had albums by Bill Monroe, Flatt and Scruggs, and acts Brooke had never heard of. It could be a match made in heaven. Except...

"Harley, let me get to work on this for you. Is it okay if it takes a couple of days?"

"Of course. I'm just gonna be wrapping toys out here in Adelaide. And I'll pay you for your time."

"Nonsense. You're a friend, Harley. We won't take your money. Tell Miss Mary Alice I said hey."

"And you do the same to Bobby. God bless y'all."

Brooke put her work aside when she heard Bobby in the hallway.

"Hey, Dad, how was lunch?"

Bobby stepped in and went to the window. He gazed outside as he spoke.

"Good enough. Raquel told me Raven's on her way in."

"Did Raquel tell you she's driving?"

Bobby made a face. "Oh, my. I hope she doesn't decide to stop to do a little shopping along the way. Did you call Nicky Lopez over at police headquarters?"

"He has patrol monitoring her route, just in case."

"Good, good. Anything else going on?"

Brooke told him about her conversation with Harley Willard. Specifically, his inquiry about Tristan. She didn't get into why it troubled her, but she was certain that Bobby suspected.

"What did you tell him?"

"That I would get back to him."

Bobby continued looking out the window for several moments before turning and heading for the door. "Let me know when Raven gets here."

"Brooke," Raquel's disembodied voice echoed from the intercom as Bobby exited. "There's a guy on the phone who claims to be Christmas Carl. Want me to interrogate him?"

"Thanks, Raquel, but I'll take a run at it... This is Brooke Summers. Can I help you?"

The guy's voice had a gravelly tenor to it, not at all like the voice on the CD, but people's voices change when they age. He said his name was Carl Winston and he was from North Platte, Nebraska.

"The song is mine. I wrote it and recorded it. Somewhere along the way, I misplaced it. I was amazed to hear that you had found it."

"It's good that you called, Mr. Winston. What can you tell me about the recording?"

"It was a long time ago. I wrote the song and played it for some friends here in North Platte, and they said I needed to record it, that it might be a hit."

"Interesting. Where did you record it?"

"A little studio. I can't remember the name exactly. It's been so long."

"Where was the studio, Mr. Winston?"

"I can't rightly remember that either. I had a go-round with the bottle for a few years and some of my memory isn't what it should be. But I remember writing that song, just as sure as I'm talking to you on the phone. Do you need me to come to Nashville, or will you send someone to get me?"

"I'm afraid I need a little more information, Mr. Winston. Plenty of people could claim to be Christmas Carl. We just need to make sure we get the real one."

"Like I said, my memories are fuzzy because of the booze. But I definitely wrote it and I want to get my share of the profits."

"There are no profits yet. It's a demo tape."

"My niece heard it on the internet, so somebody's playing it."

Brooke took a different approach. More direct. "Mr. Winston, did you go to college?"

Winston hemmed and hawed. He muttered something about a junior college near Omaha, but not much else.

"How about Missouri? Did you ever attend college there?"

"I might of. It was a long time ago and I—"

"Mr. Winston, I'm going to have my assistant take your name and number. If we need more information, we'll get in touch, okay?"

"You don't believe me, do you?" Winston snapped.

"No, sir, I don't. You've given me nothing to prove that you're Christmas Carl. If you come up with something, call back. Thank you."

Winston was still yakking when Brooke disconnected. It was one-thirty. Time for Raven to make her appearance.

"Brooke, she just pulled into the garage," Raquel mumbled into the intercom. "And she's not alone."

Brooke stood up, checked herself in the hand mirror she

kept in her drawer, and went to Bobby's office. "She brought someone with her."

"I'll bet you an egg cream from Mike's that it's him," Bobby said. He didn't have to say which *him* he was referring to. Brooke suspected the same, but any treat from Mike's Ice Cream and Coffee Bar was worth the wager.

"You're on. Let's meet in the conference room."

Raquel made them wait a couple of minutes before leading their guests up the stairs and into the conference room. It had been the master bedroom when the office was still a stately home a century before, and the large fireplace that kept it warm back then hadn't been used since Bobby bought the property. Brooke had asked about it once, but Bobby was worried about burning the place to the ground.

Raquel held the door open for them. Brooke stood to greet them. Bobby didn't. Raven stepped in as if she owned the place. She had recovered nicely from the previous day's meltdown and seemed fine with putting everything behind them. Travis Horton was close behind. His eyes cased the room as if he knew he was the unwelcome outsider. Very intuitive, Brooke thought. And very handsome, too. She hadn't been that close to Travis, and he was as gorgeous up close as he was on TV and stage.

"Thank you for agreeing to see me this afternoon," Raven said cheerfully. "Travis and I decided to go for a drive, and I said, why don't we stop by Bobby's office?"

"Is there anything else you need from me?" Raquel appeared bored with the situation.

"Yes, Raquel," Brooke said. "Please call and make sure that the agency has enough temps to handle—"

"Already done. I just had another Carl call. Not ours. I got rid of him." Raquel closed the door behind her. Travis pulled out a chair for Raven, then sat down next to her. He wore jeans and a University of Tennessee sweatshirt. He placed a UT cap on the table. Raven had her hair in a ponytail and wore large eyeglasses that gave her a studious but sexy look. She also had a UT cap on but didn't take it off, jeans that were expensive, and a sweater that cost more than a decent used car. She had done a commendable job of concealing her identity. The glasses and hat would throw most people off, even at close range.

"How is the search for Carl going?" Raven asked.

Brooke answered, "Slow, but we aren't giving up."

"I have a proposal that I think is going to make your lives a lot easier," Raven said. "Let's give the song to Travis. He talked to the folks at his studio, and they can record it before the weekend. It will be uploaded to the public by Monday."

"That's pretty fast," Bobby said.

"Real fast," Travis said in his twangy East Tennessee drawl. "And Bobby, don't think we're gonna cut you out. There's a five percent share built in for your agency."

Bobby leaned forward and placed his arms on the conference table. "Five percent?"

Travis nodded.

"But what if the writer steps forward for his cut?"

Travis waved off the question. "There's no way he has the resources to take us on. I figure twenty-five hundred will get him to go away fast enough, assuming he has the cajones to push us."

Brooke saw what she expected to see when she looked at Bobby. His mouth twitched, something the average person would never pick up on. Bobby had a distaste for people who used business jargon.

Stuff like, *I'll have my people call your people.*
Come to Jesus.

Buy-in, brainstorming, lots of moving parts, thirty-thou-sand-foot view.

Just say what you want to say was his way of doing business. And Brooke suspected he was about to do just that.

"Travis," he said slowly. "Where's Larry on this?"

Travis's left eye twitched at the mention of his agent. "This doesn't involve Larry. It's just me and Raven. And you guys."

Bobby nodded, getting ready, Brooke knew, to pin Travis's ears back.

"You would record the song?"

Travis nodded.

"This week?"

Another nod.

"You get ninety-five percent of the profits?"

Raven said, "Of course not, Bobby. Travis and I split the profits."

"For a song neither of you wrote?"

"It's not like you can stop us," Travis said, a not-so-handsome smirk crossing his handsome face. "The song is fair game. I mean, hells bells, it was in a box of Raven's stuff. It ain't yours, Bobby, no more than it's anybody else's."

Bobby stared at Travis like he would a pile of dog poo on the sidewalk, then turned his attention to Raven. "Is this how you want to do things?"

"I just thought that Travis could do the song and it would make it easier for you and Brooke."

"Thank you for thinking of us, Raven. Was this your idea?"

Brooke knew it wasn't. She was right.

"Tell you what," Bobby said as he stood and headed for the door. "We're going to find Christmas Carl if Brooke and me have to go door to door. And Travis, when we do, I'll pay for the lawyer he uses to sue you from one end of Davidson County to the other."

"Screw you, Bobby," Travis said, rising to his feet. "You don't own this song. I can record it if I want."

"I don't own this song and neither do you. And I'm going into my office to call your record label and tell them exactly what I told you." He paused at the door. "Now, Raven, honey, if you want to stick around, you're more than welcome. We're always happy to see you, but your...whatever he is to you these days...is free to get the heck out of my office."

Raquel was straightening her desk when Brooke came through. "Seven more Carls called in this afternoon."

"Any of them the real one?" Brooke asked, knowing the answer.

Raquel shook her head. "One was a woman. Another sang the entire song in reggae. That was pretty awesome, really. The others were too young or too old, or couldn't provide any information that would make me believe they were in Missouri twenty years ago."

The temp had dropped steadily throughout the day, typical for Nashville in winter. Brooke buttoned up her coat as she said, "The temp agency has forty operators on standby for the announcement tonight, so you're officially relieved of your duties as chief interrogator of Carls."

"It was kinda fun," Raquel admitted. "I felt like a lawyer cross-examining a witness. And Brooke, if you don't find the real Carl, I would go with the reggae guy. He was excellent. Oh, there's one more thing, something I think you should know."

Brooke sat down. She could see that something was bothering the usual unflappable Raquel.

"I don't know what happened upstairs with Travis Horton, but when he came down here by himself, he stood just inside the door over there and was talking on the phone to somebody about how he had just put Bobby in his place. It pissed me off royally, I'm telling you. Made me want to kick his fine backside back to Chipmunk's Elbow or whatever they call that little town he comes from."

Brooke and Bobby never discussed what went on behind closed doors, even with Raquel. Brooke was about to remind her when she continued. "But that's not what I wanted to tell you. Travis was asking whoever he was on the phone with about a party. I didn't hear when or where, but before he hung up, he said he was coming and was bringing Raven with him."

Brooke tried to push away the worry. She knew Travis's reputation for partying. And for overindulging in everything from booze and cars to women.

"I feel sorry for Raven sometimes," Raquel said as she shut down her computer. "She's got more money and stuff than a hundred people could ever need, but she just doesn't seem happy sometimes. I think she gets lonely."

"Dad and I think so, too. Some of it comes from the crush of fame."

Raquel nodded. "We've had some big names come through here over the years, but none have achieved what Raven has. The city has changed, too. When Bobby was starting out, our headliners could still go to the grocery store or a movie."

"Try that with Raven and we'll have a riot," Brooke said. "I understand why she would be attracted to someone like Travis. He doesn't let that stuff bother him. He likes the crowds and the attention." She glanced toward the stairs, just to make sure that Bobby wasn't on his way down. "And he's damned good looking, too."

"Um-hmm," Raquel said, drawing it out. "If he ever decides that he's into seventy-year-olds, I'll dump Wilbur and throw myself at that boy's feet. Provided he doesn't say anything else bad about my boss."

They chatted for a few more minutes. Brooke sometimes forgot how intuitive their longtime office assistant could be, and how much she had seen. If she was worried about Raven, she and Bobby needed to worry too. But what could they do? Raven was entitled to live her life. And if that life included Travis Horton, there wasn't much anyone could do.

"What time is the big announcement?" Raquel asked.

"Two of the television networks and all three of the cable news companies have agreed to carry a piece between seven and ten."

"The crazies will be ringing the phones off the walls," Raquel said. "How will the call screeners determine if the real Carl is one of them?"

"We have four questions that only the real Carl would know the answer to. The operators screen the calls and ask the questions. The answers go into a computer program and the contact information for anyone who hits four of four will be sent to me." She patted Raquel's hand and stood up. "Let's hope our Carl watches TV news."

It was time to bury the hatchet with Tristan. Brooke would have preferred to wait until he reached out first, but she couldn't expect more than he could give, and saying "I'm sorry" had always been hard for Tristan, even when he was one-hundred percent wrong like this time. She knew how it would go. She would bring a food peace offering. He wouldn't say much at first. They would eat in silence until Tristan decided it was time to put everything behind them. They would make love and everything would be fine. Until next time. Heck of a way to live, huh? She almost envied Raven's solitude at the house out in Brentwood.

Almost.

So, what to use as a peace offering?

The answer loomed in front of her as she headed away from the office. Hattie B's. One of their favorite hot chicken joints. Nashville's reputation as the birthplace of hot chicken was undisputed, but there were plenty of pretenders and only a few places that legitimately turned out quality hot chicken. Though it hadn't been around as long as some, Hattie B's was good and it was close. She pulled in and found a parking place, then picked up her phone to call Tristan. It barely rang before he answered.

"Did Harley Willard call you?" he asked right off the bat.

Brooke fumbled for a moment. How had Tristan found out?

"He...yeah, he called right after lunch, but I've been in meetings and—"

"What did he say?"

"He was asking if you might be available to go on the road with him, but—"

"Damn it, Brooke, why didn't you call and tell me? You know how much this means to me."

Something in the way he said it, perhaps the swearing, pushed all the wrong buttons.

"Watch your tone with me, Tristan."

Tristan raised his voice to match hers. "You know how much a gig like this would do for my career!"

"And you know Harley is a recovering addict. He has expectations of the people who tour with him."

"He's an old man, Brooke. It's been years since his troubles. And if you're saying I have a drinking problem, you're freaking nuts. There's a helluva difference between abusing something and enjoying it once in a while."

"And *you* fall on the side of enjoying it once in a while, Tristan?"

He laughed. "What are you saying? You think I have a problem?"

"I'm the one with a problem, Tristan. Harley Willard has been a family friend for a long time. He came to me and asked for help. It's a heck of a bad position to be in, but I'm there and have to deal with it. His rules are simple. No drinking, no junk. Walk the straight line. Your best friend deals grass, and before you start in on how stupid it is that grass is not legalized, I'll remind you that Harley has every right to decide who he wants to play with him."

"So you're going to call and tell him not to hire me because I smoke weed once in a while? Is that what I mean to you, Brooke?"

Brooke could feel her heart pounding. A roaring noise was building in her head. Was it time to take a stand? Was it time to say what she had been thinking for weeks?

Yeah. It was.

"Are marijuana and alcohol all that you...enjoy once in a while, Tristan?"

The line was quiet. One beat. Two. Brooke wondered if he was still there.

He was. "Are you going to give Harley your blessing or not? Because if you're not, we're through."

Brooke wasn't sure what to say next, but it would have nothing to do with which pieces of chicken he wanted her to bring home. They were way past that. Then she remembered how Bobby had spoken with Raven the day before. He had challenged her, tossed the ball into her court. It had worked.

But would it work with Tristan?

"I'll make you a deal, Tristan. I'll call Harley back and recommend he add you to his tour."

"Yeah, and what do I have to do?"

"Take a drug test."

"No problem. I can set one up for this weekend."

"You take it tonight."

"What the—Are you nuts? I said I'll get it done this weekend. Is my word not good enough for you anymore, Brooke? Are you saying you don't trust me?"

"Do you want the gig or not?"

Tristan started laughing. He sounded kind of scary. "I guess you hold all the cards, don't you?"

"I wouldn't put it that way, but yeah I guess I do."

"Little princess is calling the shots. Bobby would be proud, wouldn't he?"

She knew he would, but there was no sense telling Tristan.

"I'm my own person. My reputation is riding with yours on this. I'll let you damage your reputation, but not when it extends to mine. So, are you ready to get the test? If so, I'll come get you and take you to a place I know."

"Brooke, is this necessary?" His tone had changed. Less direct, more pleading. "We've been together for two years. You know that performing is what I've always wanted to do."

It would have been easy to let down. Go along to get

along. But Brooke had done enough of that when it came to Tristan.

"I can be at the apartment in ten minutes. Are you going?"

She heard him take a deep breath. Then he unleashed a torrent of expletives. Mean, personal, cutting. Things about Brooke—deeply hurtful things. And about Bobby and how she would never be anything without him. The barrage lasted only a few seconds, but that was all the time she needed to decide her next step.

She disconnected the call, backed out of the parking lot, and headed east. Toward Percy's Crossroads. She was on Murfreesboro Pike passing the Nazarene college when Tristan called back. She had her finger on the button to decline the call when she reconsidered. She hit accept instead.

"Yeah, I'm a daddy's girl, you bastard. And someday I hope someone loves me enough to treat me with as much love and respect as he does. It's taken me too long to realize that you're not that person."

"Brooke, I'm sorry I—"

"I'll come by and get my stuff tomorrow afternoon. Don't be there. I've paid the rent through December. After that, it's on you."

She could hear him crying. It felt strangely reassuring.

"Don't call me or come see me. And if you ever want to work in Nashville, don't mess with me. Because, Tristan, whether you like it or not, this daddy's girl can make sure you never play your guitar in this town again."

Bobby was out. Brooke had no idea where he was, but in some ways she was glad. It was seven when she let herself in the house. She was still numb but hadn't cried. And Tristan hadn't called back. She was famished. And exhausted. More exhausted than famished. Plus there wasn't much in the house to eat, so she went up to her old bedroom and crawled under the sheets.

She awakened with a start when her phone rang. Ten-fifteen. Probably Tristan. She checked the number. It was from a Kentucky area code. She answered, expecting a deal on a timeshare or cable TV. Nope.

"Is this Brooke Summers?"

"Yes. Who's calling?"

"Miss Summers, I'm Deputy Chief Kendra Johnson with the Bowling Green, Kentucky Police Department."

Brooke was suddenly wide awake.

"Oh, no, is it my father? Has something happened to him?"

"No, ma'am." The Deputy Chief lowered her voice. "It's Raven McCloud. We have her at the station. Can you come up?"

"Raven? What happened?" Brooke was already getting out of bed.

"She's fine. And safe. But there was an incident. I don't want to say much over the phone, but can you come and get her?"

"Of course. It will take me an hour, but I'll leave right now."

"Don't speed. Take your time. Like I said, Miss McCloud is fine. And she's not under arrest. Yet."

Brooke ran into the bathroom and nearly blinded herself when she flipped on the light. She squinted at her reflection in the mirror and was taken aback at how rough she looked. She found an old comb and ran it through her hair. There was no makeup in any of the drawers, so she quickly washed off what she was already wearing. She stopped by Bobby's bedroom to get him, but when she heard him snoring, she decided to go alone.

Bowling Green was a pretty college town about seventy miles north of Nashville. The trip north on Interstate 65 was traffic free. Brooke used GPS to navigate through the Western Kentucky University campus and the city's old downtown area. She was two blocks from the police station when she fully realized the magnitude of the situation she was about to encounter. Four TV trucks were parked along Kentucky Street. She drove past and saw two more on the Main Street side of the building. Four of the trucks were from Nashville, another was local. The fifth was from one of the news networks. How had they gotten to town so fast?

Brooke considered her options before driving into an alley on a side of the building the TV cameras seemed to ignore. It didn't work. A man in a parka and University of Kentucky scarf approached to check her out.

"Who are you?" he asked.

Brooke didn't answer. Directly in front of her was a side entrance to the police station. She walked to it as if she belonged there, but when she pulled at the door it wouldn't open. That got more attention. She heard someone say, "That's Bobby Summers's daughter." People came running, lights and cameras in tow. They surrounded Brooke and peppered her with questions.

"What happened tonight?"

"Has Raven McCloud been arrested?"

"Can you confirm that a police officer was transported to the hospital?"

"Is it true that Raven and Travis Horton are being held?"

"What is your relationship to Raven and Travis?"

Brooke held up her hand, but the questions continued to come. She was about to give up and make a run for the front entrance when the door behind her opened and a pair of hands reached out and pulled her inside. They belonged to a brunette woman of about forty who introduced herself as Deputy Chief Kendra Johnson. Brooke started to speak, but Deputy Johnson raised her finger to wait, then led her down a hallway to her office.

"Brooke Summers, right?"

"Yes."

"Coffee?"

"No, thank you."

Deputy Johnson motioned to a chair across from her desk, then surprised Brooke by taking the seat next to her instead of on the other side. She had kind eyes and a calm manner. There were no pleasantries, though.

"Miss McCloud was at a bar up the street this evening. Things got a little out of hand when word got out. A couple of our officers went down to keep the peace." She consulted a laptop. "Miss McCloud's friend became physical with one of the officers and was arrested. He's in custody for the night. The entire situation scared the dickens out of her, Miss Summers. She didn't cause any trouble, and we were able to get her out with no further issue."

"Was it Travis Horton?"

"Yes, ma'am. His manager has already been in." She smiled as she shook her head. "I suspect he exceeded the speed limit to get here. Anyway, he's out trying to find a judge willing to let Mr. Horton out tonight. We suspect he was the one who alerted the press."

"Where is Raven?"

"She's in one of our conference rooms. I've checked on her a couple times."

"Thank you so much, Deputy Johnson. And I'm sorry your officer was hurt."

"We've had Mr. Horton here before. He has cousins in Bowling Green and comes through now and again. He's a handful."

"That's an understatement," Brooke said, feeling a bit of relief that they may have dodged a bullet.

The deputy stood up and motioned for Brooke to follow. "I'll take you to Miss McCloud. When you're ready to leave, we'll help you get out of Bowling Green. You'll be on your own after that, but I suspect the press isn't up for a seventy-mile tail at this time of night."

Bobby met them at the bottom of the stairs, clad in blue plaid sleeping pants and a gray Vandy t-shirt. His hair was a mess. To Brooke, he looked suddenly older.

Raven was quiet. She had said little on the ride back, other than to apologize for making Brooke come so far and to ask if she could stay at her apartment. Brooke didn't get into details about why they would go to Bobby's instead, and Raven didn't ask.

"The press wants a statement," Bobby said as he shuffled to the kitchen for a glass of water. Brooke didn't ask how he had found out, but she suspected he had awakened to go to the restroom and saw he had messages.

"I'll write one as soon as I get Raven settled," Brooke said. She led Raven upstairs to the spare room. She was still shaken, but when Brooke asked if she needed anything, she said she only wanted to go to bed. Brooke closed the door and headed back downstairs. It was two-forty in the morning. Bobby was sitting at the kitchen table with a cup of instant coffee. He offered Brooke a cup, but she turned it down.

"So," he said, cracking a crooked smile. "How was your day?"

Brooke rubbed her eyes, then her neck. Her feet hurt too, but those could wait. "Where to start. Our star client has been a handful, but she's only part of why this has been a shitty day." She glanced at Bobby and gave him a grin of her own. "I've handled it, though."

"Wearing your big girl bloomers, are you?"

"I've crapped in about five pairs of big girl bloomers today, Dad, but I'm still alive. Have you ever had four TV news trucks on your tail?"

"Well...yeah. But it's been a while."

"I lost them when I did a double-back in a little town called Mitchellville."

"Good job, Brooke. I'm proud of you."

Brooke smiled. She liked it when she made him proud. "Otherwise, it was a pretty yucky day."

"Want to tell me about it?"

"How much do you know about what happened with Raven and Travis?"

"Just what I've read on social media."

"How about Tristan and me? Anything on social media about that?"

Bobby shook his head. "Not that I read."

"Well, thank goodness. Needless to say, he won't be going out on the road with Harley Willard."

Bobby wasn't surprised.

"Can I stay here for a spell?"

"As long as you want. I love when you're here."

"If you love me being here so much, please get some food in this house. We can't survive on Diet Coke and Ritz crackers."

Bobby promised he would.

Tomorrow.

THURSDAY, DECEMBER 1

NASHVILLE AND GARLAND GROVE

Brooke yawned, then rolled over and checked the time.

Ten-thirty.

Ten-thirty?

She bolted from the bed and went to check on Raven. Her bed was neatly made, but she was gone. Brooke ran back to her room and grabbed the fluffy robe that Bobby had bought her at one of those luxury hotels, back when she was in high school, then went downstairs. She didn't expect Bobby to be there, and he wasn't. She looked out the back window and saw him stacking kindling for the living room fireplace. Fresh kindling meant he and his chainsaw had already been out to the woods that surrounded the farm on three sides. How did he do it? She opened the door and called out, "Where's Raven?"

Bobby smiled when he saw her framed in the door. "I took her home two hours ago. She wanted to get ready for rehearsals this afternoon." He pointed to the stack of kindling and said, "Give me ten minutes and I'll be in."

Brooke poured a cup of coffee and checked the internet to find out what was being said about Raven's adventures in

Bowling Green. It didn't take long to determine that she was getting off easy, especially compared to Travis Horton who was justifiably being demonized for punching a cop. The Bowling Green police had done an exceptional job providing the basics of what had happened without a lot of extraneous quotes. Brooke made a note to call Deputy Johnson later to thank her for not allowing the matter to become a media circus.

There were a couple of websites that tried to make more of the situation. One flat-out lied, saying Raven was being held on bail. Others had a field day speculating about the relationship between country music's good girl and bad boy. Brooke had to admit that some of their conjecture was pretty interesting. If there was one criticism she had with Bobby's management of Raven, it was that her public persona was not indicative of who she really was. Not that Raven was a terrible person, but she had her faults. Brooke had heard the stories of stars who struggled to be someone they weren't, and how their falls were epic fodder for the public. Had Brooke been old enough and mature enough to voice an opinion back when Bobby was molding Raven into who she was, it would have been to let her be a little bad once in a while. Then, when she was caught in a Kentucky dive bar it wouldn't be the big story it was becoming.

She was flipping from website to website when Bobby stepped inside. There was frost on the ground, but he had worked up a good sweat chopping wood.

"Why don't you hire someone to do that?" she asked as she poured him a cup of coffee.

"At my age, I'm afraid that once I stop I may never start again." He took the cup and leaned against the counter. "Good job on the statement you released last night about Raven."

"Thanks, Dad. It was crazy. Hopefully, it will all blow over. What did she say about it this morning?"

"That it was dumb to go and that she was sorry for getting you out so late. I tried to get through to her about how he wasn't the right guy for her. Whether I was successful or not remains to be seen." He sipped his coffee, then said, "What kind of response are we getting on the news stories about Christmas Carl?"

Brooke opened an email that had arrived a couple of hours earlier. "Three-hundred and eighty-six callers claiming to be Christmas Carl. None could answer the qualifying questions."

"Dang it."

"Yeah. There is still some hope. The local TV news programs started picking up the story from the network feeds. A lot of them will run the story today and tonight, but after that, I'm afraid we will have taken it as far as we can."

"That's too bad," Bobby said as he stretched to work out some kinks. "Gary Gene Pickler called earlier on his way to the station. Our mystery man is getting airplay all over the south. It's the most requested song in Birmingham, Shreveport, and Oklahoma City. There's money to be made by selling the song, but we're stuck."

"Maybe we'll have some luck today," Brooke said, getting to her feet. "I need to go get my stuff at the apartment."

She knew Bobby wouldn't pry into why she was moving out. It wasn't his way. He said, "Need any help?"

"No, Dad." She went to him and hugged him. "Just be here for me like you always are. Maybe when things slow down, we'll go out back and wet a line together."

"I'm always here for you, darlin'. And we can go fishing anytime, just as long as the temperatures are high enough to get 'em to bite." He checked his watch. "Raven and the boys are rehearsing at her place at three today. I'm thinking about heading out and seeing how they sound."

"You enjoy the day," Brooke said. "I'll go to the rehearsal. I spoke to Mickey yesterday. He said everything's coming together really well. The band is sharp and Raven sounds great. I just hope that last night doesn't affect her."

It wasn't their plan to eat the entire extra-large convenience store pizza—pepperoni and onion on Craig's half, Hawaiian on Jenna's—but they did. Two thousand calories for Craig, slightly less for Jenna because she ordered light cheese. They worked through the pizza slowly and methodically as they decorated Craig's Christmas tree. If it had been up to him, they would have tossed the ornaments onto the tree so they could go to bed. The memories of their epic Monday night lovemaking had carried him through the past three days. She had been tied up Tuesday night and couldn't come over. He had rehearsals for the Christmas concert on Wednesday. She never slept over on Thursday night, but then she had never slept over on a Monday night either, and other than the fight over something he still hadn't figured out, Jenna had been amazing.

Could there be a repeat performance?

When they were nearly done decorating, he rubbed against her and nuzzled her neck a few times, sending out the signals that he hoped weren't too strong, but strong enough to get her attention. She moaned softly and placed her hand on his cheek when he came up behind her. So far, so good.

When the only thing left was the star atop the tree,

Craig carefully unwrapped it and handed it to her. He didn't have to say why. It was the same thing they had done on both their trees the year before and the year before that. She turned so he could lift her up. He did, and she gently placed the heirloom star that had belonged to Craig's grandmother on the tree. Once it was in place, she was supposed to turn herself in his arms and kiss him. Christmas tradition and all that. Craig loosened his grasp enough for her to turn. She did. Their eyes met. He lifted his chin as she lowered hers and kissed him like...like...

Mehhh.

"C'mon," Craig teased. "You can do better than that."

Jenna smiled and kissed him again. Better, but still mehhh.

"I really need to get home," she said.

Craig continued to hold her, continued to hope.

"I have an in-service class tomorrow and need to get a good night's sleep."

"Well...you can get that here." Craig tried to sound casual when he was feeling desperate. "I mean, after we, you know. Sex always helps a person sleep."

Jenna giggled but didn't bend over to kiss him again. "Yeah...no, I really need to get my rest."

"Aren't all your in-service classes online? Like, you can take them any time you want?"

"Not all of them. Some are face-to-face."

"And this one is face-to-face?" As the words spilled from his mouth, Craig could sense a change. Jenna's brow furrowed and her eyes grew cold.

"Why all the questions, Craig? It's just like Monday night."

Craig set her down. "Is it wrong to want to know about

what you have going on in your life? I've always asked questions in the past and you've never complained."

She shook her head. "Not like this. It's an interrogation. Like you don't trust me."

"I trust you completely, Jenna."

"Are you sure? Maybe I shouldn't be trusting you. All these questions. It's like you want to know where I am every minute. Are you up to something I should know about, Craig? Is that it? Do you need to know where I am so you know the coast is clear to—"

"This is ridiculous," Craig snapped as he lowered her to the floor. He could feel his pulse quickening. "I'm not *up to anything* as you put it. I hoped you could spend the night, especially after how crazy good things were Monday night. I put—"

Jenna's voice rose to match Craig's. "We had sex. We also fought, which is something we never did until you started asking so damned many questions. Would it make you feel better if I put some kind of tracking device on my phone so you know my location 24/7?" She pulled her phone from her pocket. "Here it is. Let's download one of those tracking apps and then you can check on me every fifteen minutes."

Craig was about to protest when Jenna's eyes filled with tears. He reached for her but she stepped back and stuck her hands out. "I need to go."

"Jenna," he said quietly. "You can't leave like this. Let's settle things and part on good terms."

She wiped her eyes with the sleeve of her sweatshirt. "We'll be on good terms when you stop playing detective."

"I promise I'll stop. I didn't know it had become an issue."

Jenna's shoulders trembled as she struggled to regain her composure. "Look, I really need to get my sleep. We can get together this weekend, okay?"

Craig raised his hands. "Can we? Are you available? I mean, will you... Jenna this is ridiculous. For the past two years, you and I have gotten together every weekend. I build my life around my time with you and thought that you did the same."

"Maybe that's the problem, Craig," she said matter-of-factly. "Maybe you've gotten to where you just expect me to be there. A girl likes to feel special sometimes."

He couldn't believe what he was hearing. Craig had always considered himself a romantic. Little gifts at unexpected times. Cards for special occasions and sometimes just because. Three weeks earlier he had made Jenna a pot of vegetable beef soup and left it on her doorstep when he went by and she wasn't home. Come to think of it, she had never mentioned the soup.

But it wasn't the time to bring it up. He was suddenly exhausted. And confused.

"Okay," he said, aware of the strain in his voice. "I'll walk you out. I would love to get together this weekend. Whatever you want to do, we can do. Just let me know when you want me to pick you up...if you want me to pick you up."

She reached up for a goodnight kiss when they were outside, which after the tenseness inside offered a glimmer of hope.

"I'll call you," she said before driving off. Craig went back inside and turned off the Christmas tree lights. It was nine-fifteen, and if he went to bed, he knew he wouldn't be able to sleep. He considered calling Jenna on her way home to apologize for asking so many questions, but as he thought back to Monday night and the disagreement they had just had, he couldn't see where he had done anything wrong. Was he really that far off base? He grabbed his laptop and went through a half-dozen search variations of *my girlfriend thinks I ask too many questions*. Depending upon which website he chose to believe, either Craig was too controlling or Jenna was seeing someone else. Both options were ridiculous. There were pages of lists, too. *Ten Relationship Mistakes People Make* and *120 Good Questions to Ask a Girl*.

He set the laptop aside and turned on the TV to the local news from the tiny station in Freeport. The faces seemed to change every few months, as Freeport was the lowest rung on the climb to network fame and fortune. The guy presently manning the news desk was more of a kid, really. Probably just out of college, bad haircut, cheap jacket. He could read the news well enough, though, which meant he would probably be some place like Paducah, Kentucky or York, Pennsylvania by Easter. The next step of the rung. Craig turned the sound up just enough to not disturb him as he continued his search. One online psychologist recommended couples draft a relationship contract, whatever the hell that was. Another suggested counseling at a hundred bucks an hour. A sex therapist advocated kinky stuff that could even make a pharmacist blush. There were preachers and yogis and acupuncturists who promised to clear the hostility from any relationship. It was ten-twenty-five when he finally set the laptop aside. The anchor kid with the bad haircut was wrapping up the newscast with a report from Nashville about a star in trouble with the law. Travis Horton was a name that Craig didn't recognize, but the report gave the impression that he was a bad boy who had done another bad boy thing in some Kentucky town. His ears perked up, though, when it was reported that Raven McCloud was with him, but had not been arrested. Craig reached for his phone to call Jenna and tell her but reconsidered. He laid his head back on the sofa as the story concluded and the anchor kid told of a nationwide search to find the singer of an old Christmas song that appeared to be the next big thing.

The singer's name was Carl, a long-ago friend of Raven McCloud. The anchor kid said the song was recorded twenty years before and had been found in a box of Raven's old music, and if anyone knew who Carl was, they needed to call an 800-number. Then he played the song.

It was okay, Craig thought. Kind of cute. Kind of catchy. Kind of familiar.

The report only included a few lines, but as they ended, Craig picked up the melody and hummed the next line. And the next.

He sang the next verse. And the chorus. And the verse after that. Hearing it again after so long made him smile. Made him happy. Made him almost forget about the tension with Jenna.

The song was his. Not Carl's. His.

And the singer?

That was him, too.

He hit the back button on his remote and listened again.

Yep. Definitely him. Younger. Stronger singing voice, perhaps, but still him.

He remembered recording it at that rundown little by-the-hour studio in Springfield. But it never went anyplace after that. He couldn't even remember when or where he got rid of the tape. How did Raven McCloud get ahold of it?

There was only one way to find out.

He picked up his cellphone and called the 800-number.

Brooke tensed when she opened the apartment door and found Tristan asleep on the living room sofa. Alone. In the dark. Had she been too hasty in her decision to leave the can of pepper spray in the car? Tristan had never struck her, but then again, he had never spoken to her as he had on the phone the previous day.

When she closed the door and flipped on the hallway light, she saw that the living room was immaculate. The old food containers and remnants from Tristan's football party were gone. The carpet was vacuumed, and the air smelled of lemon. Tristan stirred, then rolled over and nearly fell off the sofa. He sat up and rubbed his eyes before getting to his feet.

"I thought you were coming earlier. I—" He motioned to the bedroom. "You can get your stuff. I won't get in your way."

He sounded sober. His voice was low, but not menacing. More like a whipped boxer. Is that what they had been? Two fighters sparring with one another?

"I sat in on Raven's rehearsals. Her tour starts here in Nashville tomorrow night." She nodded toward the bedroom and said, "I'll get started," She went down the hall to the bedroom they had shared, stopping at the hall closet for her luggage. She laid three suitcases on the bed, high school graduation gifts from her Aunt Penny which had held up well for over a decade, and started pulling clothes from her dresser. She was folding sweaters when she received a text.

Are you okay?

It was Bobby.

Yes. I'll be another hour, then back to the house. Thanks for checking.

She received an immediate reply. *I love you.*

I love you too, Daddy.

Daddy. It was what she had called him from the time she could say the word until college when it seemed uncool. At the moment, it fit. He was her father, her protector, and her best friend. There used to be plenty of friends. People she went out with on Friday nights, girlfriends she shopped and gossiped with. Somehow, since she had been with Tristan they had drifted away. One or two at a time, until there were none left. Sure, they emailed and spoke on the phone occasionally, but everyone had moved on.

And Brooke hadn't really noticed that she was alone.

Except for Bobby. Her Daddy.

"Brooke?" Tristan had stepped in. She continued to fold sweaters.

"Yes?"

"I know it's too late now, but I apologize about the way I spoke to you."

She had no idea what she was supposed to say. What she wanted to say. The pause grew longer, until Tristan said, "I couldn't have passed the drug test."

She nodded but kept folding.

"I'm doing some stuff I shouldn't be doing. I won't burden you with the details, but I'm messed up."

Brooke said nothing.

"I just want to be good at something. At something that matters." He moved just enough to the side to be in her peripheral vision as he leaned against the dresser. "Right now, I'm good at convincing old people to spend money they don't have on stuff they don't need. It pays the bills, but it sucks. I had to look for ways to make the pain go away, and I found them."

Brooke placed a sweater in her suitcase and turned to face him. She still didn't speak, though. Tristan rubbed at the side of his face. She used to find the gesture endearing like a little boy just waking up.

"Today was my first clean day in months. I start meetings tomorrow."

"That's good to know."

"Yeah... I'm going to spend more time practicing my music. Maybe the next time someone is looking for a musician who's clean and sober, I can answer the call."

Brooke turned back to her packing.

"I was hoping...that if I get this worked out, that maybe you and I might try again?"

Brooke closed the last of her suitcases and took a quick look around the bedroom to see if she had missed anything. When she was certain she hadn't, she placed the largest suitcase on the floor and wheeled it toward the door.

"Let me help," Tristan said, grabbing the other two. She let him. They passed through the apartment and into the dark parking lot. She popped the trunk of her car and allowed Tristan to load the suitcases. When they were tucked away, she turned to him.

"I'll pray every day for your recovery, Tristan."

"Thank you." He moved toward her as if to give her a hug. A part of her wanted to hug him and tell him things would be okay, but she stepped back to avoid the advance.

"I can't give you an answer about us," she said. "I need time to heal and remember the person I used to be. If I get that figured out, and you're doing well..." She paused and looked skyward. "All I can say is maybe, Tristan. But don't do this for me." She opened the car door and got in. "You need to do this for you and your future. That's the only way it will ever work."

She closed the door and drove away.

FRIDAY, DECEMBER 2

NASHVILLE AND GARLAND GROVE

*W*hen Brooke walked into the office a little after ten, Raquel was at her usual post, sipping a Diet Coke and closing out the November financials.

"How are things looking for Raven's opening night?" she asked without looking up.

"Everything's good, except Mickey Cox has to find a fill-in for Dexter on bass."

"What happened to Dexter?"

"His wife Patsy had a baby girl this morning. Seven pounds, one ounce. They named her Penelope Jane."

"I'll send flowers." Raquel set aside the ledger she still kept by hand and reached for the phone. "How's Raven?"

"Okay. Not saying much about Wednesday night, though. Musically she sounds perfect as always."

Brooke headed upstairs. Bobby was working from home, though he had indicated that he might head to a little club out in Lebanon later that night to hear a drummer who was new to the local scene and was getting some attention. Mickey Cox, Raven's long-time musical director, was always in the market for a good backup drummer, and Bobby still enjoyed scouting talent in little out-of-the-way places.

The decision to open Raven's Christmas concert tour in Nashville was a given. The local audience considered her their own, and if there were any kinks to be worked out regarding sound or stage issues, they were easier to solve there before heading out. In less than ten hours, she would take the stage at Bridgestone Arena in front of 20,000 devotees. The cheapest tickets, in the rear and wings, sold for $60. For those more affluent or willing to take out a second mortgage, the VIP packages included front-row seats and a meet and greet with Raven, all for the low price of $999.00. The prices paled in comparison to Justin Bieber and Taylor Swift, but it was a Christmas concert after all. And, to her credit, Raven always purchased two hundred seats at each concert venue for underprivileged fans. That had been Bobby's idea, back when Raven was trying to gain traction on the national scene. All those years later, it was automatic.

Even on their home turf, there were a hundred little details that fell to the star performer's manager. Brooke opened her planner and started making calls. She was halfway through marking off to-do's when Raquel buzzed in with a phone call.

"Hello, Miss Summers, I'm Kaitlyn Spinelli with Search Specialists. We have an individual who has responded to the news reports for Christmas Carl. He answered the questions correctly, but we're still not certain he's the one. Would you like to talk to him?"

"Very much."

Brooke took down the number and called immediately. A woman answered the phone.

"Callaway Drugstore. This is Stacy. Are you calling to refill a prescription?"

"Hello. No, I'm not needing a refill. I'm returning a call to..." she double-checked the name she had scrawled down. "Craig?"

"Craig went home for lunch. I can help you, though. What's the name on the account?"

Persistent thing, this Stacy. "No account. Craig called and asked me to call him back at this number. Is there any way to reach him?"

"I guess I can give you his cellphone number. He's out of sorts today, though." The woman named Stacy lowered her voice. "I think he had a fight with Jenna. Do you know Jenna? Please say you don't, because if you do and I said something I shouldn't have said, then—"

"I don't know Jenna, and I would appreciate Craig's phone number."

THE OUTSIDE TEMPERATURES had plunged into the single digits overnight, and homemade chili sounded good. Craig dug through his freezer until he found some left over from the pot he had made back in October for himself and Jenna.

Jenna.

He had expected to hear from her, but nothing. It was Friday. They often went to Café Americana on Friday nights for the $16.99 prime rib special. Jenna loved prime rib. He put the chili in the microwave, punched in her number on his cellphone, but disconnected before the call went through.

Just call her.

He was about to try again when a call came in from a 615-area code. Telemarketer?

"Hello."

"Is this Craig?" The voice was female, with a nice southern lilt. She sounded nice, but so did a lot of telemarketers.

"I'm not interested," he blurted.

"Don't hang up!"

He almost had, but he'd never heard a telemarketer react so forcefully, so he didn't.

"My name is Brooke Summers, Craig. I'm following up on your call last evening about the song."

"Yes. I wrote and sang it. How did you get it?"

"We represent Raven McCloud. The song was mixed in with some other songs she recorded years ago."

"I never met Raven McCloud. We run in different circles. And if you're asking if you can have the song, go ahead and take it. I don't have a claim on it."

"Well, you kind of do, Craig. If you wrote it, you deserve credit. Can I ask a couple of questions, just to make sure you're who you say you are?"

"I didn't say who I was. I'm just Craig Callaway. I own a drugstore in a town called Garland Grove."

"Where did you go to college, Craig?"

Craig wasn't sure if he should answer her questions. Was she even legitimate? What was next? Probably a scam.

We can make you a star! Just pay us twenty-five hundred bucks and watch your music career take off!

But what could it hurt to tell where he went to school?

"Missouri State University in Springfield."

"What years?"

❄

IT WAS HIM! It had to be!

The enrollment dates matched perfectly. Craig and Raven were freshmen together. Brooke was getting excited. The guy seemed reasonable, even a bit standoffish. If what the girl at the drugstore had said was true, maybe he was in a bad mood after a fight with his wife or girlfriend. Brooke could certainly relate to that. She still had to be certain he was the one. Certain beyond a shadow of a doubt.

"Did you ever go by the name of Carl?"

"Never."

Was it possible that Raven had forgotten her college boyfriend's name? Hadn't she said they dated for a couple months? Brooke had no problem remembering Chip Hollis's name, and they had dated for just two weeks. Of course, Chip Hollis had barfed on the adorable new pair of kitten heels Brooke had bought for a fraternity mixer. A girl remembers guys who barf on their shoes.

"What do you remember about recording the song?"

"Just that a group of us went together. The studio wasn't much, really. Just some old equipment and a cranky guy who kept telling us to hurry up or he would charge us for another hour."

Yep. They were getting very close. Either he was Christmas Carl or he was batting a thousand with his guesses.

Don't get too excited yet, Brooke.

"Do you recall who wrote the song?"

Brooke heard him take a deep breath. "I said earlier that I wrote it. It was an assignment for a music theory class."

"You're a musician?"

His laugh had a nice ring to it. "I play a little, but I took the class because it sounded interesting. It wasn't, though. Do you want me to play the song for you?"

"You still remember it?"

"That's what got my attention in the first place. The local news played a snippet and I found myself singing along." The line was quiet for a moment, other than some background sound before Craig said, "I'm getting my keyboard out of the closet. It's...right...okay. I have it. Let me plug it in."

Brooke's hands were shaking. There was no evidence of deception. The guy seemed to be the real deal, at least on the phone. Now she would find out if he could sing. She heard him running through some of the same old warmup techniques kids learned while taking piano lessons.

"You ready?" he asked.

"Fire away."

And he did. The keyboard playing was good enough to pick up the melody on the phone. And when he started to sing there was no doubt. He played through the entire song and even added some flourishes to the last verse. And then he was done.

"And that's 'Making Santa Smile,'" he said after returning to the line.

By that time Brooke was jumping up and down in her office. Her intercom squawked to life, with Raquel asking if she was okay.

Craig chuckled. "My professor thought it was too risqué and only gave me a B-minus."

"I cannot believe we found you." Brooke was practically shouting into the phone. "I'm coming to see you in person. I'll fly out of Nashville late this evening and be in Garland Grove tomorrow."

"I work tomorrow, Miss Summers. The pharmacy is open until noon. Why the big deal? It's just an old

Christmas song. A B-minus one at that. Just do whatever you want with it."

"Call me Brooke. And I'll call you Craig. It's actually a very big deal. Can you find someone to cover for you?"

"Well, no. I'm the owner."

"How about the girl who answered the phone when I called? I can't remember her name."

"Stacy Pike. She's not a pharmacist, but I guess she can cover things for a few hours. Are you sure you want to come all the way up here, Brooke? I'm afraid you're just going to be disappointed with what you find."

"If what I find is anything close to what you are on the phone, it will be a very worthwhile trip, Craig, I assure you. Will you make me two promises, though?"

"Probably. What are they?"

"Don't tell anyone about your association with the song."

"Why not?"

"Just trust me on this, Craig. Will you promise?"

"Okay, though it would be fun to tell my friends. And Jenna."

"And second," Brooke continued. "If anyone shows up offering you a contract or wanting to buy the rights to your song, promise you won't sell until we talk."

"What if they offer a million dollars?"

Brooke could tell he was teasing. She also knew that if he was anything like he seemed, the chance to make a lot of money was there. "Even if they offer a million dollars," she said, going along with the joke.

"I promise again. Do you need to know how to get here? It's too far to drive from Nashville, but you can probably catch a plane from there to Chicago. Then you take a commuter flight to the regional airport. It's about a half-hour away, but—"

"I'm chartering a plane, Craig. We'll let them figure out the logistics."

"Holy smokes. You must really be somebody important."

"I wouldn't go that far, but it will be good to meet you tomorrow. I'll call you in the morning, okay, Craig?"

"It works for me. I'm getting excited."

His humility made Brooke smile. "Do you have any questions for me?" she asked.

"Yeah. What does Raven McCloud have to do with this?"

"You really don't know?"

"No idea. I'm not much of a country music fan. I saw her on that Nashville Christmas special Sunday night, though. I watched with my girlfriend, or whatever she is to me now. That's a story for another day, though. But, no, I've never met Raven McCloud and if she's claiming to know me, she's—"

"Do you remember Megan Stackhouse?"

"Yeah. Megan and I dated freshman year, but I don't know what she—"

An image popped into Craig's mind. Megan Stackhouse. And him. One of their last times together before she... What exactly happened to Megan? She was there, then she wasn't. Anyway, they were in Springfield at that new downtown restaurant, the one owned by the guy who became famous for trying to find a wife on that TV show. In the memory, Craig sat across from Megan, watching her tear through a pile of chicken wings while she talked about her plans for Thanksgiving break. Any recollection of her plans was long gone, but the image of how beautiful she was and how excited she was for Thanksgiving break remained. He could see a future with her at that moment. They had progressed through handholding and kissing, and Craig thought Megan might be ready to...but maybe after Thanksgiving break.

And then another thought. More recent. Very recent. Just a few days before. The Nashville Christmas special. Raven McCloud.

And those eyes!

The same eyes as...

"Wait a minute! Brooke, are you trying to tell me that Raven McCloud is...no. Just no. There's no way."

"One and the same, Craig."

"I don't believe you. Megan was... She was pretty... beautiful, really. Is this some kind of joke?"

"I assure you it isn't."

"Holy cow... Megan is... No, sorry, but it just can't be."

"She is. I wouldn't be flying to Garland Grove if she was anyone else."

"That's exciting. I really liked Megan." Craig's voice took on a dreamy quality. "I liked her a lot, but..."

"But what?"

"Oh, nothing. It's just that..."

"What, Craig?"

"She kind of disappeared."

Brooke had forgotten that part. Raven had mentioned that she left college and didn't speak to him again.

"Things change, Craig. People grow up. Let's continue this chat tomorrow morning, okay?"

"We sure will... Megan Stackhouse is Raven McCloud? *Damn!*"

Brooke did a happy dance after hanging up. The vibes were good. His name wasn't really Carl, but it was close enough. She just had to get to Garland Grove and see if she could transform small-town pharmacist Craig Callaway into Christmas Carl.

Bobby needed to know, but first things first. Brooke dashed downstairs and tripped on the bottom step. A lucky grab of the rail kept her from sprawling out on the floor in front of Raquel's desk.

"Let me guess?" Raquel said. "You found him."

"We found him, Raquel. Can you charter a plane? He lives in a little town called Garland Grove. I don't think they have an airport, so we may have to land someplace else."

"When do you want to leave?"

"Right after Raven's concert tonight. I would prefer to fly out of John C. Tune instead of Nashville International."

Raquel whistled. "Do you know how much that's going to cost?"

"I know. I'm hoping we can earn it back on sales of the song and maybe some future work. Before booking the return flight, see what commercial flights might be available to get me to Memphis in time for tomorrow night's show."

"Brooke, honey, you're going to wear yourself out."

"You know this business, Raquel. Hustle or get hustled. Can you please get someone from Leland Suddarth's firm on the phone for me?"

"The private investigator?"

"That's right."

Raquel seemed confused. "We don't use them, Brooke. Bobby always uses J.R. Potter."

"Honestly, Raquel, as much as I love J.R., he's so slow sometimes. I need information by the time I arrive in Garland Grove."

Brooke returned to her office and opened Facebook to

check out Craig's presence. He had a page but didn't appear to have kept it up to date. The most recent picture was from four years earlier. He was unremarkable in almost every way, from his haircut and glasses to his khakis and blue polo. He wasn't unattractive, but he wasn't Travis Horton handsome, either. If she had to describe him, she would say he looked like a thirty-something midwestern pharmacist.

But she could work with that.

"Brooke, Leland Suddarth is on the line."

"Hello, Mr. Suddarth. I wasn't expecting to speak to you personally."

"Miss Summers, a pleasure. I'm very familiar with your agency and am happy to be of assistance. What can I do for you?"

"It's a small job but has very important ramifications. Let me tell you what we need."

"CRAIG, have you heard the latest about the Christmas concert?"

In the ninety minutes since returning to the drugstore, Craig had heard the latest about the Christmas concert from four people. Eighty-two-year-old Anna Barclay was the fifth.

"That the tickets went up in price? Yes, Anna, but we have a special treat this year. A professional who is coming to perform."

"I don't go to the Garland Grove Christmas concert to hear professionals," Anna groused. "And I don't even know who the guy is."

"You've not heard of Hal Richie?"

Anna blew air from between her lips. "Nope, and for an extra five dollars a ticket, I would expect Bing Crosby."

"That would be big news. Bing's been dead for a long time, Anna."

"How about Raven McCloud, then? I would pay five extra dollars to hear her."

Craig felt his muscles go weak at the mention of her name. "You...you're a fan of Raven McCloud, Anna?"

"Of course. She's a handsome woman, don't you think?"

"Yes, ma'am, I certainly do. In fact, Anna, I used to..."

What the heck are you doing, you idiot?

"You used to what, Craig?"

"Did I say used to? I meant that I—Jenna and I—saw her on that Grand Ole Opry Christmas special last Sunday night."

"She's certainly a wonderful singer. And a handsome woman. Speaking of Jenna, is this the year you ask her to marry you, Craig?"

Craig tried to hide the burn on his cheeks, but even with her macular degeneration, Anna saw it. "You know that everybody in town is wondering the same thing," she said matter-of-factly. "Just yesterday when I was eating lunch at the Park-Rite, Mazie was saying—you know Mazie, don't you Craig? The waitress out there?"

"Yes, ma'am."

"Mazie said, 'it's about time that Craig Callaway asks that poor little veteran girl to marry him.' I said, 'Jenna's not a veteran, Mazie, she's a veterinarian, an animal doctor.'" Anna reached across the counter and patted Craig's hand. "You're a handsome couple, Craig. You'll make good-looking kids, too. But you shouldn't wait much longer. You're what? Thirty-five?"

"Something like that, Anna. Let me get your prescription."

BROOKE WAS BARELY in the house when she heard the gentle thump of Bobby's boots on the hardwood floor. She hung her coat inside the door and turned to find him entering the hallway.

"Hey, Dad, we have great news!"

"Raquel told me," Bobby said. "Congratulations."

"Darn it," Brooke said. "I wanted to tell you personally."

"Don't blame Raquel. I called in to check on something and she said you were on the phone with Leland Suddarth."

Brooke felt guilty for not using Bobby's long-time friend and private investigator. "I'm sorry, Dad, but I just felt that Leland would—"

"Nothing to apologize for, sweetheart. J.R. isn't the fastest cat in town these days. Raquel also said that you're hiring a plane to go see Carl."

"There are no commercial flights that can get me up there after the show tonight. If I can find one to get me back to Memphis in time for tomorrow night's concert, I'll use that and save money."

"Nonsense, Brooke. You need to take care of yourself. Chasing through airports trying to get from one place to another is too much. I told Raquel to book the charter both ways, and I'm planning on going to Memphis with the tour tomorrow night so you can come home and rest."

"No, Dad, I really prefer to do it myself, if you don't mind. You gave me the responsibility and I want to show you I'm up to it." She paused before adding, "I want to show *myself* that I'm up to it."

He leveled her with that look. Not the Bobby Summers sideways glance that everyone else knew. The look he reserved for her included a gentle smile with his head tipped just so, his left eye slightly scrunched. It was the look that communicated to her that he loved her more than anyone in the world. And that he was proud of her and concerned for her and always thinking about her.

"There's no doubt that you're up to it, honey," he said. "Just don't kill yourself to prove it, okay?"

"I promise."

He took a deep breath. "I have to admit that I'm enjoying the downtime. I'm getting some winter jobs done out here at the farm and I even went grocery shopping earlier this afternoon. Darndest thing I'm telling you, Brooke. I still can't figure out where Publix keeps the barbeque sauce."

"It's by the ketchup, Dad. And thank you for the charter flight. I promise to do everything I can to make it worth the expense."

Sixty fans were scheduled for the meet and greet with Raven. Brooke did a quick check of the backstage space where they would be escorted. Members of the road crew had been drafted to make sure that only people with VIP badges were admitted. Meet and greets were tightly choreographed to ensure no surprises. VIP ticket holders were usually corporate types and their spouses who did their best to act like it was no big deal being so close to the star. A few superfans might also find their way in, perhaps after scrimping on luxuries like food and car payments to afford the thousand-dollar tickets.

Brooke checked her messages while waiting for their arrival. She had missed a call from Leland Suddarth, so she quickly got him back on the phone.

"Mr. Suddarth, I only have a couple minutes. What can you tell me?"

"Brooke, Craig Callaway is squeaky clean. Other than a speeding ticket four years ago in Henderson, Minnesota, he has no arrests, citations, or complaints. His pharmaceutical license is blemish-free. He has never been married and is currently dating a large-animal veterinarian named Jenna Waite. I can't find out how serious things are between them, unfortunately."

"They had a fight a few days ago, Mr. Suddarth, so things might be shaky."

Leland Suddarth laughed. "You seem perfectly capable of doing your own background investigation, Brooke. Anyway, Mr. Callaway has always paid his taxes on time. He sporadically attends a local protestant church in Garland Grove and is the music director of the town's annual Christmas concert. His drugstore has seventy-four five-star ratings on Google. His parents are deceased. His mother was the most recent to pass away, and that was two years ago. As you know, he attended Missouri State University, where he maintained a 3.4 GPA in General Studies with an emphasis on biology. Pharmacy school was at Drake University."

"So no dirt, huh, Mr. Suddarth?"

"We can certainly dig deeper, but I suspect that your intuition from talking to him on the phone was on the mark."

Brooke heard voices coming from the backstage entrance. "Thank you so much, Mr. Suddarth. You've done well."

"Keep us in mind for future projects, Brooke. It has been a pleasure."

She put the phone away just as a swarm of fans came around the corner. Four roadies were in front, but it didn't appear they were needed as the group seemed excited, but harmless.

"Hello everyone, I'm Brooke Summers, Raven McCloud's manager. We'll go inside and have a seat. Once everyone is in place, Raven will join us. Any questions before we go in?"

Brooke knew there would be questions, and even what they would be.

"Will Raven sign autographs?"

"Yes, sir, she will. One per VIP, please. We don't want to delay the show."

"Can we shake her hand?"

"I'm afraid not. Raven needs to make sure that she doesn't contract a cold or sickness that could compromise the tour."

There was a groan that quickly went away when Brooke added, "But she will be happy to pose for pictures."

The VIPs applauded.

"Okay, folks, let's go inside."

It was funny to watch a group of people, mostly in their forties and older, dash for the seats in front. They would soon learn that it was unnecessary, as Raven moved easily around the room while she answered questions and posed for photographs. She was a master at working VIP gatherings, and the sixty people scrambling for seats were in for a treat. Once they were settled, Brooke stepped out and went down the hall and around the corner. She knocked two times, waited a second, and tapped twice more.

"C'mon in, Brooke," Raven called out. Brooke opened

the door and had to control the urge to gasp. Even though she had been a part of Raven's tours for the past two years, she was still awestruck at how beautiful she was. Concerts seemed to make her glow. Even more surprising was the outfit she had chosen to meet the VIPs. Jeans were typical, but the Missouri State University sweatshirt?

"I figured that since you outed me I might as well go loud and proud," Raven said when she saw Brooke eyeing the shirt. "They've already emailed to ask for a donation."

"Oh, Raven, I'm so sorry."

"Don't be, sweetie. I enjoyed my time there, even if it was only a few months."

"That reminds me," Brooke said. "We found Christmas Carl."

This appeared to surprise her. "Where on earth is he?"

"Up north. He's a pharmacist in a small town. And the biggest surprise is that his name is actually Craig, not Carl."

Raven contemplated this for a moment while she said his name several times. "Craig... Craig... Craig Cartwright?"

"Craig Callaway."

Raven snapped her fingers. "That's it. Why couldn't I remember that?"

"Because you ghosted him?" Brooke teased.

Raven shook her head. "Not so much ghosted him as moved on. Did you speak to him?"

"Yes, and I'm leaving right after tonight's concert to go see him. His song is getting airplay and downloads all over the southeast, and we want to sign him to a contract."

Brooke had wondered how Raven would take the news, considering the power play Travis had tried to pull on Bobby. It didn't faze her, though. In fact, she went the other way.

"If I can do anything to help, let me know, Brooke. And

I would love to see Carl—Craig again. Did he remember me?"

"He remembered Megan Stackhouse. He flipped out when I told him you were one and the same."

"Then definitely bring him to see me, Brooke."

"I'm still not sure he's interested in any of this. He seems pretty entrenched in small-town life."

"How are you gonna keep 'em down on the farm, after they've seen Nashville?" Raven sang the old turn-of-the-twentieth-century ditty as she checked her hair and stood up. "Now, take me to my VIPs, Brooke darlin'."

CRAIG HAD NEARLY SPILLED the beans twice. First to Stacy Pike when she asked if the woman who called during lunch had gotten in touch with him. The second was when Sam called to see if he and Jenna were going to Café Americana that night. He didn't have it in him to tell Sam that they had argued the night before and that he didn't know what they were doing and not doing, but he did slip and ask if Sam had heard the song the radio stations were playing about "Making Santa Smile." Sam had heard it twice that day on the Freeport radio station he played in the office. "Catchy tune," he said.

"Would you believe that—" Craig had caught himself and changed the subject before Sam became suspicious. But it was getting harder and harder to keep to himself, and there was one person more than anyone he wanted to tell. And the best way to tell her was face-to-face. So as soon as he closed down the drugstore at five-thirty, he drove to Jenna's bungalow. Her car was home. He started to get out and go to the door, but he still had some doubts about whether it was a good idea. Would she still be chilly toward him? Still angry?

"Just don't ask any questions," he muttered to himself as he approached the front door. He knocked and waited, but no one came. He knocked again. And waited some more. When Jenna still didn't reply, he tried to open the door, but it was locked. Concerned, he pulled out his phone and was dialing her number when a black pickup stopped in front of the house. It was too dark to see the driver but easy enough to see Jenna crawl out of the passenger side. She waved to whoever was inside and came his way.

Don't ask questions.

"Hey, Jenna," he exclaimed. "I have some news to share with you, but you have to promise not—"

"I was going to come to your house to see you," she interrupted.

"I guess I saved you the trip. You won't believe what happened today. Have you heard—"

"Craig, there's no use dragging this out." She nodded in the direction the black truck had headed. "That was Owen Braden. He's the new vet in Templeton."

Even as the words were coming from her mouth, Craig knew something was not right. And he suspected he knew what. "The one you've been helping out for the past couple months?"

"The one I've been sleeping with for the past couple months."

Craig shook his head, trying his damndest to unhear what he had just heard. He felt himself processing a hundred things at once, and couldn't get a grip on what to say. His stomach threatened to toss back the chili from lunch. He felt like he might cry. Or punch a wall. Or scream. Or run.

Instead, he said, "Why?"

Jenna said she didn't want to get into the why and how, but when Craig repeated, "Why?" with much more force, she took a deep breath and said, "I'm tired of this, Craig. I'm tired of us. You're almost forty, but you act sixty. We do the same things day after day after day. Eat at the same places. See the same people. It's driving me nuts."

Craig sighed. "It's called small-town life, Jenna."

"It's called boring. And I find myself getting sucked into the same boring life."

"I thought we had a good life together."

She appeared to be fighting tears. "We have...had an okay life together, Craig, but it's not who I am."

There was so much more to say, but Craig wasn't sure he could say any of it without breaking down or losing his shit. He wasn't sure he could say any of it without cussing a blue streak and calling Jenna a tramp and a cheater. She wasn't those things. They had never said they were exclusive to one another. It had just happened. The only thing he thought he might be able to say without losing it was the news about his song and Raven McCloud.

"Craig, you really should go."

"Can I tell you one thing?"

"Please don't. Let's not hash this out tonight."

"No, Jenna. It's not about us. It's about...it's..."

And he knew at that moment that he would not share such awesome news with someone who had treated him so shabbily. He pulled up the collar of his coat, took a deep breath, and stepped off the porch.

"It's nothing. See you around."

RAVEN HAD the VIPs in the palm of her hand from the moment she sashayed into the room, winking at the men and patting the women on their arms. It was Raven at her best—fully engaged and enjoying every minute.

"We have time for a couple more questions," Brooke announced.

"I have one!" A woman about Brooke's age stood up. She appeared to be alone, which was rare among VIPs.

"Go ahead, darlin'" Raven called out as she made her way to where the woman was seated.

"What's going on between you and Travis Horton?"

The room became stone silent. No one had spoken so directly, content as they were to fawn over the superstar. Brooke considered intervening but figured that would only make things worse. For a split second Raven appeared to be caught off-guard, but Raven being Raven, she recovered nicely.

"He's just a friend I go to bars with," she quipped. Brooke hadn't expected the laughter that followed, but Raven seemed to have thought it out in advance, casting a look around the room that communicated that they were all in on the joke together. When the laughter died down, she said, "Travis has a good heart. Sometimes he just doesn't consider the consequences." She lowered her voice so the VIPs had to lean in to hear. "And I'll let you in on a little secret. It gets lonely sometimes in that big old country house of mine. Sometimes a girl has to get out and kick up her heels. Any of you ever feel that way?"

It was clear by their response that they did, and when Raven blew kisses and took her leave, they stood as one and applauded. Brooke grabbed one of the road crew and said, "Wait five minutes and make sure they all get to their seats."

She headed to Raven's dressing room, knocked twice and twice again, and stepped inside.

"That was freaking awesome!" She practically shouted the words, not noticing that Raven, seated at a dressing table with her back to the door, didn't move.

"Brooke," Raven said evenly. "Never come into my dressing room without being invited."

Brooke's stomach dropped into her big girl bloomers. "Raven, I'm sorry, I knocked like we always do, and—"

"You knock and you wait for me to say come in. Understand?"

"Uh...yes. I understand."

"And if you can't screen the VIP's better, I'll tell Bobby he needs to come back on tour. That bitch's question was embarrassing and could have easily been avoided by a manager who uses her head."

"Raven, it wasn't—" Brooke stopped before saying something she shouldn't.

Something like, *that could have been avoided if you hadn't gone to that dive bar*.

Or, *that could have been avoided if you would accept that Travis Horton is going to bring you down*.

Screw it.

"I'm sorry for barging in," Brooke said, lowering her tone. "You go on in thirty minutes."

Craig pointed his truck toward downtown and drove. Sam's car was parked outside Café Americana. That meant that he and Beth were at their usual table. Beth was having a steak salad with light vinaigrette because she had eaten more than her share of their kids' cookies during the week.

Sam was chowing down on prime rib with a loaded baked potato. They both would have a glass of wine, then Beth would have a second because being a stay-at-home mom was, in her words, damned hard.

Craig knew all of that because it was the way things went down on Friday evenings in Garland Grove. Everyone had their routine. They found comfort in doing the same things with the same people, whether it be knocking down pins at Grove Bowl, bingo at the lodge, or taking the family to the latest Hollywood release at the Strand. Routine. It was the thing that small-town life was made of.

For everyone except Jenna.

When had routine become too routine?

And why hadn't he picked up on it sooner? *Two months?*

She had been sleeping with another man for *two whole months?*

But what about the previous Monday? That crazy night when they had argued, then made love. It was exhilaratingly different from before. Jenna had been the aggressor. She had done things that...that...

Oh my God. Had she been thinking of *him?* The other guy? Was that how they...? No, he couldn't let his mind go there. He continued down Main Street, past Manny and his bike, past Buckshot Kelly's Gun and Jewelry Shop. Just the day before, he had contemplated stopping by Buckshot's to check out his selection of necklaces. Jenna loved necklaces. Many people in town would have expected that he was buying Jenna something other than a necklace, but it just hadn't seemed like the right time. Yet. Thank goodness he had held off on the necklace and on an engagement ring. Imagine how awkward it would be to get down on one knee and ask the girl you love to marry you, only to have her say no thanks, that she was sleeping with the small animal vet because you were boring.

Yeah, that would have been hard.

When he reached the end of the street, Craig considered turning around and going back to the restaurant. He could take one of the two empty seats at Sam and Beth's table, and make up some story about Jenna being too busy or too tired to join them. But he knew they would see through that. Beth had a sixth sense that way. Like when Craig's mother had passed two years before. When the sense of loss was hitting harder than he expected. He had tried to play it off when around others and was pretty successful. Even Jenna had remarked about how well he was handling the loss. Not Beth. She had come in one afternoon for a contact lens case. Craig thought he was being his usual jovial self, but Beth saw through it and pulled him into the back and told him it was okay to grieve. It was good even. It helped. She helped.

So, no, he wouldn't be taking one of the empty seats at their table.

Instead, he drove. Out of Garland Grove on the main road to Templeton. That was probably where Jenna was. The new vet lived in an old farmhouse there. They were probably curled up in front of a roaring fireplace. She was recounting how difficult it had been to give old Craig the heave-ho. The vet was consoling her, telling her it would be okay. He would rub her back. Jenna loved having her back rubbed. It always seemed to lead to...

Stop it, Craig. Dammit, stop!

No, he wasn't going anywhere near Templeton. He turned around at the end of a farmhouse lane and drove back toward home. Brooke from Nashville would arrive in the morning, and somehow he had to have himself ready.

He had to be chipper and cheerful and full of polite conversation. Fortunately, she was a stranger. Unlike Beth Griffin, Brooke from Nashville wouldn't see through the façade. She wouldn't know that he had just gotten dumped by his girlfriend of two years.

Back at the house he went to the closet and retrieved his old guitar. It was out of tune, but Craig didn't want to spend the time tuning it, so he sat it against the wall, turned off the lights, and went to bed. It was nine o'clock. About time for dessert at Café Americana. Sam would have a large slice of chocolate cake. Beth would have another glass of wine.

Jenna would have apple pie a la mode. Craig would have a bowl of strawberry ice cream.

No, they wouldn't.

Not anymore.

Nothing new in Nashville. Raven killed it. From the old Christmas standards, when she invited the audience to sing along to the new stuff from her most recent holiday album, she knocked it out of the park. She gave the audience a solid seventy-five minutes, then returned for a five-minute encore. Afterward, Brooke made the rounds, checking in on Mickey Cox and the band and backup singers, thanking the road crew. Her last stop was Raven's dressing room. When she arrived, there were the usual half-dozen well-wishers who always found their way backstage. Brooke allowed ten minutes before she stepped inside and cheerfully cleared the room. When it was just the two of them, Brooke said, "I'm headed out to visit Craig Callaway. I'll catch up with you in Memphis. Milo is waiting outside to take you home and he'll also pick you up tomorrow afternoon to take you to the airport. I emailed all the details."

"Thanks, Brooke!" Raven had that post-concert glow that comes when the lights go down and the audience has gone home happy. "See you in Memphis!" There was no mention of how much of an ass she had been earlier. No apology or walking it back. She treated the whole thing as if it had never happened, so Brooke did, too.

"Great show!" she called out as she headed for the exit. Then, when she was out of earshot, Brooke mumbled, "Get me the hell out of here."

The charter was called an executive turboprop, which meant it had propellers rather than jet engines. The pilot's name was Monique.

"There is a small private airport near Garland Grove that has night landing capability," Monique explained as she helped Brooke get situated. "A rental car is waiting for you there."

"Will you be staying the entire time?" Brooke asked.

"No, ma'am. We got lucky, which means you got lucky. I have another customer who I pick up at the regional airport about forty miles away. They're going to Chicago. I'll be back by two, which is plenty of time to get you to Memphis tomorrow evening. You aren't even having to pay for my wait time."

Brooke took a seat in the rear of the cabin. There was room for six, and while it wasn't as luxurious as the big jets the stars used, it was pretty uptown for a kid from Percy's Crossroads. The charter company had stocked a cabinet with snacks and the fridge contained soft drinks and bottled water, but all Brooke wanted to do was put her head back and rest. The next thing she knew they were on the ground. It was one-fifteen in the morning. She said a quick see-you-later to Monique and walked off the plane into the kind of cold that took your breath away. A foot or two of snow was on the ground, but a path had been cleared from the plane to a tiny Quonset hut where a lone car was parked. The keys were inside. She started it and allowed it to warm up while she checked her email from Raquel.

You have a reservation at the Park-Rite Motel. I hope it's okay. There are only a couple of motels in Garland Grove. Good luck!

Brooke located the motel on GPS and took off. She hadn't driven in a lot of snow in her life, but it didn't matter. The roads were mostly clear and dry. Ten minutes later she pulled into the parking lot. The Park-Rite Motel was connected to the Park-Rite Diner. Both were dark. She approached the hotel office and found an envelope with her name on it. Inside was a single key to Room 7. The quaintness made Brooke giggle. *Room 7.* And a genuine 1970s-style key. She drove down the row of rooms that opened to the parking lot. There were probably twenty and just three cars in the lot. A quiet night at the Park-Rite. She grabbed her overnight bag and opened Room 7. It was dated, like the key, but looked clean and smelled good. She pulled back the comforter and was delighted to find the sheets were brilliant white and fresh.

Another ten minutes and the lights were off. The heat was set to seventy, and Brooke was tucked into one of the most comfortable beds she had ever experienced.

"Garland Grove, I like you already."

SATURDAY, DECEMBER 3

GARLAND GROVE

*B*rooke had expected to have trouble getting out of bed after her early morning arrival at the Park-Rite, but that wasn't the case. She awakened at six-thirty, refreshed despite just a few hours of sleep. After a hot shower, she dressed in black slacks, a turtleneck, and a wool blazer and stepped out of the room into the bitterly cold morning air. The three cars she had seen the night before were still parked in front of their respective rooms. A frigid breeze brought with it the smells of breakfast and made her stomach growl. The Park-Rite Diner was close by and, judging by the number of cars already in the parking lot, quite good. Breakfast sounded perfect, but first, she needed to stop by and pay her bill.

The motel office was at the far end of the building, closest to the restaurant. It was the largest part of the structure, and Brooke suspected the owners lived there. She stepped inside and giggled when she heard "Making Santa Smile" playing over tinny overhead speakers. If only they knew.

There was one of those old-fashioned bells on the

counter that you were supposed to ring for service, but Brooke decided she could wait a couple minutes. The office was small, with a counter that separated front from back. There was a small Christmas tree on one end of the counter, and someone had taken time to hang garland from the ceilings. Behind her, next to the door, was a rack of brochures from area attractions. The only one actually in Garland Grove was Blankenship's Christmas Tree Farm. It advertised a wide selection of fresh trees, gifts, teas, and coffees. There were also brochures for an outlet mall, lake resort, and a church retreat in a town called Freeport. On the wall above the display of brochures was a flyer advertising Garland Grove Memorial Hospital's Christmas Baby Contest. Brooke read down the list of prizes for the first baby born on December 25. Everything from photo sessions and bronze baby shoes to a four-hundred-dollar recliner. Pretty impressive. She laughed when she saw that the previous year's winning baby had been named Christopher Claus Griffin. The flyer included a picture of little Christopher Claus with his smiling parents and four siblings.

"Adorable family, aren't they?"

Brooke turned to the desk where a petite lady with brown hair going to gray had appeared.

"They certainly are. And I love the baby's name."

"The Claus part is all Sam Griffin's doing. My husband and I were surprised that Beth went along with it. Beth is Sam's wife. And I'm guessing that you're Miss Summers in Room 7. I'm Fran Mason. My husband Willis and I own the place."

"Good to meet you, Fran. The room was so comfortable I slept without waking up."

Fran beamed at Brooke's compliment. "I'll be honest.

We saw you were from Nashville and were worried you might think our place is kind of old-fashioned."

"No, ma'am. The bed was incredible and the water was hot. I came by to pay my bill before I get on with the day."

"Everything's taken care of, Miss Summers." Fran checked a computer screen. "A woman named Raquel Doney paid in advance. We emailed the receipt to her first thing this morning. The email address kind of piqued Willis's and my curiosity. Summers Management from Nashville, Tennessee. What do you folks manage?"

Brooke should have expected the question, what with Garland Grove being a small community. She had to be careful how she answered. The last thing she needed was for word to get around town that a talent manager was spending time with Craig Callaway.

"We manage...assets, Fran. And we assist people with planning and scheduling."

"Kind of like in a bank? We have a guy at the bank here who helps people find places to invest their money."

"Some of that, but more. We're a combination of finance manager, travel agent, and marketing company. What we do depends on what our clients need."

"Maybe you could help us give the Park-Rite a new image," Fran joked. "I keep telling Willis that we need to do better at promoting this place."

"Fran, your comfy beds and clean rooms are your best advertising. You must be doing something right if Raquel found you from all the way down in Nashville."

"That's a good point. And we're adding flat screens to the rooms as we can afford it. We're about a third done." Fran paused, debating, it appeared, if she should probe further. "So, what brings a pretty young Nashville management expert to Garland Grove?"

"You're sweet, Fran. I'm here to see an old friend."

Fran waited for more. Brooke realized there was no way around providing a name, so she said, "Craig Callaway."

"Oh, Craig," Fran gushed. "Such a nice man. He came to town and fit right in, at least as well as anyone can fit in who's not from here. You appear to be younger than him, though. Family friend?"

"Sort of. Craig was a college classmate of someone I'm close to. We've spoken in the past, and I decided I wanted to meet him and visit Garland Grove."

The response appeared to put Fran's curiosity to rest. "That explains a lot, then."

"What do you mean?"

"Craig usually has lunch next door once a week, twice if they have the open-faced beef plate special. He never comes in on Saturday, though, but I just noticed his truck is parked in the lot. Are you meeting him for breakfast?"

"I guess I am, Fran. Do I look okay?"

Fran's cheerful demeanor gave way to something more guarded. She studied Brooke for a moment, then said. "You're beautiful, but...I'm not sure if you knew this, but Craig and Jenna Waite have dated steadily for two years."

Brooke's cheeks grew hot. Real hot. How had she screwed up so completely? Of course, it would be strange for a young single woman to come to town with the soul intention of seeing a young single man. It wouldn't cause a ripple in Music City but in Garland Grove? Brooke knew she had probably marked herself as the other woman unless she could do something to correct Fran Mason's misperception.

"Oh, goodness, Fran, I'm not here to...you know. It's nothing like that."

"You just came to what? Say hello?"

"Something like that."

Nothing like that.

It was time to change the subject.

"Fran, the music you're playing, is that a local radio station?"

"Yes, it's the AM station out of Freeport. They play Christmas music from the day after Thanksgiving until New Year's Eve. I love my Christmas music."

"That song they were playing when I walked in? The one about making Santa smile? Did you hear that?"

"I hear it every couple hours. They play it all the time. Cute little song. Kind of off-color, but still cute."

"Very cute," Brooke said. "They play it in Nashville, too." Brooke glanced toward the restaurant. "I guess I'll head over and meet Craig. Thank you for your hospitality, Fran."

"You're welcome, Miss Summers. And one more thing..." She lowered her voice. "If Craig seems a bit out of sorts, word in town is that he and Jenna had a little spat the other day."

Brooke didn't let on that she had already heard. The Garland Grove rumor mill was quite effective.

"Yeah, Maizie at the diner heard it from Stacy Pike," Fran continued. "Stacy works for Craig at the drugstore. I'm sure there's not much to it. Willis and I get sideways with each other a couple times a week, but a lot of people think that this is the year Craig pops the question. I hope this doesn't mean we have to wait another year."

"Thanks for telling me, Fran. I'll be more under-standing if poor Craig seems out of sorts."

175

From his booth on the motel side of the diner, Craig watched a young blonde-haired woman walk from her room to the motel office. It had to be Brooke Summers. Knowing there was little chance of her escaping Fran's clutches for a few moments, he motioned for Maizie to bring him a refill of coffee.

"Everybody's wondering what's up with you," Maizie commented as she clutched her left hand with her right to hold off the tremors that were getting more noticeable as she entered her seventies.

"What do you mean?" Craig asked, knowing full well what she meant.

"Word is you and Jenna weren't at your usual table with Sam and Beth at the café last night. You look to me like you haven't been sleeping so good, and you come on a Saturday morning, which you never do, and sit over here by yourself." She nodded toward a table in the far corner where the usual group of farmers and shop owners dished gossip like bored housewives. "Pete and them are wondering if you're mad."

"I'm not mad." Then, getting to his feet, Craig called across the dining room, "I'm not mad at you guys."

The guys waved, then went back to gossiping.

"Are you ordering breakfast, then?" Maizie asked.

"Maybe. It depends on..." As he was speaking the motel office door opened and the blonde-haired woman stepped outside. The bracing north wind caught her hair and made a mess of it before she used her hand to push it back into place. She was younger than she sounded on the phone. Pretty, but not in the glitzy way of Raven McCloud. Why had he even thought she would look anything like Raven? She was an agent, not a performer. But she was from Nashville, and she represented the industry's biggest star.

Craig was ready to jump up and catch her if she

headed for her car, but she came toward the diner, no doubt having been tipped off by Fran that he was there. She came inside and glanced around before her eyes locked on Craig. He waved. She smiled and came his way. The closer she got, the prettier she was. What was more noticeable was the way she moved. Craig guessed her to be in her late twenties or early thirties, but she walked with a confidence and self-assurance that gave her a presence. The men at the corner table noticed too. Craig saw how they watched her pass through the crowded diner. And when she stopped at his table, their mouths dropped open almost as one.

"Craig?"

Craig tried to project some level of coolness as he got to his feet. The booth was tight, though, and his backside sliding across the vinyl seat made a farting noise.

"Sorry, that wasn't... I didn't... It was the booth."

Brooke laughed. "I just assumed it was a big breakfast. May I join you?"

He cringed, then said, "Please do."

She slid into her side of the booth and made a similar farting sound that made them both laugh.

"Now that we've got that out of the way," she said brightly. "What's for breakfast?"

"Maizie will bring you a menu, but I recommend the corned beef hash."

Brooke gave him a thumbs up. He waved Maizie over and introduced Brooke.

"Are you the girl from Nashville?"

"Yes, ma'am. Born and raised in Percy's Crossroads, which is a half-hour east."

"Never heard of it. I sure would like to get to Nashville someday, though. That George Strait, umm-hmmm-hmmm.

Now that's the way a man needs to be. Have you ever run into George Strait?"

"If you live in Nashville long enough you run into everybody. I used to get my hair done at the same place as Wynonna."

Maizie gasped. "Oh, that girl has good hair. Ever see her under the hairdryer?"

"No, but I know for a fact that it was her hair under my chair one time."

Maizie whistled. "I woulda been down there scooping it up to sell, I'm telling you."

They had a good laugh. Craig could see that Brooke was enjoying the back and forth. She was definitely a city girl, but she seemed to have a country girl's heart. And when Maizie asked why she was in Garland Grove, Brooke had no problem stretching the truth just enough to appease Maizie without giving anything away. She took their orders and marched off.

"I'm betting that you've met George Strait," Craig said when Maizie was out of earshot.

"He and my father are friends, though we don't represent him. They fish together a couple times a year." Brooke did an abrupt about-face. "Now, tell me how you're doing, Craig. I heard you and Jenna had a disagreement a couple nights ago."

THE WORDS WEREN'T OUT of her mouth before Brooke worried she had spoken too soon. Craig studied his coffee cup for a few moments before looking up again. There was something in his eyes that she hadn't noticed before. Something that wasn't in the pictures Brooke had found on his Facebook page. Pain. Vulnerability.

"Oh, gosh, I am so sorry I said that," she said. She started to reach out and pat his hands as they cradled his coffee cup, but pulled back. She didn't know the man, yet she had felt comfortable enough to comment on his personal life. "Craig, there's no excuse for me saying what I said. Will you forgive me?"

Their eyes met, and he held her gaze for a few seconds before his smile returned. "I'm going to guess that Fran at the motel told you."

"Maybe, but I'm the one who tried to make light of it."

"And Stacy Pike probably told Fran. Stacy works for me. She was worried about me when I showed up for work yesterday."

"Actually," Brooke said, leaning in. "Stacy told Maizie. Maizie told Fran. Fran told me."

Craig shook his head. "Small towns."

"And if I can be completely transparent?"

"Please do," Craig said, motioning for her to continue.

"Stacy told me, too. When I called the drugstore."

Craig laughed. "It sounds like we have a problem with confidentiality at the drugstore."

"Oh, my. You're not going to fire Stacy, are you?"

"Not a chance. She's too important. And if I let her go she would have a dozen job offers by the end of the day. Besides," he said as he took a deep breath, "Stacy's like family. And lately, it seems like family is in short supply."

There was an awkward pause where Brooke wasn't certain if he wanted her to pursue that further or move on. After the careless way she'd mentioned his girlfriend issues, she let it go. "So," she said instead. "Have you been able to digest what we talked about on the phone?"

He began to speak but stopped when Maizie showed up with their corned beef hash. Brooke leaned close and breathed in the heavenly scents of potatoes, onions, and corned beef. And something else. She picked up her fork and dug around until she discovered the jalapenos. Her stomach growled as she dug in.

"Delicious!" she said through a mouthful.

She was adorable as she spoke through a mouthful of hash. Brooke Summers was very down-to-earth. And quite charming despite her attempt to make humor out of him being tossed into the local rumor mill. And even that was okay.

"Back to your question. I Googled the song and learned that it's all over the place."

Brooke said, "I heard it played in the motel office this morning."

"It's nuts, and I'm not sure I understand why a song recorded twenty years ago is such a big deal."

"There's no accounting for what the public listens to," Brooke said. "My father found it in a bunch of Raven's old stuff. He has an ear for what will sell." She explained how "Making Santa Smile" had snowballed from a box in Bobby Summers's attic to a minor hit. "That's why I'm here. We want to bring you to Nashville and record it again. A better version that we can sell to the public."

"And what's in it for me?"

Brooke pulled a small notebook from her purse, then reconsidered and left it on the edge of the table. "Craig, I'm going to assume you have no experience with entertainment contracts and that kind of stuff, right?"

He smiled again. Brooke liked when he smiled. "If I say no, am I setting myself up to be fleeced?"

"Yes, in some cases. But that's not the way we operate."

"How do I know that?"

"Frankly, you don't. And we won't fault you for consulting an attorney. But let me explain the difference between us and some others in our field."

Brooke spent fifteen minutes providing a primer about the music industry, but most of it was unnecessary. Craig had always considered himself a pretty good judge of character, and he found himself drawn to Brooke's sincerity and desire for his little song to be heard and make money. He found himself drawn to other things about her, too, but pushed those aside as best he could. Those were the thoughts, he suspected, of a man who had just been dumped without seeing it coming, and who found himself drawn to someone who was smart, young, and attractive. Because she was all of those things and more, she probably had a man in her life, anyway. She didn't wear a ring, and she still had the same name as her father, but there must be someone. Some lucky man who envisioned a future with Brooke Summers, just as Craig had envisioned a future with Jenna. The biggest difference was that Brooke's guy wasn't boring. He probably didn't take her to the same restaurant every Friday night for the prime rib special. He was probably high-powered and successful at whatever he did, miles ahead of some small-town drugstore owner whose biggest claim to fame was being the director of the town's Christmas concert.

"So, do you have any questions, Craig?"

He sensed by the perplexed look on her face that Brooke might have already asked him that once already. "Yes, as a matter of fact, I do have a question."

She scraped the last of the hash from her plate as she said, "Shoot."

"You work with a lot of big acts."

She looked at him curiously. "That's not a question, but yes. My dad has run the agency since before I was born. I grew up around show business."

"You probably have seen a lot of performers who weren't as famous, too."

"Sure. We're always scouting for acts that have the potential to get to the next level. That's why I'm here."

"Okay, then," Craig said as he pushed away his empty plate. "What do you know about Hal Richie?"

Brooke thought about it for a few moments. "The name isn't familiar. Should it be?"

"He used to front the Hal Richie Quartet."

"Nope. Doesn't ring a bell. Where might I have heard of them?"

"Oh, maybe they're not as big an act as I thought." He quickly changed the subject. "Would you like me to show you around Garland Grove?"

She smiled that lovely smile. "I would love that. But we also need to sit down someplace and talk about what happens next. And I would like to hear you play the song in person."

"We can do that at my house. I just need to run by the store and fire Stacy Pike."

Brooke's mouth dropped open. "I thought you said—"

Craig waved her off. "Just kidding." He laughed. "C'mon and let me show you around."

CRAIG WENT OUTSIDE to bring his truck closer while Brooke picked up the tab for breakfast. Maizie seized the opportunity to let her know, just as Fran at the motel had earlier, that Craig was spoken for.

"They had a spat the other day, but everybody thinks they'll get married sooner or later." She leaned in so as not to be overheard by nearby diners. "They spend the night together now and then, mainly on weekends, and only at Craig's house. Everybody wishes they wouldn't, but times are different from when I was young. They just need to get married and put all that to rest."

Brooke wasn't sure why Maizie felt the need to keep her voice down. From what she had seen of Garland Grove, everyone knew everyone else's business. She thanked her, pocketed the receipt, and made a dash for Craig's truck.

"Was Maizie giving you an earful?" he asked as they pulled from the parking lot.

"She wanted to make sure that I know you're spoken for."

Craig took a deep breath and began to say something before catching himself. "Let's start downtown."

In addition to providing a running narrative of Garland Grove's most outstanding attributes, Craig tossed in the occasional question about the music business. Not so much behind-the-scenes stuff as what he could expect.

"We'll record the song in a professional studio, then send it to radio stations and upload it for purchase."

"What about all the copies that are already out there? Like the ones I saw online?"

"We can get most of those taken down easily enough. The new version will sound so much better that people will gravitate toward it anyway."

"And you really think people will buy it? Actually pay money for it?"

"If we can add to the number of stations already playing it, we have a chance to sell a lot of downloads. And who knows? If it can find its way onto a top-forty chart, it could really take off."

"Like a hit song?"

"Exactly. The thing with holiday songs is that they have a short shelf life. As soon as the holidays are over, people go back to regular music. Sales of songs like yours fall off a cliff. That's why we were in such a hurry to find you."

Brooke checked out the scenery as Craig processed everything. Garland Grove was lovely in that idyllic fifties small-town way, before big box stores and online companies gutted downtowns. Storefronts were festively decorated. Santas, candy canes, and angels hung from lampposts. The recent snowfalls were like icing on an already beautiful cake.

"My house is up this way," he said as he turned off the town's main drag and proceeded through a tidy residential area. Streets were lined with stately oaks, barren in the winter cold. Brooke could see why Jenna preferred to spend the night at his place, away from the prying eyes of anyone other than a handful of neighbors. After they pulled into the driveway Craig retrieved her bag and led the way up the front walk. He opened the front door and allowed her to step in ahead of him. The living room was nicely furnished in a comfortable, lived-in way. Nothing ostentatious or fake. The couch and one chair were leather. A cloth recliner faced the television. A table next to it contained two coasters, a remote, and a couple of paperback novels. A large Christmas tree dominated one end of the room. Brooke took a seat on the sofa and accepted his offer of hot apple cider.

The kitchen was just a few steps away, and Craig kept up a running conversation about stuff like Garland Grove winters and how he had come to own a small drugstore in a town where he was an outsider.

He reappeared with two mugs. Christmas-themed, Brooke was pleased to see, with a cinnamon stick in each. He set one on the coffee table in front of her and took the other to the leather chair placed at an angle to her left. "You're very good at getting me to tell you everything about myself," he observed as Brooke sipped the delicious cider. "But now I want to hear more about you.

"Oh, I doubt you've told me everything."

Craig grinned. "Probably not."

"What do you want to know about me?" Brooke asked. "I've already described our company and what we do."

"I could have Googled that. I want to know about Brooke Summers the person."

Brooke thought about it for a moment. If Craig Callaway had a dark side he certainly did a good job of concealing it. She decided to open up a bit more and see where things went. "My parents divorced when I was very small. I barely knew my mother."

"Knew?"

"Yeah. Past tense. She passed when I was in middle school, but she hadn't been a factor in my life. Dad had full custody from the start and I was completely his little girl."

"He sounds like a remarkable man."

"He really is. And not just for what he has accomplished in the business. Bobby Summers is the same man when it's just the two of us at the house in Percy's Crossroads as he is when he's negotiating concert tours or television appearances. There might be people who don't like him, but I've never met them."

Craig motioned for her to continue.

"I went to college at Vanderbilt, so I've never really left home. After I graduated, I spent two years in event management for the larger Nashville concert venues, but it was always a given that I would eventually come to work with Dad."

"So why didn't you just jump in? Why wait?"

"Dad wanted me to get a feel for the industry that wasn't clouded by his experiences. It turned out to be an excellent idea. I saw the music industry from the other side for a time, and I think it helped me when I returned to Summers Management."

"Kind of like learning from the ground up?"

"Exactly. It was six years ago that I went to work with Dad. He had me start with some of the detail work that is boring as heck but necessary to the business. Scouting concert venues, making sure equipment is packed and shipped, and finding rehearsal spots. I eventually started reviewing contracts. Then he had me take responsibility for some of our second-tier acts while he handled the headliners."

"That's what I would be," Craig laughed.

"Maybe, but you'll still get our best effort. We've had a bunch of acts that transitioned from regional performers to bigger acts. A few even became headliners in their own right."

"Like who?"

Brooke named three acts. Craig admitted he wasn't a big fan of country music and had only heard of one, but Brooke was undeterred. She described how those groups made the jump.

"Some leave us for other managers. That happens in our business. There are agencies that have twenty agents, and they can promise a lot more individual attention to a lot more bands. We're just Bobby and me, so we keep our stable of acts small, but it works for us."

Craig sipped his cider, then set it on the coffee table. "You veered back into the business stuff. What do you like to do when you're not representing Raven McCloud or hustling up nobodies like me?"

"Sadly, not much. I feel like I'm still learning, so I put a lot of time and energy into it. I love good food and can cook a little. I can't remember the last time I went to the movies. I go to small venues to listen to music, but it's almost always for work." Brooke had a thought. "I love to fish! We have several ponds on our farm, and I love going out on a warm afternoon with a fishing pole in my hand and a good podcast on my phone."

OKAY, Craig, you've pushed far enough. She'll think you're a creeper.

She's said nothing about a guy in her life, though. Do you think...?

Don't be stupid, dude. Jenna dumped you just two days ago. You're still not thinking straight. And probably won't be for weeks.

And besides, she's probably only being nice because she wants to make some money off your song.

Give her credit, though. She and her father saw the potential to make money on some old song you had long forgotten about. And speaking of which...

"Did you say you wanted me to play for you?"

"Yes, please." She pulled the cinnamon stick from her

mug and stuck it in her mouth. Craig excused himself to retrieve his guitar. He returned and took a seat.

"I need a couple minutes to tune it," he said as he glanced at a clock over the sofa. "What time do you need to leave?"

"I'm supposed to be back at the airstrip between two and three."

Craig played a few chords until satisfied. "Don't hold back. If my playing isn't good enough, let me know, okay?"

"I have nothing to gain by lying to you. Who is your favorite guitarist of all time, by the way?"

"Jerry Garcia."

Brooke laughed. "A Deadhead, huh?"

"He was so versatile. Rock, blues, even country. The beginning of Uncle John's Band pulls me in every time. How about you?"

"Chet Atkins. The inventor of the Nashville sound. He's my dad's favorite, and he passed that love on to me."

"Probably a frequent visitor to the Summers home back in the day," Craig joked as he plucked a few notes of some old country tune.

"Nope. I wish I had met him before he passed away."

Craig shook out his hands. "Ready?"

HE PLAYED THE SONG THROUGH, with only a brief pause as he struggled to recall some of the lyrics of the third verse. Having heard it several times over the past few days, Brooke hummed along softly. She had always liked to watch a musician's fingers as they played. You could tell a lot, like if they were nervous or at ease, or if they were feeling the music or just playing. Craig kept his head down at the beginning as he concentrated on rediscovering a song he hadn't played in years. Once he became comfortable, though, he gazed at her while he played. Eyes communicated even more than fingers. His were kind. He was a good man, she could tell.

He reached the end of the song and set the guitar aside.

"Well?" he asked.

"Did you write the lyrics?"

"I did. Like I said, it was part of a class project in music theory."

"B-minus. I remember. And the melody? All yours?"

Craig shrugged. "I need to be honest. The melody is from an old Paul Simon song I liked as a kid."

He laughed when her eyes grew large. "Nah, I'm pulling your leg."

She pointed her index finger at him. "Watch it."

"So, how did I do?" he asked.

"Your guitar playing isn't very good."

He clutched his chest as if having a heart attack. "So honest," he whined good-naturedly.

"It's the only way to be. Your voice is great, though. A lot of men lose their range as they move into their thirties, but you can still hit all the notes."

"But pitch the guitar?"

Brooke nodded.

"I can play the keyboard, too."

"Not really. I heard you on the phone, remember?"

He laughed. "So, all I have is my voice?"

"Yep, but it will be plenty. When can you come to Nashville?"

Craig sat forward in his chair. "Seriously? Just like that?"

"Just like that."

"How long will I need to be there?"

"Two, maybe three days. For starters."

"For starters?"

"If the song continues to do well, we might want you to make some appearances. The morning news programs, maybe the late-night shows."

Craig turned pale. Brooke had seen it before. It was that moment when someone whose life has cruised along on a steady path realizes they might have something special. His first thought would be that he wasn't capable or worthy of the adulation. His second thought was probably that he didn't even want to try. Bewilderment, then self-doubt.

Then, acceptance.

"Craig," Brooke said, trying to help him past the skepticism. "People love your song. It makes them happy. They want to meet the person behind the song. And the fact that you're not some big-name singer makes your story even more fascinating."

"Yeah, sure," Craig said. "Let's buy the Christmas song that small-town pharmacist sings, Craig whatshisname."

"Carl," Brooke replied. "That's the name the public knows you by. Raven thought your name was Carl, so we started calling you Christmas Carl. We can't change that now."

"I can't even use my real name?"

Brooke shook her head. "Sorry, buddy. We don't want to confuse your adoring fans."

"Carl," Craig said, more to himself. "Just Carl."

"Christmas Carl. So, do you still want to come to Nashville and cut the record?"

The few moments Craig took to consider the question scared Brooke a little. She felt she had done a good job of helping him understand everything, but was he wavering?

Then, thankfully, it passed. He stood up, grinned, and said, "Absolutely."

"Wonderful!" Brooke jumped to her feet and stepped around the coffee table with her arms open. Craig met her halfway. Her forehead just cleared his shoulder, and his body felt firmer than it looked under layers of winter clothing. The hug lingered beyond what might seem normal, probably because there was something more there. She felt as if he needed that hug.

"Tell me about Jenna," she said softly. He pulled away and she wondered if she had pushed too far again. When he sat back down, his eyes had become uncertain.

"What do you want to know?" His tone gave Brooke the impression that she hadn't overstepped. "She's a vet. We started going out a couple of years ago. Things were going pretty well, I thought, until I found out Thursday night that she's been sleeping with a colleague."

"Oh, Craig, I'm so sorry."

He shrugged and looked away. "She said she was bored with things...with me." He looked up and flashed a pained grin. "I guess we do kind of do the same stuff all the time, but I thought she enjoyed our life together. I guess not."

Brooke knew she needed to say something, but with everything being so fresh, she wasn't sure what would help. She got to her feet and moved closer, taking a seat in front of him on the coffee table, hoping it could support her weight. It creaked but held strong. When she reached for his hand, he didn't pull it away.

"A few days away might be just what you need."

He nodded. "I'll have to find someone to cover the drugstore. And make airline reservations. Maybe I'll just drive down instead. The money I save driving can go toward a motel room."

"No, Craig," Brooke said, laughing. "We're paying for you to come to Nashville. Your airfare, hotel, food. Everything. In fact," she paused and reached into her purse. "Here's a contract we drew up. Take it to someone you trust and have them look it over. If it's acceptable, sign and bring it with you when you come."

He was still holding her hand as he opened the envelope and removed the contract. He scanned the two-page document and laid it aside. "Brooke, I feel I can trust you."

The words touched Brooke's heart. "I give you my word I have your best interest at heart," she said. She removed her hand from his, grabbed the contract and a pen, and made a notation. She held it up and said, "In fact, I've added an out for you. If at any time you feel you're not getting the best representation, you can void this contract. My dad would say this was a rookie mistake, but I know better."

"I can talk to Henry Dinwiddie about filling in for me. He's a retired pharmacist who is always looking for something to do. How about I fly out tomorrow night?"

"Now that's quick!" Brooke exclaimed. "I'll be in Cincinnati with Raven, but our assistant Raquel can set everything up for you."

Brooke could see his spirits lifting as their venture shifted into gear. They spent the next couple hours talking about what he could expect while in town and what might happen if the song continued to perform well. He made them lunch, leftover chili, and before they knew it, it was one-fifteen.

"I guess I should get back to the airport," Brooke said. The prospect of leaving was saddening. Craig Callaway was a very nice man. A very down-to-earth, sincere, and guileless man. Nashville's entertainment community could eat up someone like Craig Callaway and not think twice about it. Whether he lasted for three weeks or three decades, Brooke would do everything she could to make sure that didn't happen.

THERE WAS SO MUCH GOING through Craig's mind as he drove Brooke back to the Park-Rite Motel. He was still in disbelief that he would soon be heading to Nashville to record an old song he had written as a class assignment two decades before. That kind of stuff didn't happen to him. There was also the uncertainty of not knowing what to expect next. Brooke had mentioned the possibility of late-night TV shows and concerts. Ridiculous, wasn't it? Who wanted to hear a nobody like Craig Callaway sing a silly Christmas song? And what about beyond Christmas? He would probably be back stocking shelves and filling prescriptions by January, but so what? Even if a little of what Brooke said might happen actually happened, it would be life-changing.

And what would Jenna think of everything? Would she still think he was boring when she heard his song on the radio? How would she react if someone actually stopped them to ask for his autograph? Nothing boring about that. Would she come back after his few minutes of fame? Would Jenna apologize for saying he was boring?

Or was she already in love with the vet? She had wasted no time falling into bed with him, that was for sure. It had been six months before she and Craig first made love. The new vet had been in town for four months, and...

Stop it! There's too much going on to let yourself get bogged down with that stuff!

But what if she did apologize? What if she said she had

made a terrible mistake, and that she missed what they used to have? The Friday dinners with Sam and Beth. Picking out Christmas trees at Blankenship tree farm. What if she wanted those things again? With Craig?

Would he say yes?

"What are you thinking about over there?" Brooke asked as they drove through downtown.

"A lot of stuff," he said softly. "You've certainly given me plenty to consider."

"Can I ask a personal question?" She turned in the seat so she was facing him. He already liked that about Brooke. She listened with her entire body, leaning in, tipping her head toward him as he spoke. Nodding at the right moments.

"I guess so."

"Do you love her?"

It seemed a forthright question to ask, particularly since they had known each other for just a few hours. Yet it also seemed somehow appropriate. He sensed she cared, and that was enough to earn a reply.

"I've asked myself that a million times since Thursday night."

She waited for him to elaborate.

"Maybe I'm not sure what real love is, Brooke. Does it seem ridiculous for a thirty-nine-year-old man to be admitting something like that?"

BROOKE HAD EXPECTED him to avoid her question. Most guys would respond with something that was more face-saving or made them look like they were doing better than they were. Craig's response showed vulnerability. And complete honesty. His honesty caused her to ask herself the same question. Had she ever really loved Tristan?

But that was her personal battle. Craig had admitted his struggle with knowing what love was, then asked if it seemed ridiculous. He deserved an answer.

"It's not ridiculous at all. In fact, I suspect that there are many people who are in the same boat as you. Sadly, they're already married or have families, and finding out what they have isn't genuine love can probably be scary as hell."

"You're pretty wise," he said, his eyes dancing. "Are you sure you're only... How old are you?"

"Thirty, but Dad calls me an old soul."

They rode in silence for the few minutes it took to reach the Park-Rite.

"Look," Brooke said, pointing to her rental car. "Someone cleared the snow from my windshield."

"Small-town hospitality," he said as he pulled up next to her car. "Well, I guess this is it."

"Only until Tuesday," Brooke said. "I've already texted Raquel about your flight and accommodations. I won't see you tomorrow night, but I'll pick you up at your hotel first thing Monday morning. And remember, keep it to yourself, please."

As they shared farewell pleasantries, Brooke found something tugging at her, a desire to spend a few more minutes getting to know the kind pharmacist who was about to enjoy his first glimpse of a completely different world. Would it change him? She suspected not, but she had been wrong before. Much depended upon how much adulation he received. She was certain Craig could handle the sudden notoriety, but what about the bigger picture?

The answer, she knew, would come quickly.

SUNDAY, DECEMBER 4

GARLAND GROVE

*A*re you going to church?

The alert that announced Sam's text message made Craig jump. The drugstore on a Sunday morning, without the pumped-in background music and coming and going of customers, was eerily still.

Craig texted back, *I have work to catch up on. Sorry.*

Sam replied immediately. *Don't apologize to me, you heathen. It's God who's going to be mad at you!*

A couple minutes later, as Craig checked in shipments that had arrived the previous day, another text came. This from Amy Bennett. *I convinced Andrew to attend church today and you're not coming? Shame!*

Sorry, Amy. Hey to Andrew.

We forgive you. I'm making my world-famous taco salad for lunch today. You and Jenna want?

He loved—*loved*—Amy's taco salad. It hurt seeing Jenna's name connected to his, though. Word hadn't gotten out yet. He had to eat, though, and his flight to Nashville didn't leave the regional airport until six, so there was time.

I'll be there. Then he added, *Just me.*

Be here at noon. Ask Andrew what he learned in church. He never pays attention.

Craig stocked shelves and caught up on bookkeeping until Henry Dinwiddie showed up at ten. A sweet cherubic man who was approaching his eightieth birthday, Henry had owned the drugstore until selling out to Craig nine years earlier. "Those big pharmacies are the future," Henry had said the day he handed over the keys. "But people in Garland Grove will always support their own." He had been right. Even though the neon sign changed from Dinwiddie's Drugstore to Callaway's Drugstore, customers remained loyal. And having Henry fill in every so often served as a bridge to the past that Garland Grove residents happily embraced.

"Little vacation planned, Craig?" Henry said as he took a seat behind the counter.

"Just a quick out-of-town trip. I should be back Wednesday night."

"Well, don't worry about things here. I'm available all week. It's good to get out of the house."

"How about your car, Henry? Does it do okay in snow?" Henry's purchase of a flashy red convertible soon after his retirement had been the talk of the town. He was on his fourth in nine years and while they all looked and ran great, they were questionable in winter conditions.

"I've started calling on Wally Darnell's taxi during the winter," he explained. "Wally has four-wheel drive, and goodness knows he can use the extra spending money. Don't worry about me."

The two spent the next hour talking business and catching up until Henry said he needed to get back to the house. Craig offered a ride, but Henry insisted that Wally Darnell needed the money. It was eleven-forty when Craig locked up and headed home to freshen up for lunch at the Bennetts'. The others were already there when he arrived. The sun shined brightly through the large oaks and evergreens in the front yard of the Bennett home. The place had once belonged to the hospital until Andrew convinced them that allowing him and Amy to purchase it might result in their putting down roots. Craig rapped on the door before letting himself in. He followed their voices to the kitchen where Amy, decked out in a Christmas apron, was at the stove stirring ground beef. The others were at the table with wine glasses in hand.

"Pastor Markwell asked about you this morning," Sam said. "I told him you were sleeping in after going to one of those erotic massage places in Minneapolis."

The others laughed good-naturedly at the verbal jab. To know Sam was to love him. It also meant that you were going to be on the receiving end of his witticisms. Andrew, Amy's husband of one year and Sam's medical practice partner, received most of Sam's abuse. He was quieter and more retrospective than the others. He was also, like Craig, an out-of-towner who had settled in Garland Grove.

Beth stood up and came to give Craig a hug. "Why isn't Jenna coming?" She must have seen something in Craig's eyes because she immediately grabbed his hand and led him to the wine bottle. While she poured, Craig debated how to broach the news. He didn't want to unload on Jenna, nor did he want his best friends to find out from someone else. He took a sip of wine and charged in.

"We're not seeing each other anymore."

That wiped the smile from Sam's face. Amy dropped her spatula. Andrew shook his head as he stared at the floor. Beth looked as if she might cry. No one spoke for a few moments. He suspected they wanted to know what happened, but he wasn't sure he could tell them. Unlike Brooke Summers the day before, they knew Jenna. They considered her a friend. And they were comfortable with Jenna and Craig together.

Of the four, the one he would have expected to reach out first was Beth. She had a knack for picking up on things. But it was Sam who came forward first. He leaned in close and placed his hand on the back of Craig's head.

"We're here for you," he said quietly.

What followed was one of those awkward moments when no one knew what to do or say next. The cat was out of the bag. Lunch was nearly ready. What Craig needed to do was pull his friends out of the pot of misery he had tossed them into. And there was only one thing he could say that would do that. Confidentiality agreement be damned.

"I'm flying to Nashville this evening to cut a record."

Craig laughed at their blank faces. "Okay, maybe that was a bad transition, but I really am." He told them everything, from hearing the song on the news to Brooke's visit the day before.

"That's you?" Amy said, rushing to give him a hug. "I've heard that song a lot the last few days."

"Me, too," Andrew added as he shook Craig's hand. "It was playing in the office Friday."

"I heard you were eating breakfast with a strange woman," Sam said. "But I just assumed it was your sister or somebody."

"He doesn't have a sister, Sam!" Beth scolded. "You need to pay better attention."

Amy dished out taco salad while Craig dished on everything leading up to the flight he would catch for Nashville in a few hours. The questions came. And came some more. Beth wanted to know about the song, as she was the only one who hadn't heard it. "All we listen to around our house is Disney tunes," she complained. Andrew asked what it felt like to hear himself on the radio.

And Sam?

"You dated Raven McCloud?"

"I guess so."

"The real Raven McCloud? Not some stunt double?"

Amy looked skyward before addressing her longtime friend. "Singers don't have stunt doubles, you knucklehead."

Undeterred, Sam exclaimed, "That woman is a stone-cold fox, Craig. A looker. A hottie. A dreamboat. A knockout."

"Are you almost done?" Beth asked as she scooped herself another helping of taco salad.

"Not even close. Raven McCloud is one bad kitty. She's a Betty, a yummy mummy, a PYT, a dish, a hot mama, a—"

"Where do you learn this stuff?" Amy asked. "Or do you just make it up as you go? I mean, really, a Betty?"

"Late-night TV. If you newlyweds didn't run off to bed at eight-thirty, you might know some of this stuff." Sam turned to Craig. "And speaking of running off to bed, I have to ask. Did you and Raven ever—"

"Sam." Beth didn't raise her voice. She didn't have to. Sam shrugged and let it pass.

"When will this be public knowledge?" Andrew asked.

Craig answered, "There's supposed to be a press conference while I'm in Nashville."

"A real press conference," Amy effused. "Our Craig is about to become a big-time celebrity." When she raised her iced tea glass the others did too. "To Craig."

"To Craig," they echoed.

Feelings of family and friendship filled the achy reaches

of Craig's heart that were still reeling from Jenna's rejection. They were his best friends. They loved him and supported him, and made Garland Grove feel like his own hometown.

Sam took a big slug of tea and set his glass aside as he leaned in. "I want to circle back to the lady from Nashville."

"Brooke Summers? What about her?" Craig asked.

"Maizie told me you two looked pretty chummy when you drove Miss Summers back to get her car yesterday afternoon." Sam wiggled his eyes in a way that was supposed to appear suggestive but looked more like Groucho Marx telling a dirty joke. "Could there be a spark there?"

"You don't know when to quit, do you?" Beth said. "It's getting so I can't take you anywhere."

They spent the next hour chatting excitedly about Craig's adventure. Andrew and Amy offered a ride to the airport, but he turned them down. "I have no return flight scheduled yet," he explained. "I don't want to put anyone out."

"You could never put us out," Amy said quickly. And Craig knew she meant it.

They were, after all, his best friends.

Brooke knocked twice, then twice again. And waited.

She had learned her lesson in Nashville.

"C'mon in, dear!" Raven called out. She had been cheery since Brooke caught up with the tour in Memphis the night before, an hour before Raven took the stage.

"Everything looks good," Brooke said as she stepped into the dressing room and sat on the arm of a loveseat. "No VIPs tonight, so you can relax until showtime."

Raven said nothing as she fussed with her hair for a

couple of moments. Her phone buzzed incessantly while she primped. Raven would pick it up periodically, return a text, and go back to her hair. Brooke pulled out her own phone and sent a text to Craig Callaway.

I saw where your flight to Chicago was delayed a few minutes. All okay?

His response came right away. *All good. Twenty minutes until boarding. I'm indulging in a quesadilla salad at Chili's. I hope I'm not spending too much.*

Raven looked up when she heard Brooke giggle. "Did your boyfriend say something funny?"

Her tone was playful, which helped Brooke relax. "No," she replied. "Yours did." Then, realizing Raven might think she was referring to Travis Horton, she added, "Craig Callaway is having dinner at Chili's and was worried he is spending too much money."

Raven rolled her eyes. "Mickey said his song is getting more airplay than my new release." She paused for a moment, then added, "What would you think of adding him to the tour?"

CRAIG CHECKED his watch and signaled for his check. He nearly fainted when he saw the price of dinner. "Airport prices and taxes," the server said when he asked. When his phone buzzed, he expected to see a return text from Brooke, but it wasn't.

Hi Craig, how are you? I'm sorry for the way I broke the news to you about Owen and me. I had hoped we could remain friends. Do you have time to talk?

Jenna.

So his name was Owen. How had he not remembered

that? Jenna had been sleeping with Owen for two months and Craig hadn't even known his name. Talk about oblivious.

Talk about stupid.

He handed his credit card to the server and skimmed Jenna's text again before writing one of his own.

Hey Jenna, sorry I can't talk right now. I'm at O'Hare Airport about to board a flight to Nashville. So much has happened the past few days. A song I recorded in college has become a minor hit. A Nashville talent agent came to visit and ask if I would like to record the song again and maybe do some personal appearances. I'll be in Nashville for a few days and don't know how busy I'll be, but maybe we can talk sometime. Oh, by the way, I discovered that I dated Raven McCloud in college, except back then she was Megan Stackhouse. I hope to see her while in Nashville. Talk to you later.

"Here's your credit card and receipt, sir." The server said.

Craig pocketed the card and took another look at his text to Jenna. He was about to hit send when he reconsidered. Why did she deserve to know?

Was he thinking that the news might make her want to drop Owen the veterinarian and come back to him? He wasn't just Craig the pharmacist anymore. He was Craig the singer. And soon would be Craig the Nashville recording artist.

That had a nice ring to it.

He read the text once more, deleted it, and headed for his gate. He was just arriving when he heard an overhead page.

Nashville Passenger Craig Callaway, please report to the ticket agent.

Uh-oh.

There might be an issue, he texted Brooke.

"Your tour?" Brooke asked, getting to her feet. "You want to add Craig to the Christmas tour?"

Raven sat aside her brush, stood up, and checked out her awesome outfit in a floor to ceiling mirror. "Sure. He can come out during the time I take a potty break. Maybe we can tell his story and sell some music."

Brooke couldn't believe what she was hearing but was smart enough to know that Raven's thoughts were subject to change without notice. "How about this?" she suggested. "Meet him tomorrow and see if you're comfortable with him joining the tour. If so, and he is interested, we can discuss it."

"Why wouldn't he be interested, Brooke?" Raven scoffed. "You said he works in a drugstore, right? Singing on a sold-out Christmas tour has to be better than that."

"He's a pharmacist. He actually owns the drugstore. Getting away for an extended time might be hard, but let's keep the option open, okay?"

Brooke wished Raven well and stepped back out. She saw she had two messages from Craig.

There might be an issue.

And then, *I CANNOT BELIEVE THIS!!! YOU GUYS BOUGHT ME A FIRST-CLASS SEAT!!*

She laughed, then texted, *It's the least we can do.*

Craig's response came quickly.

THIS IS AMAZING! TAYLOR SWIFT IS SITTING ACROSS THE AISLE AND ONE ROW UP!!!

His follow-up text, no longer in caps, said *I was wrong. It isn't Taylor Swift, but she could be her sister.*

Taylor doesn't have a sister. Enjoy your flight. Our driver, Milo, will pick you up at the airport. We have a room reserved for you near our offices, but Dad and I were wondering if you would prefer to stay at our farm. Either is fine.

CRAIG CHECKED AGAIN JUST to make sure the woman seated a row ahead of him really wasn't Taylor Swift. There was no way it could be, though. She was eating a sub sandwich while chatting with a man who kept calling her Pamela. As the flight attendant announced the door was about to close, the Taylor lookalike glanced past her seatmate and smiled at Craig. She had a piece of lettuce on the corner of her mouth. That clinched it. There was no way Taylor Swift would have lettuce on her mouth. He glanced at a text that had just come in from Brooke. Her family house or a hotel? Easy choice.

First class and a limo? Is this really happening? I happily accept the offer to stay with you and your father.

MONDAY, DECEMBER 5

NASHVILLE

*B*rooke awakened at six-fifteen, road weary after arriving home so late from Cincinnati, but intent on chatting with Bobby before Craig Callaway made his appearance. She threw on her robe and slippers and trudged downstairs. The coffee was on, which meant Bobby was up and around. That wasn't a surprise. He was always an early riser, even on mornings following road trips. What was a surprise, though, was seeing Craig seated at the kitchen table with him. Brooke was about to dart out of view, but he was looking right at her.

"Good morning, Brooke!"

"Uh...hi, Craig... You're certainly up early."

"Hi, darlin'," Bobby said as he raised his coffee mug. He was already dressed for the day, down to his boots and Stetson.

"Hey, Dad. I thought that... I guess I should go back up and get dressed."

"Eh, nonsense. Get in here and have some coffee. We want to hear about the tour, don't we, Craig?"

"We sure do. And thanks again for everything, Brooke.

The trip in was great. I can't wait to tell my friends I flew first class."

Brooke grabbed a mug and pulled out a chair. She must look a mess, but Craig was too kind to mention it. "Three shows down, thirteen to go. The audio system in Cincinnati gave the crew some trouble, but they got things squared away. Raven did two encores last night. The second was completely unplanned, and really caught Mickey and the band by surprise, but they handled it."

"She'll do that sometimes," Bobby said in his slow drawl. "She gets so caught up in the moment. How has she been otherwise?"

There was no need to air the dirty laundry from opening night. Raven scolding her for coming into the dressing room before being invited, then blaming her for the VIP question about Travis Horton. She had been charming and full of Christmas spirit the last two nights, so perhaps things were looking up.

"Raven flies to Pittsburgh for Wednesday night's show, then we switch to buses for the next four."

"Tour buses?" Craig asked. "I've seen those on TV. Pretty ritzy, from what I could tell."

"Ritzy for Raven," Bobby said. "Her coach is loaded with everything she needs. Two big screen TV's and even a jacuzzi tub. The rest of the crew sleeps in cramped bunks or the back of equipment vans."

Brooke continued. "From Pittsburgh, we go to Richmond. Then it's on to Charlotte, Atlanta, and Tampa before we come back home."

Craig was hanging on every word. "How do you keep it all straight?"

"She's real doggone smart," Bobby said. "I write everything down and check my notes fifteen times a day. Brooke just remembers."

"How about you, Craig?" Brooke steered the conversation away from herself. "Are you ready to record your song today?"

"I hope so. I could barely sleep last night. I was so excited."

"The studio guys will make it easy for you," Brooke said as she downed the last of her coffee. "Mickey Cox is Raven's music director. He'll oversee everything.

"Mickey is the best there is," Bobby said. "You're in good hands." Then, to Brooke, "What have you got planned for the rest of the day?"

"I'm not sure yet. Maybe show Craig around Nashville. Want to go along?"

Bobby shook his head. "Raquel needs me in the office for a spell. After that, I'm going quail hunting with some boys out near Gallatin." He turned to Craig. "Do you quail hunt?"

"No, sir. I grew up in a small town, but we never did much bird hunting."

Brooke put a stop to the conversation before Bobby did what he always did, which was extend an invitation. The last thing they needed was for Craig to wind up tromping through the woods. "Maybe another time. I think we can find plenty to do in town today."

"Too bad," Bobby said. "The boys would enjoy meeting you." Craig's eyes were as round as saucers when Bobby nonchalantly named off his hunting buddies. Two were already in the country music hall of fame, and another would be there soon.

Brooke washed out her mug and headed for the stairs. "I'll go get ready. Dad, can you keep Craig occupied?"

"I'll show him around the place, then maybe we'll run up to the store and see what flavors of pie Maude has."

"Just be back in ninety minutes. Craig, you're in good hands."

BOBBY SUMMERS WAS A HECKUVA GUY. If someone were writing a movie script about an aging Nashville talent agent, Bobby would be the model. He was gracious and well-spoken and every inch the country boy who made good, but never forgot where he came from.

And perhaps his crowning achievement was his daughter.

Brooke was smart and quick-witted. She cared very much about Bobby, and Craig could already tell she cared about him.

Oh, yeah, and she was beautiful. Goodness, was she beautiful. Even when she showed up in the kitchen without makeup and her hair mussed from sleep, she was lovely.

And later, while hiking along the ponds, when Bobby good-naturedly mentioned that he had noticed the way Craig had been looking at his daughter, Craig surprised himself by responding that he had indeed been checking her out. He apologized, but Bobby seemed unbothered. "She's a good one," Bobby acknowledged before pointing to a deer stand he and a couple music legends had constructed in the nineties.

Brooke was in the living room flipping through a magazine when they returned. Her jeans and tan sweater fit to perfection. Craig tried not to stare, but when he saw the way Bobby was watching him, he knew he was busted.

"I hope you brought another pair of shoes," Brooke said,

nodding at his muddied Timberlands. He had, and he hustled upstairs to put them on. When he returned, Brooke was outside waiting.

BROOKE SENSED that Craig's nerves were rearing up as they drove to the studio. She said the things she needed to say, but nothing would help more than just getting on with it. They parked in a visitors' spot at the studio and entered through a side door. They were barely inside before they heard the melody of his song. Craig appeared shellshocked.

"Brooke, this is... Am I really the person to do this?"

"You wrote it and sang the original," she said casually. "There's no one else."

Mickey Cox smiled when they entered the studio. He raised his hands, and the seven musicians seated around him paused mid-song. "Hey, everybody, y'all know Brooke already, but this here has to be Mr. Craig Callaway. Craig, welcome to Nashville!"

The others echoed Mickey's greeting before returning to their sheet music. Mickey ambled over and shook hands. "They might not look like much, but these are some of the best session players in town." He pointed to each and told Craig about some of their previous work. Craig was growing greener by the moment. Mickey picked up on his doubts. "You're going to do just fine. Brooke wouldn't have brought you to town if she thought otherwise. Our job is to make your song sound the best it can. We're all on the same team. If you mess up, we stop and do it over. So relax and take a seat off to the side while they run through the song another time or two. We'll record the instrumental parts first, then we'll cut the musicians loose and get to you.

❄

THE MUSICIANS WERE AMAZING. Brooke had been spot-on in her assessment of Craig's guitar playing. Compared to the two men and one woman who were playing his song, he was a butcher. A hack who could spend hours practicing each day for years and not come close to the talent in front of him. They were into their second run-through before Craig realized that Brooke had pulled up a seat beside him.

"Your turn is coming," she whispered.

"I'm in a different league than these people."

"Nope. You're the guy whose name is on the song. You're Christmas Carl."

Mickey appeared satisfied with the quality of the rehearsal and instructed the guys in the control booth to prepare to record. The mood in the room, calm and steady, moved to a different level as musicians tuned their instruments and double-checked their parts. Mickey's eyes canvassed the group before motioning to the booth. "Okay, everyone. This is it."

It took three takes, but even Craig could tell they nailed it. And after playing the final note the musicians took a collective sigh. They knew, too. Even before anyone in the control booth gave the thumbs-up, they knew.

And fifteen minutes later, they were gone.

It was Craig's turn. Mickey handed him a headset and led him to the center of the studio where a lone microphone was placed. He demonstrated how close to stand and what cues to look for.

"Are you ready?"

Craig shook his head. His hands were shaking, and he wasn't sure he even remembered the words. "Can I have a copy of the sheet music?"

"Nope," Mickey said. "You know the song, Craig. You wrote it. And you're gonna kill it."

When he asked a second time if Craig was ready, he nodded that he was.

"First take," Mickey said as he stepped away.

The music started playing through Craig's headphones. It sounded so natural and so familiar. He flashed back to the night he'd written the song in his college dorm room. Raven was there, except she was Megan back then. She was working on some of her own stuff for the same class. They swapped lyrics and melodies and sampled each other's songs. Even then, her music seemed so much more advanced than his, but he would never have predicted that she would wind up where she was.

And now he was there, too. Certainly not on her level. He was no Raven McCloud. But he was about to record his song. A song people wanted to hear.

Yep, it was all so familiar. And so natural.

Until he missed his mark.

By the time Craig realized he was supposed to be singing, it was too late.

The music stopped. A guy in the control booth with a soft Tennessee drawl said, "Let's back up and go from the top."

And they did.

Craig missed his cue again.

And again.

By the fifth take, his knees were shaking. Mickey motioned for him to hand over his headphones. Craig thought he was being dismissed.

"Gosh, Mickey," he stammered. "I'm so... I apologize for wasting everyone's time. This is just so much..."

"Take ten," Mickey said. "Step outside and get some air. You're gonna be fine."

Craig kept his head down as he shuffled to the exit. He stepped into the studio hallway and toward a back door. He stepped out onto a covered stoop that appeared to be a smokers' hangout. He leaned against a railing and breathed in the cool December air, uncertain if he should be mad or disappointed. He had to fight to head off tears of frustration. He bit his lip and took a deep gulping breath, and then another. He felt lightheaded. And sad that he had come all the way to Nashville at others' expense. And failed. Failed miserably.

The door opened and Brooke stepped out. She took one look at him and came to his side.

"Relax," she breathed.

Craig tried to speak, but the words wouldn't come. He stared off into the alley that separated the studio from a cooking school and a pottery shop, then, after a few moments he turned so he was facing her. When she looked into his eyes, he saw kindness.

"Brooke, I just can't..." He gathered his thoughts. "It'll be better if you and Mickey find someone else—"

Brooke raised up and kissed him on the lips. Gently, but with enough force to make him shut up. She kissed him until he returned the kiss. Instead of one person kissing another, it became two people kissing each other.

And it was nice.

Very, very nice.

After a few moments, Brooke gently pulled away. She tapped his chin with her finger and said, "Get back in there and finish the song."

Craig headed toward the door, turning back when

Brooke playfully swatted his butt. He started to speak, but she cut him off.

"They're waiting for you."

SHE HAD GONE OUTSIDE INTENDING to calm him. He was as frightened as a kitten when Mickey told him to take a break. She just wanted to make sure he didn't run away.

How many times had an agent kissed her client into performing his song?

And smacked his butt?

Holy crap, Brooke, what was that?

That was sexual harassment, you idiot. Unwanted touching. Had someone slapped her butt, Brooke would have turned on them like an angry mama bear.

It was so unlike her. And yet, she did it.

It must've been the kiss. Yeah, that was unwanted touching, too, and if she had it to do all over again, she would... What would she do?

Kiss him again, because that was a darn nice kiss. There was electricity in that kiss. Sparks flying, lightning striking. Wow! Who would have thought that the guy from Garland Grove could kiss like that?

He felt it, too. Not at first, but he'd gotten with the game pretty quick.

Yeah, she would probably do it all over again. It was her job to calm the talent and help them perform at the top of their game.

But the pat on the derriere? She would need to apologize for that.

Not only did Craig not run away, he returned and performed his song flawlessly on the first take. Even Mickey, who was never impressed, was impressed. While the others clustered into the control booth to listen to the playback, Brooke stepped aside to text Bobby and tell him the song was complete. And to figure out how to apologize to Craig for her actions.

She had missed a text from Raven.

Please drop off Carl at my house for dinner. 7:00 p.m. Thx!

Carl?

Please drop off *Carl?*

The message was clear. Dinner was for Craig only. Brooke was to drop him off.

Forget the fact that she had spent the day prepping him for his big recording. Forget that she had flown to Garland Grove to find him. Forget that she had made all the arrangements.

Forget that she had just kissed him.

And smacked his butt. Ack!

Raven's instructions were clear.

Drop. Off. Carl.

Brooke fumed while she waited for the session to conclude. It was after one, and they had missed lunch. She was hungry. And angry. They called that hangry. And the word fit. It would be another fifteen minutes before Craig stepped out of the studio. He was on top of the world.

"I don't know what to say except thank you," he said happily.

Brooke charged ahead. Best to get it out of the way. "Before we go any further, I need to apologize."

"For what?"

For what? Really?

"For... I should never have never gotten physical..."

Gotten physical? Geesh, you moron, you pinched his ass.

215

You didn't drop him with an uppercut to the chin. Say what you need to say.

"I mean...kissing you. And..."

Craig grinned and raised his hand to cut her off. "You helped me get past my fear."

"Yeah, there are other things I could've done to—"

Craig suddenly picked her up and spun her around. She felt incredibly light as she looked down into his eyes. "The recording is done!" he exclaimed. "Mickey said it was perfect!" When he set her down, Brooke thought she detected something else in the way he looked at her. A wondering? A hopefulness? Would they kiss again? When?

Or maybe not? Maybe she was only seeing what she wished was there. She had already screwed up enough for one day. Time to back away. *Put the brakes on, Brooke.*

"Some news," Brooke said casually as she led him from the studio. "Raven invited you to dinner."

"I'm game if you are," he replied.

"No...not me. Just you."

He appeared disappointed, and that made Brooke a little less hangry.

"It's really fine if you go," she said. "I have some work to do, anyway. I'll drop you off and come back for you later."

Craig gave this a few moments' thought. "Cool. What are we doing until then?"

"Let's grab a quick lunch. Then, how about if I show you how Nashville turns out for Christmas?"

"I would love it!"

CRAIG WAS ENTHRALLED as they strolled among the trees and decorations outside the Opryland Resort. Brooke pointed out some of her favorite displays while asking Craig questions about his childhood in a small Iowa town.

"It was a lot like Garland Grove," he said as they strolled side-by-side. "Smaller, but the same feel. I think that was what helped me decide to buy the drugstore." He paused at a concession stand to study the selections of coffee and hot chocolate. "Would you like something?"

"Yes, but I'll pay. Remember, you're our guest."

Craig smiled. "Please let me. Hot chocolate?"

"Yes. With marshmallows."

Brooke watched him wander off to join the concession queue. She found the way he took in his surroundings to be quite endearing. Christmas was special to him. Perhaps that came from living in a small town where the mad rush of Christmas shopping was softened by visiting with neighbors and friends along the way.

Nothing further had been said about the kiss. He must have sensed it wasn't a romantic gesture. He hadn't as much as tried to hold her hand, yet there was undeniably something there. She felt it in the way he gave her his undivided attention when she spoke. It was so different from Tristan's habit of listening with one ear or barely letting her finish before jumping in with some story he wanted to share. Tristan's stories dominated their conversations, particularly over the last few months. Brooke had assumed that it was just a guy thing, that men were incapable of listening fully and completely.

But perhaps her assumption was wrong. Maybe there were men out there who listened. Men like Craig, rather than guys like Tristan.

Tristan.

Tristan?

She spotted him coming around a decked-out evergreen.

He carried his guitar and wore a cheerful red sweater emblazoned with Christmas trees and a corporate logo. He rushed over.

"I can't believe I ran into you!" he exclaimed as he opened his arms. Brooke hugged him quickly, then stepped back. "What's this?" she asked, motioning to the sweater.

"I'm a Toy Maker!" he laughed. "Well, not really a toy maker, like one of Santa's elves, but I'm playing Christmas music with a group that's called the Toy Makers. I got the call yesterday. A couple of musicians bailed on them at the last minute. The gig lasts through the holidays."

"Congratulations, Tristan," Brooke said, daring a glance over his shoulder to where Craig was at the front of the hot chocolate line.

"Are you with someone?" Tristan asked.

"Yeah, he's getting hot chocolate."

She knew Tristan well enough to see her reply hurt him. The slight droop of his shoulders, the furrowing of his brow. He looked toward the concession stand just as Craig turned their way. Their eyes met, and the smile on Craig's face slipped away for the briefest of moments.

"Oh, sorry," Tristan said, backing away. "I didn't mean to... I just figured you were by yourself."

"Don't leave," Brooke said. "You'll want to meet Craig."

Tristan shook his head. "No, really. I need to get back to work."

"Nonsense." Brooke waved for Craig to join them. "Craig, this is Tristan Fleming." She turned to Tristan. "Say hello to Craig Callaway, better known as Christmas Carl."

"Oh, my goodness, Brooke!" Tristan exclaimed. "You found him!" He shoved his hand out, but Craig's were both holding hot chocolate.

"Good to meet you, Tristan," Craig said, smiling as he

handed Brooke a cup and extended his hand. "The Christmas Carl thing is still like a dream. I flew first-class to Nashville and got to record with a group of amazing musicians. And to think it's because of a song I had forgotten about."

"That's the way things happen here sometimes," Tristan replied. "Congratulations, man. I'm happy for you." He gave Craig a thumbs-up, then said, "And I need to get back to chasing my dream. Great meeting you, Craig." He looked at Brooke. "Good to see you, Brooke."

Brooke watched him disappear into the crowd. His eyes were clear. There was color in his cheeks that meant he had probably spent time outside over the weekend. She had considered asking him about it, but didn't want to give any false impressions. Still, he did look good.

"How long?" Craig asked from behind her. Brooke pulled her mind back to the moment.

"How long what?"

Craig came up beside her. He sipped his hot chocolate and said, "How long since you and Tristan split up?"

Brooke tightened the grip on her cup. "Am I that obvious?"

"You aren't," Craig replied. "But Tristan is. I'm not the most observant guy in the world, but there was something in the way he looked at you." He glanced away as he said, "I can imagine myself looking at Jenna that way if we ran into each other, but we've only been apart since last Thursday."

"I broke things off with Tristan last Wednesday."

"Goodness," Craig said. "We're both on the rebound. You're certainly handling it a lot better than me."

She smiled, though it hurt a little. "Don't be so sure. Tristan said some very unkind things, but it was me who broke it off. You got blindsided."

"True, but I still feel bad that I poured out my misery to you in Garland Grove. If I had known your breakup was so fresh, I would have kept quiet."

Okay, enough of that. The last thing Brooke wanted was for the conversation to digress into a rehash of broken hearts and hurt feelings. Especially amid the lights and pageantry of Christmas. She checked the time and said, "We should be getting out to Raven's. Are you excited to see her after all these years?"

BROOKE WAS DOING her best to move the conversation beyond break-ups and old loves. Her attempt was sudden and a bit clunky, but Craig appreciated her for it. It was apparent that she wasn't completely over Tristan any more than he was Jenna. He had mentioned the way Tristan looked at her but refrained from saying anything about the way she had gazed at him as he drifted away. Her eyes said things, too. Tristan certainly seemed like a good guy, but who knew what lurked beneath the surface?

Oh well, it wasn't Craig's inclination to dig into the matter. Not when she had already pushed the conversation ahead. And now she was asking if he was excited to see Raven.

"Well," he said as they moved toward an exit. "I'm not sure what to feel. She dumped me, too. That hurts as much as my breakup with Jenna."

The *oh crap* look on Brooke's face made him lose it. He laughed good and hard. His sudden change in countenance seemed to confuse her. "I'm kidding! I haven't thought about her in years."

Brooke punched his arm. "Maybe it's your terrible sense of humor that keeps chasing the girls away," she teased.

"Maybe," Craig laughed. "Seriously, though, yeah, I'm excited to see her. If only to find out if she remembers me."

"It's not a good sign that she thought your name was Carl."

"Ha, ha. Do you remember every guy you dated?"

"Not every guy, but every guy I was serious with."

"Name the first one," Craig challenged.

"First college crush or first crush?"

"Both."

"Chip Hollis was the first guy I got serious with in college, but it only lasted two weeks. He had a drinking problem."

"Oh, no. That's terrible. Any idea if he ever got treatment?"

"His problem wasn't addiction. It was keeping it down. He belched his Budweiser all over my favorite pair of shoes at casino night sophomore year."

When Craig laughed, Brooke paused and pointed her finger at him. "You obviously don't understand how important a girl's shoes are, Craig. It's no wonder you've never found the right girl." The grin on her face let him know she wasn't serious. He liked how she could poke fun. Somehow, she had sensed that he was okay with it. And he was.

"That was college. How about the first crush?"

Her grin softened into a smile. Her pretty green eyes focused on something in the distance. Probably a happy memory. They were stepping out into the parking lot. She pointed to their left, where she had parked, and said, "It was tenth grade. His name was Jared Langston, and he was incredibly sweet to me."

There was a dreamy quality to her voice that made

Craig feel good that it was Tristan and not Jared Langston they had just run into. He waited for her to share more.

"He was such a nice boy. Handsome and smart. I didn't think he knew I existed until he sat behind me in chemistry class."

"Why wouldn't he know you exist?" Craig asked as they approached her car. "I'm sure you were one of the prettiest girls in class."

Brooke pushed a button that unlocked the car. They were seated inside when she said, "No I wasn't. I was skinny and had a long neck. Kids in junior high called me Ostrich Neck." She started the car, then turned to Craig and shook her head. "Good luck getting past a nickname like Ostrich Neck."

Craig didn't laugh. He'd never had a nickname of any kind, good or bad, but remembered and hurt for Janice Busby, a classmate who had lost her left eye in a car accident. Kids could be merciless, and junior high kids were often the worst of the worst.

"Jared Langston started talking to me every day, and not the usual kidding around that high school kids engage in. He would ask how my day was and what I was doing over the weekend." She checked for traffic as they pulled onto the highway. "After a few weeks, he asked if I wanted to come to a party he was having. Five girls and five boys. I assumed there was no way that Dad would let me go, but I was wrong. He knew Jared's father a little and since his parents were chaperoning, and the party was only from seven until ten on a Friday night, he let me go."

Nightfall was descending, making it harder to see Brooke's facial expressions as she drove. "Was it a fun evening?" Craig asked.

"Really fun," she said softly. "It was the first time a boy kissed me."

"Wow. Even with his parents there?"

"Jared went to the kitchen to get snacks. He asked me to go along. His parents were in the next room watching that TV show, Cops."

Craig sang the hook from the show's theme song. "Whatcha gonna do?" Brooke laughed.

"That's how I knew what they were watching. Anyway, they were engrossed in their show, so Jared and I talked while we got out the snacks. We were pouring drinks. Soda, juice, that kind of stuff, when he asked me if I wanted to go out with him."

"Go out? Like on a real date?"

"Not like that at all. Our school was out in the boondocks and pretty small. Going out meant you were a couple."

"So going steady?"

"Yeah. And when I said yes, he put down the bottle of Dr. Pepper and came over and kissed me. It was heavenly." She giggled. "And then he kissed me again, and that was when I heard the Cops theme song, which meant the show was over. We heard his mother's chair squeak, and by the time she came into the kitchen we were pouring Dr. Pepper again."

"She never figured out a thing, huh?"

"Oh, yes. She had it all figured out. I guess it was the look on my face. I would have been a terrible poker player back then. My neck and cheeks would turn beet red." Brooke paused. "And when you have a neck like an ostrich, that's a lot of red."

The way she related the story made Craig laugh out

loud. Brooke was the rare person who could laugh at herself. But still, he had to know the rest of the story.

"So...did you and Jared start going out?"

"We sure did. Eleven months."

"That's a long time for high school. Now, if you don't mind me asking, what caused the breakup?"

Brooke sighed deeply. She took a second deep breath, then, barely above a whisper, said, "There was a shooting...a hunting accident."

Oh my God. No. Craig felt his muscles become weak. Why did he ask? Why did he have to know?

And then Brooke started giggling. Just a little at first, then louder. The giggle became a laugh. Craig was still trying to sort out the feelings of tragedy and loss when she said, "I'm pulling your leg. Jared didn't die. He started dating Sarah Bristow. They got married after college and still live here in Nashville."

"You!" Craig took a deep breath of his own, which made Brooke laugh harder. "Just pull over right now," he sputtered. "I'll walk from here."

"No, you won't," she replied, gasping to get her laughter under control. "You've got a date with the current queen of country music."

"And what about you?" Craig asked. "Are you performing at a comedy club or something? Because you think you're pretty funny."

His response made her laugh harder. Her entire body was shaking. "Please...don't make me laugh...I'll...pee my pants..."

It was too much. Craig lost it, too. They drove for a few moments without speaking. Without being able to speak. Laughing like kids. And having a wonderful time.

Time that was about to be cut short by his visit with Raven McCloud.

"What can I expect?" He could finally say. Brooke glanced at him and smiled.

"About Raven?"

"Um-hmm."

"She's...her home is beautiful. She'll welcome you with open arms."

Brooke's tone, unlike her smile, was guarded. What was she not telling him?

"Does she act like a big-time star? Or will we just chat like two old friends?"

She was definitely holding back. Perhaps she didn't want to color his impression. Maybe Raven was difficult to deal with. One thing was for certain—there was no way he would enjoy Raven's company as much as he was enjoying Brooke's.

"Raven will visit with you like two old friends," she finally said. "For what it's worth, I think she can be a driving force behind your success in music."

"You're saying I should suck up to her?"

"Quite the contrary. Raven would see right through that. Just be yourself, like you've been with me."

They passed through a neighborhood of large stately homes that became larger and statelier the further they went. Then the houses disappeared behind large gates and hedges. A few turns later, they came to the end of a small road. Brooke pulled to a gate and waited for it to open.

"And here we are."

She drove slowly through the gate and up the drive. Too slowly. Like *a person can walk faster than this* slow.

"Is there someone standing next to that tree over there?" Craig was pointing into the darkness a few yards off the driveway.

"That's Khalid. He's one of the night security guys."

"Wow, even with that fence and gate? Raven still needs security people?"

"Yep. It's pretty remote out here."

They rode in silence at a speed approaching four miles per hour. After a couple turns, Craig asked, "What's wrong?"

"Nothing's wrong." Brooke tried to sound casual but didn't think she succeeded.

"Ten minutes ago, you were cracking jokes about your dead boyfriend. And now, you're...different."

Brooke's mind raced. What should she say to that?

It's because I'm about to drop you off at the home of the most successful and beautiful recording star in America.

And single. Did I mention single?

And did I mention how I'm supposed to go someplace and wait?

While you and Raven McCloud renew your friendship.

And whatever else you had back then.

And did I mention she's drop-dead gorgeous?

And single? Don't forget single.

Just you and her.

And not me.

And even though she's seeing Travis Horton, who is pretty drop-dead gorgeous himself, she will probably think you're pretty cute.

And since you already have a history, who's to say she doesn't try something? Just for old time's sake?

Did I mention that I'm kind of jealous? And hurt at being excluded?

That's what's wrong, Craig.

But those are things I'll keep to myself.

"I'm sorry. I was just thinking of some things I need to get done this evening."

I actually have nothing to get done this evening. I'll probably sit in a parking lot and stare at my phone until Raven calls for me to come get you because it's too far to run all the way to Percy's Crossroads and back.

"That's too bad," Craig said. "I wish you could stay."

Brooke pulled onto the circle that led to Raven's front door. Every light in the house was on. The Christmas tree glowed brightly through the large double doors. And while Brooke couldn't see it, she knew the fireplace was fully stoked in the living room. That's where Raven would take him first, the living room.

And after that?

Craig turned to her as they came to a stop. "Are you sure you're okay, Brooke? You're gripping the wheel like it's going to fly out of your hands."

"Really, I'm fine. It's just that—"

There would be no time to finish as Raven opened the door and swept down the steps like one of those actresses making her grand entrance in an old Hollywood classic. She pulled open the passenger door. Craig's eyes grew wide with wonder. Brooke saw his hands shaking.

"Craig Callaway! Is it really you after all these years?"

Craig nearly tripped getting to his feet. "Hey, Megan— Raven. It's great to see you!"

Raven pulled him into a straight-on head-to-knee hug that probably wiped out any memory of Brooke's silly little kiss back at the studio. She grabbed his hand and pulled him toward the house, pausing only after they were back on the landing.

"Brooke, honey, thanks for bringing Craig out."

"You're welcome, Raven." Brooke tried her damndest to sound unaffected.

"I'll text you when you can come back," she said. Then, to Craig, "Let's get inside and start catching up. I have a special bottle of wine just for the occasion. You like wine, don't you Craig?"

"I sure do!"

That was all Brooke heard before the door closed. Craig never looked back. Raven did, though. Once they were inside, and the door was closed, she glanced over her shoulder and winked at Brooke.

Yep, she winked.

RAVEN TOOK his hand and led him into an oversized living room that was the whitest white he had ever seen. Blindingly white.

"I'll give you a tour, but first let's open the wine." She named a vintage and waited for his reaction. Craig didn't have the heart to tell her he didn't know the good stuff from the crap they sold at the Superstar Food Market in Garland Grove.

"That sounds perfect," he exclaimed. "And a lot better than the junk we drank in college."

"Oh yeah," Raven said absently as she retrieved the bottle from a wine cooler in a corner of the living room. "I guess we drank some bad stuff back then."

Craig offered to uncork the bottle, but Raven did it herself, tittering when a bit of the bubbly ran down her hand. She poured two glasses and handed him one. He assumed they would sit on the large living room sofa, but she had other plans.

"Let's go in the kitchen. I love entertaining in the kitchen. The best friends are kitchen friends, don't you think, Craig?"

Craig followed her, admiring the view and trying to reconcile the Raven of today with the Megan he'd known twenty years before. Her choice of clothing was better. Megan Stackhouse preferred shorts and sweatshirts, a combination Craig used to think of as rather strange. Raven's jeans fit to perfection, and even an idiot small-town pharmacist could see that her sapphire blue sweater was the perfect complement to her jet-black hair and sky-blue eyes. She was stunningly attractive, probably the most beautiful woman he had ever seen. Everything perfect. Not a hair out of place.

They entered a huge kitchen with a refrigerator that would have held three of Craig's old Frigidaire. The appliances were brands Craig had never heard of. She pulled out a stool at an oversized kitchen island and motioned for him to do the same. When they were seated, she held up her wine glass.

"To old friends and new adventures," she said, her eyes locking on his as they toasted and sipped. Then, setting aside her glass, Raven leaned in closer. Proximity only made her more lovely. She smiled sweetly, and said, "Can I ask you a question?"

Oh, God, yes. Anything. Any. Thing.

"Of course."

"It's something I've been wondering ever since Brooke said she found you."

Craig held her gaze. It was hard, but she was good at it. Her eyes seemed to see right into him. "Ask away, Raven."

She nodded. "Back in college?"

"Yes?"

She picked up her glass and took another sip, then asked, "Did we do it?"

NASHVILLE WAS home to some of the country's best restaurants.

Southern cuisine. Hot chicken. Meat-and-three.

Some pretty good Memphis barbeque also found its way to Music City. Some outstanding pizza, too.

But sometimes a girl just needed comfort food. Something to stick to her ribs and remind her she was okay.

And for Brooke, that was Waffle House.

There was one just a few miles from Raven's home. Brooke pulled into a sparsely filled parking lot and stepped inside.

"Sit where you want, hon," a skinny server called out. Only a few tables were occupied, but Brooke sat at the counter. She enjoyed watching them prepare the food; the codes they used, and especially the secret way of arranging things on plates to help cooks remember who ordered what. She chose a seat with an opening on one side and a guy in a Santa suit on the other. Santa gave her a sideways glance, smiled, then returned to his pork chop and eggs.

"What can I get you?" Lucille was the name on her badge. If there was ever a perfect name for a hash-slinging server, it was Lucille.

"I'll have a patty melt and an order of hash browns, scattered, smothered, and covered."

"Large or small?"

Brooke's stomach growled. "Large, please."

"Sure you don't want those peppered, too?"

Brooke considered the option. She certainly liked jalapenos. But would she be able to eat it all?

She didn't even know how long she would be there. Might be a few minutes. Might be hours.

"Yes, please. Peppered, too."

Lucille smiled. "And what to drink?"

"Diet soda."

Santa looked at her and laughed.

"What?" Brooke asked.

"You ordered about ten thousand calories of food with a diet soda."

What business was it of Santa's?

"Habit, I guess," Brooke said, forcing a smile. "I always drink diet soda."

Lucille brought the soda while Brooke perused her email. After a few minutes, something caused her radar to go up. She glanced up and found Santa looking at her. He winked.

Like Raven had winked.

What was with all the winking?

"You're not a regular?" Santa said, turning in his seat and placing his chubby Santa elbow on the counter.

"Nope," Brooke replied, trying to make it clear that she didn't want to chat.

"I live just up the pike a few miles," Santa said.

Brooke didn't look up from her phone. "Oh. I thought you lived at the North Pole."

Santa snorted and blew a bit of egg onto the sleeve of Brooke's coat.

"This is just a part-time gig. I'm a singer."

Isn't everybody? Brooke thought.

"That's nice."

Santa rattled off the names of several bars where he had performed over the years. "Still hoping one of the local talent agents will pick me up. There's one old boy, Summers is his name, who came and saw me play a year or two ago, but I never heard from him again. That's kinda rude, don't you think?"

If he only knew how many acts Bobby had checked out over the years. "Maybe he got busy."

Or maybe you just weren't very good.

"I tore it up that night. I really expected something to break for me." Santa paused and pulled down his beard. He was in his thirties and forty pounds overweight. That worked well for Santa but made it difficult to get a foothold in a business that held looks in such high regard.

"Maybe you would want to come hear me play some-time," he said. "Maybe get dinner before. Might be fun, you know?"

Brooke glanced around. Lucille was watching from the other end of the counter. When Brooke met her gaze, Lucille gave her a *sorry, honey* look.

"Oh, Santa, I would love to, but...I'm moving. Next weekend. All the way to...Montana. Ever been to Montana?"

That did the trick. Santa hadn't been to Montana, and his interest in Brooke ended about the same time as his eggs did. He wished her well, paid his bill, and wandered off into the night.

"Not too often a girl gets hit on by Santa Claus," Lucille said as she plopped down two plates of food in front of Brooke. "Made me think of that song they're playing on the radio. You know the one, hon? That song where the woman gets it on with Santa?"

"Making Santa Smile?" Brooke said. "Yeah, I've heard it."

Brooke ate slowly as customers came and went. The level of intoxication ratcheted up after nine, but at least no one else hit on her. Lucille came by several times to refill her soda and make sure she was okay. While they dealt with all kinds of people, it was probably rare for servers at Waffle House to have someone stretch out their hash browns for two hours. Even Brooke was starting to feel uncomfortable. She scraped up the last of the potatoes, left a generous tip for dear Lucille, and returned to her car. She was putting on her seatbelt when she received a text from Raven.

Craig is spending the night. I'll text you tomorrow. R.

TUESDAY, DECEMBER 6

NASHVILLE

*B*rooke awakened to the rumble of Bobby's truck behind the house. It was pitch dark outside. She hadn't slept well to begin with, but her sweet Daddy didn't know that. It wasn't his fault that she was miffed at the world because of the way Raven had left her hanging the night before. It wasn't Bobby's fault that Craig had spent the night at Raven's place.

Doing who knew what. Sleeping who knew where.

Nope, she couldn't lay any of it on Bobby. Nor did she want to burden him with her hurt feelings. It wouldn't matter anyway, because when Bobby was heading out before daylight in that old truck, it meant he was going duck hunting.

There was no need to roll over and try to get back to sleep. She picked up her phone and checked for messages from Craig. She had texted him after getting back to Percy's Crossroads a little after eleven. *I hope you're enjoying the evening with Raven. I'll catch up with you tomorrow.*

No reply.

Brooke got up and showered. There was always work to

do at the office. And she could make sure Craig's recording from the day before had gotten to the right people. With any luck, it would be available on the big music sites by evening. She had no idea when she was expected to meet up with Raven and Craig, and frankly, it felt like Raven relished keeping her in the dark. They had a rehearsal set up for noon with Raven's backing band. If she heard nothing else, she would just show up there.

Breakfast was coffee and half a grapefruit. Her stomach was still agitating from the previous evening's hash browns. Or maybe from being treated so shoddily. Bobby preached family to their clients. When a performer signed with Summers Management, they could expect the same loyalty and dedication they received from their own kin. Raven was acting like the spoiled big sister.

There was no traffic at the early hour, and the drive to the office was cut in half. Brooke was letting herself in the back door when her phone chirped with a text.

Sorry I missed your message. It was a wonderful evening. Raven is amazing. Not sure what the plans are, but if I find out I'll let you know. Craig.

Brooke turned on her desktop computer and checked the entertainment dailies for any mention of their clients. It had been a quiet night, and there was nary a whisper of Christmas Carl's arrival in Nashville. That would change the following morning at a press conference scheduled for a nearby hotel ballroom. Their usual venue, Wainwright's Chop House, was booked, and while the owners would have made it work, Brooke didn't want to put them out. She considered how things might go when the public got their first official look at Craig. He didn't have that traditional country presence about him. No hat. No boots. His attire consisted of khaki pants matched with sweaters or button-down oxfords. With his glasses and combed and parted hair-cut, he looked every inch the small-town pharmacist. That was okay with Brooke. She felt they could sell that image. Position Christmas Carl as the shy newcomer to the music scene. The little guy who made good. Fans loved an under-dog, especially when he looked like one of them.

By seven-thirty, Brooke's email was cleaned out, three contracts were in the mail, and Craig's recording was on its way to cyber-heaven where the experts would make it available to the world. The marketing firm they used for special projects was in the loop and would have a full-on campaign ready to roll out later that afternoon. Everything would culminate with the next morning's big announcement. It was a glorious plan, and Brooke was proud she had put it together so quickly. She heard a noise downstairs and figured it was Raquel showing up for work. She got up to go say hi, but her cellphone rang.

Raven.

Brooke put on a cheerful face and gave herself a pep talk, then answered.

"Good morning, Raven."

"Hey sweetie, are you on your way?"

"I didn't know I was supposed to be."

She heard Raven's heavy sigh. Then a few moments of silence. "Brooke, I told you I had a doctor's appointment this morning. Didn't you write it down?"

Oh, snap.

"I'm sorry, Raven. I have it on my calendar, but I didn't think about how it would affect Craig."

Because you changed everything around last night without notice.

"Well, I can't just leave him sitting around here twid-dling his thumbs, Brooke. That would be inhospitable.

Someone needs to come get him. I just assumed that you would be here."

You have no problem with me twiddling my thumbs for three hours.

"I'll be there in twenty minutes."

"Make sure you are, honey. If Milo doesn't leave by then I'll never make it on time."

Brooke apologized again, but Raven was already gone. Two minutes later she was gone too. She made the drive in fifteen minutes, weaving through Franklin Pike traffic like Dale Earnhardt Jr. and gunning through more yellow lights than she could count. She checked herself in the mirror on the car's visor as she pulled to a stop out front. It was in the mid-fifties, and Craig was waiting on the porch.

"Good morning," he called out as he came down to the car. He got in and said, "Raven is getting ready for a doctor's appointment. I guess you're stuck with me this morning."

He was wearing the same clothes as the day before. They appeared pressed and clean. When he noticed her checking him out, he said, "Raven washed my clothes."

Oh, really?

And what did you wear while they were agitating, big guy?

"That was very nice of her," Brooke said as they headed down the driveway. She tried her darndest to be chipper but was growing frustrated with how things were playing out. Of course, none of that was Craig's fault. He seemed on top of the world. Practically glowing. Being close to someone so famous could do that. Until you got to know them better and realized that even the biggest stars had their own faults and peculiarities.

"Are you hungry?" she asked as she headed toward the city.

"I had a huge breakfast. Raven makes the best blueberry waffles I've ever tasted."

Craig went on and on about how good breakfast was. Then, after Brooke asked about his evening, he took off on that.

"I learned she didn't really break up with me as much as she fell in love with Nashville." Brooke didn't let on that she already knew that, and that she had kidded Raven about ghosting him. "She's not the same Megan at all, but after a few hours, I started to see things about her that I remembered from college."

"Like what?"

"Like how she runs her hand through her hair. She doesn't know she does it, but I remembered. She couldn't believe that I remembered that."

Especially since she couldn't even remember your name.

"Missouri State didn't even realize she went there until you inquired."

Hmm. Did she tell you how she scolded me for that?

"And now she's thinking about doing a concert there next summer. And she asked if I would want to go as her special guest. Can you imagine that, Brooke? Me appearing with Raven McCloud. It's nuts. I can't wait to tell Sam Griffin. He thinks Raven pretty much walks on water."

"Don't get too excited," Brooke said, feeling the need to assert her role as manager. "Raven can say she wants to do something, but there are a lot of hoops that need to be cleared to make it all happen. That's where Bobby and I come in."

"Raven thinks the world of you guys," Craig exclaimed. "She thinks of Bobby as a second father."

And me as the wicked stepsister, Brooke mused. "We

have a couple hours to burn before your rehearsal. Is there anything you want to see?"

"Well, there is one thing, but I know you're busy, so I can do it another time."

"I'll make time, Craig. What is it?"

"The Ryman Auditorium. I would love to see the birthplace of the Grand Old Opry."

Brooke smiled at his enthusiasm, but there was one problem. "I'm not sure I can get us in so early in the day."

Craig pulled out his phone and glanced at a text message. "No problem with that. When I told Raven I would like to see it she made a call." He held up a screen with a name and phone number. "She spoke to this man and he said to just ask for him."

THE MAN RAVEN knew was as good as his word. He said a quick hello to Brooke, then gave them the run of the place. While country music had never been his thing, Craig was thrilled to stand at center stage and look out over the rows of wooden pews, trying to imagine how it would feel to perform before a packed house. He also contemplated the many stars who had stood in that same spot. And when Brooke encouraged him to sing a few lines of his song, he didn't need any prodding. His audience would consist of her and a maintenance worker changing lightbulbs near the back of the theater. Craig took his mark and looked up into the beautiful stained glass windows at the rear of the hall while he tried to imagine a full band warming up behind him. He took a deep breath and started singing, and was instantly amazed at how his voice reverberated from the walls, and how rich his tone sounded compared to the old

Vogue Opera House where they performed the Christmas concert in Garland Grove. It was dreamy and surreal, and Craig did not know if anything in life could top the experience. He reached the end of the song and bowed when Brooke applauded from a seat in the second row.

"Bravo!" she shouted. She was smiling, but something seemed different about her. She wasn't the cheerful, witty Brooke from the day before. Work issues, perhaps? The evening before, she had mentioned having a lot to do. That was probably it. She was a major force in the music business. That undoubtedly came with a lot of demands on her time. She met him as he stepped off the stage.

"Now that your voice is all warmed up, let's get to the studio."

Brooke was friendly on the drive across downtown Nashville, but there was still something off. Finally, after a few moments of awkward silence, Craig asked her about it.

"Did I do something to offend you? Because I'm getting different vibes than yesterday."

"Of course not," she said with a bit more force than Craig expected. "Bobby and I are so glad you're here. And how you've hit it off with Raven...that will make things even better." She paused while waiting for a light to change. "We need to start looking ahead. There's a press conference scheduled for the morning where we'll have your coming out party. By the time you leave for Garland Grove tomorrow afternoon, you'll no longer be the mystery man who recorded 'Making Santa Smile.'"

Craig laughed. "Yep, I'll be Christmas Carl, which still isn't exactly me, but it'll be good enough. Can I ask you something else, Brooke?"

"Uh...certainly."

"If you ever see me screwing up, will you tell me?"

WHEN BROOKE GLANCED over and saw the look on his face, she realized she was worried about nothing. Raven wasn't going to change Craig Callaway. Sure, he was star-struck but was still the same charming, down-to-earth man she had met for breakfast at the Park-Rite Diner.

Just give it some time, Brooke.

Raven will not mess him up.

"I promise I'll tell you if you screw up."

He reached out his hand. "Shake on it?"

She laughed as they shook. His hand was soft, but his shake was firm. His was the hand of someone who worked with his brain, and who was comfortable enough in his own skin to not be pulled into a lifestyle that went against his beliefs.

"Thank you for finding me," he said sweetly. And Brooke knew he meant it. The rest of the ride was better. She pointed out landmarks while he oohed and aahed. They arrived at the studio a few minutes before noon. That was when he became nervous.

"You'll be fine," she said as they pulled into a parking spot. "Just like yesterday."

"Yesterday, after you kissed me," Craig said. "Is that part of your treatment strategy for nervous clients?"

"Not until yesterday." She turned away to conceal her embarrassment. Was he thinking of that kiss like she was? Was he thinking of how she'd patted his backside? *Oh, please don't be thinking about that. I don't want to wind up making the news for sexual harassment.*

"If I get the jitters again, can I count on you?" he asked as they crawled out of the car.

"Yep, but you won't. Shall we get inside?"

❄

CRAIG EXPECTED to see the same faces from the previous day's recording session, but other than Mickey Cox, they were different.

"This is Raven's touring band," Mickey explained as he escorted Craig into the rehearsal area, a converted warehouse with lots of sound equipment. "Most of them have been together for a couple years now, and with the Christmas tour in full swing, today's session is mainly to run through some new stuff. And Raven wanted me to see how y'all sound together, too."

"Is she thinking she wants me to do a show or something?"

Mickey shrugged. "You'd have to ask her that. More than anything, we need to know if you can carry your weight in a live performance. Now let me introduce you to everyone."

The band was comprised of six musicians. Chester, an older man with a gray beard that extended to his chest, had played slide guitar with some of the biggest hard rock bands of the early seventies. The drummer, Lindsey, spent two years touring with a chart-topping punk band. The others shared backgrounds in country. One, a bassist named Denise, was making her professional debut on the Christmas tour. She appeared as nervous as Craig felt. Mickey had Craig take a seat while they ran through the song set for the concert. The music from up close was louder than he had expected. On a couple songs the keyboardist, a cheerful guy named Steve, sang Raven's lyrics. When Brooke pulled up a stool next to him, Craig asked, "Why isn't Raven here?"

"She's at the soundchecks before each concert, but

Mickey wants to make sure his people are one-hundred percent ready."

"Do they also record her songs?"

"Some of them. Mostly we go with studio musicians. As you've probably started to pick up, Raven McCloud is a brand all to herself." She pointed to bearded Chester. "A few hardcore fans know Chester Beeks, and he attracts a pretty good crowd when he does his show at some of the local clubs, but it's not important that the faces behind Raven change from time to time."

"As long as the face singing the songs is the same?" Craig asked.

"You got it. Are you ready to jump in and give it a whirl?"

He took a deep breath. "I guess so. I keep telling myself it's the same as the Garland Grove community choir, except louder."

Brooke laughed and, as Mickey closed out an old carol about angels on high, she said, "You're about to find out. Try to enjoy the moment. It's what thousands of people dream of."

Several band members stepped away to check their phones or use the restroom. Mickey and Steve the keyboardist remained. Mickey motioned Craig over. Steve was playing the opening notes from "Making Santa Smile." "The song is pretty simple," Mickey said. "Craig, you and Steve run through it a couple times, then we'll bring back the others."

Steve riffed through the song, double-checked the sheet music, then said, "Ready for a trial run?"

Craig said he was. And they did. It sounded perfect.

"Okay," Steve said. "Let's do it again. Make sure you hit your marks this time."

Craig thought he had hit all the marks. His stomach fluttered. The next time through sounded better, though. And the third was even better. By the time the band returned during their fifth run-through, Craig felt he and Steve were on the same page. The others, except Chester and a guitarist who weren't needed on the song, took their positions.

"Craig, front and center," Mickey said, motioning to a spot in front of the band. "Now pretend there are seventy-five-hundred people seated in front of you."

"And try not to crap your pants," Chester called out from the side.

"Like Denise did opening night," the drummer shouted from his perch in back. Denise, proving she was already part of the band despite her recent arrival, flipped the drummer the bird.

The familiar tune came at Craig like a wall of sound, pouring from speakers in front and to his sides. And just as he had in the recording studio, he missed his mark. The band didn't stop, but they did circle around and pick it up from the beginning. Very impressive. Craig hit his mark the second time and, other than blowing a line in the second verse, he nailed it. They reached the end and when he turned around, he could tell that the band was impressed.

"Not bad, rookie," the drummer called out.

"Do you think you can find him a gig, Brooke?" Chester called out from the sideline. "Maybe a YMCA or a junior high sock hop?"

The band ribbed Chester about his archaic references. Keyboardist Steve came over and said, "You did well, Craig. Now let's see how you do the second time around."

❄

CRAIG'S IMPROVEMENT was immediately noticeable, and as she watched from the side, Brooke considered where she might find opportunities for him to perform live. Nashville venues were a given, but if the song was going to continue to attract a national following, she needed more. There were several cable networks that were possibilities. Again, she thought Craig's everyman appearance would appeal to a wide audience, particularly those from flyover country who would view him as one of their own. The possibilities were whirling in her mind when she felt a tap on her shoulder.

Raven.

"How's he doing?" she asked.

"He's doing well, but listen for yourself," Brooke replied. Craig was wrapping up what was supposed to be his final run-through, but when Mickey spotted Raven, he called for one more. Raven listened intently until the last verse. Then, turning to Brooke, said, "You're right. He's very good. Do you think he can chat up an audience?"

Brooke shrugged. "He only has one song now, so how much chatter would he need?"

"Good point," Raven laughed. "By the way, I hope you don't mind, but I would like to borrow Craig for the afternoon."

What? Borrow?

"Well...sure, Raven. Should I plan on meeting you someplace later?"

"No, sweetie, I'll have Milo bring him back to your house." She sighed. "I promise not to keep him all night this time."

What the hell was with that dreamy sigh?

Had something happened or was Raven just being catty? Could she tell that Brooke had feelings for him? Please, not that.

"It's good for you guys to spend time together, with Craig headed home tomorrow and all. And I have so much stuff to get done. Are you sure you don't mind having Milo bring him back?"

"Of course not, Brooke honey. We'll have a grand old time, and I'll have him back to you in time for supper. Give Bobby my love."

Raven floated into the midst of the band as they finished Craig's song. She whispered something to Steve that made him frown, hugged Mickey, and intertwined her arm with Craig's.

"You're spending the day with me, sugar. I just cleared it with Warden Summers over there."

Warden Summers?

Why that...

"Enjoy your day," Brooke said with a forced grin. "The warden will see you this evening."

And just like that, they were gone. Raven spirited Craig from the building like Elvis at the end of a concert. The band dispersed as well. Brooke was gathering her things when Steve stopped by and whispered, "She sure can get under a person's skin sometimes, can't she?"

Brooke watched as the others headed for the door. She had known Steve for years. He was the consummate professional. "What did she say to you?" she asked.

"That I needed to get my shit together if I want to be on the next tour. That I lagged behind on a couple songs in Cincinnati. She said it sounded like I was getting lazy, and she knew plenty of keyboardists who would kill to step into my spot."

Brooke gasped. "Steve, I'm sorry. I didn't notice a thing. And Mickey never said a word."

Steve waved her off. "I've had my ass handed to me by

some of the best, Brooke. But you know what the damndest thing is?"

Brooke shook her head, not sure she wanted to know.

"The entire time she was dressing me down, she never stopped smiling. It was like she was asking about the wife and kids."

"WE NEED to work on your look," Raven said as they hurried to the limo. Milo had the door open and ready. "Mr. Callaway," he said amiably.

"Call me Craig."

"Certainly. Where to, Miss McCloud?"

"Downtown. I'll let you know when I figure it out." Then, to Craig. "Do you own a nice pair of boots?"

"Of course. You can't live in Garland Grove and not have boots. We can get two feet of snow sometimes."

Raven laughed. "Not snow boots. Cowboy boots."

Craig didn't. "I've never really been into cowboy boots. I have a wide foot, and they always seem to pinch."

"Not the ones we'll get." Then, to Milo, "Jim Campbell Custom Leathers, please. Do you know the address?"

"Yes, ma'am."

Raven turned to Craig. "If Jim doesn't have what we need, he'll make them by hand. You'll love him. Now, how about contact lenses?"

"I've never worn them. I've always been a glasses guy."

"Not anymore." She grabbed her phone and made a call to someone named Quincy. Moments later, Craig had an appointment with a local optometrist.

"Now let's talk about your clothes."

"Seriously, Raven, this isn't me. I prefer—"

"It's not about what you prefer, boo. It's about what your audience expects." She paused and looked him over from head to toe. "You're cute enough. I knew that back in college. We just have to country you up a little. Trust me, sweetie. Raven will have you looking like a country stud before suppertime."

CRAIG HAD HEARD of none of the stores they stopped at. More upholstered chairs and plants than merchandise. Sedate lighting. Even the air smelled rich. Employees who outnumbered customers three to one eyed Craig's khakis and green sweater skeptically but did an about-face when they recognized who he was with. Even in Nashville's most exclusive stores, amongst the wealthiest of the wealthy, Raven McCloud stood out.

First were boots. Jim Campbell Custom Leathers had the perfect pair. Blue jeans were next. Not the brands they sold at Werner's Western Wear in Garland Grove. "They might be pricey, but they'll last for years," Raven explained as they entered a place with minimal décor and an owner who offered bourbon as they browsed. An employee took Craig's measurements, asked questions about his preferred fit, and led them to a small room where three selections were set out.

"Try those on," Raven said after choosing two pairs. Craig carried them to a small dressing area behind a sheer curtain. He stumbled as he pulled the jeans over his leg and fell against the wall before catching himself.

"Mr. Callaway?" The employee called out. Raven pulled back the curtain and exclaimed, "Are you okay, sweetie?" He was, other than the embarrassment of her seeing him stumbling about in his tidy whities with one leg stuck in a pair of three-hundred dollar jeans. Raven ogled him for a few moments, recommended he use the chair, and stepped back out. Four pairs of jeans and two shirts later, they exited the store.

"You didn't have to buy these," Craig said to Raven. "I'll pay you back as soon as I can."

"What's the point of having money if you can't spend it on friends, sugar? And they look really nice on you. You have a great butt, by the way."

Craig snorted. "Thanks. People in Garland Grove are going to wonder what's come over me when they see me filling their prescriptions in designer blue jeans."

"They won't wonder at all. By the time you get back home, the world's gonna know all about you. Those local girls will expect you to dress like a star. Now, let's go see my friend, Dr. Hadley."

Milo was parked by a fire hydrant two doors up. Craig was surprised by how little attention locals paid to Raven as she passed. Sure, they looked. A couple gawked. But no one approached to ask for an autograph.

"Are you always able to move about like this?" he asked.

She shrugged. "It depends on where we are. The more tourists there are, the harder it is to get around. I can't do the fast-food joints or run into Walmart, and I haven't been to a movie in forever."

Craig felt a twinge of sympathy for her as he remembered them going to several dollar shows at a Springfield cineplex back in the day. "Is it hard?"

"Is what hard, sweetie?"

"Being isolated? Not being able to go where you want when you want?"

She paused a few feet from the car and appeared to give

Craig's questions some thought. Someone called out her name and she waved. Craig put himself between Raven and the man who had spoken to protect her in case he came too close, but he was already on his way across the street.

"I guess it's hard sometimes," she finally said. "But you have to look at both sides of it. I mean, yeah, I have to plan out my movements, but I've made out pretty well in a ruthless business that can cut you down while you're not looking."

"Do you ever worry about that? About falling from the top?"

"Sweetie, there's no need to worry about that. It's going to happen someday. Nobody gets to the top and stays there." She stepped past Milo and into the backseat of the dark sedan. "There's an expression I learned from Brooke's daddy. A rooster one day, and a feather duster the next." She ran her hand through her hair, told Milo where to go next, and said, "I just hope I can avoid being a feather duster for a few more years."

They were pulling from the curb when Raven exclaimed, "Hold it a minute, Milo. There's Millie Spacey!" She lowered her window and called out to an attractive, middle-aged redhead coming out of an office building. "Hey, Millie!"

Millie smiled when she spotted her. "Well, I declare! What are you doing in this part of town, Raven? Aren't you on tour?"

"We head out again tomorrow afternoon. Hey Millie, crawl in here with me. I have somebody I want you to meet." Raven turned to Craig and said, "Slide over and sit between Millie and me."

Craig did as he was told. Millie came around the car just as Milo was opening the door. She slid in and smoothed her dress. She smelled like flowers. She smiled at Craig. "Well, who do we have here, Raven, dear?"

"You won't believe it when I tell you, Millie. You just might have the biggest story in all of Nashville sitting with his leg against yours."

Craig blushed and shifted his leg a few inches away. Millie took another look at him. Something clicked. "Don't tell me this is Christmas Carl!"

Raven grinned. "Yep," she nodded. "In the flesh. His real name is Craig, but we'll stick with Christmas Carl for now."

"Oh, my heavens," Millie exclaimed. "You found him!"

"I sure enough did. And it wasn't easy. Of course, you news people know how hard it is sometimes. Kinda like a needle in a haystack. But in this case, the needle was in a little town called Garden Grove."

"It's actually Garland Grove," Craig said. "Good to meet you, Millie."

"The pleasure is all mine. Will you come down and be on with us at six tonight?"

"Oh, no, I really shouldn't. I think we have a press conference set for tomorrow, but thanks for the—"

"Of course, we'll come by, Millie." Raven grabbed Craig's hand. "Millie's evening news is first in the market, and she's been real good to me over the years."

Millie clapped her hands. "I'll get it all set up." She hugged Craig and reached across and took Raven's hand. "Thanks so much. We'll make a big to-do out of this."

Millie dashed out of the car. Craig felt as if things were moving a lot quicker. "Shouldn't we clear this with Brooke first, Raven? She had a press conference set up for the morning, and I feel like we should—"

"Brooke and Bobby work for me, sugar. And they do a

marvelous job, but in this case, I'm afraid if we wait another day the word will get out and ruin everything." She took his hand in hers. "Trust me on this. I'll make sure you're treated the way you deserve. First chance I get I'll call Brooke and let her know about the change in plans." She paused, then said, "And little ol' Raven might have a surprise of her own."

Craig slid back to his side of the car as Raven gave Milo their itinerary. "If we're going to be at that studio by six, we've got a lot to do. There's contact lenses and a haircut. And we can't forget a good-looking hat too, can we, darlin'?"

"Is anybody going to recognize me by the time you're done?" He wanted to sound as if he was teasing, but something about the transformation felt slightly off. Was he Craig Callaway? Or someone he didn't know? A stranger in his own body?

A stranger by the name of Christmas Carl?

Brooke was reading a novel in the living room when she heard Bobby pull up in his truck. She had been home for a couple hours and was anticipating Craig's return so she could begin prepping him for the next day's presser. Bobby came in the back door and called her name.

"I'm in here."

She heard his footfalls as he passed through the kitchen. He usually removed his boots out back but hadn't this time. He stepped in, still in his hunting gear.

"You spent a long day out there." As she spoke, she realized that Bobby's usual calm manner was missing. He seemed bothered by something.

"Hector Caldwell down at Channel 25 called me as I was pulling in."

Brooke's first thought was that there might be an update on the previous week's incident in Bowling Green, Travis Horton's bar fight.

If only it were that.

"Hector wanted to give us a heads-up that Raven and Craig Callaway are going to be on the six o'clock news."

Brooke shot out of her chair. "What?"

Bobby picked up the remote and turned on the large TV mounted over the stone fireplace. Brooke grabbed her phone and called Raven's number. When it went to voice-mail, she tried Craig's. Same thing. She tossed the phone on the sofa. "Did Hector say anything else?"

Bobby shook his head and took a seat with her on the sofa. "I guess we'll find out pretty quick."

Quick was right. The anchor led with breaking news, a Channel 25 exclusive. They cut to Millie Spacey, a veteran reporter and big-time music fan, who sat in a fake living room set. She seemed almost beside herself as she proclaimed that the week-long search for the mysterious Christmas Carl had ended successfully and that he and country superstar Raven McCloud were live in the studio.

"Well, I'll be a son of a gun," Bobby uttered. Brooke held her breath as the camera panned back to show Raven, dazzling as always, seated next to someone she barely recognized as Craig Callaway.

"What did he go and do to himself?" Bobby asked.

"I have a feeling Raven did it to him," Brooke replied, not taking her eyes off the TV. Gone were the glasses that had given him a studious appearance. Also gone were the shirt and khakis he was wearing earlier that day. Brooke recognized his new jeans as being from one of the more exclusive shops in town. The white shirt was snug and untucked at the waist. The boots were western. And the hat was Stetson.

"Darn nice hat," Bobby observed.

Brooke exclaimed, "She changed everything about him. I can't believe she—" She shushed when Bobby pointed at the screen. Millie Spacey asked Craig about his past. He did his best to give the short version. It still wasn't short enough, as Raven interrupted to give a completely bogus account of their college friendship. When Millie asked if it had blossomed into something deeper, Raven laughed and said she would never tell. Craig glanced away in embarrassment. Bobby noticed his discomfort.

"What's going on with his eyes?"

"New contact lenses, I suspect."

Raven's account of finding Craig was short on facts and long on embellishment. She said plenty about how they had recorded the demo tape in college, but conveniently forgot to mention Brooke's investigative work and trips to Missouri and Garland Grove.

"I was elated to find him again after all these years!" she exclaimed in a syrupy voice that made Brooke want to gag.

To his credit, Craig handled the spotlight well, other than blinking like his eyes were on fire, which they probably were. He deferred to Raven at every turn and even called out Brooke and Bobby for helping him get to Nashville. That was nice.

But Raven?

She wasn't done yet.

When Millie Spacey asked if they had anything to add, Raven sat forward in her chair in anticipation of a close-up. She got it, then announced to the public how thrilled she was that Christmas Carl would join her on her holiday tour.

"Carl will be with me for the last ten stops on the tour,

beginning this Saturday in Atlanta. I hope y'all will come out and support him just as you support me."

"The shows are already sold out," Bobby muttered. "There's no tickets left."

She had completely sabotaged their planned announcement. That would piss off a lot of press members who were loyal to Bobby and Brooke. People who showed up at Wainwright's Chop House for every press conference and faithfully reported news updates that helped propel the careers of lesser stars.

Yep, they would be pissed.

Bobby's phone rang first. He moaned when he saw who it was.

"Hey Mary Jo...yeah, I'm watching it right now... I reckon we'll cancel tomorrow's presser... Yeah, me too, Mary Jo...I owe you one for sure."

He disconnected and looked at Brooke. She started to speak, but her phone buzzed. She took a confused and irate call from one of the press regulars, promised to do better, then turned to Bobby.

"Dad, she's driving me nuts."

"Now let's think this through, sweetheart." Bobby was back to being Bobby. And that only made Brooke madder.

"We had everything planned out," she snapped. "We located Craig. We brought him to town and recorded the song." Brooke felt her pulse racing and knew she needed to chill, but it was Bobby she was talking to. And if there was one person with whom she could let fly, it was him. "And then she swoops in and takes credit for everything."

If there had been something throwable nearby, Brooke would have let fly. The only thing within arm's reach, other than a couple of pillows, was one of the many awards Bobby had earned over the years. That was strange; Bobby never displayed his awards.

"Why is that out?" Brooke asked.

Bobby smiled. "I was looking for some double-aught buckshot in the closet and the dang thing fell off the shelf and busted me in the head." He leaned over so she could see the lump. The absurdity of the moment made her laugh.

"Are you okay, Daddy? Let me look at that."

Bobby bent over so she could get a good look. He winced when she touched it, but it didn't appear life-threatening. She kissed his forehead.

"Look, Brooke, darlin'," he said as he sat back. "I know you're hurt with how Raven is acting, but look at it this way. We wanted to get Craig's name and music out there, and we did. Granted, it wasn't the way we planned, but it's done. And now he's going to be joining Raven on tour. It could be the best thing that happens for that boy's career. He's going to sell a lot of records over the next few weeks, and we're all going to make a lot of money."

Dammit, he was right.

Again.

CRAIG WAS STILL in a daze when they left the studio. And the new contacts felt like sandpaper.

"Are you serious about me joining you on the road?" he asked Raven. He wasn't sure she heard him, as she was sending and receiving texts.

"Our ride is on his way," she said finally. "Let's wait near the front door. What did you ask me, sugar?"

"What happened to Milo? I left my phone in his car."

"I let him go. We'll be fine. Now, what were you saying?"

"I didn't know you wanted me to go on the road so soon. Brooke hadn't mentioned it, and—"

"It wasn't Brooke's decision to make," Raven snapped.

What was going on? Were Brooke and Bobby okay with the sudden change of events? And what about Garland Grove? Could Henry Dinwiddie handle the drugstore while Craig was away? If not, what would he do? He couldn't shut down until January. People needed their medications, and he didn't want to lose business to the big pharmacy in Freeport.

"Raven, I really need to check on some things before I can commit."

"You're already committed, sweet pea. If you didn't want to be a performer, you should have stayed in Shady Grove."

"It's Garland Grove, and I didn't know—"

"Here's our ride!" Her face lit up as they watched a white sports car roar to a stop in a loading zone a few feet from the door. She turned to Craig and said, "follow me," as she stepped outside. Streetlight and neon signs illuminated the area, but Craig could see the car was a Lamborghini. Absolutely beautiful. Something he had always hoped he might get to ride in someday. There was just one problem.

"Stupid Travis," Raven groused. "He was supposed to bring his truck."

There was no back seat.

She pulled open the passenger door and scolded the driver, "Travis, did you forget I had Craig with me?"

"Oh, shit, honey. I was already out when you called, so I figured we could make do." The guy looked every inch the country heartthrob. He extended his hand. "Hey, bud. Travis Horton. Damned glad to meet you."

"Hello, Travis." Then, to Raven, "You guys go on to wherever you're going. I can catch a taxi back to Brooke's. She'll be expecting me."

"Nonsense, darlin'. We'll just make this work. Get in."

Craig slid into the front seat. The leather was so soft it felt as if it might swallow him up.

"Now get ready," Raven teased. "Because you're gonna have the sweetheart of country music sitting in your lap." She climbed in and arranged herself across Craig's legs. Between Raven and the dashboard, there was no room left to move. Travis Horton laughed as he watched them get situated.

"Now watch your hands there, bud. Don't let me catch you feelin' up my girl."

"Stop it, both of you," Raven admonished them playfully. She wiggled her butt and smiled at Craig. "You like that, don't you?"

Craig was at a loss for words. The evening was taking off in a direction he was unsure about, and he suddenly wanted nothing more than to just go back to Brooke's place and call it a night.

That wouldn't be happening for another few hours, though.

So what if she had seen Titanic thirty times?

And so what if it was on commercial TV, which meant...commercials. The breaks gave Brooke time to think. To mull over what the heck was going on between Raven and Craig. Bobby had encouraged her to sleep on it, to get some rest and see that things would be better in the morning. And she had wanted to. But just before going upstairs, she had tried calling Craig.

Voicemail.

That was nine-thirty.

Ten o'clock, same thing. Eleven, too.

It was three minutes before midnight when she heard the low growl of a car coming up their driveway. She flicked off Titanic just as water began seeping into the room where Jack was chained. She didn't need to watch the rest. There are no surprises when you've seen a movie thirty times. Brooke only wished there were no surprises when it came to Raven and Craig Callaway.

She followed the sound of the car as it moved around the house to the back door. She stepped out onto the screened porch, shivering in the darkness as the fifty-degree temperatures cooled her bare feet and hands. She had changed into an old pair of jeans and a Vandy t-shirt. Comfort clothes.

The car was white. A two-seater with the rumble and low profile of an expensive make. The driver hit the brakes hard when he reached the end of the drive, then turned so the passenger side was closest to the house. The door opened, and Raven practically fell from the front seat. Behind her, scrambling out to ease her fall, was Craig. A dome light inside the car provided enough light to see Travis Horton. He laughed as Craig helped Raven to her feet. She was drunk. Travis appeared to be, too, and the knowledge that he was driving caused Brooke to step out of the darkness. Raven was crawling back into the car as she approached.

"Raven, you can't go with him. He's had too much to drink."

259

"Oh, hush, Brooke," Raven said, slurring her words. "Travis is fine. He's been driving all evening."

Brooke glanced at Craig, who appeared shellshocked. "Is he okay?" she asked.

When Craig spoke, Brooke could tell he was sober. "I thought so, but the further we drove the worse he was."

"Travis," Brooke said, approaching the passenger door. "Give me your keys. I'll give you a ride home."

Travis swore at her. His angry words frightened her, and she felt as if she couldn't move. Raven said nothing.

But Bobby did.

"Travis Horton, park that car and get out."

Travis swore at Bobby, too, but without the same effect it had on Brooke. "Get Raven out of the car," he said to Craig. He then walked in front of the car to the driver's side, pulled open the door, and yanked Travis out like a rag doll.

"I'm gonna sue your ass, Bobby!" he sputtered as Bobby clutched his left arm. Raven, watching from a few feet away and starting to fully grasp the situation, began to sob.

"Bobby, I'm so sorry. He said he wasn't drunk. I would never have—"

"Take her into the house," Bobby said, his voice low and steady. Craig led her away. "Brooke, honey, call Travis's people and tell them to get out here and get him. Then call Milo and tell him to come take Raven home."

"He'll be in bed by now, Dad. Why don't I just take—"

"You've been through enough." Then to Travis. "Sit down on that porch and don't move. Someone is on their way to get you."

"Hell with that," Travis snarled. "I can drive my own damned self."

"I'm calling the sheriff right now, boy. He'll have a car at the end of the lane in about three minutes. Try to leave and you'll be in a worse bind than you were in Bowling Green."

Travis looked to his car, then back at Bobby, sizing up the situation as best he could in his drunken state.

"Dad," Brooke said, putting her phone in the pocket of her jeans. "I just texted Larry. He says one of his people lives in Lebanon. They'll be here to get Travis in twenty minutes. I couldn't raise Milo, though."

Bobby said, "I'll run Raven home myself. You stay here and make sure that Craig is okay, darlin'."

After a few minutes of stewing on the cold porch, Travis banged on the door, demanding to be let inside. Bobby went out and sat with him for a bit, and whatever he said seemed to quiet Travis until his people showed up. One took his car. The other took Travis. Raven paced the living room, alternating between belligerence and remorse.

"Do you think people will find out?" she asked Brooke at least a half-dozen times. Brooke's answer was always the same. Probably not. What she said and what she felt, though, were different. If Raven insisted on running around with Travis Horton, she would eventually have to pay the price. And that price was her reputation as the squeaky-clean diva of country music. It wasn't the time for that conversation, though, so Brooke stayed with her until Bobby came to take her home.

And Craig? If there was ever an example of a small-town boy out of his element, it was Craig. He sat quietly while they waited. Brooke thought she saw fear in his eyes when Travis was beating on the back door. What had he witnessed over the course of the evening? Where had they gone?

He also continued to rub his eyes, and during a moment when Raven stopped crying, Brooke asked about his glasses.

"I left them in Milo's car," he said glumly. "With my cellphone and my wallet."

"We'll get them in the morning," Brooke replied. "Why don't you go upstairs and take out those contacts before they do some damage?"

She didn't have to say it twice, and by the time Craig returned, Bobby and Raven were gone. It was just the two of them. He sunk down onto the sofa and placed a warm cloth over his eyes.

"I understand why the doctor tells you to only wear contacts for a few hours until you get used to them," he moaned.

Brooke giggled, and it seemed to release some of the tension. "Yeah, it looked like they were giving you trouble on TV earlier."

Craig raised the cloth and looked at her. She smiled and blinked several times. He whimpered and replaced the cloth. "I think it's time for me to head back to Garland Grove."

"Things went off the rails a little, didn't they?" Brooke said, getting up from her chair and taking a seat next to him on the sofa.

"You mean it's not always like this? Because if it is, no thank you."

"It depends. Why don't you tell me about your day?"

He did. From clothes shopping to his trip to the optometrist. From a two-hundred-dollar haircut to cramming three into a two-seat roadster. "It was fun for a while," he said wearily. "Raven was so kind. I saw a little of the Megan Stackhouse I knew in college." He paused and removed the cloth from his eyes so he could see Brooke. "I'm sorry if the TV thing ruined your plans. I just assumed that Raven knew what she was doing."

Well, it did kind of ruin things, but as Bobby had gently reminded her earlier, their goal was to introduce Craig's name and face to the world, and that had been achieved.

"How do you feel about Raven including you on her tour?" Brooke asked.

"I didn't see that coming. I need to figure out how to handle the drugstore. This weekend doesn't worry me so much, but the eight shows in eight days will be hard. That's why I need to get back home."

Brooke could see he was exhausted. He hadn't gone into detail about the evening's later activities, but judging from what she'd seen of Raven and Travis, it had to be crazy. The fact that Craig wasn't wasted like they were made Brooke feel good. Her initial feelings about him had been on the mark. He was a good guy. Over his head a bit, perhaps, but a good guy, nonetheless. When she reached out and patted his shoulder, he leaned in. He was vulnerable and out of his comfort zone. And it would be her responsibility to make sure that he didn't have to go through another day like he'd just experienced. Even if it meant she had to go toe to·toe with Raven.

"You go on to bed," she said softly when she noticed his eyelids becoming heavy. "I'll book your return flight to Garland Grove."

He smiled, happy it appeared, to be going home. "Can you make it early enough for me to be there by six? We have Christmas Concert practice."

She promised she would. And when he stood up she did too. She hugged him and said, "It's going to be okay, Craig."

"I know," he whispered. "I'm just glad I have you."

That made some of it worthwhile. He headed for the stairs, turned, and said, "I'm not sure who that woman was I spent the day with, but she sure as heck ain't Megan Stackhouse anymore."

Craig went on to bed. Brooke logged onto one of the airline sites and booked his ticket home. She was still up when Bobby returned home an hour later.

"Everything okay with Raven?" she asked.

He shrugged. "She's becoming a problem." His eyes were dark. It was well past his bedtime and he had mentioned an early-morning fishing trip. He would probably be getting up again in about four hours, yet he still cared enough to say, "How about you, honey? Are you okay?"

She went to him. He opened his arms and pulled her in. "I'll be fine, Daddy, but I'm starting to wonder about working in this field after you hang up your spurs."

Her head was against his chest, and she could hear the comforting rhythm of his breathing and the steady thump of his heart. "I don't plan on hanging up my spurs for a few more years, Brooke, but when do I have no doubt you'll be up to the job."

She smiled. "I know I'm up to the job, Dad." She pulled away and looked up into his soft eyes. "The question is, do I want it?"

WEDNESDAY, DECEMBER 7

NASHVILLE AND GARLAND GROVE

*B*rooke worked on her phone while she sat on the edge of the bed and waited in the darkness. Minutes passed like hours. At seven-fifteen, she decided she would wait fifteen more minutes before waking Craig up. She could just make out his face. His mouth was open, but he wasn't snoring. His left hand was tucked under his pillow. His right was curled under the comforter. Peaceful and serene, and completely unaware of the hell that was rearing up.

The first text had awakened her at five-forty. It came from an obnoxious reporter from a fan website notorious for printing half-truths. The text was vague and asked for a call-back. Brooke ignored it. The second and third texts arrived within seconds of each other. The wording was identical.

Can you confirm that Raven McCloud was with Travis Horton last night?

Brooke didn't reply. Her gut told her that something bad had happened, but wouldn't Craig have mentioned it? She watched the clock until seven-twenty-nine, then leaned over to tap him on the shoulder. She was within a few inches when his eyes flew open.

"What?"

Brooke pulled back as he jolted into a sitting position. "Did I oversleep? Oh, my goodness. Am I going to miss my flight?" He tossed back the covers and threw his legs over the side of the bed before she could respond. Then, realizing he was in his underwear, he jumped back under the sheets. His bashfulness was adorable and kind of sexy, and if the crap weren't about to hit the fan, Brooke might have enjoyed the moment more.

"I'm sorry, Craig. And no, you didn't miss your flight. It doesn't leave until eleven-thirty."

He took a breath, scrunching his eyes as he tried to see her in the dim light. Brooke turned on the bedside lamp. "I need to ask you about last night."

He sat up against the padded headboard, keeping the comforter over his legs. He rubbed his eyes as they adjusted to the light.

"What about last night?"

"Were you with Raven the entire evening?"

Craig's face twisted as he thought about it. "Yes...well, most of it. I went to the bathroom a few times. And I stepped outside once to get some fresh air."

"And that's it?"

"I think so. Brooke, what's wrong?"

"Was Travis Horton there?"

"He might've stepped away a few times, but mostly, yes."

"Did you see him slap someone?"

Craig's eyes became wide. "No!"

"Did you see someone ask for his autograph?"

"That happened several times. Raven, too. Are they in some kind of trouble?"

"Can you give me a rundown on what happened between the time you left the studio and when you came back here?"

"Sure, but I never saw Travis hit anyone."

"A pipefitter from Kenvil, New Jersey claims he was taking a cellphone photo of Travis and Raven when Travis slapped him and took his phone."

"Holy smokes. I didn't see anything like that."

"Tell me about a place called…" Brooke glanced at her notes. "…Risky Rick's."

Craig thought about it for a few moments. "That was the last place we stopped. And it was the only place where we had to pass through the general seating area to get to a private room." He paused and shook his head. "Who knew so many places have special seating areas for famous people?"

"It's a Nashville thing. Celebrities know where they are. But you didn't see Travis slap anyone?"

"Not at all, except…"

"Except what? If you saw anything, even if you aren't sure what it was, Craig, tell me."

"We were getting ready to leave Risky Ricks, but I had to go to the restroom first…"

"Yes?"

"It's kind of embarrassing, Brooke."

She patted his hand. "Tell me, please. It's important."

"We ate some Nashville hot chicken from a place downtown. I had never had it before, and it really messed up my stomach, so…" Craig lowered his gaze. "I *really* had to go, if you know what I mean."

In most situations, Brooke would have found this funny, but dealing with a crisis outweighed poking fun at Craig's gastric distress. She waited for him to continue.

"I was in the restroom for ten or fifteen minutes, and when I came out, Raven and Travis were gone. Part of me hoped they'd left me so I could just Uber back here. I looked for them in the bar, but the place was nuts. People were practically crawling over one another to see something that was happening. I was kind of curious, but I was also exhausted and ready to end the night." He took a deep breath. "We have a place in Garland Grove called Smacks. It gets a little loud sometimes, but nothing like that. Anyway, I figured they had already left, so I did too. I was in the parking lot when Travis pulled up and told me to get in."

"And nothing was mentioned about what happened inside?"

"Nothing. Travis was pretty obnoxious all night, but I never thought he might hit someone."

Brooke leaned against the headboard and shook her head. Craig was watching her. "Should I have not left them alone?" he asked. "Frankly, it was hard keeping up with them, and if I hadn't stepped away now and again..." He shrugged. "Is Travis in trouble?"

"Probably, but Travis isn't my responsibility. You and Raven are. Fortunately, no one has identified you. Plenty of people recognized Raven, though. We just went through a situation in Kentucky last week involving her and Travis. The last thing we want is more bad publicity."

"That Travis is a mess," Craig said.

"He is. And he's dragging Raven along for the ride." Brooke squeezed his hand. "It's not a ride we want her to take. I suspect the police will talk to them later this morning. I figure that since no one has identified you, we might as well get you out of here and onto a plane back to Garland Grove."

"You cannot imagine how good that sounds," Craig said. "I'll get ready."

THE FANCY NEW jeans were packed in his suitcase with the belt and boots. The contact lenses, too. Craig combed and parted his new haircut to make it look like his old one. The only thing he couldn't stow away for the flight home was the hat. He had to wear it or carry it. He carried it. It felt good just being Craig Callaway again. And even as he arrived at the regional airport and heard his song over the terminal speakers, he was content with his anonymity.

He reached Garland Grove at five-forty. Downtown was bustling with Christmas shoppers, but in the darkness, no one recognized his pickup. He would have preferred to stop at home first, to check the mail and make sure everything was okay, but Christmas program rehearsal was at six, so he headed straight to the theater. He entered the lot with minutes to spare. It felt good to be back.

He pulled open the stage entrance expecting to hear the buzz of friends sharing the latest gossip, but instead encountered silence. And the smell of ham.

Ham?

He passed through the theater's backstage area and nearly passed out when he was greeted by a thunderous ovation. All six-hundred and twenty-seven seats appeared to be occupied. Craig stopped in his tracks, unsure what to do or how to acknowledge what was happening in front of him. His first thought was that he had somehow forgotten the concert was that night. Sam Griffin rushed to his side.

"S-Sam," Craig stuttered. "What's this?"

"It's for you!" Sam exclaimed as the applause continued. "Come up on stage and take a bow."

Sam pulled him onto the stage. Craig looked out over the faces and worried again that he might faint. "Stay close," he whispered to Sam.

Sam raised his hand for quiet, then went to a microphone at center stage and said, "Ladies and gentlemen, here he is. Just back from his big coming out party in Nashville, the one...the only...our own Craig Callaway!"

The audience erupted again. And while the nerves didn't approach what he had felt in the recording studio two days earlier, they still jangled his insides. He waved and held his hands to his heart in a show of appreciation and love. They were there for him. They were excited for him.

They were proud of him.

Sam patted him on the back and stepped away. Craig's emotions threatened to get the best of him. How could he adequately express his appreciation? How could he let them know how much they meant to him? He felt tears welling up and wasn't sure he could stop them. "I just don't know what to say... I—"

"Don't say anything," Sam called out from the wings. He came onto the stage carrying Craig's guitar. "Just sing."

More applause.

"How did you get this?" Craig whispered.

"Everybody knows you hide your spare key under the planter next to your back door. I helped myself to some chili I found in your fridge, too."

Craig gazed into the faces looking back at him in anticipation. Standing on stage at the Ryman had been a memorable experience, but it didn't compare to what he felt as he placed the guitar strap over his shoulder and prepared for his first official performance.

"I've never felt more a part of this wonderful community than I do right now." His voice was strong. The emotion had passed. It was time to perform. "I'd like to play a song I wrote in college. One that I had forgotten until I was reminded of it last week." The audience, fully aware of his recent good fortune, laughed. Craig paused to find his chord and let the anticipation grow. "It goes something like this..."

He watched their reactions as he sang the first verse. Faces lit up. Many sang along, and by the time he reached the chorus, everyone had joined in. The feeling was beyond description, so much so that Craig didn't want it to end. So, when he reached the last verse, he circled back to the beginning. The Garland Grove faithful would have been happy for him to circle back all evening, but twice was enough.

"Thank you, Garland Grove," he said as he set aside the guitar. Sam rushed back to the stage.

"And now we have time for a few questions!" he exclaimed. Hands shot up. Craig pointed to the second row where police officer Greg Claggett was waving his hand.

"Greg, aren't you supposed to be on patrol?"

"Yeah, Craig, but everybody's here, so I figured I would come too."

The audience laughed warmly. Greg asked, "Why didn't you tell anybody you dated Raven McCloud in college?"

"Good question," others called out.

"We want to know," said others.

"I didn't date Raven McCloud. I dated a nice girl

named Megan Stackhouse. Unbeknownst to me or anyone else at our college, she later became Raven McCloud.

"Did she remember you?" a farmer called out from the rear.

"Well, she thought my name was Carl, so what do you think, Hank?"

That got a laugh. The questions came nonstop for the next fifteen minutes. What was Nashville like? How did it feel to record a song? What famous people did you meet? When Nancy Parker, a crusty, two-pack-a-day smoker, asked Craig if her daughter's antifungal cream would be ready the next day, Sam hurriedly returned and brought the session to a close. For the next twenty minutes, friends came forward to let Craig know how proud they were. The Bennetts and Griffins stayed back until everyone else was gone. Amy hugged Craig and planted a big kiss on his cheek. The usually reserved Andrew slapped him on the back. Beth Griffin hugged him, too, then said, "You owe us for a babysitter."

"What do you mean?"

She grinned. "We're flying down to see your concert in Atlanta Saturday."

"All four of us!" Amy added. Sam came closer. "Do you have any freaking idea what last-minute tickets to a Raven McCloud concert cost?"

Craig didn't.

"I'll be working nights and weekends for the next three months."

"You deliver babies," Craig replied. "Nights and weekends are part of the job."

"It was worth every penny," Beth said, slapping Sam playfully on the back of his head. "We're staying at the Omni."

"Andrew thought it was too expensive and wanted to share a room," Sam said, shaking his head. "Can you believe that? Beth and I get a weekend away from the kids and Andrew thinks we're going to share a room with him and Amy. And to think the dude has only been married for a year."

It felt good to be with them, and Craig would have loved nothing more than for all of them to head over to Smacks because he was starving.

"Did I smell ham when I came in?"

"Yeah," Beth said. "There was a VIP dinner in the lobby before you arrived. Amy set it up after your big announcement. Fifty dollars got dinner and a seat in the first five rows for your return."

Craig laughed. "How did you know I would make it back?"

Amy said, "A nice lady in Brooke Summers's office gave us your flight information. We tracked you all the way back. We knew you wouldn't miss concert practice."

"It was a fundraiser for new stage curtains," Andrew said. They all turned to look at the Vogue's faded maroon curtains.

"The old place is definitely needing a facelift," Sam lamented.

"I just hate putting too much money into it," Amy added. "The city council still brings up the possibility of selling the theater. Every so often someone makes an offer to buy the land and replace the Vogue with something else."

"Even the hospital has their eyes on this parcel," Andrew said.

"But don't despair, buddy," Sam exclaimed. "Your Christmas program will go on as scheduled. Unfortunately, we're still about a thousand bucks short of what we need for the new curtains, but there's next year, right?"

The Christmas concert.

Craig glanced toward the rear of the hall where the thirty-some participants chatted and visited among themselves, perfectly content to wait their turn. "I'd better get rehearsal started," he said.

The Griffins and Bennetts took that as their cue to depart. Craig followed them up the center aisle to the lobby, said goodbye, then turned to the singers. "I'm sorry to keep you waiting. Something unexpected came up."

They laughed. Most of them, anyway. Sadie Trout and Willa McKenzie didn't laugh. Willa started to laugh, then stopped when she noticed Sadie wasn't. What was up with them? Probably unhappy with the delay. Craig was in too good a mood to worry about the czars of the Christmas Program Committee. There was music to perform. Craig asked David and Joe, a couple of farmers with rich baritone singing voices, to wheel the grand piano to center stage.

"Okay, everybody, let's take it from the top." Craig nodded at Joanne Sayer, a middle-aged woman who was the town's best pianist when she wasn't working as administrator at Garland Grove Memorial Hospital. "Joanne, did you get that interlude worked out that we talked about?" When Joanne said she had, Craig waved for everyone to head for the stage. He hung back, waiting for Sadie to catch up with him. She didn't, so he stopped and turned to her.

"Sadie, how are things with Hal Richie? Has he let you know which songs he plans to sing?"

"Not yet," she said crisply, then looked away. That was a very un-Sadie-like thing. When they reached the stage, Joanne Sayer whispered, "Tickets aren't selling very well.

People don't like the five-dollar price increase, and no one has heard of Hal Richie."

That explained it.

"Look everyone," Craig called out as they moved to their positions. "Don't worry about ticket sales. We always sell out, and we will this year, too." He turned to Joanne, who nodded she was ready. "Now let's get started."

FIVE REPORTERS RUSHED toward Brooke as she entered Pittsburgh's general aviation terminal.

"Is Raven on the plane?"

"Is Travis Horton with her?"

"Did the police question Raven about what happened last night?"

"Can we talk to her, Brooke?"

Fortunately, a quick-thinking airport employee pulled Brooke aside and recommended they have the waiting limo proceed directly to the tarmac. It was quickly arranged, and Brooke and Raven were soon on their way. Two of the reporters tailed the car all the way to the evening's venue, going so far as to attempt to gain access through the restricted entrance into the arena itself.

"Might as well let 'em on in," Raven said with a nonchalance that defied the shitstorm that encompassed her and Travis Horton. "I'll get this thing quieted down soon enough."

"How do you plan to do that?" Brooke asked.

"Do you doubt my communication skills, Brooke?" Her tone remained casual, but Brooke could tell when Raven's irritable edge was about to show itself. And if she was upset with Brooke, too bad.

"Have you looked over the talking points I sent you?" Brooke asked.

Raven waved her off. "I've got this. I may wait a few days, though. Keep the media away from me, Brooke, honey."

As the limo pulled to a stop on a loading dock, Brooke decided to ask the question that had been bugging her all day. "Did you see Travis strike the man?"

Raven rolled her eyes like a petulant teenager. "I'm not discussing what Travis Horton did or didn't do, Brooke. I'm here to perform for the wonderful people of Pittsburgh. Now, if you will just keep those parasites from the papers and websites away from me, I'll get ready." She stepped out of the car and was intercepted by two security officers. "Hi, boys," she called out, amping up the southern charm. "Will y'all handsome men take little ol' Raven to her dressing room?"

The guys appeared as happy as hogs in slop, practically falling over themselves to escort the lovely Raven McCloud. Brooke gave last-minute instructions to the limo driver, then followed Raven from a distance. She had put off speaking to the Nashville police, and according to Bobby, they still hadn't located Travis Horton. The only people talking were New Jersey pipefitter Ruben Stefano, the alleged slapping victim, and his attorney, a pain-in-the-ass named Mary P. Patterson, whose billboards loomed over Nashville highways. Too many questions were unanswered, and the press was circling like sharks.

It was going to be a long Christmas tour.

CRAIG HAD STRIPPED to his skivvies and was ready to collapse into bed when someone knocked on the front door. He ignored it. The craziness of the past twenty-four hours was catching up with him. His head was pounding, and he had no energy left to deal with a late-night visitor. Whoever it was knocked a second time, then stopped.

Thank goodness.

Craig pulled back the sheets and crawled in. He turned off the lights, then nearly jumped out of his skin when someone knocked on the bedroom window above his head.

Who?

And why?

Ten-fifteen in Garland Grove was like midnight anyplace else. People didn't drop by at ten-fifteen, and they certainly didn't bang on bedroom windows.

Unless it was an emergency.

Was someone hurt? Had someone died?

Craig started to lift the shade, but the low-budget horror films of his youth stopped him. What if a hockey-masked killer was staring back at him?

Don't be stupid. It's Garland Grove.

Still, a person couldn't be too careful. He silently rose in the dark, went to the closet, and retrieved the bathrobe he only wore when he had out-of-town guests, which was almost never. He stuck his feet into the slippers he also never wore and plodded toward the back door. He pulled aside a curtain and peered into the night.

Whoever it was, was still there. Standing under his bedroom window with their back to him. They appeared to be of medium build and wore a dark hooded parka and snow boots. Craig silently unlocked the door and was about to step out and confront whoever it was when he reconsidered. He retraced his steps to the bedroom and grabbed the baseball bat he used each summer when he played leftfield for the merchants' softball team. If whoever was out there came at him, he would be ready.

Then, a thought. Should he call the police? Maybe, but that would entail dispatch rousing Greg Claggett who was probably fast asleep behind the Moose Lodge. Just like everyone knew where Craig kept his spare key, they knew how Greg spent most of his night. It was the only way he could handle the eight-to-noon shift at his brother's auto parts store. Nope. Calling the police would take too long. Craig took another look out from the kitchen window. The intruder was still there. Still waiting for him to open the bedroom shade.

Well, Mister Intruder, you have another thing coming.

Craig turned the lock and pulled open the door. The frigid air rushed at him, but the intruder didn't hear a thing. They reached up and rapped on the window again. Craig stepped out onto his back stoop and pulled the bat close, leaving the door open just in case he needed to flee back inside. Creepy horror film music played in his head, and when the front doorbell rang inside the house, he dropped the bat. The backyard intruder turned, but Craig didn't wait to see who it was. He hurried back inside and locked the door, then raced through the house to the front door. Had a neighbor alerted the police? He took a deep, ragged breath and debated his next move.

"Christmas Carl? Are you in there, man?"

He knew that voice.

"C'mon, dude. Open the door. It's cold as shit out here."

Craig unlatched the lock and opened the door. He grabbed Travis Horton's arm and pulled him inside. "Quiet," he hissed. "There's somebody in the backyard. I think it might be a burglar or—"

"Is it her?" Travis said, pointing toward the kitchen. Craig spun around just as the kitchen light came on.

"Jenna?"

Jenna?

And Travis Horton?

What the hell was going on?

"Why didn't you let me in before? I knocked twice." She came closer. She was carrying Craig's bat. "You dropped this out back." She looked past Craig. "Did anyone ever mention that you look like Travis Horton?"

"One and the same, darlin'. Who are you?"

"She's Jenna..." Craig stammered. "She's my—she used to be—Travis, why are you here?" Then, turning back to Jenna, "And why are you here? And how did you get in? I'm sure I locked that door when I heard the doorbell."

"Everyone knows where you keep your spare key, Craig," she said. "I came over to talk."

"And I came to hide out," Travis said as he dropped an overnight bag on the floor and moved toward the sofa. "As you probably heard, I'm in a bit of a spot back in Nashville, so I just jumped in my truck and came up here."

"That's at least ten hours," Craig exclaimed.

"More like twelve." Travis pulled off his cowboy hat and tossed it on the sofa. "I left Nashville at daybreak. My head was still crackin' from last night, but by the time I got to Illinois, I was feeling better. I'm tired as hell now, though, so I figure I'll stay here until things blow over back home."

"Stay right there," Craig said. "Let me get back to you." Then to Jenna. "Come into the kitchen."

There was no door between the kitchen and living room to mute their conversation, but Travis didn't look like he would be long for the world. Craig motioned for Jenna to have a seat, considered offering coffee, then decided he didn't have it in him. His first thought was that she had come by to make up. To tell him she had ended things with the vet, Owen-what's-his-name. And that she had heard about his newfound fame and wanted to let bygones be bygones. Heck, she probably would even spend the night.

How would he feel about that?

"I came by to apologize for how I spoke to you last week, and how I've been acting in general."

Craig pulled out the chair across from her. "At ten-fifteen in the evening?"

She pursed her lips. "I was afraid that if I didn't come as soon as you got back that I might never do it. I treated you badly, Craig, and you didn't deserve that."

She glanced away as she rubbed her hands together. *Was she about to broach the subject of their getting back together?* Craig leaned forward in his chair, still not sure how he would respond.

"Anyway, I felt the need to tell you I was sorry." When she returned her gaze to him, she was smiling. "And to congratulate you on becoming famous."

"Oh, it's not..." What was he about to say? That it was nothing, really? That being flown to Nashville to record his own music was no big deal? It was a huge deal. A really huge deal, and he didn't need to minimize the accomplishment.

"Thanks for the kind words," he finally said, as he stood back up. "And if you don't mind, Jenna, it's been a long couple of days and I still have to deal with him." He nodded toward the living room where Travis was snoring.

"If what I read about him is true, he's quite the piece of work."

Craig laughed. "Try being the third person in his two-seater Lambo when he's going a hundred and ten on a two-lane road."

He walked Jenna to the door. She turned before leaving and looked at him tentatively. Was there supposed to be a hug before she left? Probably, but she had already hurt him enough for one month.

"Good night, Jenna."

"Good night, Craig... Maybe you can call me when you get back." She flashed that sweet smile that always did things to him. "It would be fun to hear about your adventures."

She reached out and caressed his forearm before leaving. Craig pushed the door shut, then jostled Travis awake.

"You can't stay here."

Travis looked around uncertainly. "Where the hell—" The fog seemed to lift, and he remembered where he was. "You can't toss me out on the street, Carl. I drove all damned day. I'm staying here and that's that."

Craig left the room, returning with cellphone in hand. "You have two minutes to get out. The police are looking for you and I'll not let you hide out here. Go now or I'll call them."

They remained there for several moments, eyes locked on one another. Craig looked away first, but only because he glimpsed his reflection in a small mirror on the wall. How menacing could a guy look in a bathrobe and slippers?

"You would really do that?" Travis snarled. He stood up and Craig had to fight the urge to take a step back. "After all that Raven did for you, you would give me up like that? You know she gave me your address, right?"

"I don't care. You assaulted someone. I won't be party to that."

Travis grinned. "Once the whole story gets out you

might not have a choice." He grabbed his hat and put it on, then reached for his bag. "It's a shame you're tossing away whatever career you might have had for something like this." When he moved to within a few inches and stood nose-to-nose, Craig realized for the first time that Travis Horton was a couple inches shorter than him. No wonder Bobby had little problem pulling him from the car the previous evening. Craig wracked his brain to come up with the expression he'd heard Bobby use to describe someone he considered a pretender. Something about a hat.

Then it came to him.

All hat and no cattle.

That described Travis Horton to a tee.

He had been dismissive of Craig from the moment they'd met. He possessed every characteristic of a bad boy celebrity. He was dragging his career into the mud and had nothing against taking Raven with him.

Travis was everything Craig didn't want to become. Not that his career would ever approach the level of success Travis Horton was experiencing, but still, why didn't he handle it better?

But what statement was Craig making by sending him off into the night? He was far from home and exhausted from a short night followed by a long day of driving. What if he fell asleep at the wheel?

What would Bobby do?

What would Brooke do?

They wouldn't let him stay, nor would they send him off into the night without someone there to catch him.

And since there was no one to catch Travis, it fell to Craig.

Travis was still eyeing him, trying to appear tough, but there was an insecurity in his gaze that wasn't there before.

Unlike the previous day, Craig didn't feel like they were on separate plains. Travis wasn't a high-and-mighty singing star. He was just a person. And Craig had always strived to treat people with respect, even if they didn't always deserve it.

"Get your stuff," he said. "You can have the guest room."

Travis relaxed. He extended his hand. Craig shook.

"I won't forget this," he said.

And for once, Craig believed him.

SATURDAY, DECEMBER 10

ATLANTA

"Good Morning, Mr. Callaway, I hope you slept well!"

The woman on the other end of the line had the most perfect southern lilt. In fact, everything about Atlanta had been perfect.

"Yes, ma'am, I did. This suite is incredible. Are you sure someone else isn't supposed to be staying with me? There are two enormous bedrooms, and I think the living room sofa folds out, too."

"No, Mr. Callaway, when Miss Summers made the reservation, she indicated you would be the only guest. How can I help you today?"

"I was hoping you could recommend a good place to get breakfast."

"There are several quality restaurants within walking distance, Mr. Callaway, but meals are included with your accommodations. If you check the desk in your room, you'll find a complete room service menu."

Craig spotted the menu among some other items. He gulped when he saw the prices, then remembered it was covered. The nice lady with the accent took his order and promised to relay it to room service. Twenty minutes later there was a knock at the door. He pulled it open, still wearing the complimentary plush robe he had found in the closet.

"Good morning, Mr. Callaway! I'm here with your breakfast."

"Brooke!"

She looked incredible in a dark green sweater dress over leggings and leather boots. She pushed a serving cart into the room, and with a flourish, removed three silver lids. Bacon and scrambled eggs, hash browns, and waffles. Also, coffee and juice. It smelled heavenly.

"Your breakfast, sir!" Then she came to him with her arms open. They hugged. She smelled even better than breakfast.

"Sorry I'm not dressed," Craig said.

Brooke eyed him from head to toe, then quipped, "Last time we were together you jumped out of bed in your Fruit of the Looms. If you're trying to get my attention, sailor, you're succeeding." She pushed the tray to a table in the corner of the suite's expansive living room. "You need to eat. It's a big day."

"I didn't know it would be so much food. Will you join me?"

"I ate two hours ago, but..." She eyed the heaping dishes. "Yeah, I might try some of those eggs."

They spent the next hour cleaning their plates. Craig was enthralled by how down-to-earth Brooke was. She wielded her fork like a precision instrument, swooping in and snagging bits of egg and waffle. They shared a laugh when she beat him to the last bite of bacon.

"I trust your flights were good?" she asked.

"Everything on time. Atlanta's airport is huge, but the driver met me just past security. I could get used to having someone waiting for me with my name on an iPad."

"I enjoy doing it for you," Brooke said. "You deserve it."

"And this room." Craig paused mid-bite to gaze at his surroundings. "Who knew hotels had rooms like this?"

"Wait until you see your dressing room at the concert venue," Brooke said. "Now tell me how your time in Garland Grove was. Did you get recharged?"

She had been so busy traveling with Raven the past few days that Craig had avoided bothering her with the minutiae of his life. They had exchanged a few texts, but most of his conversations had been with Raquel. Brooke didn't know about the surprise reception, or that his friends would attend that evening's show. Nor did she know how reluctant Mr. Dinwiddie had been to fill in for him at the drugstore this time, and how much coaxing and pleading it had taken to get him to agree to cover through Christmas.

She didn't know that Travis Horton was staying at his house.

It was time to clear the air about some things.

So he did.

The reception. She loved hearing about that. "I envy you living in a community where everyone knows everyone."

The impending arrival of the Griffins and Bennetts. "I want to meet them. We'll get them backstage passes."

Mr. Dinwiddie's reticence about filling in at the drugstore. "I'll arrange for Raquel to send him a very special gift. Maybe we can set him up with a weekend trip to Nashville this spring. Would he like that?"

Travis Horton at Craig's house? Nope, he couldn't do it.

Brooke needed to know, but not yet. She was in such a cheerful mood and seemed overjoyed that he was in town.

Yep, better to leave that one for later.

Craig was like a kid at Christmas. Everything from the size of the suite to the spa robe and room service breakfast left him wide-eyed with wonder. Sure, she had splurged for the nicest suite in the hotel, not usually the type of accommodations a first-time performer received, but he was worth it. Whether music became his life or just a quick stop on the road through life, Brooke wanted him to fully experience it.

And maybe she wanted him to like her a little bit, too.

With all that in mind, she kept things light. No mention of the incident at Risky Rick's. Craig didn't need to know that Raven was living in her own little cocoon, refusing to acknowledge being anywhere near Risky Rick's the previous Tuesday night. Acting lovey-dovey to everyone she met, except Brooke. She continued to run hot and cold when it was just the two of them. Demanding and irritable one moment, sweet as pie the next.

But Craig didn't need to know that, just like he didn't need to know Travis Horton had dropped from the face of the earth. Brooke wanted his attention focused on that evening's concert. His debut. And judging by the way he put away breakfast, nerves were of no concern. He seemed happy to be in Atlanta and ready for what lay ahead.

Raven's soundcheck was in full gear when the limo dropped Craig off a little after three. Brooke met him at the stage entrance and took him around back where he could see the venue from the band's perspective.

"It's huge," he exclaimed as the first butterflies took flight in his stomach.

"Twenty-one thousand," Brooke said. "But don't worry about that." She pulled up a schedule on her iPad. "Raven will take a potty break between these two songs. We'll make sure you're in the wings and ready to go. She'll finish her song in the darkness, then you'll be announced. The band will play a transition piece while you make your way to center stage." She paused and placed her hand on his arm. "Don't be surprised if people get up and walk out, though. It's common in shows like this where there's no inter-mission."

"Don't take it personally if people walk out," Craig repeated slowly. "How about if they boo?"

"They won't boo." Brooke giggled. "But they will prob-ably sing along, so be ready."

"What if I get out there, see all those faces, and freeze?"

"The lights will make it hard to see much at first, and you're only doing your one song, but if you get nervous, just concentrate on singing to one person."

"One person?"

"Yes," Brooke continued. "Trick your brain into believing you're not performing in front of twenty-thousand people."

Craig looked past the band to where Raven was seated on a stool. It was only a soundcheck, with frequent stops and starts while Mickey Cox made minor corrections, but the vastness of the arena and the noise and lights were over-powering to the senses. How much more would it be with all those seats filled?

"So I pick one person and sing to them?"

"That's right."

He turned to face her. "Will you be out there someplace?"

She glanced toward the empty seats. "I'm usually back here, but I can go out front if you like."

He nodded, making no effort to hide his uneasiness. "If I'm singing to one person, I want it to be you. Just like last week at the Ryman."

Brooke looked into his eyes. "That's very sweet of you, Craig. I'll be honored to have you sing to me."

They remained where they were. Facing each other while the band ran through one of Raven's Christmas medleys. She might have sounded perfect, or she might have been off-key. Craig couldn't say for sure. He was sure, though, that he felt something for Brooke Summers. And he wanted to tell her. And maybe see if she was feeling it, too.

"Brooke?" he said, barely above a whisper.

Her smile was sweet and warm and gave him hope. "Um-hmm?"

"I hope I'm not out of line in saying this, but—"

"Christmas Carl!"

"But, I think I'm—"

"Carl, you're up!"

"Mickey is calling you," Brooke said, a trace of disappointment in her tone.

Craig turned toward the stage. He had barely registered the sound of his name coming through the speakers. "Yeah, I guess I'll go out there."

He reached out for her hand. Hers met his.

"I'll be there for you," she said, before turning and walking away.

"My one person," Craig called to her. He turned and proceeded past the band toward center stage. Raven was flipping through a stack of sheet music. She looked up and smiled.

"Hi, darlin'!"

"Hey, Raven. I guess I'm up."

"You sure are, sugar, and don't forget your fancy duds tonight. The ladies are going to be swooning over you when they see you in those sexy new blue jeans."

Mickey motioned Craig over and explained much of what Brooke had already told him.

Except for one thing.

"Have you thought about what you're going to say?"

Craig laughed. "Sorry, Mickey. I'm a singer. Not a talker."

"Not good enough," Mickey responded. "When you finish your song you'll need to throw it back to Raven, but first you need to acknowledge the audience and chat with them for a few moments."

"Yeah, sugar," Raven said from her stool. "If you don't chat with them a little, I'll still be in the little girl's room."

"Just general stuff," Mickey said. "Maybe a joke or two. A little about your past. Tell you what, man, we'll pretend it's tonight. Take your spot and do your song, then give me five minutes of dialogue before calling Raven back out."

It was becoming more complicated. Singing. *And talking?*

"Oh, I nearly forgot," Raven said. She pointed to a stagehand. "Get my little gift for Christmas Carl, honey." The stagehand disappeared for a moment before returning with a guitar. Craig's heart rate escalated.

"Raven, I'm not ready to do that. Brooke said I wasn't good enough to play."

"Don't worry, sweetie. It won't be plugged in. And it'll give you something to do with your hands."

Several band members laughed, but Craig suspected they laughed at anything remotely funny, provided it came out of the mouth of Raven McCloud. Still, she had a point. He had given no thought to how he would stand or what he would do with his hands. And it was a sweet-looking guitar, even if it was only a prop.

"Okay, Christmas Carl," Mickey called out. "Let's take it from the top. You've just been introduced and come onto stage."

The band broke into the intro for "Making Santa Smile." It sounded different than it had the two previous times he'd sung it. The music reverberated off the rear walls, but Craig was set on not missing his mark. He stepped into the spotlight and started strumming his mute guitar for all it was worth. When he looked out over the empty arena, he noticed there was one seat occupied near the back. He smiled and nodded at Brooke. And when the band turned the corner, he was ready.

As SHE HAD the previous three nights, Raven cancelled the meet-and-greet. She promised she would pick back up the next evening in Tampa, but she had said the same thing each night. Her last-minute decision resulted in hours of work for people in ticketing and guest relations, but Raven never experienced that side of things.

Brooke decided it was about time she did.

She knocked twice, waited, and knocked again. Raven called her into the dressing room where she was seated on one of two sofas, browsing the latest entertainment news on her phone. She was looking, Brooke knew, for mentions of their trouble at Risky Rick's. There was plenty out there.

Brooke had already looked after getting Craig situated in his dressing room. He had been ecstatic when he saw it. Raven was probably less thrilled about what she was reading.

Country Bad Boy Disappears Into the Night.

Travis "Slap and Run" Horton Still On the Lam.

Assault Victim Files $2 Million Suit Against Horton. Is Raven McCloud Next?

"Do you know where he is?" Brooke asked.

Raven was slow to answer, and Brooke wasn't sure if it was because she didn't want to say anything or didn't know.

"He hasn't texted or called," she said quietly. "I figured he might stay with relatives, but the papers have checked that out already."

Brooke took a seat on the other sofa. "Where does a guy as well-known as Travis Horton hide out?"

She had planned to have Raven take a walk to the ticket office with her. She needed to see the insanity that ensued after her cancelled meet-and-greet. How minimum-wage employees were phoning VIPs to break the bad news. But she seemed legitimately concerned about Travis. And about her own situation. Raven was a lot of things, but she wasn't dumb. She understood that sooner or later she had to issue a statement. But when would that be?

And then, she said something completely unexpected.

"I want to manage Craig's career," she said.

Brooke rolled her eyes, then checked to make sure Raven hadn't seen it. She was still scrolling through webpages on her phone. Brooke waited for her to finish.

"Since I'm the reason he's here, I feel I have that right."

Okay.

"I've learned from the best. Bobby has done a wonderful job managing my career."

Brooke gritted her teeth. *Just Bobby? No mention of Brooke's hard work?*

"Not having him on the road this Christmas has made me realize how good he is."

"Look, Raven..." There was no way Brooke could keep the hostility out of her voice. "I'm the first to admit that I'm not Bobby, but you need to take responsibility for your actions, too."

She continued to study her phone, not even bothering to look up as she said, "Brooke, honey, this isn't the prom decorating committee back in high school. And if you're going to succeed you need to understand that the whole world doesn't revolve around pretty little Brooke Summers. You might have Bobby wrapped around your finger, sweetheart, but I'm my own person."

The way she said it, as casually as if they were two old friends catching up on the latest gossip, only made Brooke angrier. She kept her voice level and hoped she gave no indication that she would enjoy kicking Raven's ass. "Will you take a walk with me?"

This got Raven to look up from her phone. "Now? So close to concert time?"

"The gates don't open for ninety minutes. I want you to see something."

"Really, Brooke? Can't it wait? I'm busy here."

"Five minutes. That's all I ask. If you won't do it for me, do it for Bobby, because he would want you to see what I have to show you."

Raven sighed as if she was being severely put upon. She stood and said, "Lead the way."

"What are you doing answering your phone? Don't you have a concert coming up?"

It was Sam.

"It doesn't start for two hours, and I don't go on for another hour after that. Are you guys in town?"

"We sure are!" Sam was practically shouting. "We're checked in. Separate rooms, despite Andrew's suggestion otherwise. We're going to get a bite to eat in a bit, then we'll head over to see you."

"How about after? Plans?"

"Just to come back to the room and remind Beth why she married me."

"Well, I wouldn't want to intrude on that, but I was wondering if you guys might want to come backstage and then go for a late supper."

The line was silent for a few moments, making Craig think they had been disconnected. Sam finally spoke. "Can I meet Raven McCloud?"

"I think that can be arranged."

Craig pulled the phone away from his ear when Sam practically screamed, "Yes!" After he got his friend calmed down he gave him instructions about where to get his backstage passes.

By the time Raven understood where they were, it was too late to turn back. Brooke counted fifteen workers in a large room, placing calls to disappointed VIPs.

"Why did you think I needed to see this?" she hissed.

"Because you caused it, Raven."

"It's their job."

"No, they have other things they're supposed to be

294

doing. Most will be here through the night getting the things done they had to put off because you cancelled the meet-and-greet."

Raven threw her hands into the air and turned away. "There's enough stress in my life without this. And Bobby would not have brought me here."

"Bobby wouldn't have allowed you to cancel the meet-and-greet."

Raven didn't respond. She knew Brooke was right.

"I'm giving you the space to make your own decisions, Raven. But it's things like this that chip away at your public image. You choose not to listen to me. Or you belittle and disrespect me, but I'm trying to protect you from yourself."

Did her words hit the mark? Brooke couldn't be sure. Raven stared past her for several moments before opening the door into the phone room. Fifteen harried operators did double-takes when she stepped in, but none stopped making calls. Even as Raven went from person to person, patting them on the shoulder and whispering her thanks, they kept calling. They were only in there for five minutes, but Raven's reaction gave Brooke reason to hope things might get better.

Until they stepped back out into the hallway.

"I'm going to my dressing room," Raven said tersely. "Make sure I'm not disturbed."

CRAIG PUT on the cowboy hat and turned to Brooke.

"How do I look?"

She rose from the chair next to his lighted dressing table, came over, and straightened the collar of his shirt. "Like a genuine country-western superstar."

Her smile helped calm some of his nerves, but not enough to push away the nausea. "Do country-western superstars sweat like this?" he asked, grabbing a tissue and wiping his face.

"Usually not until they're on stage, but you get a pass this time."

"I think I might throw up."

"That would be something to remember. You won't though. Remember, you're singing to one person."

He glanced at himself in the mirror and smiled. "I don't even look like myself."

Brooke shrugged. "It's part of the act. You're still you."

"Maybe, but I don't feel—"

Craig jumped when a stagehand rapped on the dressing room door. "Three minutes!"

"Oh, God..."

He took a step and staggered. His color was ashen, and his pupils were the size of quarters.

"Brooke, I'm not sure I can—"

Her kiss came without notice, just as it had the day he recorded his song. His lips were trembling but softened after a moment. Brooke held on to him until she felt the trembling subside. He searched for what to say, but words eluded him. Brooke grinned at him, then stepped to the dressing table, returning with a small container of face powder. She dabbed a little on his cheeks and forehead. "This will help with the sweating."

"Maybe you should rub it all over me," he said.

"Yeah, you would like that, wouldn't you?" she teased.

Craig stammered, "I didn't mean—"

"Stop talking," she said, leading him from the dressing room. "It's show time."

SHE HELD his hand as they stood offstage. It was nice, but felt a little like kindergarten, too. Back when his mother had dropped him off the first day. Raven commanded the arena from center stage, and as she finished an assortment of Christmas classics, the audience gave her a thunderous ovation. She basked in their adoration, waving and holding her hands to her heart. Sweeping gestures of appreciation. And when they quieted, she said, "Tonight is one of the most special performances of my life…" She had to wait for another round of applause to subside.

"She's going off-script," Brooke murmured in Craig's ear.

"What does that mean?"

"She was supposed to leave the stage before you came out, but I think she's going to introduce you herself."

"What do I do?"

"Just go with it. Listen and respond, just like a regular conversation. Let them see the real Craig Callaway."

Raven continued. "As y'all might know, I recently discovered some old recordings from my college days."

You discovered them…right, Raven. Her voice was starting to grate on Brooke like fingernails on a chalkboard.

"Among those old songs was one that was written and sung by an old and dear friend of mine…some might even say an old flame."

The audience cheered. As always, Raven had them right where she wanted them. "Well, one thing led to another, and after a nationwide search, we found him and he's hiding out backstage. Now he's a shy fella, so it might take some encouragement to get him to come out here and sing his little song for y'all. Will you help me welcome him?"

The arena was nuts. Raven rode the wave of noise like the pro she was. Craig was starting to have some waves of his own and hoped he could last long enough to get through the song.

"Y'all know him as Christmas Carl, and his song is an adorable little holiday thing called 'Making Santa Smile.' Will you welcome my special guest...my friend...and..." she paused and covered her lips as she stage-giggled. "And who knows, y'all? He's kinda cute and all, so maybe he'll be something more than my friend. What would you think of that?"

"Oh, for the love of..." Brooke muttered.

"Christmas Carl!"

"Go," Brooke said, giving him a gentle shove toward the stage. Craig took five steps before emerging into the bright lights of the stage. The band played a festive holiday song with a rocking melody while the audience stood and welcomed him. The last thing he had eaten was a slice of pepperoni pizza two hours before. The taste of pepperoni stung his tongue, but that was as far as it got. He glanced at the band as he passed, and for some reason he would never fully understand, he waved to them. Then he waved to the audience. And grinned. He was still grinning when he realized he had walked right past Raven.

"Hold on, cowboy," she called out. "Get back over here!"

The audience thought it was the funniest thing ever. Craig turned and feigned surprise when he saw Raven behind him. He turned and opened his arms wide. Cameras and cellphones flashed as they embraced.

"You're doing fine, sugar," she said into his ear. "Now

I'm gonna chat with you for a minute or two, then you do your song while I go pee."

She stepped out of his embrace and took a seat. A second stool had been placed next to hers. Craig sat down and waved to the audience again.

"Isn't he adorable?" Raven called out. Then, after the audience had quieted enough to continue, she said, "Carl, how does it feel to be up here in front of all these wonderful folks?"

Craig looked from Raven to the audience. He squinted to see through the spotlights, which were much brighter at the front of the stage. "It's...a lot different from Garland Grove."

"Garland Grove is where you live these days, right darlin'?"

"Uh...yes. I have a drugstore there."

"That sounds...interesting," Raven teased. "What else do you do back in good old Garland Grove, Carl? Is there a special lady in your life?"

"Yeah...well, not anymore. There was, but she was seeing someone else, so we...she broke things off."

The audience moaned.

"I'll go out with you," someone shouted from the arena's upper reaches.

"Come get me, Christmas Carl!" another called out.

"Carl, honey, you might just be cut out for this business," Raven said, grabbing his hand. "Your life kinda sounds like a country song, don't y'all think?"

They did. Craig didn't want to come across as a total loser, so he quickly added, "I direct the community Christmas concert, too."

"Now there's something," Raven exclaimed. "How are rehearsals going? Any big name acts this year?"

The audience laughed. "As a matter of fact, yes. Hal Richie is scheduled to appear this year."

Silence.

More silence.

"I'm afraid I don't know who Hal Richie is, sugar," Raven said.

"He used to lead the Hal Richie Quartet."

Crickets

"Anyone familiar with the Hal Richie Quartet?"

Raven's question was met with more silence.

"Yeah," Craig said, "That's probably why we're having trouble selling tickets."

"Oh, that's so sad, Carl, dear. I wish there was something we could do about that."

Someone shouted, "You could show up, Raven!" The audience expressed its approval.

"Aren't y'all forgetting I've got this little concert tour of my own going on?" Raven asked, sugar practically dripping from her tongue.

"The Christmas concert is the night after our last concert," Craig said.

"Do it!" the audience cheered.

Raven beamed. "Well, maybe I just might. You never know where this little country girl might show up."

BROOKE STEPPED into the aisle and wound her way to the rear of the arena's lower level. Craig wouldn't be able to see her from stage, but she had promised she would be there. She had to stretch to see over the heads of the rows of Raven McCloud fans between her and the stage. He looked good. Raven was doing a nice job of making him feel comfortable.

Her phone buzzed with a text from Bobby. *How is he doing?*

So far, so good! Grinning from ear to ear.

I'm having our people look at some other songs for him. Think he'll be up to an album in January?

Brooke thought about it while Craig and Raven chatted on stage. He was holding his own, even when Raven took his hand like they were college sweethearts. But would he still be interested in the Nashville lifestyle after that wild night with Raven and Travis?

Oh yeah. Travis. She texted Bobby, *What's the latest on Travis?*

Nothing new. No sightings.

Raven broke off the chit-chat. "Okay, sugar," she said as she rose from her stool. "It's time for you to give these people what they came for. Are you ready?"

"I sure am."

He looked good. There was color in his face and he appeared at ease as he strapped on his guitar and rose to his feet. He even said hello to the stagehand who swept in and removed the stools.

"Thank you, everybody." He turned to the band. "Mickey?"

Mickey kicked it off perfectly. And when they reached the part where Craig was supposed to begin singing, he sang. The cheering threatened to drown out his voice, but by the second verse, many were singing along. Just like the Vogue in Garland Grove, except with a lot more people. The only thing amiss was Craig's guitar. It hung from his neck like a giant necklace. Untouched and unplayed. The audience didn't seem to mind, though. And four minutes later, when he reached the end of his song, they roared their approval. He handled it with grace and poise, and when Raven reappeared, they clasped hands and bowed together.

"Ladies and gentlemen, that's Christmas Carl!" she called out as he exited the stage. Brooke turned to head back to Craig's dressing room and was on her way when she received another text from Bobby.

Have you talked to Steve today?

Steve the keyboardist?

Yes.

Brooke had crossed paths with him and noticed he was quieter than usual but figured he had a lot on his mind. Bobby's next text filled in the missing details.

He told me he's leaving the band after tomorrow night.

Departing band members was nothing new. Many headliners weren't above poaching talent, even mid-tour if a need arose.

Who is he going with? Brooke texted back.

Nobody yet. He said he can't take Raven's abuse any longer. He's going to tell Mickey later tonight. I'm on the phone looking for a replacement.

CRAIG HAD NEVER SEEN Sam Griffin rendered speechless, but when he and the others were escorted to Craig's dressing room, Sam seemed overwhelmed.

"He was actually crying while you were singing," Beth said, not afraid to throw some shade her usually boisterous husband's way.

"I have to admit that I might have too," Amy said. "It was incredible, Craig. I mean, it was you, but it wasn't. I kept trying to think of you as our Craig, but on stage, you were like a big star."

Craig had relaxed in the forty-five minutes between his performance and the end of the concert. He ditched the cowboy threads and contact lenses in favor of khakis and glasses. He had hoped that Brooke might make an appearance, but so far she hadn't. It was just him, alone in the dressing room, experiencing everything from euphoria to worry.

Wow, that went great!

Did it? Or was the audience just being kind because he was Raven's friend?

Did he sound okay?

Oh crap, he forgot to play his fake guitar.

Where was Brooke? She would lend perspective to everything.

As much as anything, Craig was hungry. The snacks that had been left in his dressing room didn't sound appealing. He needed more. He needed substance.

"Are you guys ready to go find something to eat?" he asked the Garland Grove gang.

They were. Craig grabbed his phone. "Let me see what's close."

"Can you really go out into public?" Andrew asked. "I mean, you're sort of famous."

Craig hadn't considered it. And he wouldn't get the chance. There was a knock at the door. When it swung open, his friends froze at the sight of Raven McCloud standing in the doorway.

"Well, who do we have here?" she exclaimed.

Silent Sam sank back onto a sofa as if he was having a stroke. Craig made introductions, then said, "We're thinking about getting some late dinner, but I wasn't sure where to—"

"Let me take care of it," Raven said. "Meet me at the loading dock in ten minutes."

BROOKE KNOCKED TWICE. Waited and knocked twice more. The damned code.

"Come on in!" Raven called out.

She went in all right. She went in loaded for bear.

"Raven, what happened between you and Steve?"

Brooke's question wiped the smile off Raven's face. "He's not pulling his share of the load. I've warned him before. I think he's lazy and—"

"He quit. Tomorrow's his final performance."

Raven blinked several times. "He can't quit like that."

"He just did."

She stood up. "I'll go see him and get this straightened out."

Brooke held up her hand to stop her. "No. He's hurt and insulted and refuses to see you. In fact, he told Mickey that if you spoke to him again, he would leave immediately."

"He can't do that. We have a contract."

"You want a keyboardist playing for you who doesn't want to be there? Really, Raven?"

"I'm sick and tired of this," Raven said, throwing up her hands. "And Brooke, I place the blame on you. When Bobby tours with me this never happens."

"Then maybe you need to fire us, Raven because this is the way things are going to be."

Raven gasped. Brooke had struck a blow. She plopped down into her dressing table chair. "Bobby can't quit. He is the reason that I..." She grabbed her phone and punched in a number.

"Bobby, you have to help me. Brooke is—"

She became silent as Bobby spoke on the other end of the line. Brooke couldn't hear him until Raven put the phone on speaker.

"You there, Brooke?" Bobby said.

"I'm here, Dad."

"Good, because I'm only going to say this once. Raven, you need to cut the drama."

"It's not me, Bobby, I swear. I'm trying to make sure the band is strong, and Steve has not been—"

"That boy is one of the best keyboardists in the country," Bobby said brusquely. "He'll have another gig before the end of the weekend. And your actions left us with four days to find a replacement, and so far I'm coming up empty."

"I'll make some calls when I get home, Bobby. There are plenty of keyboardists who would love to join our tour."

"Really, Raven? Name one."

When Raven didn't reply, Bobby continued. "Because what I'm finding is that most good musicians are already on tour or taking the month off to be with family over the holidays. And you know as well as I do that once you get past a handful of people, the talent level drops off pretty quick. And don't forget we need someone who can jump in and learn the music in four days."

"I'll take care of it, Bobby. I think I—"

Another knock at the door.

"Go the hell away!" Raven yelled.

"I won't," Mickey said, as he entered. "Brooke, I'm glad you're here. Two more guys just dropped out." He glared at Raven. "They won't put up with your bullshit anymore."

Raven scowled at Mickey. "You've let things get away from you, Mickey!" she snipped.

"Wait a damned minute, you—"

Bobby's voice remained calm as he spoke through the phone speaker. "Mickey, can we replace them by Thursday?"

"We can try, but it'll be hard. Denise just joined us on bass at the beginning of the tour, and it took two solid weeks to get her up to speed."

Bobby sighed. "That's what I was afraid of. Let me mull this over and get back to y'all."

"We need to get to Tampa for tomorrow night," Brooke said. "I'll tell the crew to start packing things up."

"Good idea, honey," Bobby said. "I'm not sure what we'll do beyond that."

THEY'D BEEN WAITING on the loading dock for an hour. Sam had finally found his voice.

"I think we've been stiffed by Raven McCloud," he said.

"She probably got busy," Amy said, ever the optimist.

Craig felt terrible. They had left Garland Grove before sunrise that morning, just to see him perform. It was now ten-thirty. Everyone was hungry and tired. He had tried calling Brooke a couple of times, but she wasn't answering.

"Maybe they took off without you," Sam said. "Where is your show tomorrow?"

"Tampa. Brooke and I have airline reservations for tomorrow morning. The others are going by bus."

"Well," Sam said between yawns. "We can always go back to our hotel and order pizza. It's just a short walk."

"No," Craig said, trying to hide his disappointment. "You all go on. I probably should wait here."

They hugged him, repeated how awesome he had been,

and trudged off. Craig was on his way back to his dressing room when Brooke found him. She looked exhausted.

"I'm so sorry," she said. Then, after glancing around, "Can we go back to your hotel and talk? I really need to get out of here for a while."

They passed several custodians and a squad of people armed with brooms and mops.

"You're scaring me a little," Craig said after she closed the door. "Did I not do very well?"

Her smile was a weary one. "You were great, Craig. It's just that... I don't know how to tell you this, but the rest of the tour is cancelled."

BROOKE ACCOMPANIED him back to his hotel, but she was far from her usual happy self. Once they were in his room, she filled him in about what had taken place. "We can't continue without a band," she said sadly. "Bobby spent the evening working the phones, but there's just no one available." There were tears in her eyes when she looked at him. "I'm so sorry. You've worked so hard."

She looked frail and defeated. Her biggest star was crashing and burning, yet she was more distraught about his disappointment. He wanted nothing more than to go to her and tell her that things would be okay. That he would be okay, and she would, too. But there wouldn't be a chance.

"I've booked a charter back to Nashville. I'll accompany Raven, though spending two hours on a plane with her is the last thing I want to do at this point." She rose to her feet and rubbed her eyes. "At least we haven't had to worry about Travis Horton. He's still on the lam."

"Brooke," Craig said tentatively. "About Travis?"

"Um-hmm?"

"There's something you need to know."

SUNDAY, DECEMBER 11

GARLAND GROVE AND NASHVILLE

*T*hree cups of coffee had left Craig feeling like a zombie. His flight from Atlanta had departed at five-fifteen. It was nine-forty when he reached the Garland Grove city limits. Bright sunshine reflected off snowdrifts as families headed to church. It was going to be a beautiful winter day, but Craig was too sad and sleep-deprived to enjoy it.

His singing career was over as fast as it started.

But that wasn't what had him feeling so down.

Brooke leaving his room the night before was the reason for his sadness. They had parted with a hug and promise to keep in touch, but Craig felt that part of him walked out that door with her. He had wanted to tell her, to chase her, and let her know his feelings went beyond agent and singer. Or whatever he was now that he wouldn't be singing anymore.

But he hadn't chased her. She was so beaten up by the way Raven was treating her and others. Craig knew she was suppressing her emotions so that she didn't disappoint Bobby. She didn't want him to think she couldn't handle the job. And that, Craig thought, was silly, because she could handle it. She was great at her job.

She was great at everything.

When he admitted that Travis Horton came to his house, she hardly blinked. She understood why he took Travis in, and when he mentioned Travis had planned on returning to Nashville the day before, she had calmly texted his management team and told them to get ready.

Then she had gotten up to leave. Oh, how Craig wished she would have stayed. Even if it was just long enough to tell her how he felt about her. And about how sad he was that they might not see one another again.

"Early morning tomorrow," she sighed. "For both of us."

"Yeah, but at least I get to go home and relax," Craig had said, though he wanted to say much more. "You have to go put out more fires."

And that had been that. His eyes were heavy as he made the final turn onto his street. Craig knew his day would be nothing like poor Brooke's. A million-dollar tour was cancelled and the work that entailed would probably keep her up for days.

Nope, his day would be nothing like poor, sweet Brooke's.

Beautiful, sexy, intelligent Brooke.

His bed was calling, and if that meant he didn't see anyone until the next day at the drugstore, all the better. He placed a quick call to Henry Dinwiddie to let him know he wouldn't be needed that week. The call went to voicemail, which meant Henry was at church. He left a quick message, then noticed he had several of his own. Three were from well-wishers, left before the previous night's concert. Before everything blew up.

The fourth was from Willa McKenzie.

Craig, the Concert Committee has voted to replace you as the concert director. There are some who feel the song you sing on the radio is dirty and indecent, and that your association with that... The line was silent while Willa took a breath and searched for what she intended to say...*that woman, Raven McCloud, is inappropriate. I'm sure you understand.*

"Well, at least I won't have to deal with Hal Richie," Craig mumbled as he turned onto his street. He was relieved to see that Travis Horton's truck was gone. The sight of Jenna's car in his driveway gave him pause, though. *Why was she there?* Had she somehow heard the news that boring old Craig was on his way home with his tail between his legs? Had she come by to share her condolences? He remembered her kindness the previous week. Was that her way of leaving the door open for something more? She wasn't Brooke Summers, but perhaps Jenna was going to be as good as things could be for him in Garland Grove. He parked next to her car and fished out his house key, then stumbled sleepily toward the front door. He unlocked and stepped inside, and was about to call her name when she appeared in the hallway leading to his bedroom. She was wearing one of his favorite dress shirts. And nothing else.

BROOKE FOUND Bobby at the kitchen table with a cup of coffee and a ham and cheese sandwich. He was working on his laptop computer.

"Isn't it kind of early for a sandwich?" And then she saw the time. "Eleven o'clock already? Oh, gosh, Dad, I needed to be up hours ago. I thought I set the alarm on my phone, but I couldn't find it when I woke up."

Bobby pulled it from his shirt pocket. "You needed some rest, and I can handle the clean-up. The cancellation penalties are going to wipe out the profit from the tour stops Raven already made." Bobby glanced at the computer screen, smiled, and said, "It's a lot of money, but she's not gonna miss it. There's plenty more where that came from."

"Yes, but what about the cost to her reputation?" Brooke mused as she went to the coffee pot and poured a cup. She hadn't changed out of the sleeping pants and pink Dolly-wood sweatshirt she'd had for years. "Craig said that Travis was supposed to be back in town by now. How long before his people get him down to police headquarters to make a statement?"

"If they're smart, they'll do it quick but don't get your hopes up. Larry from his office called this morning to see if we might know anything about his whereabouts. I told him that his boy Travis was the least of my worries."

"Jenna?"

She was disheveled like she had just woken up. Her eyes were red, and she seemed stunned that he was there. Why? It was his house.

"I thought you weren't due back until tonight," she said tentatively. And when she glanced over her shoulder, Craig had an uneasy feeling that the surprises weren't over yet. Then Travis Horton stepped out of the guest bedroom. He was wrapped in a bedsheet but still wearing his cowboy hat.

"You're home early, sport!" Travis called out. "Me and her were planning on clearing out before you got back. What happened? Did they kick you off the tour already?"

Travis grinned with pride at his wittiness. Jenna's eyes

darted from Travis to Craig, waiting for the other shoe to fall. Craig pulled out his phone and dialed the local police station.

"Marcie? Hey, it's Craig Callaway." He was speaking to Marcie Walker, the weekend dispatcher, but he locked his eyes on Travis and Jenna. Travis was still grinning, clueless as to the nature of his call. Jenna knew. She turned and headed back to the bedroom. "Marcie, can you connect me with the Nashville Police Department? And stay on the line when you get them because I think they'll want your help."

Travis's face clouded. He took a couple of steps toward Craig. He was trying to appear menacing, but the bedsheet dragging behind him only made him look silly.

"Don't do it, man," he ordered. Craig shrugged and waited for Marcie to place the call. Nothing was likely to happen, but it should prove enough to get Travis Horton out of his house. They played their own little game of chicken while they stared at one another. Travis gave up quickly, though, and stalked back to the bedroom. When Marcie returned to the line, Craig quietly told her he was mistaken. He ended the call but kept the phone to his ear while he waited.

Jenna appeared first, fully dressed and wearing her coat.

"Have a nice day, Jenna," Craig said, keeping the phone to his ear. "Tell your boyfriend, Owen, I said hey."

Okay, maybe the crack about Owen was unnecessary, but it made Craig feel a little better. Jenna didn't apologize or explain. She wouldn't even make eye contact. She just left. Travis was a couple minutes behind her. He looked terrible.

"Did she leave?" he asked. Craig shrugged, then said into the phone, "Nashville police? Yes, I would like to report the location of a suspect in a high-profile crime that was recently committed in your city."

"Dude, hang up the damned phone," Travis snapped. "If the girl left, I got no way to get out of here. I stashed my truck in her garage."

A horn sounded from outside.

"*The girl* is still here," Craig said. "Her name is Jenna."

Travis flipped him off before stalking out the door. Craig went to the window and watched them drive away. Travis was riding shotgun.

Still wearing his hat.

MONDAY, DECEMBER 12

GARLAND GROVE

*C*raig should have been on his way to Phoenix in a couple of days, the first stop on a westward swing of eight concerts in places like Dallas, Phoenix, and Los Angeles. The tour was to have concluded in Minneapolis the night before the Garland Grove Christmas program.

So much for that.

No Dallas. No Los Angeles or Minneapolis.

And now, not even the Garland Grove Christmas concert. Unless he bought a ticket.

But worst of all, no Brooke.

Craig let himself into the drugstore and flipped on the lights. The sun hadn't yet made its appearance and the stark fluorescence stung his eyes. It was a dreary day, with a forecast of cloudy skies and the possibility of several more inches of snow. Gray and bleak. Like how he felt.

The store wouldn't open for another twenty minutes, but that never stopped needy customers from showing up early. It was part of life as a small-town pharmacist, so when Craig heard someone rapping on the door, he forced a smile to his face, threw back his shoulders, and went out front.

Beth Griffin waved at him. She was smiling, but it wasn't her usual everything is great with the world smile.

She knew.

He unlocked and held open the door for her. "I'm betting you aren't here for a refill of Sarah's allergy meds." He returned her smile, but his was no more convincing than hers.

"Not this time." Beth stepped inside and removed her coat, then opened her arms for a hug. "I don't know everything that happened, and I don't need to unless you want to talk about it," she said softly. "I came to make sure you're okay. Sam would be here too, but he's home with the kids."

"I appreciate that, Beth. I really do." Craig motioned for her to follow him to the back of the store. He took a seat at a worktable and she did the same. Then they spent the next fifteen minutes trying to make sense of everything.

Raven's behavior.

The band's implosion.

The end of the tour.

Travis Horton.

Jenna.

Travis and Jenna.

Craig wasn't going to mention his feelings for Brooke, but always-intuitive Beth zeroed in.

"I wish we had gotten to meet her."

"Yeah, me too. She was really good to me."

"Um-hm," Beth said slowly. "I can tell." She paused before saying, "You really like her, don't you?"

Craig nodded. "She is so good at her job."

Beth smiled, and this time it was more a smile of hope than sadness. "It's not just being good at her job. You really *like* her, don't you Craig?"

Craig realized he had been staring at the table

throughout their conversation. He looked up and met Beth's gaze. "I do. But there's not much we can do about that."

"Why would you say that?"

"Come on, Beth. She's a high-powered Nashville talent agent. I'm a drugstore owner in Garland Grove." He thought back to that moment at the Ryman when it was just the two of them—him onstage, her seated in the second row. He sang while she beamed at him. Even then, before she gave him the advice to pick out one person and sing to them, he realized now he was already doing that at the Ryman. No band, no lights. Just him and his audience of one. That, he knew, was the moment he'd fallen in love with Brooke Summers.

"It just can't..." he searched for words to describe the ache he felt. Perhaps, had he been able to continue his singing career, they could have built a relationship. But now? He shook his head and glanced away from Beth.

"You started a love story," Beth said quietly, but with a confidence Craig wasn't feeling. "Now you have to find a way to finish it." She stood up and came around and gave him a peck on the cheek. "You have friends here, Craig Callaway. You will always have friends. Now go finish that love story."

"*R*aven is here."

Raquel's voice through the tinny speaker sent Brooke scurrying into Bobby's office. He was straightening his desk. Despite already having discussed strategy for an hour, Brooke was feeling uncertain. Not Bobby.

"It's the right thing," he reminded her before instructing Raquel to send Raven up.

Brooke had not seen her in person since the charter flight the previous Sunday. Despite the events of the past week, Raven appeared as put-together as always. She stepped into the office like the queen arriving for a ceremony, and it wasn't until she realized that Bobby nor Brooke were about to stand to acknowledge her arrival that the first sign of worry flittered across her beautiful face. She sat on the edge of one of the guest chairs and leaned toward Bobby. There was a chair between her and Brooke. When there would typically be chitchat and gossip, there was silence. Bobby had made it clear that it was a business meeting.

"Raven," Bobby began in his usual slow cadence. "Do you still wish to be represented by Summers Management?"

"Not if you're going to tell me who I can and cannot see," she replied curtly. "And not if you're going to take a band member's word over mine."

Brooke hadn't seen that coming. She also hadn't expected that Raven would attempt to freeze her out of the conversation, but she was making a point to not even look in her direction.

"When did we say anything about who you run around with?" Bobby asked pointedly.

Raven rolled her eyes. "Do I really need to answer that, Bobby?"

"Yes, you do, because I don't recall ever telling you not to date Travis Horton."

"You didn't exactly say it, Bobby, but it's pretty obvious that you don't approve."

"Raven, Brooke, and I help you manage your career. It would be remiss of us not to let you know if we have concerns, don't you agree?"

"Not when it comes to my personal life."

Brooke wanted to speak, to explain that it was impossible to separate the personal from the professional when Raven's every move was scrutinized by hundreds of websites, bloggers, and media members. When Bobby glanced at her, though, she held her tongue. Like it or not, Raven would be more open to advice if it came from Bobby. He picked up a single sheet of paper and held it up for Raven to see.

"Travis Horton has eleven arrests over the past three years. Six speeding tickets, including one for going a hundred and seventeen miles an hour on a two-lane road. He's been arrested for drunk driving twice and twice for assault." He laid the sheet aside. "The incident at Risky Rick's is going to cost him a lot of money, and it's only because of Brooke's hard work that you might slide by without being pulled into it."

Raven glanced at Brooke for the first time but quickly turned back to Bobby. He wasn't done. "Brooke cleaned up this mess better than anyone could...much better than I could. She's savvy and has a way of convincing people to see the good in others."

Brooke looked down at her lap and allowed his kind words to wash over her. God, she loved that man. He made her feel like she could accomplish anything. The big question was, how would he respond when she told him about the opportunity she'd discovered earlier that week?

That conversation would take place as soon as they were finished with Raven.

"Look, Bobby, if you are planning to fire me as a client, you need to know that the people in Travis's office have made me a very lucrative offer."

Bobby didn't miss a beat. "Is that what you want, darling?"

His use of 'darling,' the simple term of endearment, did something to Raven. Her lip quivered, and Brooke saw the way she dug her nails into the arms of her chair. She remained tough, though.

"I need time to figure out who I really am," she said. Then, turning to Brooke, "I think I'm in love with Travis. I know it's crazy, but I am."

A hundred thoughts flooded Brooke's mind. Ninety-nine of them centered on the text she'd received from Craig earlier in the week about returning home to find Travis and his ex-girlfriend Jenna in bed together.

Nope, Brooke. Not your place.

"If it's what you feel, Raven, then it's not crazy."

Well, yeah, she thought. *In this case, it's pretty crazy.*

Brooke reached across the empty chair and squeezed Raven's hand. She squeezed back.

"You realize that the way we promote you has to change," Brooke said. "Perhaps your entire image has to change. People are talking about how some of the band quit on you, and the police reports from Risky Rick's are starting to circulate, too."

"Maybe not," Raven said quietly. "Perhaps I can help Travis get straightened out. He called me this weekend to let me know he's thinking about getting help with his drinking."

Brooke couldn't remember all the Nashville stars who had hung their hopes on guys who weren't worth the effort. A few turned out okay. A lot more continued their slow swirl down the drain. But if there was one thing she'd learned over the past few weeks, it was that Raven McCloud was becoming her own woman. She wanted what she wanted, and if she stayed with them, it would be their responsibility to help her find it.

Provided it didn't tarnish the image of Summers Management.

Because when push came to shove, Summers Management was Bobby's life. And there was no way he would let Raven McCloud diminish what he had spent his life building up.

"Okay, Raven," Bobby said, leaning forward in his chair. "Here's what I propose we do."

Wainwright's Chop House had several individual booths that were closed off from public view. They were typically reserved for small business meetings, but even on a busy Friday afternoon at five-thirty, Ernesto made one available for Bobby and Brooke. After the server took their dinner and drink orders, Bobby removed his hat and placed it next to him.

"Well, sweetheart, you've done great work this week."

"Thank you, Daddy. You, too."

He grinned. "I'm proud of you, little girl. You know that, right?"

Brooke loved when he called her that and couldn't imagine she would ever not love it. "So," she said. "What do you think Raven's next move will be?"

"She needs to get back on the road, but finding top-flight musicians might be hard."

"I loved your idea of an acoustic tour," Brooke said as the server returned with their drinks. Sweet tea for Bobby. Beer for Brooke because beer sounded awesome after the week she'd had.

"Yeah, I agree," Bobby said. "Legally, she's going to be okay. At least she didn't hit anyone like Travis did. Image-wise, as you know, the press is kicking her backside. She's never been through anything like that. She's always been sweet Raven McCloud, the darling of country music. A tour of just her and her guitar might be just the thing she needs. Small venues, though. No more arenas for a while. Let her spend time connecting with her fans until all this blows over, then we'll see where we are."

They sipped their drinks and enjoyed the solitude. It had always been like that when they were together. No need for constant chatter. Bobby was comfortable with silence and had raised Brooke to be the same. Dinner arrived and they dug into hearty steaks that Ernesto had specially selected. A big ribeye for Bobby, a juicy Delmonico for Brooke.

"So, what about you, sweetheart?" Bobby asked between bites. "Where does all this leave you?"

Brooke's mind raced. Oh, goodness. Where to begin?

"Daddy, I think I'm in love."

That seemed as good a place to begin as any.

He cut a sliver of ribeye but laid it aside. "Craig Callaway."

Brooke dropped her fork. "How did you know?"

"The way you talk about him." Bobby grinned. "I've never seen you that way about any man."

"Not even Tristan?"

Bobby shook his head. "Not even that Langston boy you liked so much in high school."

"Jared," she replied, smiling to herself as she remembered the outlandish story she'd told Craig about how that relationship ended. "He was the first boy to kiss me. But, yeah, I'm pretty smitten by Craig. He's so kind."

"Any idea if he feels the same?"

Brooke shrugged and took a sip of her beer. "Everything was so crazy when he was here that it's hard to tell. Maybe... I hope so." Then, doing an about-face, she said, "It will probably be better if he isn't in love with me. Our lives are so far apart."

"If it's love, Brooke darling, none of that other stuff matters."

How did he know so much about so much? There had been nothing in life Brooke couldn't bring up to him. Even during those awkward years when she was becoming a young woman, Bobby was her rock. And here he was, offering wisdom on love and life. How much love had there really been in Bobby Summers's life, anyway? He had married her mother when they were teenagers and, other than the occasional date every so often, he had remained out of the romance game.

His love—all of his love—Brooke realized, had been lavished on her. And for that, she owed him the world. And when he reached into his pocket and withdrew a piece of white paper and unfolded it, she knew instinctively that he was about to give her a push in the right direction.

It was a recording contract.

Not a huge one. Certainly nothing like Raven's and other big stars. Not even close. Probably not even enough for Craig to give up his day job. But for a man in Garland Grove who still might want to break into the music business, it represented a start.

"I'm planning on closing the offices through the holidays," Bobby said. "Why don't you book yourself a flight up to Garland Grove and see if Craig still wants to get into this mess of a business?"

"I don't want to leave you alone, Daddy. Maybe you should come with me."

Bobby laughed. "That's just what y'all need, sweetheart. You'll be trying to get to know Craig while I'm in the next room waiting to find out where we're going for supper." He leaned in closer and said, "Besides, a couple of old boys asked me if I want to try some wahoo fishing off the Bermuda coast. I've never done that before, but I was holding back in case you needed me around."

That was settled. Brooke felt a tingle of excitement at the possibility of getting to see Craig and visit Garland

Grove again. It would be a great time to get acquainted away from the glitz and pressure that accompanied life in Nashville.

But first, there was one more thing.

"Dad, when I was visiting the manager of Risky Rick's the other day, we kinda hit it off."

Bobby cocked his left eye at her. "Another guy? I thought you were gonna chase Craig Callaway."

"No," she giggled. "Nothing like that. The manager's name is Latisha. She's happily married and has four children. I expected she might make things difficult for Raven, but she was very kind."

"Yeah," Bobby said, his eye still cocked. "And?"

"Have you ever thought of owning your own music venue?"

Bobby rubbed his chin. "As a matter of fact, yeah. A long time ago, before things started taking off with the agency. I thought it might be a good investment and give me a place to showcase some of our newer acts."

"What changed your mind?"

He pointed at her. "You did. I didn't want to be away from you a minute longer than I had to."

Brooke liked that. It was the rare Bobby Summers tale that she hadn't heard before. And it offered a nice segue. "Latisha told me that the owners of Risky Rick's want to unload it."

"Kinda run down as best as I remember," Bobby replied. "But it's been five or six years since I was in there."

"It's not in the greatest shape, but they have a big back room they use for storage. Do you remember it?"

She saw the moment the light came on. Bobby nodded slowly. "Yep. They used to do shows six nights a week in there. Conway did a few sets when he was working on new material. He would show up totally unannounced. Eddie Rabbitt, that Whitley boy who died way too young. A lot of up-and-comers passed through there."

"The venue has table seating for two hundred, so it's not real big, but with our connections, we could bring the old place back to life."

Bobby pushed his plate aside. "Are you thinking that's something you'd like to do, baby girl?"

She nodded. "Yeah, Dad. I do. I mean, you made your name in the music business, and I would like to as well." She hesitated to go on, not sure how he might take her next revelation. "I think I would enjoy operating a music venue. Maybe more than what I do now."

She looked at him closely for any sign of disappointment, praying she wouldn't see any.

"Make no mistake, Brooke. You can surpass anything I've achieved in life. You're smarter than I am and you have a good way about you. Maybe you're a little in the dumps because of what happened with Raven, but that's not on you, honey."

"I know that. And I believe in myself. But your side of the business doesn't excite me like it does you. Now owning a venue? Helping performers get started? That excites me." She reached into her purse and pulled out a folder. "I want you to look at the financials and tell me what you think."

She slid the folder across the table. Bobby didn't touch it. "Have you already looked at them?" he asked.

She said she had.

"And?"

"They're solid, even without using the space in back. I got ahold of a couple people who know about that kind of stuff and they said the costs to bring the stage area up to code would be recoverable in under five years, provided I could attract the right type of acts." She smiled at Bobby. "Do you know anyone who can help me get the right type of acts?"

Bobby nodded. "I just might. And I would love to be a part of it if it comes to pass, but..."

"Conflict of interest," Brooke interjected.

"Yeah, and you would have to step back from the agency for the same reason."

Was there a tinge of sadness in his words? She thought so at first, but as she listened, Brooke realized there was no sadness at all. The longer they talked the more Bobby's eyes danced with excitement.

"But what about Summers Management?" she asked.

Bobby clasped his hands on the table in front of him. "I can hire a couple of good young associates without any problem. It won't be the same as having you around, but you have to remember, Brooke honey, the company was my dream." He looked into her eyes and held her gaze. "You need to chase your own dream, and if this is it, you go after it with everything you got."

Those might have been the most heartfelt words he'd ever spoken to her. She rose from her chair, tossed her napkin on the table, and came around to his side. She hugged him hard and kissed his cheek.

"I love you so much, Daddy," she said.

"You're my world, sweetheart."

She gave him one more good squeeze, then said, "The owners of Risky Rick's aren't planning on doing anything before Christmas, so I have time to make sure it's the right move."

"That's perfect. And that gives you time to visit with

Craig and sort out what might be percolating between the two of you."

She clapped her hands like the little girl she sometimes felt like with him. "I can't wait to find out, Daddy. Would it be okay if I leave on Monday?"

It was fine.

Just fine.

MONDAY, DECEMBER 19

GARLAND GROVE

*C*raig flipped on the lights and turned on the OPEN sign. It had been seven sucky days since his return to Garland Grove. Customers entering the previous week were stunned to see their regular pharmacist back on duty. Then, as word got around, their surprise gave way to sympathy.

"It's terrible how she cancelled the show."

"You deserved better, Craig."

"Those show biz types can't be trusted."

Word had also gotten around that Jenna Waite was seeing Owen the vet. Rocky Spangler had spotted them together at the Red Lobster in Freeport and carried his account of the sighting back to the Park-Rite. Maizie picked it up from there, broadcasting it to everyone who came in for the lunch special. Jenna's weekend fling with Travis Horton hadn't become public knowledge yet, so as far as people in Garland Grove were concerned, poor Craig had lost his chance at stardom and been dumped by his longtime girlfriend, all within a few days.

It was excruciating being the object of pity. Even when

the sympathy pies and cakes had started showing up the previous Friday, Craig just wanted to lock up the drugstore and escape. He didn't have the option, though. Henry Dinwiddie had made it clear that he wasn't to be bothered again until after the holidays. "I remember now why I retired," he had said when he returned Craig's call.

Nope. Keeping Callaway's Drugstore open fell to the only Callaway in town. And when Friday had rolled around, it was easy to turn down Sam's invitation to dinner with the Bennetts at Café Americana. "I just want to sit in my recliner and do nothing," he had said. Beth had checked on him later that afternoon but didn't push the invitation.

Then came the call that changed everything.

Friday evening. Late. Craig was watching the end of one of those newsmagazine shows. He figured it was a spam call, or maybe Beth was checking in one more time. But it wasn't.

When he saw Brooke's name on the screen, his heart raced.

She wanted to come to town.

To visit. And talk business.

If it was okay with him.

If it was okay with him?

Oh, God, was it ever okay with him!

She said something about booking a room at the Park-Rite. Craig blabbered on about how he had a spare room and that it had its own bathroom and its own closet and its own dresser. He had been about to tell her it had its own lamp and pictures on the wall when he realized how dopey he sounded. He paused for a breath, and during that pause, Brooke said that she would like very much to stay at his house.

And her saying that made all the sadness and embarrassment of the past week slip away.

Things were going to be okay.

Brooke was coming to town.

Henry Dinwiddie had been surprised to receive his call Saturday morning. Craig told him about Brooke and all she had done for him and how much he cared about her. He asked—nearly begged—Henry to cover an hour here or there. And Henry had, despite his earlier protestations, said he would be happy to cover the entire week.

"Have I ever told you about Gladys?" he asked. He had many times. It was a sweet love story about a young druggist and the new schoolteacher. A story that Craig had barely listened to in the past, but hung on every word as Henry repeated it over the phone.

"If Gladys were still here, she would tell me to get my tired old self down to the drugstore so that Craig can spend time with his new friend."

Brooke would arrive that evening. Craig had offered to pick her up at the regional airport, but since she was also coming for business, the agency would spring for a rental car. She took him up on his offer to make dinner. He had put a pot roast in the slow cooker before leaving that morning.

Things were looking up.

Amy Bennett was his first customer of the day. She commented on how upbeat he was and squealed with delight when he told her the source of his joy.

"Any idea what the business part is?" she asked.

Craig hadn't really given it much thought. "There's probably some paperwork involved when a guy's career goes down the drain." He was joking, but it still hurt a little.

"They're still playing your song about a hundred times a

day on the radio," Amy said. "Maybe there's been a change of plans. Maybe Raven patched things up with the band and the show will go on."

Craig knew better but didn't let on. They moved on to other topics as Amy brought him up to speed on Garland Grove gossip that didn't have his name attached to it.

"I heard that they've only sold seventy tickets to the Christmas concert," she dished. "People are mad that Willa is running things, and that she's paying that Hal Richie guy so much money. I'm afraid the concert is going to be a big flop."

Craig had every right to not care, but he did. The concert had been a big part of his time in Garland Grove, and to think it was not pulling the community together like it used to was sad. "I haven't purchased my ticket yet," he said. "Maybe I can convince Brooke to go along."

"If you do, let us know and we'll all sit together." Amy paid for her purchases and rushed back out into the cold. It was a sunny day with temperatures in the mid-thirties. Snow was predicted for later in the week, but that was all well and good. Whatever happened, happened. Brooke Summers was coming to town.

THERE WAS something comforting about driving along a clean, dry road with snow piled along the sides. A secret passageway that belonged only to her. Brooke's experiences with snow were limited to occasional dustings, though she remembered the time a few years before when Nashville had received eight inches. It was pretty, but people down there were snow-driving novices, motoring around like, as

Bobby joked, pigs on skates. Within days, temperatures rose, and the town was a wet, muddy mess.

Nothing like the area surrounding Garland Grove. Snow was everywhere. Lots and lots of it. Still beautiful and pristine in the headlights of her rental car. She wondered if Craig ever went outside and played in it, or if he still built snowmen. She had never built a snowman and wanted to very much. Was it considered cool to build a snowman in a town where the snow arrived in November and stuck around until March?

But more than anything, she was excited to see Craig. To spend time with him and get to know him at home, where he could be himself. There were no pressing tasks on her work schedule. The music world was mostly silent since Raven's cancellation. It would be a few days of just her and Craig.

And that sounded heavenly.

She double-checked GPS and pulled onto a street of brightly decorated homes. Santas waved from snow-covered porches and yards. Wise men bowed before baby Jesuses under wooden shelters in front of at least a third of the homes along the block. Two men deep in conversation under a streetlight took time to smile and wave. It was very warm and homey and inviting, and made Brooke realize what she had missed while spending the past several years in an apartment complex where no one knew anyone else's name and the faces were always changing. She smiled when she saw Craig had shoveled the snow from the driveway, leaving plenty of space for two cars. She pulled in next to his pickup and was retrieving her bag from the trunk when he opened the front door and bounded out to meet her.

"Hey, you made—"

That was as far as he got before he slipped on an icy patch and was tossed headfirst into a snowdrift.

"Oh, no, Craig!" Brooke left her bag and hustled to where he had taken his fall. The snow was several feet deep, and all she could see of Craig was his backside. She peered over the snowdrift just as he was attempting to turn over. It was dark, but the snow provided a luminescence that made it easy to see his face when he looked up. He was smiling. No, he was laughing. His glasses were crooked and his nose was as red as Rudolph's.

"Doggone it. I thought I had put down plenty of salt," he said as he extended his hand. "Can you help me up?"

She reached for his hand and pulled him from the snowdrift. He got to his feet, straightened his glasses, and wiped snow from his shirt and pants. Then he turned to her and threw open his arms. They hugged for a few moments, neither saying a word. It was good. Brooke had missed him, and his hug made her realize how much.

"I took six years of gymnastics, but never had moves like those," she teased as she stepped back to get a good look at him. His laugh was full and happy and seemed to come from deep in his soul. And before she knew it, he had picked her up and tossed her. She was airborne for what felt like a long time, but probably was only a second or two before gently landing in snow as soft as a cloud. It felt cold and fluffy and heavenly, and when Craig launched himself into the snow next to her, it was even better. They laughed like kids, and when he reached for her hand, she let him take it.

"I've never done this before," she said as she gazed at a sky so dark and full of stars that it seemed only a few feet above them. A light came on in front of the house next door and while it was impossible to see anyone over the mounds of snow, Brooke heard a woman call out, "Craig, did you slip and fall? Are you okay?"

"I'm fine, Tammy. My friend Brooke is visiting from down south and I invited her to join me in a snowdrift."

"Is that the pretty girl who you had breakfast with at the Park-Rite a couple weeks ago, Craig?"

Brooke giggled and elbowed Craig.

"One and the same."

"Oh, good for you. Fran said she was a sweet girl. Does she know Jenna broke things off with you?"

Brooke's giggle became a snort.

"She heard about it, Tammy. Maizie told her."

"Maizie heard from Stacy Pike," Brooke called back.

"Okay, then. You two enjoy yourselves. Merry Christmas!"

"Merry Christmas!" they answered together.

Craig turned in the snowdrift so he was facing her. "Welcome to Garland Grove, Miss Summers. Where everyone knows everything about everybody."

"I'm delighted to be here, Mr. Callaway. Now, will you help me crawl out of all this snow?"

CRAIG RETRIEVED her bag and led the way inside.

"What is that heavenly aroma?" she exclaimed as soon as they stepped into the house.

"I put a roast and veggies on this morning. Are you hungry?"

She pulled her coat off and hung it on the coatrack just inside the door. "I had pretzels and apple juice on the flight from Nashville to Chicago, and nothing on the flight to the regional airport. If you don't dish up some of that roast in about two minutes, I'll start eating right out of the pot."

"I'll save you the embarrassment of slurping from the pot," Craig said. "Come into the kitchen."

"Do you mind if I take my boots off first? We southern girls have soft feet, and these have been pinching me since O'Hare airport."

Craig watched as she sat in one of the living room chairs and started tugging at the brown leather boots she wore with jeans and a pink cashmere sweater. She struggled for a few moments, so he offered a hand, getting down on his knees in front of her. She lifted her foot and he pulled one boot loose, then the other. She wiggled her sock-clad toes to get the blood circulating. Craig couldn't take his eyes off her.

"Much better," she sighed. "Now, let's eat."

Craig got plates from the cupboard and filled them with roast, carrots, and potatoes. He offered wine, but Brooke said no.

"I'll stick to water. I love wine, but I'm afraid of what it might make me do," she said. "But tomorrow, after a good night's sleep, ask me again."

She dug in, calling to mind the morning they met at the Park-Rite on her earlier visit. Craig was hungry as well. They cleaned their plates and went back for seconds. The conversation never waned. Nor did it veer back to the events of the past weekend. She asked more questions about his childhood and life in Garland Grove. He was surprised at how much interest she showed in the drugstore. She talked about life at Percy's Crossroads, and how Bobby had shielded her from the trappings of being in such proximity to stardom. The more they chatted, the more clear it became that, despite all the differences in their lives, they had been raised to respect people and remain humble.

"Would you change anything?" Craig asked. He was surprised that she didn't take long to consider his question.

"As a matter of fact, I am thinking about something along those lines right now."

"Care to talk about it?" he asked as he stood up to refill their water glasses.

"Sure. It's—"

Someone was at the door. Craig glanced at the clock. Nine-fifteen. He excused himself and went to the living room. He was surprised to see Joanne Sayer.

"Joanne, come in. What brings you out so late?"

"I'm sorry to bother you, Craig, but I didn't know what else to do." She stepped in and spotted Brooke's suitcase in the middle of the room. "Are you on your way out? I can make this quick."

"No, that belongs to..." He glanced toward the kitchen just as Brooke stepped through the doorway.

"Hi," Brooke said.

"Hello," Joanne replied.

"Joanne, this is Brooke Summers. She's a...friend who is visiting for a few days."

Joanne backed up toward the door. "I should never have come by without calling first. I'll get back to you another time."

"Nonsense, Joanne, come in and have a seat. We were just finishing dinner. Would you like something?"

"Thank you, but no. I'll keep this quick so you can get back to your friend. Things are a mess with the concert."

"I heard tickets weren't selling."

"Willa McKenzie announced today that she is resigning from the committee. Our singers are upset with her and how she treated you. People are hearing about it and seem to be boycotting the concert." Joanne took a breath. "I'm afraid that the entire thing is going to blow up."

"I'm sorry to hear that, Joanne, but what can I do? The concert is Thursday night. Maybe it would be better to cancel it for this year and try to regroup."

"We—and I'm speaking for the others—were hoping you might come back. We can fire Hal Richie and try to salvage the concert as it used to be."

"Oh, Joanne, I don't think I should—" Craig's cellphone rang in the kitchen.

"Want me to get it?" Brooke offered.

"It's okay. Probably someone who needs an emergency prescription filled. I can call back." Then, to Joanne, "I'm touched that the performers think enough of me to want me back, but I've been gone all week and have so much to catch up on that—"

Craig's phone again.

"I'm sorry, Joanne, maybe I should—"

"I'll get it," Brooke said, disappearing into the kitchen.

"Craig, I wouldn't have come by if the situation weren't so dire, but I'm afraid there are so many hurt feelings over the way Willa has handled things. We may never have the concert again."

"You might be right, but why me, Joanne? Willa said that people were offended by my song. She said the lyrics were too—"

"Willa was offended. Everyone else thinks your song is the best thing ever. Willa McKenzie has wanted to run the concert for years, but you were so good at it she knew there would be trouble if she cut you out. She seized on your song to make it seem she was doing the community a favor."

"I'm sorry, Joanne, but so much has happened that I just don't think I can—"

"Craig?" Brooke was back. She had his phone. "You really need to take this. It's important."

Joanne glanced from Craig to Brooke. "I'll leave. I just hoped you might reconsider once you heard what people were saying."

"Don't leave," Brooke said, coming closer. "Craig, it's Raven. She needs to speak to you, and Joanne might be interested in what she has to say."

Raven? Now?

Craig took the phone and held it to his ear.

"Raven?"

"Craig, I've been self-centered and bitchy and incredibly unfair to you. There are a hundred other things I could say, but it all comes down to this: can you forgive me?"

"Well...uh, Raven, of course, I can forgive you."

"I'm so glad. I have about twenty more calls like this to make, but I wanted to start with you. I heard Travis hid out at your house last weekend. You would have been justified in kicking him out, but you didn't. That shows the kind of person you are." The line was quiet for a few beats. Craig sensed Raven was composing herself before continuing. "I need to be more like that, Craig. I need to be kinder and more thoughtful."

Talk about uncomfortable. Raven was apologizing and pledging to clean up her act. Brooke had taken a seat on the sofa. Joanne was nearby, poised to leave. Neither could hear what Raven was saying, though Craig suspected Brooke knew what the call was about. But if she did, why had she asked Joanne to stick around?

"I'm sure you can figure things out, Raven," he responded. He considered asking her if she knew Jenna had spent the weekend at his house with Travis, but that wouldn't help matters. What was between Raven and Travis was between Raven and Travis. "Was there anything else?"

"As a matter of fact, sweetheart, there is." She sounded more like the Raven everyone knew and adored. And what she said next nearly bowled Craig over.

"Remember when I said I might come sing at your little Christmas concert?"

She couldn't mean it. Could she?

"Uh, yes, I recall you mentioning it, but I don't think anyone really thought it would happen."

Raven laughed merrily. "Well, it's not like I have anything going on now, is it darlin'? Your show is this Thursday, right?"

"Yes, but I'm not—"

"Have Brooke send me the details, sugar. It will be a nice way for me to get back out there again. And maybe help spit-shine my image."

"Uh...Raven, can you hold on a minute?" Craig took the phone from his ear. "Joanne, what would you say if I told you I think I can help sell out the Christmas concert?"

"So," Craig asked after Joanne had departed and it was just him and Brooke. "Can we count on Raven to show up?"

"She'll be here. Dad texted me just before she called to let me know. They're chartering a plane for her and everything. No band, though. Just Raven and her guitar."

They were in the living room. Craig was on the sofa with his legs extended on the coffee table. Brooke had considered joining him but opted for a chair to his right.

Close, but not too close. Not that she wouldn't have welcomed a little closeness, but it was late and she was exhausted. No need to start something she couldn't finish.

"We do have some business to discuss, but how about we put it off until morning?" she proposed.

"Is it good news or bad?"

"It depends on how you look at it, I suppose."

He laughed. "You're being evasive."

"Yes, I am." She stood and stretched. "Now, if you don't mind, I would love to get some sleep."

He stood and came to her. When he embraced her, she didn't object. It felt familiar and good, and when she leaned into him, she thought about how easy it would be to stay that way. To spend the evening in his arms. That had been in the back of her mind since she'd planned the trip three days earlier. Getting close to Craig was why she was there. More than business. More than anything. And the opportunity was right in front of her, with his arms around her waist. She rested her head against him and liked how it felt.

But not quite yet.

"You know," she murmured into his shirt. "I'm not some fair little maiden who hasn't seen a thing or two."

He didn't reply. She heard only his breathing and the steady beat of his heart.

"And I'm not some loose woman like in those old country songs people like so much."

Still no reply. But that was fine. Brooke sensed he knew where she was going.

"It would be so easy to follow you down that hallway."

"Um-hm," he said softly. "But that's not what's best."

She raised her head to meet his gaze. "It's not what's best *yet*."

"Yet," he echoed.

"But given time..." she continued. "It might be the best thing ever."

His response was to kiss her forehead. It was good, but not quite good enough. She raised her chin and their lips met. They had kissed twice before, spur-of-the-moment encounters when he was nervous about performing his song. This was slower. Searching. Deep and lingering. His arms held her when she felt herself going weak in the knees. If she followed him down that hallway, to his bedroom, she knew what was happening between them would only get better and deeper. And real.

Craig knew it, too. She could tell by the way she felt him responding. And they were adults. Perfectly capable of making adult decisions.

But she was worn out from a morning in the office, followed by an afternoon of travel. And from the pressures of the past week. And even if she went with him he wouldn't be getting her at her best. And Craig Callaway deserved the best she had to give.

"Will you show me to my room?" she whispered.

"Of course."

TUESDAY, DECEMBER 20

GARLAND GROVE

A soft knock at the door brought Brooke fully awake. She wasn't sure where she was for a moment until she noticed the snow-covered windowpanes.

Garland Grove.

Craig's home.

The thought made her happy.

His being on the other side of the bedroom door made her panic. She scrambled out of bed and tiptoed to the dresser mirror. Her hair was a mess. She wore no makeup. There was sleep in her eyes. She needed a couple of minutes to make herself presentable, but he was just a few feet away and would probably hear her plodding around.

Heck with it. She ran her hand through her hair, wiped the sleep from her eyes, and crawled back into bed.

"Come in," she said cheerfully.

He had on his usual khakis, topped with a white quarter-zip sweater. What he wasn't wearing were his glasses. His eyes were bright and alive, but what really grabbed Brooke's attention was the tray of food he carried.

"You made all this for me?"

"I certainly did," he said as he placed the tray across her legs. He unfolded and handed her a cloth napkin. "I don't have plate covers like the hotel in Atlanta, but I only had to bring the food from the kitchen, so it's still warm."

Brooke leaned closer and inhaled. Eggs scrambled to perfection, thick slices of crispy bacon, and biscuits that appeared to have been...what?

"Deep fried," Craig explained. "It's Stacy Pike's specialty. I begged her to make them so many times that she finally gave me the recipe and told me to make my own." He picked one up and cut it in half, then slathered it with a thick brown concoction.

"Oh, my goodness. Is that apple butter?"

"Yep. Locally made by Beverly Blankenship. She and her husband have a tree farm a few miles out of town." He handed Brooke half of the biscuit. She took a bite and moaned in ecstasy at the deep-fried sugary explosion of apple goodness.

"I have to meet Beverly Blankenship," she exclaimed. "I just want to follow her around and learn all her secrets, because that is the best apple butter I've ever had in my life. And those biscuits..." she took another bite and moaned again.

Craig sat on the edge of the bed and appeared delighted with the way she put away breakfast. Brooke couldn't remember the last time someone had served her breakfast in bed, then realized it was a first. But something she could easily become used to. She cleaned up the eggs, except for the last bite, which she held out for him. He had no reservations about sharing a fork, so she also gave him a couple bites of bacon before he said, "No more. I ate while I cooked." She polished off the last crumbs, took a sip of orange juice, and dabbed at her face with the napkin before declaring, "Okay, I'll cut to the chase. Will you marry me?"

Craig's eyes became huge for a moment, then he laughed. "Breakfast in bed is all it takes? If I had known that, I might not still be single."

"Lucky for me you are," she teased. "It would be awkward to be served breakfast in bed by a married man."

Craig removed the tray from the bed and sat back down. "So, what do you want to do today?" he asked.

"A lot of things," she answered. "I want another look around town and maybe window-shop a little. And I definitely want to meet Mrs. Blankenship and get a couple gallons of apple butter to take back to Nashville. And of course, we have that business to discuss." She paused and made sure she had his full attention. "But more than anything, I want to spend time with you."

They gazed at one another for a few moments. He appeared uncertain about what his next move should be, so Brooke made it easy for him by sitting up and moving close. She was nearly there when he realized what was about to happen. The kiss was slow and searching. Mmm, he was good at that. His lips lingered on hers. His hand came to her cheek and caressed. She moaned again, but this time apple butter had nothing to do with it. He started to pull back, but she wrapped her hands around the back of his head and kept him right where he was. One kiss became another. His tongue searched for hers, and that connection nearly short-circuited everything. She wanted to pull him down next to her and see if he was as gentle at other things as he was at kissing. She knew he would be, but the fun was in the discovery.

"I got a call earlier from the Grasshopper," Craig murmured when their lips finally separated.

"Did it chirp?" she replied with a grin.

"Very good," he laughed. "Grasshoppers actually do chirp, but this was the *Garden Grove Grasshopper*. Our local paper. They heard about Raven coming to town and want to run a story on the front page of tomorrow's paper."

"That should help sell your tickets," Brooke said as she reclined against the headboard and pulled him along with her.

"Yeah, but they want to interview me for the article. I said I would stop by before noon."

Brooke pursed her lips in a pout. "Does that mean the kissing is over?"

Instead of answering, he kissed her again. Still sweet. Still searching. Still giving Brooke crazy good feelings in her tummy and other places.

"Do you want to go along?" he asked when they came up for air.

"I didn't come all this way to sit around by myself, mister," she teased. "Now that I'm here, you're stuck with me."

"I like that," he said, following with another kiss. Then he stood up. "I'll get the kitchen cleaned up. We'll leave when you're ready."

CRAIG HELPED Brooke from the cab of his pickup and kept one hand on her arm as they crossed the *Garland Grove Grasshopper's* ice-glazed parking lot. Her cheeks were red, and her eyes danced. His eyes were probably dancing too, after those intimate moments back at the house. A bell over the door announced their entrance. There was no receptionist, so they waited until Randy Hastings appeared from someplace in back.

"Our prodigal son returns!" Randy exclaimed. He came to the counter and opened the swinging gate that separated visitors from staff. "C'mon back and let's talk."

Craig made introductions. "Randy has been editor of the *Grasshopper* for thirty years."

"You've probably covered a lot of big stories," Brooke said as they stepped into Randy's pine-paneled office.

"Not really, young lady. A few big stories, but a lot of city council and school board meetings. We're strictly local."

The way Randy delicately lowered himself into his overstuffed desk chair communicated to Craig that the man continued to have problems with his back. Were it just the two of them, he might encourage him to swing by the drugstore and refill his pain meds. "Anyway," Randy continued when he was seated. "The news about Raven McCloud has me champing at the bit. She'll be the first famous person to pass through Garland Grove since Alex Trebek."

"Alex Trebek?" Brooke asked. "The Alex Trebek who used to host Jeopardy?"

Randy nodded. "One and the same. He was traveling back to California and detoured off the highway to see somebody he used to know."

"Did you meet Alex Trebek, Craig?"

"He was here before I arrived, but I've seen his picture on the wall at Smack's."

"Sure enough," Randy interjected. "He had the chicken and dumplings special. Told the manager at the time they were the best dumplings he'd ever had. He even gave me ten minutes to ask him some questions. One of the greatest days of my career."

"That certainly is impressive," Brooke said. Craig liked the way she validated Randy's brush with greatness. Particularly given how many famous people she had rubbed shoulders with. After Nashville, Garland Grove had to be pretty boring.

Then, an alarming thought hit him. Would Brooke find *him* boring?

Jenna had. Dinner with friends, movies at home. She was raised in a small town, yet she had described their relationship as boring. If Craig Callaway was too boring for Jenna Waite, what was there to stop Brooke from feeling the same?

And then she reached for his hand and those worries disappeared. They were seated next to one another, across the desk from Randy. He noticed. His eyes zeroed in on their hand-holding, and he didn't say anything about it for a moment, choosing to chat a bit more about Alex Trebek before circling back.

"So, should I take it you two are an item?" he asked. Craig's face became hot, but Brooke didn't flinch. "It seems so, Randy." She leaned in and motioned for Randy to do the same. "So tell me, am I making a smart decision or should I run straight back to Nashville?"

It was Randy's turn to blush. "Well, I guess he's okay. He has the drugstore, which I imagine does alright for him. He just broke up with Jenna Waite, though, so watch yourself in case he's on the rebound."

"Oh, that's okay," Brooke said without a trace of concern. "I'm on the rebound, too. Maybe we'll bounce straight to each other."

Randy chuckled and reached for his writing pad. "Well,

then, how about you tell me what Nashville was like, Craig? I figure I can talk to you about your singing and get a story about Raven McCloud coming to town this week. Two for the price of one, I guess you'd say."

Craig covered the basics, leaving out any mention of the incident at Risky Rick's or Raven's harsh treatment of the band. It was already page one fodder on the big entertainment websites, anyway, but Randy didn't deal in gossip. He finished up by asking if he might be able to conduct a quick interview with Raven. Brooke took that question.

"She'll be delighted to chat with you, Randy."

THE COLD, dry air nearly took Brooke's breath away as they stepped back outside.

"Do you ever get used to the climate?" she asked Craig.

"I don't even notice it until it gets into the negative numbers. And the summers are the best. I might turn on the AC for a few days in July, but mostly it's open windows and low humidity." He glanced up the street, then said, "You wanted to talk business. How about we grab some coffee at Lula's? Unless you're ready for lunch."

"After that wonderful breakfast? I can't eat another bite. But coffee sounds nice." Brooke pulled up the collar of her coat as she looked up the street. "How far is Lula's?"

"Close, but if you want we can jump back in the truck."

She considered it. Her cheeks and ears were numb. Fortunately, she'd remembered to bring mittens. "Let's walk. I need to toughen up if I'm going to be spending time here. But promise me we'll go see the apple butter lady later."

"I promise. You'll love Beverly." He took her hand and

led her along the sidewalk, past adorable little shops selling everything from apparel to knickknacks and gifts. Brooke paused in front of a window display of beautiful jewelry and, interestingly, firearms and ammunition.

"I know," Craig said with a laugh. "It's weird. Buckshot does quite a brisk business, though."

"The jewelry is exquisite," Brooke said as her eyes lingered on engagement rings. "I can't say much about the firearms, though. That's Bobby's area of expertise."

Only a handful of customers were in Lula's. The menu of coffees and pastries was on a blackboard behind the counter. Craig ordered a vanilla latte. Brooke studied the menu like there might be a test later.

"How is the cocoa?"

"Decadent," the barista replied. "We make it with gourmet chocolate. And the whipped cream is from a local dairy."

"Ooooh, I'll have that. Extra whipped cream, please."

They took their drinks to a table in the rear of the cozy shop so they could talk privately. Brooke had left the paperwork back at Craig's house but had everything on her phone. She took a sip of cocoa and savored the smooth, sweet burn. "Wow, that's good," she said, smacking her lips.

Craig laughed. "We're not Nashville, but things are pretty nice here."

"Okay, first things first," Brooke said, opening a spread-sheet. "We haven't talked about royalties."

"Will there be enough to cover our drinks?"

She looked up from her phone. "I should have done a better job explaining things. You're the singer *and* the song-writer, so any profits from the sale and download of 'Making Santa Smile' are yours." She paused. "Except the percentage that comes to us for representing you. Remember? From the contract?"

He remembered. "Whatever it is isn't enough. I had my few minutes of fame because of you."

Brooke smiled appreciatively. "You're sweet, you know that?"

"I mean it, Brooke. It was crazy, and there were a couple times in Travis's car when I wondered if I would survive the night, but I wouldn't trade those memories for anything." He gazed into her eyes. "Especially getting to know you."

Brooke held his gaze. The guy was really something. So gentle and unassuming. So appreciative. So *real*. Living a life he enjoyed, reveling in the special moments as they came. What was up with that Jenna Waite? How could she ever find him boring? Brooke wondered if she might reconsider after a weekend of being Travis Horton's plaything. Had she come to realize that Travis wasn't coming back? He would never return her calls. It was unlikely he had even given her his real number. If so, she was probably lamenting how wonderful boring old Craig really was.

Ha! Sucks being her.

"About those royalties. I've created a projection of how much the song will make over the next thirty days. Remember when you look at this that you have two things working against you. First is that you're unknown."

"Christmas Carl," Craig interjected. "Sort of hard to break out a bunch of summer hits with a name like that."

"Yep. The second is that 'Making Santa Smile' is a holiday song. As soon as people finish unwrapping the presents, sales fall off a cliff."

"Are you saying I won't be able to cover the price of your cocoa?"

"Well, maybe you'll have enough. I guess it depends on

351

how many times you bring me here." She turned the screen so he could see it, then used her finger to point to the bottom line. Craig jolted forward in his chair when he saw the number. He stood up and looked around as if someone was following him.

"This can't be right." He nearly missed his chair when he sat back down. A couple of college-age espresso drinkers a few tables away eyed him curiously. "Brooke, is this a joke?"

"It's actually a conservative estimate. You have a good song, Craig, but you also got lucky. Radio stations helped build an audience, and your connection to Raven made it take off. Sure, it's a holiday novelty song, but I believe that its sweet and slightly off-color message will help sales bounce back every year. Will it be a hit again? Probably not, but radio stations and streaming services will continue to play it. People will hear it. And some will add it to their playlists."

"This is..." Craig's breathing was heavy with excitement. He looked at the number a second and third time. "This is as much as I earn from operating the drugstore in a year. And you're saying it could be like this every year?"

"It could. Now, as your agent, I would advise you to invest it wisely and enjoy the returns. If it dries up after a few years, you'll still have the proceeds to help you later in life." She winked as she said, "but as your friend, I would suggest you spend a little of it. Buy something you've always wanted." She pointed to the number again. "Provided it's not much more than this."

Craig sat back in a daze. He tried to speak, but words didn't come for a few moments, until he could spit out, "There's really nothing I want."

"Then maybe you invest the proceeds and have a nice

little nest egg that lets you retire a few years early. Maybe do some traveling."

"Greece," he said, his voice still unsteady. "I always wanted to see the Parthenon."

"You should go."

"Brooke, can you help me invest this?"

"I can recommend people who can."

He shook his head slowly. When he lifted his coffee cup to his lips, his hand was shaking.

"So," he finally said. "Do you want another cocoa? It looks like I can afford it after all."

They shared a laugh. When Brooke caught the espresso drinkers still glancing at them, she pointed to Craig and called out, "He wrote a hit song!"

"Good," the guy called back. "Use it to stock more comic books in the drugstore. Your superhero selection stinks."

"Yeah, Craig," Brooke said, giving his hand a squeeze. "Get to work on your superhero selection."

"I will, Cameron," Craig said, turning to face the guy. "I promise. More superheroes."

The guy gave them a thumbs up. Craig turned back to Brooke. He was grinning from ear to ear. "Well, thank you for that wonderful bit of news."

"You're welcome," she said. "But there's more." She flipped to another page on the phone and said, "Caswell Music is a small boutique label in Nashville. They want you to come to town and cut an album."

"People still buy albums?"

"Not like back in the old days. Vinyl records and CDs don't sell like they used to, but record companies still package songs together. Fans can download one song or the entire album." She pulled up the Caswell Music website and handed her phone to Craig. "They aren't one of the big names, but they do okay."

"How does it work?" Craig asked as he studied the website.

"You sign a contract. They produce, market, and distribute the album, and you earn royalties on each sale. Nothing like you earn from 'Making Santa Smile' because you earn royalties as writer and singer, but it could prove to be a good deal."

She allowed him time to continue to peruse the website. "Do they want me to write songs, too?"

"No. They will provide the songs. You just sing."

"What do you think?"

"They're reputable, and I don't see any larger labels jumping in because of the seasonal angle. If you want to pursue the dream, this is the way to do it."

He handed her phone back. "Can I have time to think about it?"

"A little. They want an answer right after the holidays."

"Oh, gosh. Well, I guess I can think on it while we go buy apple butter."

"Yes!" Brooke was already on her feet. "Let's go!"

Brooke and Beverly Blankenship hit it off immediately. Brooke oohed and aahed as she perused the shelves of the little Christmas shop. Craig drifted into the background while Brooke sampled preserves, coffees, and candies. His mind wandered back to the discussion at Lula's.

Royalties from his song.

A recording contract.

It was intriguing and a lot to consider. An hour before, he had assumed his life would remain in Garland Grove, but it was clear now that Nashville could be an option, too.

And Nashville meant being closer to Brooke.

Now that would be something. And even if the recording gig didn't pan out, "Making Santa Smile" would bring in enough royalties to allow him to be picky about what he did next. Could he open his own drugstore, like in Garland Grove? Or would he work for one of the larger pharmacies? The thought of working in one of the big-box stores had always been a turnoff. Even when coming out of pharmacy school, when the big stores dangled sign-on bonuses and new automobiles, he had found the prospect very off-putting. He enjoyed being his own boss, and he liked knowing his customers.

But the possibility of recording music. Taking another run at touring. Concerts in exotic venues in faraway places. Intoxicating.

And closer to Brooke.

Because something was happening there. She liked him. And he already knew he was head-over-heels for her. Like earlier, when she was checking out the rings in Buckshot's display. He was thinking about someday placing one of them on her finger. Maybe that was far-fetched. They had only known one another for a few weeks, but still, he could dream.

Nashville meant Brooke.

Garland Grove, no Brooke. Or maybe occasional visits, but how long could they sustain a relationship that way?

"Would you like a sleigh ride?" Beverly offered. "It's a perfect time for it. The sun is low in the sky. It's lovely this time of day."

"I want to!" Brooke practically shouted her answer. "I've never been on a sleigh ride before."

"Then it's settled." Beverly reached for her cellphone. "Lloyd is in the barn. I'll have him hook up the sleigh and pick you up in five minutes."

"I love her!" Brooke exclaimed as they waited for Lloyd Blankenship to bring up the sleigh. "I hope the idea of a sleigh ride isn't too boring for you. You and Jenna probably did this all the time."

"A couple times, maybe, but not like this." He pulled her close and brushed away a strand of hair from her forehead. "This will be special."

A few minutes later, they were flying across the snow at a brisk gait. Lloyd was seated in front of them, holding the reins and keeping up a steady patter of conversation. "Loved your song, Craig," he remarked, looking over his shoulder at them. He winked as he said, "Back when we still had little ones in the house, Beverly was pretty good at making Santa smile. Certainly was a lot more satisfying than milk and Oreos."

"That's sweet, Mr. Blankenship," Brooke replied. "And I'll bet you were a pretty nice Santa."

Craig could see she was getting cold, so he grabbed a blanket from behind the seat and wrapped the two of them together. She leaned against him to take advantage of his body heat and felt perfect there. They skirted a wooded area and practically flew over a series of hills. From their seat, they could hear the horse's breathing and smell pine and cypress from the fields of trees that surrounded them.

"It's kind of like home," Brooke said. "We have areas at Percy's Crossroads that are like this. No snow though, or at least almost never."

Lloyd turned the sleigh back toward the barn and

slowed down, allowing them time to enjoy the scenery in silence. Craig put his arm around her and leaned his head against hers. She smelled exquisite. Soap and shampoo and a hint of perfume. She murmured when he nuzzled her ear and ran her hand over the side of his face, her fingers lingering along his chin. He reached for them and kissed them. Each one.

Oh, my goodness, was he smitten.

"I think I want to pursue the recording deal," he said softly.

She pulled back to look at him. "That was fast."

He nodded. "It seems like the right thing. The best thing."

She gave nothing away as to how she felt about it. Lloyd returned to the barn and helped them down. He appeared slightly embarrassed when Brooke hugged him and said thanks for the ride. They went inside and bid farewell to Beverly, but not before purchasing five jars of apple butter.

"Would you like to get a bite to eat?" Craig asked as they reached the city limits. "We have a nice Italian place. And there's always Smacks. Everybody likes Smacks."

She slid across the seat and wrapped her arm in his. "Do any of them serve dinner to go?" she purred. "Because more than anything, I want to go back to your house and be close to you."

WEDNESDAY, DECEMBER 21

GARLAND GROVE

*W*aking up in Craig's arms gave Brooke warm fuzzies on her warm fuzzies. He was still asleep. She felt the rhythm of his breathing and remained still so as not to disturb him. Staying still was just fine, particularly with her back against his chest.

And he had certainly earned his rest.

He had earned his rest for the next several nights. *Whew, boy.*

The memories made her quiver. Her quivering caused him to stir. He shifted his arm, the one over the top of her. He caressed her arm and made her feel tingly.

"Good morning," he whispered into her ear.

"Mmmmm," she replied. That was the best she had.

"Did you sleep well?"

"Mmmmm."

He chuckled. "I'll take that as yes."

"Mmmmm."

They were silent for a spell before, out of the blue, he asked, "What does it mean when someone says, 'Oh my stars and garters?'"

"It's an old southern expression."

"I gathered that, but I have no idea what it means."

Brooke turned to see his face. "It means... Where did you hear something like that?"

He kissed her ear. "You said it. Last night."

Brooke covered her face to hide her blush. "I did not. You're making that up."

"Nope. It was new to me. It was when you were—"

"No! You don't have to tell me. I think I remember now." She giggled, then couldn't stop. She snorted and sounded like a duck. Or maybe a pig. Craig started laughing, too.

"Well, is it good?" he asked through the laughter. "Oh, my stars and garters?"

His saying it again made her laugh more. "Yeah, it's really good. Like over-the-top, out-of-this-world good."

"So when I was...you know? You thought that was really good, huh?"

She turned, pulled him close, and kissed him. "Like you couldn't tell?"

"Hmm," he answered. "I might just add that one to my vocabulary. I'll use it at the drugstore. Maybe the next time Willa McKenzie comes in for her bromodosis prescription, I'll say, 'Oh my stars and garters, Willa, your feet smell like the county wastewater plant.'"

Brooke smacked his arm. "That's not the way to use it. Remember, stars and garters is for something that's really good. Why don't you try saying, 'Holler fire and save the matches, Willa. If you don't do something about those stinky feet, I'm gonna swat my hind with a melon rind!'"

It was too much. They were both overtaken by the hilarity. Like a couple of kids laughing at an unexpected fart.

Gosh, it was fun being with him.

"Speaking of the drugstore," Craig said after a few moments. "I need to run by there today. Henry said some boxes came in that are too heavy for him to unpack. Want to go?"

"I would love to, but I really should check in with Raquel and answer a couple emails. How long will you be?"

"A couple hours, tops."

"How about if I stay here and get my work done, then come to the drugstore? When you finish, we can get some breakfast." Brooke grabbed her phone and laughed when she saw the time. "So much for breakfast. How about lunch?"

Lunch it was.

CRAIG WAS STILL SMILING when he entered the drugstore.

Oh, my stars and garters.

Henry was back to his usual jovial self. The grumpiness from the previous week was pushed aside by the merriment of the holiday season. "I'm really glad I got to fill in again this week," he said as Craig got busy unpacking boxes. "Otherwise, I would just sit at home and miss all the fun of seeing old friends here in the store."

"What's the latest news around town, Henry?" Craig asked as he checked cold medicines off an invoice.

"Raven McCloud coming to Garland Grove is certainly big, and under normal circumstances, it would dominate the rumor mill. But not this year."

Craig looked up from the invoice. "What could be bigger than Raven McCloud?"

"Well..." Henry said. "You. And that pretty young lady you've been seen around town with." Henry lowered his voice, despite there being no one else in the store. "Word is you stopped by Hanson's for lasagna to go."

"Why is that gossip worthy?"

Henry chuckled. "The experience of dining at Hanson's is as good as the food, son. Nobody orders takeout unless they've got something bigger planned for home. So, everybody is assuming you and your new lady friend had... bigger plans."

Oh, for the love of Pete.

Fortunately for Craig, Stacy Pike's noisy arrival saved him from having to respond. "Darn it all, Henry. I can't believe I left my gloves in Melvin's truck. And of all the days he would have to go on the road, well—" She paused when she spotted Craig. Her face lit up. "I hear you and that Nashville girl are getting serious. Is it true that you ordered takeout from Hanson's? Amy said you did, but I told her that nobody gets takeout from Hanson's."

"Yep, but only because it was so late and we didn't want to—"

"You don't owe me an explanation, Craig, but don't be surprised if you hear about it at rehearsal tonight. Every-body's so happy for you. You have a new lady in your life. You're back directing the Christmas concert. And you somehow convinced Raven McCloud to come to Garland Grove!"

"Yeah," Henry echoed. "Everybody's thrilled. Now tell me, Craig, what was it like to date that pretty Raven McCloud? I'll bet she was a handful, that one."

"To be honest, Henry, she didn't even remember—" The bell over the front door jingled. He felt his face light up when he saw who it was.

"Henry, Stacy, I want you to meet Brooke."

She looked radiant. Her blonde hair was pulled into a ponytail. She wore a long leather coat over jeans and boots.

"Hi, y'all," she said cheerily. "I hope I'm not interrupting."

"Oh, my goodness, listen to that delightful accent," Henry exclaimed, lifting himself from the stool with more energy than Craig had seen in years. He hustled down the aisle and held out his hand. "Henry Dinwiddie, young lady. Pleasure to meet you."

"Mr. Dinwiddie, the pleasure is mine. I want to thank you for saving the day. If it hadn't been for you agreeing to tend the drugstore, I'm not sure we would have gotten Craig down to Nashville."

Henry's eyes danced at being in her presence. He laughed merrily. "I didn't do anything special. You really don't think Raven McCloud would be coming to town if I hadn't filled in for Craig?"

"Probably not." Brooke gave him a peck on the cheek that left him grinning from ear to ear. She looked to Stacy Pike. "And Stacy, all I've heard is how good you are at your job. And how everybody loves you because you're so cheerful."

"I do like my job," Stacy gushed. "So how did you like your takeout lasagna from Hanson's? Not many people get it to go."

"It was delicious! Maybe the best lasagna I've ever had. Next time, we'll eat there instead of takeout. You can appreciate that I wanted some alone time with Craig. I hadn't seen him in a few days and was kinda missing him."

"Oh, I get it. My Melvin is an over-the-road trucker. He's gone for ten days at a time. Maybe I should try that. I could send the kids over to spend the night with Grandma Pike and order us some takeout lasagna."

"I highly recommend it." Brooke winked. "Maybe pass on the garlic bread, though. If you get my drift." She turned to Craig. "How much longer? I'm itching to do some window shopping. I saw a little place down the block that sells leather goods. I'm thinking I might find something for Dad."

"Maybe you should take her by Buckshot Kelly's while you're out," Henry teased. He was clearly smitten. Stacy was checking her calendar to see when Melvin arrived home from his next trip. "They've got some really nice jewelry in there," Henry continued. "And some pretty good hunting rifles, too. If that's your thing."

"Oh, I'm much more a jewelry girl, Mr. Dinwiddie."

"I'm just finishing up," Craig said, tucking away the last of the new merchandise. "We've got a few hours before concert practice, so let's get going."

"Oh, my goodness, Craig. This is where you hold your concert?" Brooke gawked at the Vogue through the window of Craig's pickup as they pulled up in front.

"I know it looks kind of rundown, and it needs a lot of work, but it's here or one of the local churches and none have the Vogue's capacity."

"The Vogue Opera House," Brooke said as she admired the façade. "It's lovely. I love Greek Revival."

"You know architecture?" Craig asked.

"I'm more than just a pretty face," Brooke teased. "It was probably built at the end of the nineteenth century."

"1891, to be exact. Nobody remembers if there was ever actually an opera here."

"Oh, there probably was at one time or another. Quite a

few small towns had opera houses like this. They hosted plays and traveling productions. Some became movie theaters during the silent film era. Many are long gone." She turned to look at Craig. "Kudos to Garland Grove for keeping this fine old girl alive and well."

"She's alive, but not well. The plumbing is ancient. We usually blow a breaker or two during performances. And the curtains. They're...well, I'll let you see for yourself."

"I can't wait," Brooke said as she unlatched her seatbelt. They entered through one of three arched entryways. The Vogue's interior had that wonderful and distinct smell that reminded her of the lovely old theaters she sometimes visited with Bobby back in high school. The lobby was large and ornate, but also tired and tattered. She approached a glass-counter concession stand expecting to find packages of M&Ms, Sno-Caps, and Twizzlers. The counters were empty though, other than a fine coating of dust.

"See what I mean about needing a good renovation," Craig said. "Sadly, the city doesn't have the money." They proceeded through the lobby into the seating area. The stage lights were already on and two dozen people were visiting on the edge of the stage where Joanne Sayer played a lovely rendition of Silent Night on a grand piano. The acoustics were amazing. Brooke could hear every note as if she was standing next to the piano.

Several of those gathered waved and called out to Craig. They also checked Brooke out. They were smiling, but she could tell they were taking their measure of her after having heard she was in town. Craig turned his attention to the program while Joanne continued to warm up. She finished Silent Night, then rose and came down to where they were standing.

"Hello again, Brooke!"

"Hey, Joanne. You play beautifully."

Joanne's face lit up. "Thank you so much. That means a lot coming from someone like you." She nodded at Craig. "I'm thrilled to have him back. Last week's rehearsal was..." She shook her head. "Let's just say it was a struggle. Better days are ahead, though. Craig, have you heard about ticket sales?"

Craig hadn't.

"As soon as word got out about Raven McCloud the ticket committee was overrun with calls. We're sold out and have a waiting list."

"Goodness, Joanne, that's wonderful," Craig said.

"How many people can you squeeze in here?" Brooke asked.

"Six hundred and twenty-seven," Joanne answered. "We have at least another three hundred on the waiting list."

"Then I guess we need to get started," Craig said, tucking away his notes. "Okay, everybody, this is our last and best rehearsal. And as you probably know, you'll be performing before a sellout crowd!"

The performers clapped and cheered. Craig introduced Brooke before kicking things off. While the singers warmed up, she wandered up and down the aisles. The seats were padded, but threadbare. The once ornate balcony that wrapped around the back and sides was gloomy. And, as Craig had mentioned, the curtains had seen better days.

But gosh, the place was beautiful.

And the friendly folks of Garland Grove, at least those lucky enough to get tickets, were in for the treat of their lives. Raven McCloud. In person. Just her and her guitar. Brooke had seen her perform acoustically before, usually in her living room or alone on a sound stage. Acoustical performances, particularly when they involved holiday music, were the best way to experience a performer's raw talent. And Raven's ability to enthrall an audience was unmatched.

She stepped back into the lobby and called Bobby.

"Is everything ready for tomorrow?" she asked.

"Raven's flying into the same airport you used on your first trip. In fact, the pilot's the same, too. A nice gal named Monique. She remembered you."

"Any problems, Daddy?"

"None that I know of. The media storm is dying out. Travis pleaded not guilty at his arraignment, but word is that his people will reach a settlement with the guy he hit."

Had it been their client, she and Bobby would have taken the same approach, but it still made her angry that Travis might skate. That wasn't her problem, though.

"Dad, you wouldn't believe this theater. Raven will love it. They've already sold out the performance and have a bunch of people who didn't get in."

"I'll let her know when I call her in a bit. How about you, sugar? Are you and Craig having a nice time?"

"A wonderful time, Daddy. He's a very sweet man."

They spoke for a few more minutes before Bobby had to run. Brooke returned to the stage just as the singers concluded a lovely rendition of *Oh Holy Night*. It had been years since she had attended a local production, and their imperfect yet heartfelt voices gave her a warm feeling. Craig praised their effort, then noticing she was back, said, "Brooke, we were wondering about the order of things for tomorrow night. Should Raven go first or later?"

"Don't put her on before us or everyone might get up and leave," a cherub-faced man in overalls quipped from the second row.

"Save her for last," Brooke said. "Performing at the end gives her the option of adding a song or two if time allows."

The performers' excitement was off the charts. Brooke took a seat in the front row and relaxed while they ran through their program one more time. It seemed good and right, and she felt herself envying Craig for the life he had built in Garland Grove.

Why did he want to give it up for a recording contract?

That was a question she couldn't answer. Only Craig knew his reasons.

She just hoped he knew how lucky he was.

As THEY COMPLETED one final run-through, Craig's mind drifted to other things. He wanted to spend every moment with Brooke. She was leaving Friday morning. Christmas was Sunday, and she and Bobby had plans.

Craig? No plans. He and Jenna had spent the holiday together for the past two years. They had opened presents on Christmas Eve, then made love and slept in before heading to her parent's house in Freeport on Christmas Day. Not this year, though. She was likely spending Christmas Eve with the new vet, Owen, who was probably still unaware of her dalliance with Travis Horton. They would probably open presents. Or not. Maybe that was too boring. Perhaps they were going on a cruise or to one of those all-inclusive resorts. Jenna would return to work after the holidays suntanned, satiated, and full of stories.

And Craig?

"Craig?"

"Craig? Do you want us to run through it again?"

Joanne was speaking. The theater was quiet. The singers watched him curiously.

"Ah, no, Joanne. That was great. Singers, wonderful job tonight. The show begins at seven, so everyone be here ready to go by six-thirty."

They packed up, wrapped up, and headed for the exits. Five minutes later it was just Craig and Brooke. She came onto the stage and asked, "What were you thinking about?"

"What do you mean?"

"At the end." She came close and looked into his eyes. "You were a million miles away."

"Oh...just about...where we should have dinner."

She kissed his cheek. "I would be okay with a repeat of last night. Maybe not lasagna again, though. It's kind of heavy."

They turned when they heard a door creak open. Craig expected to see one of the singers returning for something they had left behind, but it was Sam. He spotted them and made a beeline their way, arms open wide.

"You must be Brooke!" he called out. Brooke glanced at Craig and saw the smile spreading across his face.

"I sure am. And you're Sam. I recognize you from the Christmas baby poster I see all over town."

They hugged, then Sam said, "We have two seats for you at our table at Smacks." He turned to Brooke. "Beth is dying to meet you. So are Amy and Andrew. Andrew is kind of shy, though. Not nearly as charismatic as me, so be ready." Then, realizing he might be moving too fast, Sam added, "You can join us, can't you? I mean, really Craig. You can't make this girl eat takeout pasta two nights in a row. You need to let Brooke see that there's more to Garland Grove than your bachelor pad."

Brooke adored Craig's friends from the minute she laid eyes on them. Sam's wife, Beth, pulled her into the kind of hug usually reserved for relatives and dear friends. She had a fun, but totally in-control vibe about her that Brooke figured she needed to rein in Sam and their five children. Amy and Andrew were joined at the hip. He was a doctor, she was a nurse. He was reserved. She chatted about everything and anything. And Sam was just as she expected him to be. Boisterous, silly, and hilarious. Throughout dinner, people stopped by to slap him on the shoulder or share a joke. Most of the jokes were bawdy. A couple were downright dirty. Dr. Sam Griffin was everyone's best friend. The others were content to let him be himself.

She hadn't been at the table five minutes before the questions started. The usual stuff at first. Life in Nashville. Famous people she knew. Then they moved on to life and family. Amy and Sam did most of the talking, though it quickly became obvious that when Andrew or Beth had something to say, it was of some importance. After a plate of chicken wings and two beers, Brooke thought she had their group dynamic figured out. She found herself drawn to Beth, the mama bear with a heart of gold and patience of a saint.

Brooke could tell by their questions that the others were hopeful something might develop between her and Craig. No one mentioned Jenna, and for that Brooke was grateful.

Until she had to go and ruin it by showing up.

CRAIG WAS WIPING wing sauce from his chin when he saw Jenna come in. She was with Owen. They were holding hands. Her smile vanished when their eyes met. She cast a furtive glance around the restaurant, looking for an open table. As luck would have it, the only one was a few feet away.

Owen led the way. Sam spotted them first. He waved, then speaking to the others said, "Uh...is this going to be awkward for anyone?" His eyes were on Craig, but it was Brooke who answered.

"Not for me." She stood up as Jenna and Owen arrived. "Hi," she said, smiling from ear to ear. "You must be Jenna. I'm Brooke. Craig's new girlfriend."

Brooke stuck out her hand and waited for Jenna to catch up. She awkwardly introduced Owen, then they sat down and ordered drinks. Beth, always the peacemaker, told Jenna it was good to see her, then asked Owen about his work. Craig heard little of what was said. His attention was on Brooke who seemed perfectly at home seated five feet from his old girlfriend. He saw how Jenna checked her out, and how Brooke paid scant attention in return. He also noticed something else. Something he couldn't quite put his finger on. Something so recognizable, yet hard to explain. He thought on it as the others returned to their conversation. Beth shared a couple hilarious stories of recent motherhood mishaps. Sam asked Andrew about work stuff. Amy and Brooke chatted about places they had visited. Brooke fit in perfectly. That quality of hers he couldn't describe came through loud and clear. Jenna never had it. Amy did to some extent. So did Beth.

But what was it?

It took something as small as the server returning to clear away plates for him to figure it out. The server's disposition had been subdued since they arrived, but as he leaned in to take Brooke's empty plate, she whispered something that made him smile. He nodded, then took off with the dirty plates. What Brooke said to the server, Craig had no idea, but there was no denying the impact she had on people. Even strangers. That was what made her different.

Brooke Summers seemed to sparkle.

Yeah! That was it. She sparkled! Not like really sparkled in the light, but her personality and the way people were drawn to her. She sparkled that way.

Craig loved that about her.

Along with everything else.

When her phone rang, she checked the number, then glanced at the others. "I have to take this. I'm sorry." They watched her head for a quiet corner near the exit. Even Jenna's eyes followed her. And when she returned a couple minutes later, she was all smiles. She grabbed Craig's hand and said, "That was Raven. She wants to know if you want her to do two shows tomorrow night."

"Oh, my goodness!" Amy exclaimed. "She would do that?"

"She certainly will. Dad told her about the sellout, so she said to schedule a later show and she'll stick around if the others will."

Craig couldn't believe what he was hearing. "It would be great, but how will we get the word out? And tickets? We don't even have extras printed."

"I can help with getting the word out," Sam said, jumping to his feet. He pushed his way through the crowd to the dance floor where a local deejay played music on weekends but was empty on a Wednesday night. He stood on a chair and shouted for the bartender to unplug the jukebox, then waited as a Garth Brooks song faded out.

"Okay everybody," he called out as the room grew quiet. "How many of you wanted to see Raven McCloud but couldn't get tickets?"

Several hands went up.

"Yeah, and there are a lot more who missed out, too. Well, we have good news. Raven has just agreed to do two shows tomorrow night!"

Smacks went nuts. There was clapping of hands, pounding of boots, yeehaws, and even a hallelujah. Sam waited for things to quiet down before focusing his attention on one table in the corner. "Nancy," he called out to a pretty brunette with a beer in her hand. "They can't do the show without tickets. Can you and Georgie fire up your presses in the morning and get six-hundred tickets ready by noon?"

Craig leaned close to Brooke and whispered, "Nancy and Georgie run a print shop in the industrial complex south of town. They charge a fortune, though."

"Sam, we can do it," Nancy called back, "But supplies and ink cost a lot and that's a short run. It'll cost at least—"

"Oh, c'mon, Nancy," Sam said, cutting her off. "You know half of what you charge is profit. If you cut out that part I'll write you a check myself. How about it?"

Craig knew how frugal Nancy and Georgie were. He also knew how persuasive Sam could be. And within minutes, they had a deal.

By early the next morning, everyone in Garland Grove would know the news.

Brooke pulled back the covers and slipped into bed.

"If the doctor thing doesn't work out, Sam could have a future in concert promotion."

Craig smiled as he pulled her close and inhaled her wonderful scent. A candle on the dresser was the only light. It was plenty, though. Snow had fallen on their way home, and the outside world was quiet and peaceful and very much like Christmas. Their lovemaking was slow and searching and intensely personal. Brooke was tucked against him, the warmness of her back warmed his chest. She fit there perfectly. She would leave in two days. He didn't want to miss a second with her, and if they spent most of it just as they were, all the better.

"There might be one good thing come out of your crazy evening with Raven and Travis," she said, as she turned to face him.

"You mean you and me?"

She smiled and kissed his nose. "There is that, though I was having feelings for you way before then."

"Me, too."

"But the other thing," she continued, "is that I am considering buying Risky Rick's."

Craig pulled back to look at her. "Seriously? A bar?"

"It used to be a pretty good music venue." She told him about her conversation with the manager, and the potential she and Bobby envisioned.

"But wouldn't that be a conflict of interest?" Craig asked. "Can you hire your own talent?"

"It's a blurry line, but if I decide to proceed I'll separate myself from Summers Management."

Craig got an uneasy feeling in his gut. "Hasn't that always been your dream? Working with your father?"

"He gave me my love for music, but everything with Raven has made me realize that I don't enjoy life on the road and dealing with big-name stars as much as he does. Bobby comes from a different era when agents didn't have to deal with things like social media and twenty-four-hour news cycles. He's been able to maintain his old-school approach, but if there's one thing I've learned, it's that catering to big acts isn't as much fun as it looks on the outside."

"You think managing a venue would be easier?"

She laughed. "Not easier. But more in line with what I enjoy."

Craig listened as she talked about how she would expand and improve Risky Rick's. Everything from changing the name to utilizing the stage area in back. There was an exuberance in the way she spoke that got him excited, too. It wasn't much different from how he felt about the drugstore. Challenges that would frustrate others kept him excited and fresh for his work. Her helping new acts get a toehold was similar to his desire to help his customers improve their health.

What nagged at him, though, was that they had to do the things they loved hundreds of miles apart.

Fortunately, he had something to fall back on.

"Any chance a Christmas-song-singing fake cowboy can perform at your place?" he asked.

She hugged him. "Of course, but are you sure it's what you want?"

THE QUESTION that had been gnawing at her was out in the open.

Did Craig really want to pursue music?

She searched his face as he thought about it. It was too

dark to make out any subtle changes, though, so she had to be content to wait for his reply.

"I believe so," he said, speaking slowly. "I love the thought of being close to you."

She caressed his cheek. "But if it doesn't work out? You would be giving up so much?"

He took her hand from his cheek and kissed it. "I don't see it that way. What I give up would be nothing compared to what I gain."

She knew the gain he was referring to was her. She felt good knowing he was willing to do that. She could see them together in Nashville. Living downtown. Maybe an older house they fixed up together. Craig would spend his days rehearsing and preparing for concerts. She would stay busy overseeing bookings and making the former Risky Rick's into one of Nashville's best small venues. New friends. Maybe a church. Kids?

Hold your horses, Brooke. Kids? You've only known him for a few weeks. No one has said a word about marriage, let alone kids.

But she could see it as clearly as she could see the venue coming together. Craig would be an amazing father, just like Bobby had been for her.

It was an ideal mental picture, but Brooke couldn't look past the potential problems.

"What if your music doesn't sell?"

"Well..." he said before pausing for a few moments. "I'm a pharmacist. I can get a job at any of those big stores. Probably for more money than I make running my place here."

"But would you be happy?"

He kissed her. Gently, then deeper. It felt divine. "If you're in my life, Brooke, everything else will work out."

THURSDAY, DECEMBER 22

GARLAND GROVE

"Craig? Sweetie, your phone is buzzing."

"No. It's too early." Craig rolled over and buried his head in the pillow, preparing to return to sleepy land for a few more hours. He didn't make it, though.

"It's buzzing again," Brooke said, her head deep in her pillow. Craig moaned as he rolled over, then moaned again when he saw the time.

Seven-twenty.

In the morning.

It was still dark outside, and while he usually arose at six-fifteen so he could open the drugstore by eight, he had taken the day off. Henry was running things. Craig nuzzled Brooke's soft, sensual neck. She murmured and went back to sleep.

And then someone was knocking on the door. With an urgency that far surpassed Clarence the UPS guy or Danielle from Amazon. An urgency that caused Craig to sit upright in bed. Brooke did the same.

Eight-seventeen.

He scrambled out of bed and grabbed the robe from his

closet. The knocking continued until he pulled open the door and found Stacy Pike on his front step. Her face was clouded with worry.

"Henry fell out of bed and hit his head," she said. "He's at Garden Grove Memorial."

"Oh, no. I'll get dressed and head there now."

"No, Craig, you don't have to do that. He's going to be fine. They x-rayed his head and bandaged him up. He'll probably go home later today. But there's nobody to open the drugstore."

As Stacy was speaking Brooke came up behind Craig. Their eyes met, but Stacy wasn't finished yet.

"If it's okay with you I want to spend the day with Henry. His daughters live down south and can't come. When they release him, I'll take him home so he doesn't have to call Wally Darnell's taxi."

"That's a good idea, Stacy. I'll head down and open the drugstore, and then—" Craig paused midsentence when he felt Brooke's hand on his right arm. He turned to her. "Brooke, I'm sorry, but there's no way to avoid—"

"Don't be silly. Of course, you need to go. And I'm going with you."

"You don't have to do that. Stay here and relax."

"Nope." She winked at Stacy. "I came to Garland Grove to spend time with you. Stacy, go take care of Mr. Dinwiddie. We'll cover the drugstore."

THERE WERE two customers waiting patiently when they unlocked the drugstore a little before nine.

"Penny... Leland," Craig greeted them as he held open the door. "I apologize for keeping you waiting."

Penny, a dark curvy woman about Brooke's age said, "No worries, Craig. We heard about Henry and knew you would be along pretty soon."

"It's all good," the man, Leland, replied. "Take care of Penny first." Then turning to Brooke. "Hello, young lady, you must be Craig's agent friend."

"Brooke Summers," she said, extending her hand. He accepted it and held on a bit too long while he checked her out.

"Leland McKenzie. I'm a lawyer in town."

"One of the best," Craig said as he started on Penny's prescription.

"He's just saying that because he has to put up with my wife, Willa, every year. She was chairperson of the Christmas concert, but fortunately for Craig, she has bowed out of that role."

Brooke had no idea what he was talking about, but she saw Craig grinning behind the counter. "I would never say that, Leland."

"Yeah, but everyone else would. Right, Penny?"

Penny had been doing a good job of minding her own business, but when asked, she didn't hold back. "I cross the street when I see that woman coming."

"You should try living with her," Leland commiserated. "And now that she's quit running the Christmas concert she's crankier than ever. And her feet? Geesh, Craig, can't you give me a double dose of that prescription? Our house smells like someone dipped corn chips in dog crap."

Brooke bit her tongue to keep from laughing. Penny didn't bother to hide her amusement.

"Sorry, Leland, but you'll have to talk to the doc about that. All I do is fill 'em." Craig handed a paper sack over the counter. "Here you go, Penny. Merry Christmas."

Penny was soon on her way with Leland McKenzie close behind. The front door had barely closed before Brooke started laughing. "What a funny guy!" she exclaimed. "Is Willa as bad as he says?"

"Goodness, yes," Craig said as he came out and kissed her. "There are lots of things to love about Garland Grove, but Willa isn't any of them."

Brooke turned so they were facing. She pulled him to her for another kiss. "So, what do you have for me to do, boss?" she asked.

"How about you sit behind the counter where all my customers can see you? They'll tell their friends about the beautiful mysterious woman at Callaway's Drugstore, then they'll all come in. Maybe some of them will even buy something."

"Sure, but I'm not exactly mysterious. Everybody already knows who I am." She glanced around, then said, "What would Stacy do if she were here?"

"Deliver prescriptions, but I can take care of them during lunch hour."

"Nonsense. Let me do it."

Craig thought about it for a moment before a smile spread across his face as he handed her the scrips. "The sad thing is that people won't have a clue that the person dropping off their Lipitor or Losartan is one of the best talent agents in the world."

"That's sweet of you to say. Maybe I'll tell them." She picked up one of the sacks, glanced at the name, and said, "Good morning, Mrs. Jurgenson, I'm Brooke, the new girl at Callaway Drugstore, and I'm here with your prescription. Oh, and, Mrs. Jurgenson, I've heard you play bass with some really kicking local bands. Would you consider a career in music? If so, here's my card!"

"You know the best part of what you just said?" Craig asked.

"What?" Brooke asked as she pulled on her coat.

"The part where you're the new girl. But could you just change it a little bit? Maybe say, 'I'm Craig Callaway's new girl?'"

She kissed him softly on the lips and didn't want to stop.

"I promise I'll say that," she whispered into his ear. "And I hope I can say it long enough to someday drop the *new* part."

BROOKE WAS PULLING AWAY from her next-to-last delivery when Bobby called.

"How's fishing in Bermuda?"

"Fun as all get out, but I cut it short a day. Guess where I'm headed now?"

Brooke double-checked the address of the last delivery against GPS as she said, "Let me guess...barracuda fishing in the Bahamas."

Bobby chuckled. "No, but maybe another time. I'm on a plane headed to Chicago. I land in about an hour, then catch another flight to a little airport I can't even remember the name of. And if things work out..."

Bobby didn't have to finish. "You're coming to Garland Grove, Daddy? Really?"

"Yep, sweetheart. I thought it would be fun to see you and make sure Raven's show goes okay tonight."

"That makes me so happy! I'll pick you up at the airport and—"

"Nope. I have a car rented. Just text me the address. I'll

pick Raven up and make sure she gets there. A little time together might do us good."

"This is wonderful! You're going to love the Vogue Opera House, Dad. It's like some of the places where we used to scout talent when I was a little girl."

"I can't wait, darlin'. I've missed you. And tell Craig not to worry about me getting in the way. Raquel has already rented me a room at the little motel there in town."

Brooke had to stop herself from skipping up the sidewalk to her final delivery. It was an older clapboard house along a street of well-kept craftsmen and bungalows, all festively decorated for Christmas. It was the kind of street that one would expect to see in a Hallmark movie. Except for the house where she was delivering. She hadn't rung the bell before the smell of cigarettes wafted out. The old lady who answered the door wore a ratty housecoat.

"Mrs. Parker?"

"Maybe? Who's asking?"

Her voice was gravelly and guarded. Brooke soldiered on.

"I'm dropping off a prescription from Callaway's Drugstore. I'm Brooke."

"Is it oxy?"

"Ma'am, I'm afraid I don't know. I'm filling in for Stacy Pike. She's with—"

"I know where Stacy Pike is. And I know about Henry Dinwiddie, so you can save your breath. Hand it over."

Brooke did as she was told. Mrs. Parker's abruptness caught her off guard after all the wonderful people she had met in town. No thank you. No Merry Christmas. The woman just stepped back inside and closed the door. "Even Garland Grove has one, I suppose," Brooke mumbled to herself as she walked back toward her car.

"Brooke? Is that you?"

The voice came from across the street. Brooke spotted Amy Bennett waving from the front porch of a pretty white house.

"C'mon in and warm up!"

ONCE WORD GOT out that Craig was closing at three, customers showed up in waves. Most were content to wait and chat with one another as he worked behind the counter. Raven McCloud was the primary topic. People who thought they had missed out on tickets were delirious with excitement at the announcement of a second show. By noon it was sold out too.

"Stanley Custer sold his tickets for twice what he paid," one customer complained. "Who ever thought there would be ticket scalping in Garland Grove?"

Stacy Pike pulled up out front a little after one and ran in to tell Craig that Henry had been discharged and was in her car. Henry seemed embarrassed when Craig came outside to say hello. "Petunia got tangled up under my feet and sent me scrambling," he explained. Petunia, as everyone knew, was Henry's miniature poodle. He apologized several times for leaving Craig in a lurch.

"I'll be back tomorrow," he promised.

"Not necessary, Henry. Brooke leaves in the morning, so I can cover things. You take care of yourself."

There were a few moments of silence after Stacy took off with Henry. Just enough time for reality to sink in.

Brooke was leaving tomorrow.

Just thinking about it made Craig sad. He didn't want her to leave.

Especially at Christmas.

He didn't want to spend Christmas alone.

Nor any other day. Alone might have been fine before, but that had changed. Brooke was in his life now, and the possibility of going days or weeks without seeing her seemed unbearable.

And where was she? The deliveries couldn't have taken this long. He tried to call her, but there was no answer.

Where was she?

BROOKE SAT across the table from Amy in a kitchen that was as homey as any she had seen. Amy's decorating eye trended toward country, with pale blue cupboards, open shelves, and a large cookie jar shaped like a bear. They each had a couple of ginger snaps from the bear. Amy was adorable and caring, and away from the others, her personality shined through.

"Craig told Andrew that he's signing a recording contract and moving to Nashville."

That was a surprise. Brooke hadn't known he had shared the news with anyone.

"In the time I've known him I've never seen him happier than last night at Smacks." Amy sipped her cocoa thoughtfully before asking, "You aren't going to break his heart, are you Brooke?"

Brooke was startled by her bluntness. She considered saying as much but reconsidered when she saw the kindness in Amy's eyes. She cared about Craig. He was her friend. And she felt perfectly justified in protecting her friend.

And she deserved an answer.

"I can't believe I'm telling you this, but I'm already in

love with him." Brooke blushed as she spoke. "I know it's hard to believe, after only knowing him for a short time, but it's the truth. Am I nuts?"

Amy's burst of laughter made Brooke wonder if she should have not been so candid.

Then everything changed.

"Let me tell you about Andrew and me," she said as she got up to refill their mugs.

CRAIG WAS LOCKING up when Brooke texted a little after three to let him know she was on her way back, and that Bobby was coming to town.

Come to the house. I closed early to get ready for tonight. Hurry! Missing you!

She had certainly been gone for a long time, but business was nonstop all afternoon, so there would have been little alone time. After two quick stops to drop off last-minute prescriptions he pulled into the driveway the same time she did.

"You might have set a record for slowest delivery speed," he teased.

"The deliveries were quick. Running into Amy slowed me down." She started to fill him in when something across the street caught her attention. Craig followed her gaze to a yard three houses up. Two girls and a boy, elementary school age, were constructing a snowman.

"I want to do that," Brooke said dreamily. "Have you ever built a snowman?"

Craig tried to remember his last snowman. "Probably in junior high," he guessed. "When you live with snow for a few months a year it gets old pretty fast."

Brooke nodded but didn't take her eyes off the kids as they worked together to lift one large ball of snow onto another. Her eyes held a look of fascination that led Craig to add, "But I think it would be fun to build another one. How about right now?"

He wasn't sure if she heard him, lost as she was in the fun the kids were having. But after a moment she said, "Do we have time? I know you have to get to the theater."

"There's time," he said, wrapping his arms around her. "Let's build it right here next to the porch.

WHO KNEW that you began with a little snowball and just kept rolling until it became big?

Certainly not Brooke. In her mind, you shoveled snow until you had enough to shape it into a snowman. Kind of like forming a sculpture from a block of granite. Nope. Not like that at all.

When Craig asked how big a snowman she wanted she said really big. Like life-size big. "Taller than me," she answered. They got to work. The base, then the body, and finally the head. They lifted the head up together, rested it in place, and paused to share a kiss or three.

"He needs a face," she said between kisses.

Craig had leftover carrots from the roast he had made earlier in the week. One worked perfectly for the nose. They considered what to use for eyes. Craig recalled how they used lumps of coal when he was a little boy. There was no coal around, but a couple of charcoal briquettes from the garage worked perfectly. While Brooke plopped them into place Craig found sticks that made perfect arms. That left a mouth.

Raisins? Maybe.

Pebbles? Brooke liked that idea, but most pebbles were buried under a couple feet of snow, so they settled on a banana. Turned upright, of course, to show the world how happy their snowman was. Happy, just like Brooke as they worked together.

"Can we put one of your shirts on him?" she asked when the face was fully formed. Brooke laughed when he returned with one of the shirts Raven had purchased for him to wear on the concert tour.

"At least someone will get use out of it," Craig said as he wrapped it around the snowman. Brooke stepped back and took a good look at their creation, laughing and clapping gleefully.

"It's perfect," she said, turning to Craig. "Thank you!"

"Who knew that building a snowman could be so fun?" he said as they hugged. She rested her head on his chest and shivered from the cold.

"Shall we go inside?" Craig asked.

"In a minute. Hold me a little longer."

They remained there, holding one another and gazing at their snowman. The late afternoon sun was low on the horizon. Christmas lights twinkled in the yard across the street. A passing driver offered a friendly toot of its horn, but Craig barely noticed. He rubbed Brooke's back and kissed her earlobe. She turned so her lips were close to his cheek.

"I love you, Craig."

The words were whispered, yet hung in the air between them for him to savor and return to. Craig had no doubt that he would forever remember that moment and the way in which she had spoken those three words into his ear. And when he remembered them, he would know that was the moment his life began again.

"I love you, Brooke. So much I can't put it into words."

They held one another and allowed the sweetness of the moment to wash over them. Craig realized that the sun had descended below the horizon. It was night.

Time to go to the concert.

Brooke waited near the backstage entrance for Bobby and Raven. It was six-forty. Twenty minutes until show-time. Two-thirds of the audience were already in their seats. Brooke sensed their anticipation. On the other side of the backstage area, Craig's talented group of singers milled about eagerly.

Oh, goodness, what an afternoon.

She hadn't planned on telling Craig she loved him, but it felt right in the moment. She had sensed he felt the same, but when he said the words they touched her soul. They were so perfect for one another, and as she had learned from Amy, sometimes with love like that a person didn't need months or years to come to that realization.

But she was leaving tomorrow.

Oh, that hurt. She wanted to stay. Or take Craig back to Nashville. But he had the drugstore to tend, so she would sit at Percy's Crossroads and pine for him from afar. It would be hard to put on a happy face and enjoy unwrapping presents with Bobby when her heart was hundreds of miles away in that adorable little house in Garland Grove. Her only solace came from thinking about him eventually relocating to Nashville after he signed the recording contract, but even that was tempered by the worry that he would be away from Garland Grove. Away from the community that had accepted him and made him one of its own.

387

They would be together, though. And that was what mattered.

A horn sounded twice from outside. Bobby's signal that they had arrived. Two volunteers had hastily cleared out a broom closet near the stage entrance. That would serve as Raven's dressing room. Brooke pushed open the door just as Bobby and Raven emerged from the rental car. Raven was dressed in a short black dress and seemed oblivious to the snow and cold. She carried her guitar case. It was the first time Brooke had seen her pack her own equipment. Her face was aglow. Her hair was perfect, and she was gorgeous.

"Brooke!" she exclaimed as she stepped inside. They air-kissed, then Brooke showed her to the makeshift dressing room.

"Sorry, Raven, but all that's in there is a chair, a folding table, and a mirror."

"Don't give it another thought, sugar. I got ready on that nice charter jet. Give me just a couple minutes to mess with my hair and I'll be good to go."

Across the backstage area, the singers watched Raven's every move. Bobby went to his daughter and hugged her.

"Welcome to Garland Grove, Daddy!"

"Good to be here, darlin'." He glanced around. "Place looks a little worse for wear."

"After the show starts I'll show you around."

Craig came over and shook hands with Bobby, then turned to Brooke. "I guess this is it. The singers are ready. Hal Richie is ready to go, too, and in fairness to Willa McKenzie, I have to admit that he is quite a gentleman."

Brooke reached up and kissed his cheek. "We'll be out front. Good luck."

"He doesn't seem nervous," Bobby observed when Craig was gone.

"After being on stage in Atlanta, I'm not sure much of anything could unnerve him." Brooke pointed to the stage exit. "We have seats in the third row, but I'm guessing you would prefer to watch from the back."

"You know me too well. Lead the way, darlin'."

They passed through the wings into the packed theater. The place was abuzz. "Things like this don't happen every day in Garland Grove," Brooke observed. An elderly woman squeezed her arm as she passed. "Hey, Miss Lettie," Brooke called out. Then, to Bobby, "She likes a bag of gumdrops delivered with her heart medicine."

Bobby chuckled. "You've been here three days or three years?"

"Three days," Brooke laughed. "But Henry fell out of bed and had to go to the hospital. Stacy Pike went to be with him, so I delivered Miss Lettie's heart medicine. And gumdrops."

"Well, okay then." Bobby took a look around. "This reminds me of Antoinette Hall down in Pulaski. A little bigger, actually. Really needs some work, though."

"They're raising money for new curtains, but—"

"Brooke!"

Brooke turned to find Amy scurrying her way.

"Craig needs your help. He sent me to find you."

"Sure. Amy, this is my father, Bobby Summers. Dad, this is Amy Bennett."

"C'mon, Mr. Summers." Amy extended her arm. "I'll take care of you."

Brooke hustled backstage and found Craig and Raven huddled in her tiny dressing room. Raven caught her eye and winked. "Brooke, tell this stubborn man that he has to do his song tonight. He can't disappoint his friends and neighbors."

"I didn't even bring my guitar, Raven." Then, turning to Brooke he said, "It never crossed my mind. And the show starts in two minutes."

"You're going to do your song," Brooke said. "I'll get the guitar."

"No, Brooke, you don't have to—"

"Raven's right. You need to sing. I'll be back in plenty of time. You'll be the grand finale."

CRAIG PREFERRED to remain off to the side, ready to jump in if something went awry. Fortunately, with Joanne Sayer on piano, and singers who knew their parts, nothing went awry.

Quite the contrary. The local portion of the evening's first performance was flawless. The performers were enthused, and it showed in their singing. Craig had never been more proud. And even though the audience knew that the great Raven McCloud was waiting in the wings, they called for an encore. Joanne and the troop happily obliged with a rousing rendition of Jingle Bells.

And Hal Richie? The man had a heart of gold. He gave everything he had for the entire fifteen minutes of his set. He was a master showman who played pretty good keyboard to boot. Craig made a mental note to let Willa McKenzie know how much he enjoyed working with Hal. Maybe that would soothe some hurt feelings.

After Hal Richie closed out his set, Craig dropped the curtain. The Vogue grew quiet. Craig retrieved a stool from the wings and took it and a microphone to center stage. The audience watched his every move, excited beyond words at what was about to happen in their little town. Craig glanced offstage to his left where Raven smiled and gave him a thumbs up. He stepped to the microphone.

"We are so delighted you chose to be with us tonight, Garland Grove. And I'm especially excited to introduce to you an old friend who I've recently reconnected with."

He expected some laughter, but it was as if he was speaking to a theater full of wax figures. Faces stared at him, eyes open wide. They heard nothing he said. They were waiting for one thing...one person. It was time to shut up and give Garland Grove what they wanted.

"Ladies and gentlemen, Raven McCloud."

Had the President, the Queen of England, and Elvis come on stage together, the reception would not have matched what 627 proud residents poured out for Raven McCloud. There was no musical introduction by a backing band. No bright lights. Just pure adulation for a person who had chosen to come to their little part of the world. Craig glanced into the audience as Raven came onto the stage. He was disappointed to see that Brooke's seat was empty. She was probably on her way back from retrieving his guitar. Bobby was seated next to Amy and Andrew Bennett. He was smiling proudly. Amy was clapping as if her life depended on it. Two seats away Sam was fanning himself with a program as if he were about to pass out. Beth was laughing at him. God bless 'em. What wonderful friends they were.

Raven approached with arms open wide, her guitar turned so it was on her back.

"Thank you for doing this," Craig whispered as they embraced.

"I'm sorry for everything," she whispered back. "But I'm going to do better in the future. Lots of changes are ahead for this little country girl."

Craig stepped away. The audience response continued as Raven situated herself on the stool, turned her guitar around, crossed her legs, and let fly.

One woman. One guitar. Bad lighting. A rundown old theater.

It was one of the best performances Craig had ever seen. Raven knocked it out of the park. She sang Christmas standards, a few of her own holiday tunes, and chatted easily with the audience. And when she asked for a volunteer to come up and help her remember the twelve days of Christmas, she chose Sam Griffin, who nearly keeled over when she gave him a peck on the cheek, then proceeded to mess up every day of Christmas from six to twelve. The audience roared with laughter and appreciation. Craig laughed along with them.

And before he knew it, she was calling him back to stage.

But what about his guitar?

Had Brooke found it?

He turned to see if there was any sign of her.

She had been next to him the entire time.

Right beside him.

She smiled as she handed him the guitar. "Are you nervous?"

He took a deep breath. "If I say yes will you—"

Her kiss stopped him midsentence. Just like before.

Except this time it was different. There was a feeling of forever in that kiss, a kiss that would be one of many. There would be kisses of happiness.

Kisses of sadness.

Kisses of gain and loss and excitement and disappointment.

Kisses of affection and longing and lust.

That day, and for every day to follow.

But first, Raven McCloud was calling.

Garland Grove was calling.

He took a step toward the stage and jumped when Brooke smacked his backside. He turned to find her laughing.

"I guess I can get away with that now?"

"Don't ever stop. And one more thing?"

"Anything."

"Will you go out front? Someone told me once that if I was nervous I should pick one person and sing to them."

"Me?" she asked.

"Always you."

BROOKE FOUND a spot in the rear of the theater to watch Craig's performance.

It was the happiest day of her life.

Yet, also quite sad.

Happy because she knew with certainty the man she wanted to spend forever with.

But sad that she had to leave the next day.

Happy because he had said he loved her more than words could say.

But sad that their lives and careers had led them to different places.

She weighed those feelings as he walked onto stage. The reception he was given matched Raven's. They loved Craig Callaway in Garland Grove. And he loved them.

And the fact that he was willing to give that up to follow her to Nashville?

And chase his dream.

Oh, my goodness.

THE AUDIENCE WANTED nothing more than to mill around and bask in the greatness they had just experienced. They hugged and congratulated members of the chorus. They clustered around a card table in the back where Hal Richie signed autographs and peddled CD's. And they scrambled for a glimpse of Raven McCloud. She returned to the stage to wave and sign a few autographs, but the second show started in thirty minutes, so Craig had to begin the process of moving people along. Fortunately, they took it with their usual good cheer. There were ten minutes between the last audience member's exit and the arrival of the first wave of second show attendees. Craig visited with Brooke and Bobby. Brooke took both of his hands in hers.

"You were so good!"

They chatted. Brooke planned to stick around for the second performance, but Bobby had other plans.

"Amy invited him to join them for supper at Smacks," Brooke said. They said their goodbyes and Bobby took his leave. It was just the two of them.

"I love you," he said as he took her in his arms. "Having you here was better than all the applause in the world."

Craig saw his love reflected in her beautiful green eyes. He also saw sadness and knew it was the same sadness he felt. She would be leaving in the morning. He considered saying something but preferred to allow the moment to linger. They had the rest of the night, and that thought burned brighter than the excitement of another performance.

"Craig," Joanne called out from the stage. "They're opening the doors for the second show."

BROOKE TEXTED Bobby with the news that Craig was running Raven to the airport.

She asked him to. Not sure why. I'll come join you guys at Smacks.

Bobby stood when he saw her come in. He said something to the others, then came her way. Brooke hugged him and exclaimed, "I've never seen Raven better than she was tonight, Daddy. The acoustic tour is going to be the best thing ever. Her fans are going to be knocking down the door to see her."

He led her to a couple of empty stools at the end of the bar, then waved off the bartender as he came their way.

"Travis Horton came with her, darlin'. He's waiting on the jet. They're headed to the Cayman Islands for Christmas."

Brooke felt a heaviness in her stomach. "Oh, Daddy, I'm sorry. Do you want me to talk to her?"

Bobby shook his head. "She's leaving us for Travis's management team. She let me know tonight. Her contract doesn't expire until July, but I told her we would release her immediately."

Brooke felt her legs going weak. She didn't fight the tears. Bobby pulled out a handkerchief and handed it to her. "Daddy, I'm so... You worked so hard for her and now she's just... I don't know what to say except...*that bitch.*"

That got a smile from Bobby. He took the handkerchief and wiped tears from her cheeks. "Pray for Raven, but don't worry about me. It ain't my first rodeo."

Brooke breathed deeply then used the handkerchief to blow her nose. "I'll be back in Nashville tomorrow afternoon. We'll figure out a strategy for how to proceed. Daddy, there will be plenty of big acts lining up to be represented by you."

"You're probably right," Bobby said as he patted her hand. "But I think I'll turn them down. I've been chewing on this all evening. It might be fun to get out and beat the bushes for talent. Kind of like I did back in the old days. In fact..." He leaned closer so there was no risk of anyone overhearing. "I signed that Hal Richie fella between shows. He ain't Luke Bryan, but I can find work for him on the fair circuit."

Brooke rolled her eyes. "It's a big drop from Raven McCloud to Hal Richie, Dad."

Bobby laughed. "I'll let you in on a little secret, darlin'. I'm pretty excited about the fresh start. There's a lot of people in Nashville who think we always get the best talent without having to work for it. I can't wait to see their faces when I find the next Blake Shelton. Or the next Raven McCloud."

If she had heard the words from anyone else, Brooke would have considered them false bravado. But from Bobby Summers, they were as good as a promise. Despite all the success and money, he still delighted in the hunt. Whether it was in the woods at Percy's Crossroads or the dive bars of Cookeville or Elizabethtown, Bobby reveled in turning over the rocks and finding what might be underneath.

"And it's the perfect time, too," he continued. "Assuming you're still interested in pursuing your music venue."

"I am, Dad. I figure I'll get in touch with the owners of Risky Rick's next week and see if we can make a deal."

"What about Craig?"

Brooke sighed. "He still insists he wants to chase a music career. Have you received the recording contract from Caswell?"

"It should be on my desk in the next week. And that reminds me. I cancelled my return ticket. I'm going to drive back to Nashville. It'll give me time to think. And who knows? Maybe I'll discover the next Raven someplace along the way."

Brooke stepped out of the hallway as Craig returned from his airport run. He knew from the look in her eyes that Bobby had told her about Raven's departure. He also suspected that she didn't want to talk about it. Those types of conversations could take place over the phone. She was leaving in less than eight hours. He went to her, picked her up in his arms, and carried her down the hallway.

It was after three, and Brooke could tell Craig was as exhausted and spent as she was. The previous few hours had been filled with romance and quiet conversation.

But there was still one thing she wanted to discuss before they drifted off to sleep.

"Amy told me that she and Andrew met and fell in love within a few weeks."

Craig lifted his head and gazed into her eyes. They left a lamp on in the living room, and it cast a soft glow across the bed. "They certainly did. And the difference she's made in his life is remarkable. Andrew always came across as aloof and standoffish. People said he would never find a wife with his disposition, but Amy crashed through all that."

"She told me all about it," Brooke laughed. "So, what do you think?"

"About Amy and Andrew? I'm happy they got together."

"No, silly. About whirlwind romances?"

Craig scratched his chin as if he was giving the question serious consideration. "I guess it can work. Sometimes... maybe."

He was milking the moment. Brooke knew it.

"Yeah...no," she said. "I don't believe in that kind of stuff. I think real love takes time. Months at least. Even years."

He looked down at her, waiting for her serious expression to change. Hoping she was pulling his leg, but suddenly not so sure.

And then she smiled and he knew they were okay.

He also knew he wanted her very much. He kissed her. She wrapped her arms around him and pulled him to her. Sleep would have to wait.

FRIDAY, DECEMBER 23

GARLAND GROVE

o Craig, it felt as if there was a hole in his heart as he went through his day at the drugstore. Nothing could fill it. Not the dozens of happy people who poured in, raving about the previous night's performance and sharing stories about how they had shaken Raven McCloud's hand or gotten her autograph. Nearly all took the time to mention how good the local performers had done too. Garland Grove always looked out for their own.

The sidewalks outside the drugstore were teeming with last-minute shoppers. Neighbors chatted with neighbors they passed along the way. It had always been Craig's favorite time of year in Garland Grove.

This year, not so much.

Brooke left for home a little after seven. He had stood in the driveway waving as she departed. There were tears. Lots of them. And the promise of a reunion in a few days, when she returned with the recording contract. Craig had placed a call earlier in the morning to a company that marketed and sold small businesses. And while a *FOR SALE* sign would not suddenly appear on the front door of

Callaway's Drugstore, it would be listed on websites that specialized in that kind of thing.

The dominoes were starting to fall.

And when they had all fallen, he and Brooke would be together again.

And that would keep him going.

SUNDAY, DECEMBER 25

GARLAND GROVE AND NASHVILLE

*M*erry Christmas, Dearest!

Craig smiled as he read Brooke's text. It had been two days since he held her in his arms, yet the ache showed no sign of letting up. She would be spending the day with Bobby, as she had every year of her life. Other than his Aunt Sally way up in Belle Plaine and cousins in North Dakota, Craig was the only person left in his family. He was spending Christmas alone. Alone had never bothered him in the past, but after his time with Brooke, it was nearly overwhelming.

There was no need for her to know that, though. She had Bobby.

Merry Christmas! Have you and Bobby exchanged presents?

In a few minutes. Can you do me a favor?

Anything!

Check the top drawer of the bedside table...my side.

Her side! Oh, how he loved the way that sounded. There had never been anyone in his life who had her side of the bed. Not even Jenna. He went into his bedroom and pulled open the drawer. He found a flat package wrapped in holiday paper.

There's a gift in here.

It's for you. Open it now.

He pulled at the ribbon and ripped the paper away to find a beautifully framed photograph of himself. On stage in Atlanta. He was surprised at how calm he appeared, despite the fake guitar hanging untouched from his neck.

It's the best gift ever! He paused, then added. *I only wish you were here to see me open it.*

Soon, darling. She replied. *Soon.*

His heart felt a little lighter when she called him darling. He might make it after all.

Thank you for the jelly samples from Mrs. Blankenship! she texted. *Bobby and I had some with our apple butter for breakfast.*

I'm glad it arrived in time for Christmas!

There was no need to mention the second mortgage he had to take out for next-day delivery. She was worth every penny.

What are you doing today, Craig?

Amy and Andrew invited me over for lunch.

Will you text me when you return? My aunt and uncle are coming in from Oklahoma, but I can break away to chat with you.

I will... I miss you so much, Brooke.

Same. Soon though!

Not soon enough. Love you and talk to you later.

Bobby admired the fly rod as he shifted it from his left hand to his right.

"How did you know this was the one?" he asked. "I've never mentioned it."

"You've never mentioned it *to me*, but you say plenty to your buddies."

Bobby nodded, but never took his eyes off the fly rod. "I'm gonna have to remind Luke and those boys that what gets said at the fishing hole stays at the fishing hole." He set the rod aside and rose from the sofa to give her a kiss. "Thank you, sweetheart."

"You become harder to shop for each year, Daddy."

He gave her that deep, soul-searching look of his as he said, "Everything I need is right here."

Butterflies. The good kind. A few weeks earlier she could have responded the same, but things had changed. A daddy's love was one of the most precious things in the world, but she had discovered a different love. And she desperately missed its source.

Bobby handed her a small Christmas package, barely larger than his hand. "I'm not much of a shopper. I hope you like it."

She plucked it from his hand and used a fingernail to pull away the paper. A key fell out, and for a moment Brooke was back in high school. It was her sixteenth birthday, when Bobby had surprised her with her own car, a red Jeep. He had wrapped the key just like this time. This wasn't a car, though. The key was the old-fashioned kind with a rounded top and long thin shaft. The kind people used a hundred years ago.

"It's lovely, Daddy," she said, admiring it like he had the fishing rod. "But I don't understand."

He sat down in the chair to her right and took her hand. "Brooke, honey, it represents the key to your heart."

She could see that there was more he wanted to say, but

emotions were making it hard. He used the back of his hand to rub his face and eyes, then swallowed. "I've held that key since you were a baby. Now there were a couple times along the way that I thought I might lose it, but so far no one has come along to take it."

He paused again. His shoulders heaved and tears came, but he soldiered on. "Someone else holds that key now."

"Craig," she said, now fighting tears of her own. "Yes, Daddy, I am very much in love with him."

"You can pass this on to him. And I want the two of you to find happiness together."

She jumped into his lap and hugged him, just as she had when she was a little girl. It was the sweetest moment she remembered. And how difficult it had to be for dear Daddy. He was acknowledging that it was time to give up the part of his life that meant more to him than anything. The love and gratitude she felt were beyond expression, so she sat on his lap and they cried together. Tears of sadness? Some, perhaps. But also tears of joy for what was to come.

"Daddy, I promise you'll always have a piece of my heart," she said when she was finally able to speak.

"There's plenty to go around," he said, his voice barely above a whisper. "And hopefully the two of you will find joy and I'll gain a son." Bobby wiped at his eyes again, then smiled. "There's another part to the gift, though."

"You've given me plenty, Daddy."

"Well, let me give you one more thing." He paused to let the anticipation build. "Do you remember Monique?"

"The pilot?"

"Yeah, honey. She'll meet you at the airport at two today. She's flying you back to spend Christmas with Craig."

Brooke shrieked, then, not sure she had heard correctly, exclaimed, "Daddy? You're sending me to Garland Grove?"

He smiled and gave her his sideways glance. "That's what I said."

"On a charter plane? On Christmas Day? That will cost a bunch."

"It was that or a sweater, honey. I can always go back for the sweater."

She slapped his arm playfully. "No! Please don't." Then, quieter, "But what about you? I don't want you spending Christmas by yourself."

"Who's going to be alone? Dave and Kelly are coming from Oklahoma. I reckon I'll practice with that nice fly rod a little bit, too." He kissed her forehead. "I want you to go. I insist that you go. Enjoy a couple days together. I'll let you know when Craig's contract shows up. Maybe we'll invite the local paper and a couple of the fan sites and have ourselves a big announcement up in Garland Grove."

AMY GREETED Craig with a hug when he arrived a few minutes before noon.

"Merry Christmas!" she exclaimed. "Come on in. Andrew is in the living room trying to figure out the drone my parents gave him."

Craig laughed when he found Andrew seated on the floor with a dozen pieces of drone and an instruction manual. He looked up at Craig and shrugged.

"Don't Amy's parents know how hopeless you are with mechanical stuff?" Craig teased.

"I hoped it would come fully assembled." He pushed the instructions toward Craig, who kicked off his shoes, kneeled in the midst of the mess, and ignored the instructions.

"It's intuitive," he said as he grabbed two parts and snapped them together. The next few pieces were just as easy, and ten minutes later Craig was hooking up the battery as Amy returned.

"Nice job, Craig." She said with a laugh. "I bet Mom that Andrew wouldn't figure it out on his own. You helped me win the bet."

"You shouldn't be making bets on Christmas day anyway," Andrew groused good-naturedly. "And what about lunch? Aren't you supposed to be getting that ready while we men do the heavy lifting in here?"

"It's almost ready, though it's not exactly a traditional Christmas lunch. I made stir-fry chicken. I hope that's okay."

Craig smiled. "It's better than okay. It's one of my favorites."

Amy's text alert sounded. "Probably Mom checking to see if Andrew hurt himself putting together the drone. Lunch in fifteen minutes, fellas."

"Want to take it outside and try it out?" Andrew asked Craig as he held the drone up for their inspection.

"Sure."

Craig put on his shoes and coat and checked his phone while waiting for Andrew. Still no message from Brooke. Not unexpected, as she was probably visiting with her aunt and uncle. He texted *I'm at Amy and Andrew's. We're testing Andrew's new drone. Miss you!*

Andrew led the way into the front yard and placed the drone on the sidewalk.

"Watch the tree branches," Craig cautioned.

"It's a clear shot from here," Andrew said as he studied the control pad.

"What is its range?"

Andrew shrugged. "It probably says in the instructions, but I'm only going to send it up and back."

"You've done this before?"

"Not personally, but Sam's daughter Sarah has one. I figure if an eight-year-old can do it, I can, too."

Craig laughed. "That's a terrible assumption. Kids are always better at tech stuff."

Andrew pushed a couple buttons and the drone came to life, beeping and whirring on the sidewalk. "Okay, here we go," he said as he toggled a switch that caused the drone to lift off.

"Hey, you did it!" Craig shouted.

Andrew grinned as they watched it ascend into the sky. "I'll make it go to the left, toward the hospital," he said. The drone did as it was supposed to, lifting and moving toward the west. Very impressive.

"Lunch!" Amy called out from the front door.

Andrew fiddled with the buttons again and caused the drone to shift back toward the airspace over the house.

"I think it's still going up," Craig said.

"Yeah, I need to stop it." More jiggling of controls. This time the drone made a sharp turn to the north and continued to rise. A few moments later Craig could barely see it in the gray sky. A few moments after that he couldn't see it at all.

"Maybe this will do the trick," Andrew said as he twisted a control.

It didn't.

The drone was gone.

"Shall we go look for it?" Craig asked.

"It will probably find its way back," Andrew said. "Don't they do that?"

"Cats do, but I don't think that's how drones work."

Andrew's face was grim as he continued to tinker with the controls.

"Are you guys coming in to eat?" Amy again.

"We'll be right there," Andrew called back. Then, to Craig, "Not a word of this to Amy."

THEY WEREN'T through their first helping of Amy's stir-fry before she knew Andrew's new drone was MIA. They debated how they might find it. Craig returned to his suggestion that they ride around and hope for the best. Andrew was sticking to his theory that it would return to the mother ship. Amy wanted to play Parcheesi. They finished lunch and left Amy to clean up while they cruised the nearby streets. They passed three sets of kids playing with drones of their own. None had spotted Andrew's. All promised to keep an eye out. An hour later they returned without the drone.

"It will show up," Amy said brightly. "Let's play Parcheesi."

"I really should be going," Craig said.

"I'm not sending you back to that empty house, Craig Callaway," Amy replied. "At least not until we've played a couple games. Now get into the dining room and let's get started."

Andrew glanced out the window. "Maybe we should make one more search for the—"

"After Parcheesi." Amy's persistence was too much to overcome. They were into the second game when Craig checked his messages. Still nothing from Brooke. He missed her and wanted to chat for a bit and find out if she was having a good day. And hear her voice.

Then, after four games, he got up to go.

"No, Craig," Amy protested. She grabbed his arm. "You haven't even tried my peanut butter balls."

"I'm still full from lunch, and I really need to get home."

"Not without trying my peanut butter balls." She hurried into the kitchen and returned with a full plate. Craig snagged one and popped it into his mouth. Sweet perfection. He had another, then another.

"Would you like something to drink?" Amy asked. "Wine? A soft drink maybe?"

Why was she so persistent?

Then it hit him. She was worried about him being at home alone.

She was being a friend.

"Really, Amy, don't worry about me. I'm used to being by myself."

Amy waved her hand. "I'm not worried about that. Andrew and I just enjoy your company, and we want you to—"

The doorbell chimed a classical Christmas piece that sent Amy scurrying from the dining room. Craig used the opportunity to make his escape. "I'll look for your drone on my way home," he said to Andrew. "Thanks for having me over."

"Good to have you, friend. Merry Christmas."

Craig stepped into the foyer and thought he was seeing things.

"What?" he said, barely above a whisper. "But you're..." He couldn't find the words to express his surprise. And delight.

It was Brooke. She was back. He picked her up and hugged her with everything he had. She hugged him in return, then kissed him deeply. It was incredible, and Craig didn't care that Amy and Andrew were watching.

"I guess another game of Parcheesi is out of the question," Amy quipped.

Indeed it was.

THEY MADE IT INTO THE BENNETTS' front yard before Craig took her in his arms again.

"I don't know what led to you being here, but I am the happiest man in the world."

Brooke laid her head against his chest, barely noticing the frigid temperatures and swirling late-afternoon wind. "It was Dad's idea. He arranged everything."

"How did you know I would still be here?"

Brooke laughed. "I texted Amy before I left Nashville. She said she would keep you here until I arrived."

"She sure did! I've never played so much Parcheesi." Craig lifted her chin to kiss her. "And if it's okay with you, I would love to continue this reunion at my house."

"Mm-hmm. I thought you would never ask."

MONDAY, DECEMBER 26

GARLAND GROVE

enry had originated the tradition of closing the drugstore the day after Christmas. Craig had considered breaking the tradition early on, but Henry talked him out of it.

"Someday you'll want that extra day," he'd said. "And since your customers are used to the store being closed, there won't be any complaints."

Craig was glad he listened.

He and Brooke slept late, then went to Lula's for coffee. They chatted about anything and everything while other customers came and went. Bobby called just before noon and said he would be arriving that evening. He was bringing the contract from Caswell Music. When Brooke asked how it looked, Bobby acknowledged that it was very fair.

"And you're sure this is what you want?" she asked Craig after letting Bobby go.

"It's Nashville, right?"

"You know it is," she said, smiling.

"And you live in Nashville?"

"I do indeed."

"Then it's what I want."

She studied him for a moment before saying, "You want to sing?"

"Why would you ask that, Brooke?"

She pushed a strand of hair from her forehead. "For this to work you have to want it more than anything you've ever wanted. Nashville is a hard place for anyone who isn't fully committed to the business."

He understood her motivation. It was Brooke's way of preparing him for the road ahead. For the possibility of fame.

And the potential for complete and utter failure.

What he didn't say—what he wouldn't say—was that it wasn't about the music. He never even thought of it, unless someone brought it up.

When he dreamed about a future in Nashville, the focus wasn't him singing his heart out to twenty-thousand adoring fans. It wasn't hanging out in a recording studio with a bunch of great musicians. Or seeing his name in lights.

It was her. Brooke. Whether he sang or filled prescriptions or drove a forklift, he wanted to do it close to her.

He cleared his throat. "I want it more than anything."

SHE DIDN'T BELIEVE HIM.

It wasn't that she felt he was intentionally lying to her. Craig wasn't that way.

But she sensed—she knew—that his motivation for the move revolved around her.

She knew because she felt the same way.

It scared her that he might not make it. It was a simple

truth of the business that some performers could put every-thing they had into their careers, yet still fall short. Many were great performers who just never got their break. Failure sometimes turned them inside out, like it had Tris-tan. Many became cynical, like the Waffle House Santa who blamed others for their shortcomings. Even if the potential for success found them, they didn't recognize it.

She and Bobby could help, but that would only take Craig so far. And while he had the financial cushion from a hit song, how would he respond if future earnings dried up? Or never materialized? Would he look back on the decision to give up his drugstore and wish he'd never taken the plunge? Or, worse, would he blame her?

That scared her.

But what could they do? He wanted to be with her. She wanted him in her life more than anything. The love was overwhelming. And Brooke already knew that she was at her best when she was with him. Bobby knew it too. She reached into the pocket of her jeans and caressed the key he'd given her the morning before.

Bobby knew.

She knew.

And Craig knew.

But if everyone knew so much, how come she felt so uncertain?

Bobby pulled his rental car into Craig's driveway a little after seven. The only change in his usual attire was a canvas duster.

"I learned my lesson when I showed up last week without a coat," he said with a grin when Brooke teased him about the duster. Craig welcomed him and directed him into the living room, but Bobby opted for the kitchen. "We need some room to spread out all this paper," he said, holding up several manila folders.

"That's a lot of documentation for a recording contract," Brooke observed as they took their seats.

"Actually, Brooke, darlin', this isn't one contract. It's three."

Craig sat up straighter. "Three contracts?"

"Yeah, son," Bobby said. "I guess you could say that tonight is decision time. Let me begin with the Caswell offer."

Bobby opened the thinner of the folders and pulled out several pages. He placed them on the table so they could all see, then went item by item. The money was good. Not as much as Craig anticipated, but still plenty. It didn't include earnings from things like concerts and personal appearances, and Bobby cautioned him that those numbers would be a direct result of the success of future songs and his willingness to go on the road.

"Right now, all you have is a nice little Christmas song. Not much demand for that on the summer circuit, so Caswell's folks will be working to expand your appeal."

"How much can you expand the appeal of a singer called Christmas Carl?" he asked.

"That's a good question. Brooke, you want to take it?"

"Sure, Dad." She turned in her chair to face Craig. "Your first album with Caswell will be released as Christmas Carl, but it will be a complete change in direction. They're thinking of calling the album something like 'Christmas in July with Christmas Carl.'"

"Country love songs with a summer theme," Bobby added.

"Exactly, Dad. If the songs from that album gain traction, they'll drop the Christmas part of your name and refer to you as Carl."

"No chance of becoming Craig?"

"We discussed that," Bobby said. "If you were in your twenties, maybe. But Caswell sees the window of opportunity to capitalize on your hit as three to five years."

"And then they put me out to pasture?"

Bobby chuckled. "Country singers aren't put out to pasture. There's the oldies circuit. Especially if you get a couple more hits under your belt. There's also country music cruises and shows that feature five or six performers. That kind of thing can more than pay the bills."

"And don't forget the royalties," Brooke chimed in.

Craig took a couple minutes to read through the contract. Most of it was straightforward, though there was some legal jargon that flew over his head. He pushed it aside and turned to Brooke. "What do you think?"

"It's a good start. As I mentioned before, Caswell's people are pretty smart. If they didn't believe they could turn a profit they wouldn't make the offer."

"Brooke's right," Bobby said. "Caswell isn't a top-tier outfit, but they're well run." He scooped up the contract and returned it to the folder. "The question isn't whether this is a fair offer, Craig because it is. The question is, are you interested in changing careers at this point in life?"

Craig removed his glasses and cleaned them with a tissue, then looked at Brooke. "If Brooke is there, I'm in. I want to be where she is."

Brooke shook her head. "But that shouldn't be why you—"

"Brooke," Bobby said, cutting her off. "I have something here for you, too."

❄

RISKY RICK's had forwarded a sales proposal to the office. Actually mailed it. Like real U.S. Postal Service snail mail. Certified. And even though it was sent to Brooke's attention, Bobby had taken it upon himself to sneak a look.

The numbers were a surprise. The sales price was about seventy percent of what she had figured when estimating the expense involved in bringing the place up to code and resuming use of the performance area in back.

"They're struggling to cover their overhead as a bar," Bobby explained. "I got that from some friends who know the owners. They don't have the contacts or experience to expand to live performances, so they want to get out."

Brooke retrieved the yellow highlighter she always carried in her purse and went to work on the offer. There were a few areas of concern, but they were minor. Financing through the bank Summers Management had used for years was a given. She could have Risky Rick's up and running, under a new name of course, by spring.

Craig would be touring and cutting records while she operated her new venue. It was what she had dreamed of when she'd arrived in Garland Grove the week before.

So why wasn't she excited?

Craig picked up on her reticence, but when he started to mention it, Bobby cut him off. Just like he had cut off Brooke a few minutes before. What was up with that? Bobby was usually the consummate country gentleman. Never interrupting while others had the floor.

Which could only mean he had something important to say.

And boy did he ever.

MONDAY, MAY 29

MEMORIAL DAY

*N*erves jangled at Craig's insides. Much worse than that night with Raven in Atlanta. It was understandable, given he was about to go onstage not as Christmas Carl, but as himself. Craig Callaway.

The first of his two songs was an old Charley Pride hit that would be familiar to country music fans. The second was a tune he had written himself a few weeks earlier, in a moment of joyous inspiration. No one had heard it yet, but he was certain it was good enough to save him from being booed off stage.

He glanced across the backstage area to where the evening's headliner relaxed with his band. He was the reason the tickets had sold out in hours. Craig was the opening act. Two songs. Hardly enough to work up a good sweat, but he was still nervous. Unlike his night in Atlanta, it would be just him and his guitar. Not the prop guitar. The real thing. He had been practicing like crazy ever since his appearance was announced.

At ten minutes until showtime, someone knocked on his dressing room door. Twice, then a pause before two more knocks. He pulled open the door and embraced Brooke. "You don't have to use your Raven knock, you know?"

"Old habits and all that," she said. "Are you ready?"

He told her about the jitters.

"I know the cure," she teased.

"I was hoping you would say that." He leaned close so she could kiss him. Almost six months together and the feeling her kisses gave him were as alive as ever.

"Remember, if you're nervous when you get on stage, sing to one person," she said, kissing him again.

"And you'll be my one person?"

"Always," she whispered before stepping away. "Now I have some stuff of my own to do. But I'll be out there when you perform, so look for me, okay?"

He turned to take one last look in the mirror, and Brooke used the opportunity to pat him on the backside. He laughed. "I love you!"

"You too," she said, then again added, "Always."

Craig said a prayer and stood in the wings as the house-lights went down. Then, from someplace offstage, a voice burst through the new state-of-the-art sound system.

Brooke's voice.

"Ladies and gentlemen, welcome to the first performance in the newly renovated Vogue Opera House!"

Six-hundred and twenty-seven people rose from six-hundred and twenty-seven newly upholstered seats and gave a rousing ovation. Brooke, savvy in the ways of the industry, let the applause play out before continuing.

"And who better to kick off our first show than Garland Grove's own... Craig Callaway!"

The applause came in waves as Craig stepped onto stage. He glanced to where Brooke had just concluded her opening. She was already gone, but the evening's headliner gave him a thumbs-up. It was time to get the show on the road.

"Thank you, Garland Grove!" he called out before launching into the Charley Pride song. The sound of his guitar filled the old building with richness and clarity. As he reached the chorus he spotted Brooke in the rear. By the second verse, many in the audience were singing along. And when it was over, the place went nuts.

"Thank you!" he called out as he took a bow. "And now, it is my pleasure to introduce a real legend in bluegrass. A hall-of-famer with twenty-four gold records. He's here all the way from his farm in Adelaide, Kentucky. Ladies and gentlemen, please welcome Harley Willard and his band!"

WHAT HAPPENED?

Craig forgot to sing his second song.

Brooke wiped perspiration from her forehead and headed backstage. She stopped halfway up the aisle when Tristan caught her eye from the stage. Her thoughts went back to that December phone call when she stopped short of recommending Tristan for a spot in Harley's band because of her concerns about his addictions. Tristan's response was explosive and proved to be the last straw in their relationship.

Harley eventually signed Tristan in March, fully aware of his past struggles, but also acknowledging that he had been clean since Christmas. It took only a few moments visiting with Tristan backstage to see he was thriving. His eyes were clear and he was much like the man she had met three years before. Harley had not only become his boss, but also his mentor and sponsor on his road to sobriety. Their exchange was pleasant and tension-free, and Tristan appeared legitimately happy that she had found someone. For Brooke, there were no feelings of remorse over what might have been. After a few months with Craig, she realized that her past relationships had been just that—relationships. What she and Craig had went far beyond that, to include commitment and dedication, and total selflessness. What was between them had deepened in the four months since she had relocated to Garland Grove to refurbish the Vogue. And while some might look askance at the two of them living together for the time being, she didn't care. It was, she suspected, only a matter of time before he popped the question. And when he did?

Of course, she would say yes.

She would say yes because he was the man she wanted to spend her life with. The man she wanted to have children with. The man who had said no to a career in music because it could never give him the same satisfaction he felt in Garland Grove. His home.

Their home.

She would marry him in a heartbeat.

But first, she had to find out what happened. Why just one song? She found him standing offstage, tapping his foot as eighty-year-old Harley Willard led his band through their paces. Bluegrass had never sounded better than it did in the Vogue. She wrapped her arms around his waist and they watched Harley together for a few moments before she raised the big question.

"What about your new song?"

He threw his hands up in the air. "What can I say? Things were moving faster than I could keep up. Maybe I'll remember next time."

Brooke pinched his cheek. "We had a deal, mister. Two

songs. I only got one. You realize that I can consider that breach of contract and not pay you."

He kissed her on the forehead. "You aren't paying me anyway."

They continued to watch from the wings as Harley and his boys worked up a sweat rolling through decades of bluegrass hits. Brooke looked around at what had been accomplished over the past few months. Walls were painted. Acoustics improved. The lobby shined, and the candy counter was stocked with M&Ms, Sno-Caps, and all kinds of sweet and salty treats.

But the icing on the cake was the curtains. Amy and the others involved with the fundraiser had insisted Brooke take the money. She had added to it, of course, and the final result was spectacular. The thick red material pulled the audience's attention to center stage. She would never forget the day when she opened the opera house for tours and how hundreds of locals and out-of-towners marveled at the improvements. And then, a few weeks later, how they had snapped up the tickets for the premier. Harley was the first of ten shows planned for the summer and fall. If all went well, Brooke planned to add more later.

Garland Grove had become home. People stopped to chat with her at Hartman's Bakery and the Superstar Food Market. The barista at Lula's prepared her favorite concoction as soon as she walked in. The familiarity might be more than some folks could take, but for Brooke each day felt as comfortable as her favorite old sweatshirt.

She wondered sometimes what Jenna had found so boring. What was boring about having a group of friends to gather with for dinner every Saturday night? What was boring about greeting the same customers each day, people who knew Craig cared for them and their health?

And as far as their time alone? There was certainly nothing boring about that. She was completely, utterly, and madly in love with him. And Garland Grove. And owning the Vogue. How many times had she thanked Bobby for quietly initiating the conversation with the city council that led to her buying the theater? Dozens, maybe, but still not enough. If it weren't for him she would probably be in Nashville, working tirelessly to breathe new life into Risky Rick's. It would have been a challenging and rewarding task, but it wouldn't have compared to life in Garland Grove.

It was perfect. And it was home.

As Harley and his band reached the final song of their set Brooke kissed Craig and hustled off to make her sendoff announcements. She reached her spot just as Harley concluded to yet another warm ovation. He set aside his mandolin and picked up the microphone.

"We had a little mess-up earlier, folks," he said in his folksy Kentucky twang. "Craig was supposed to do two songs, but by golly, I guess he just plain forgot. So, if it's okay with y'all, I'll have him come out here and play for you."

Applause and calls of affirmation from the audience followed. Brooke moved closer to the stage, hopeful that Craig knew what was going on. She spotted him placing his guitar around his neck. Then, when she checked to make sure the audience was sticking around, she spotted Bobby seated near the front in an aisle seat.

Bobby?

When did he show up?

He was supposed to be in Shreveport checking out a band that was getting a lot of attention down there. At least that was what he told her. It would be just like him, though, to surprise her at her first show as the Vogue's owner.

Craig moved to center stage and motioned to one of the volunteer stagehands who brought out a chair.

"No," Brooke whispered. "Don't sit down, Craig. Always play standing up."

Thankfully, he didn't sit.

But he did approach the microphone and ask her to come out. Her stomach dropped to the floor.

Oh, my gosh! Was he going to...?

No!

Not now!

But what if he did?

She wanted that more than anything. But there? At center stage?

No.

Well...maybe.

Why not?

She stepped out of the darkness and received a warm welcome. Craig kissed her on the cheek, then pointed to the chair. When she was seated, he turned to the audience and said, "If it weren't for this wonderful lady there might have never been another show at the Vogue. Don't you agree?"

They made their agreement known.

"And now I would like to perform a song I wrote especially for her. And I want to thank Harley Willard and his band for helping me out."

The song was called *My Brooke*, and while it wouldn't win any Grammy awards, or even get airplay, it was the most beautiful melody she had ever heard. It touched her deeply and completely, and when the tears came she made no attempt to stop them. By the second verse they flowed freely.

I'll get you for this, Craig Callaway. I spent a half-hour on my makeup, and it's a mess because of you.

She glanced in Bobby's direction and saw that he was misty-eyed too.

And as Craig reached the final verse, he lowered himself to one knee. And just as in Atlanta, the guitar hung unused as he reached into his pocket and retrieved a tiny box. As he handed it to her she recognized the logo.

Buckshot Kelly's Guns and Jewelry.

She opened it, hoping it was from the jewelry side of Buckshot's little store.

And it was.

AFTERWORD

Why Nashville?

Robin loves Nashville. She loves everything about it, including the TV series that aired for several seasons in the 2010s. Her favorite stars are in the same superstar league as Raven McCloud: George Strait, Trisha Yearwood, and Garth Brooks. She also loves Air Supply, which isn't country and Paul teases her about.

Paul doesn't care for country music, though he admits to an affinity for Dwight Yoakam since his appearance in the movie Sling Blade in the late 90s. He certainly had a fun time developing Raven's character, though his life has been more like Craig's.

As in all our books many of the settings and places are real. We've done our best to replicate the Nashville vibe. Former Music City residents Glenda and Chris Reagan were a huge help. Brooke and Bobby's office is located along Music Row. Raven humiliates Brooke after her performance at the Ryman. Hillsboro Pike is faster than the interstate if you're driving out to Raven's place. Franklin, Tennessee is a lovely place that still maintains a community feel. If you find a place there that sells peanut brittle and cider, though, please let us know.

Raven's hometown is Salmon, Idaho. That's the hometown of our friend, Amye Gillio. She says it's the most beautiful place on earth.

Two settings we made up but would love if they were real are Wainwright's Chop House and Percy's Crossroads. There aren't enough great steak places anymore. We modeled Wainwright's after our personal favorite, Bern's Steakhouse in Tampa. You can't score a reservation at Wainwright's, but you can at Bern's provided you are willing to wait a month or so. It's worth it.

Percy's Crossroads is Paul's idea of a great place to live. Quiet. Secluded. Robin not so much. Give her a condo close to the music scene. Percy's Crossroads and Bobby Summers seem to go together like peas and carrots, though, don't you think?

Other communities mentioned, like Murfreesboro and Paducah, are real. The same for Bowling Green, Kentucky, where Raven and Travis got in trouble. Bowling Green is the home of Western Kentucky University, the most awesome college in the entire world, according to Paul.

Missouri State University, Raven and Craig's former college, is also real. It used to be known as Southwest Missouri State. Another notable alum is our daughter and social media pro, Alison Correnti.

Since you've probably read Christmas Presence, our first Garland Grove Christmas Romance, you already know that setting lives only in our minds. There are certain aspects of Garland Grove, however, that are real to us. Manny the bike-peddling mannequin, could be spotted for many years in Seaford, Delaware near Paul's hometown.

The Park-Rite Motel and the adjoining restaurant are a blatant ripoff of the Park-Et Restaurant and Motel in Perryville, Missouri.

And everything else? We just made it up, because that's what we do.

BONUS MATERIAL

THE WEDDING OF BROOKE AND CRAIG

It's nearly one year later, and friends and family are gathered for the wedding of Brooke Summers and Craig Callaway.

And you're invited too.

To accept your invitation and read our bonus chapter, *The Wedding of Brooke and Craig*, go to
https://BookHip.com/ZTQMLFK

ABOUT ROBIN PAUL

Robin Paul is the pen name of **Robin and Paul Wootten**. We live on Florida's Gulf Coast and in Kansas City.

We want to get to know you. Please check out our website at www.robinpaulromance.com. We have freebies, special offers, and news about upcoming events. You can also follow us on Facebook and Instagram.

ALSO BY ROBIN PAUL

Garland Grove Holiday Romance Series

Christmas Presence (2021)

Christmas Carl (2022)

Blues Christmas (2023)

Christmas Comeback (2024)

Standalone Holiday Romances

Christmas Class Reunion - Inspired the Hallmark Channel Original Movie (2022)

Clear Christmas - A Later in Life Holiday Romance (2023)

Write Christmas - A Kansas City Christmas Romance (2023)

Bethany Beach Summer Romance Series

Drifting Together (2022)